Advance Praise for *Say the Word*

"*Say the Word* is a compelling insight into the world of substance abuse treatment facilities. The authenticity of the characters showcases the intricate complexities of the relationship between sexual trauma and drug and alcohol abuse. A great read for anyone impacted by chemical dependence!"

—Caitlin Segriff, Licensed Marriage & Family Therapist

Praise for *Easy Kill*

"E.Z. Kelly is the next, great kickass heroine."

—EmKay Connor, Award-winning Author

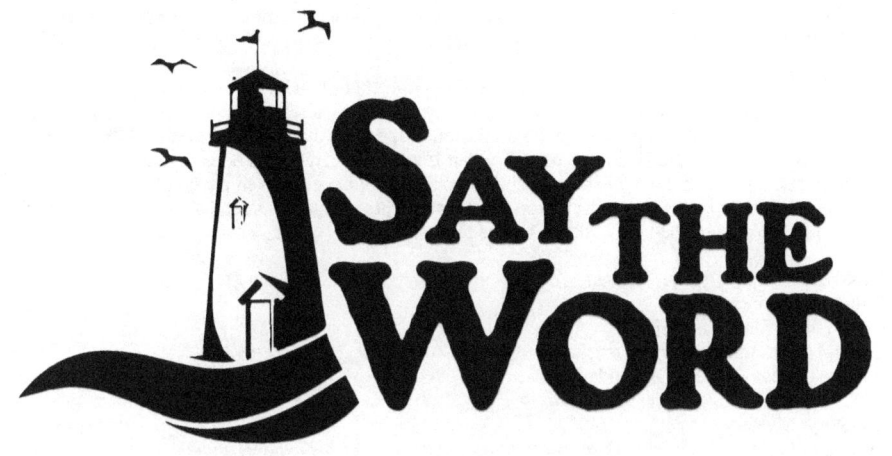

Charles M. DuPuy

Green Bay, WI 54311

Publishing Editor: Brittiany Koren
Editor: Maria Connor
Copy-editor: Dale Shepherd
Cover Art Designer: Sunny Fassbender
Interior Layout Designer: Amanda Dix

Category: Mystery
Description: *A young physician's assistant finds himself in over his head when he calls in a promise to a mafia don.*
Hardcover ISBN: 978-1-7335034-8-8
Paperback ISBN: 978-1-7335034-9-5
Ebook ISBN: 978-1-7335034-5-7
LOC Catalogue Data: Applied for.

First Edition published by Written Dreams Publishing in May, 2019.

Green Bay, WI 54311

This novel is dedicated to all the men and women whose childhoods were brought to an abrupt end by sexual predators.

Chapter One

Jim Booker had already given his notice at the hospital when he saved Nick Bonnano's life. He didn't think he'd done anything extraordinary. It was all in a night's work. He was working at the University Hospital emergency room in the heart of Newark, New Jersey when Nick Bonnano was wheeled in more dead than alive, but still salvageable, as it turned out.

Jim had begun suturing a long laceration on the left forearm of a drunken young man who thought he could win a knife fight. He hadn't. He'd come in second, and Jim got the thankless task of patching the guy up. His patient snored loudly, his slashed forearm lying inert and draped within a sterile field before him.

Dressed for work in blue hospital-issue scrubs, the pullover top showed off his solid upper body and well-muscled arms. A cloth headcap hid most of Jim's curly blond hair. As Jim began to suture, a team of paramedics popped the automatic doors and rushed a stretcher through.

"Keep an eye on him," Jim said to the nurse assisting him.

"We got a bleeder," yelled one of the paramedics.

With practiced precision, Jim set the suture needle and tweezers on the sterile field, peeled off his latex gloves, and grabbed a pair of plastic ones from a nearby cart. His tall, lean frame reached the stretcher in three long strides, his crisp blue eyes assessing the patient as he approached.

Jim saw black, curly hair, a swarthy complexion blanched from the loss of blood and a full, black mustache drooping above his gaping mouth. His coal black eyes were open, unfocused, but his pupils weren't fully dilated.

Jim noted an IV line running wide open into the young man's right arm. A glance at the IV bag confirmed Ringer's lactate, the right fluid for blood loss until whole blood could be run in. He also noted that the paramedics had placed MAST trousers on the man's legs and waist. They were firmly inflated to squeeze blood from his lower extremities up to his vital chest and head. They also applied pressure to the injured area to control the bleeding.

"Where's the bleed?" Jim asked, already guessing.

"Right groin. Stab wound," said the paramedic.

Jim saw his nametag. Peter something. No time for last names.

"Get his vitals. Type and cross for five units. Kathy, alert vascular surgery. And get a big line in his left arm," Jim ordered. "Ringer's. Wide open," he added.

Two nurses rushed to carry out his orders.

"BP ninety over fifty, pulse one-ten, thready but steady," said the nurse who'd wrapped a blood pressure cuff on the patient's left arm.

A phlebotomist stepped in, partially inflated the cuff, and deftly withdrew a vial of blood from an antecubital vein. Then she hurried off with it to the lab to get it typed and cross-matched for the transfusions.

The second nurse moved in with an IV set-up. She reinflated the cuff to distend the man's veins, now collapsed by his loss of blood. She swabbed the skin over her chosen puncture site with an antiseptic pad and threaded a 14-gauge catheter needle into the most promising looking vein.

Meanwhile, the vitals nurse was busy. She'd prepared a bag of Ringer's lactate and inserted an IV line into it, then opened the control to bleed out the air in the line. She was ready when the second nurse finished inserting the catheter needle into the young man's arm and handed her the end of the tubing.

Taking it, the nurse pushed it into the open catheter, giving it a twist to secure it. Satisfied that it was running well, she taped the catheter and tubing to the man's forearm, then secured his limb to an arm board to keep the catheter from being dislodged.

Jim guessed that the knife thrust had severed the man's right femoral vein. If it was damage to his femoral artery, it had to be slight. He knew that a well-cut artery would've been fatal in a matter of minutes. Each beat of the man's heart would spray out blood like a pulsating lawn sprinkler until there was no more blood to pump out, no more blood to carry oxygen to the brain or to the heart itself. Death would be swift.

"Was it a gusher?" he asked Peter. *Gusher* was the term for an arterial bleed.

"No," replied Peter. "When we got to him, he was lying in a sea of blood. It was oozing out of his groin."

"How long was he bleeding?"

"It was less than five minutes from the time we got the call til we were on the scene. Don't know how long he was bleeding before we got the call, though. Found him in the short alley behind Water Street," Peter said.

As if this information was vital to Jim. It wasn't. Nerves.

"What's under the trousers?" Jim asked, pointing at the MAST trousers.

"We put a compress dressing over the wound," Peter said.

Jim formed a mental picture of a nasty slash in the young man's right groin at the juncture of leg and abdomen. "BP?"

"Holding at ninety over fifty. Pulse one-ten, not so thready," said the nurse monitoring vitals.

Jim made his decision. "Okay, deflate the waist and right leg. Let's have a look. Get me a large hemostat and prepare a second one with gauze two-bys. Call out vitals every thirty seconds."

The paramedics opened the valves to release the air in the waist and right leg of the MAST suit.

A nurse slapped a large hemostat—surgical pliers that had a locking mechanism built in—into Jim's open hand.

The sound of escaping air signaled the decompression of the waist and right leg. With the tension gone out of the deflated suit, the paramedic unzipped first the waist and then the right leg to the young man's knee.

Jim peeled back the blood-soaked nylon fabric and lifted away the saturated compression dressing, exposing the young man's gored groin area. The wound oozed dark red blood. He carefully inserted the hemostat into the deep gash and spread it slowly, tentatively. Blood welled up around the hemostat.

"Eighty over fifty. Pulse one-twenty, thready," announced the vitals nurse.

With the MAST trousers off, blood was flowing from the man's decompressed right leg. His blood pressure was falling.

"Sponge," barked Jim. He was running out of time.

A nurse shoved a clump of gauze pads held by a hemostat into the open gash, paused a second, then withdrew it, dripping a trail of blood to a nearby stainless steel basin.

For the instant before the wound filled with blood again, Jim was able to visualize the severed femoral vein, its distal end pouring fresh blood into the wound cavity. He inserted the hemostat into the area where he'd last seen the severed lower vein, then squeezed them closed.

In the silence surrounding them, the faint clicking sound as the hemostat locked closed could be heard.

"Sponge," Jim called out.

Once again, the nurse pushed a fresh clump of gauze down into the gash, held it a second, then withdrew it.

All eyes were on the wound, expectant.

The wound no longer oozed blood. Jim had been successful on his first try, clamping off the distal end of the severed vein, the segment responsible for returning oxygen-depleted blood from foot and leg back to the man's heart.

"BP?"

"Seventy over forty, pulse one-twenty and thready," came the nurse's calm response.

Grabbing a handful of four-by-four gauze pads, Jim carefully encircled the hemostat so it lay flat on the man's groin. He topped it with a compression dressing. Finished, he folded the MAST trousers back into position.

"Pump them up, guys," he ordered, a tenseness in his voice.

The paramedics deftly zipped up the suit and inflated it. The pressure forced blood out of the man's legs and into his upper body. It'd result in an increase in his blood pressure.

"Vascular's ready in OR Three," someone called out.

"Get this guy to surgery," Jim ordered. "Make sure the blood bags go to Three, too, okay?"

"Okay," said the nurse in charge, respect for Jim noticeable in her voice.

"Good work, people. Looks like we saved another one," Jim said, a broad grin creasing his lean face. It was his stock comment whenever a patient survived his ministrations. His voice carried a hint of sarcasm, recognizable by everyone on the trauma team.

The young man's father wasn't on the trauma team, but he'd managed to barge his way into the emergency room as Jim made his comment. Apparently, he'd gotten word of his son's injury, then rushed to the hospital. Accompanied by four solid-looking men wearing long overcoats and deadpan expressions, the man had bullied his way into the trauma room, pushing past a security guard who'd tried to stand in his path.

At the doorway, the security guard managed to yell, "Hey, you can't go in there!"

Two of the men took up positions on either side of the security guard while the other two stayed with the father, one on each side, assuming a protective posture.

Jim returned to his suture job. The drunken young man with the slashed left arm slept on.

"No change," said the nurse.

Jim nodded. "You can go on with your duties. I can handle this." The sterile field around the man's arm was undisturbed Jim noted with satisfaction. He seated himself and began pulling on a new pair of sterile gloves.

The man approached him. "So, Nick's gonna live?"

Jim looked up, startled by the question from this unauthorized stranger in the trauma room. "Who're you?"

"Tony Bonnano." He'd said it in a way that suggested Jim should know him. "I'm Nick's father."

"Who's Nick?" Jim asked, confused.

"He's my boy," the man explained. "You just saved his life. I heard you say so."

Jim concentrated on finishing up the suture. "The young man with the stab wound?"

"Yeah, that's him. I want to thank you."

Jim became aware of the two well-muscled men positioned on either side of Tony Bonnano, unbuttoned coats held closed, eyes everywhere but on Jim.

"There's nothing to thank me for," Jim said. "His youth and physical condition were what saved him. I had hardly anything to do with it."

"Yeah, sure, Doc. Play it down if you want, but I know what kinda shape he was in when he got here. You saved his life, plain and simple," Tony said.

"Look, it was no big deal. And by the way, I'm not a doctor." Jim glanced up at Tony.

"Not a doc? Well, what are you then, besides a hero?"

"I'm a physician assistant. A PA," said Jim.

"No kiddin'! My boy was saved by a physician's assistant?"

"I kid you not."

"Hey, that's great! I gotta hand it to you, you sure know your stuff. What's your name?" Tony asked.

"Jim Booker."

"Well, Jim Booker, I won't forget what you did for Nick."

Tony stared down at the young man with the arm laceration, saw he was sleeping, then stepped in close.

Jim caught the faint smell of Italian spices. Garlic, oregano, basil, maybe. *Must've been eating pasta when he got word of his son's injury.*

He spoke in a low voice, meant for Jim's ears only. "I want you to come see me any time you got a problem, no matter how big or how small. I'll take care of it. You hear me? Say the word and I'll take care of it." He held out a business card to Jim.

Taken aback by the solemn promise, Jim reached out and took it with his gloved hand. Silently cursing his carelessness, he shoved the card into his scrub shirt pocket. As he pulled his hand away from the pocket, it was enveloped in Tony Bonnano's meaty grip and Jim was drawn up close to him.

"Remember, Jim Booker, because I won't ever forget. You saved my boy's life today and I owe you. You call me whenever you need me to take care of something for you, okay?"

Tony Bonnano's dark eyes bored into him, leaving no doubt in Jim's mind of the man's sincerity.

"Thank you. I'll keep it in mind," Jim replied, his eyes locked with Tony's.

"Good. Good. Be talkin' with you."

With that, Tony released Jim's gloved hand. He and his associates turned and exited as quickly as they'd come.

Jim shook his head. "Guess it takes all kinds," he muttered to himself.

He peeled off the contaminated gloves and began the task of putting on a new, sterile pair so he could finish the suture. The young man slept on, oblivious to the scene that had played out around him.

At the end of Jim's shift, he made his way to the male staff's locker room to change into his street clothes. When he pulled his scrub shirt over his head, the white business card slid from the pocket and fluttered to the floor, landing under the bench at his feet.

"Hey, Jim, you dropped something," said Paul Yorkston, an orderly who was in the locker room when Jim entered.

Jim glanced down, didn't see anything.

"Under the bench," Paul prompted. "Looks like a business card. You have some sweet young thing slip you her card tonight, you sly old devil?"

Taking the cue, Jim looked more closely. Spotting the card, he leaned over and retrieved it, remembering where it had come from.

"Don't I wish," Jim said, a rueful expression overshadowing his face. He examined the card for the first time. Its simplicity surprised him. It bore a name and a phone number. Nothing else. No business name. No address. Only the bare-bones information:

Tony Bonnano
(862) 555-6834

Jim turned the card over. Scrawled on the backside in black ink was a three-word message: *Say the word!*

"But I guess you could say it's some kind of an offer." Jim chuckled, considering the possibilities.

"Who's it from?" Paul asked, his tone suggesting that he didn't really care, was simply making small talk.

Jim shrugged. "Some guy named Tony Bonnano."

"Did you say *Tony Bonnano*?"

"Yeah. Why?"

"Geez, Jim. If we're talking about the same guy, he's big-time mafia," Paul breathed, clearly impressed.

"Mafia?" Jim whispered back, picking up on Paul's tension.

"Yeah, one of Newark's biggest. Describe the guy."

Jim recalled the man, the encounter. "Five-ten, stocky, black curly hair, and a small black mustache under a nose that got moved to the left some time ago. Oh, and there were four big guys with him who acted a lot like bodyguards."

"Even without the bodyguards, you described him to a tee," said Paul. "That's Tony Bonnano, no question. I hope you're on his good side."

"It looks that way. He thinks I saved his son's life tonight, offered to pay me back."

"Huh. That's something worth thinking about, isn't it?"

"You think he could find me some sweet young thing?" Jim fired back, trying to make light of the situation.

"That man could find you anything you want, no problem," replied Paul, dead serious.

Then Paul switched into his easygoing mode. "Hey, Jim, I'm out of here. Keep me posted on what you decide on. That is, unless you're too embarrassed to talk about it." He cocked his index finger at Jim. Then he was gone, leaving Jim alone in the locker room.

Jim had another look at the card, checking out both sides again. He took out his wallet and tucked it between a couple of other cards.

What the hell. You never know.

Later, when Jim opened his apartment door and saw all the boxes he'd already packed, he forgot about the card. His thoughts were focused on the move ahead, on the changes it would bring to his life. He was anticipating a much slower pace and a less stressful job.

In three weeks, he'd be on his way to Serenity.

Chapter Two

Jim glanced into the back of his pickup truck at the jumble of his belongings. *Guess that's it.* At twenty-six years old, he was happy to be single, and his possessions fit easily into a four-by-six pickup. He preferred it that way. No sea of stuff to pin him down. No big anchors to hold him in place.

He flipped the tailgate up and closed the cap door. Its dry hinges shrieked at him, reminding him of his farewell encounter with Dianne. He winced, a reaction to both the shrieking hinges and memories of the woman.

He shook off the thought while locking the hatch door. He knew securing the lock was an automatic reaction, futile, really. The boys of Newark could open his pickup cap like a sardine can if they took a liking to any of his stuff. It was daylight, though, and his street was waking up to a sleepy Sunday in early February. There would be enough activity to discourage most thieves. Besides, didn't thieves sleep in?

He stepped back and collided with his red mountain bike, nearly toppling it. His well-tuned reflexes took over as he snagged it before it crashed to the pavement. He set it upright once again.

"Sorry, old friend," he whispered.

He recalled the many miles of pain and pleasure the bike had given him as he fit the rack onto the tow bar bracket. That done, he set his bike on the rack, snugged it down with nylon straps, and secured it further with a cable lock. He double-checked his work, assuring himself it would survive the long drive ahead. He guessed it would.

One more quick go-round and I'm gone.

With long, purposeful strides, Jim bounded up the chipped brick stoop and hauled open the dirty, peeling entry door to the drab vestibule. He swept past the bank of scarred, dented mailboxes without a glance, then tolerated the slow elevator ride to the sixth floor, tapping his foot impatiently with each floor passed. He unlocked his apartment door for what would be the last time. Two years had been more than enough.

It wasn't much. Living room, bedroom, kitchenette, bath, all furnished in what he referred to as 'early East Newark.' Bulky, heavy, worn sofa and chairs, all faded to a neutral beige color. *Nothing much worth stealing, which may be why it's furnished this way.*

His final inspection took less than a minute, finding nothing in the empty rooms belonging to him. The place gave back the same feeling it had when he'd first moved in two years before. It was neutral, devoid of any personality. There was nothing inviting about it, nothing attractive here. It was a cold, lifeless space. He felt like a stranger in the place he'd called home for two years. He realized that what had been warm and inviting and alive about this apartment was outside now, packed in his truck for the move to Maine.

Time to go.

Jim pulled the self-locking door closed until it latched with a final clunk. He avoided the elevator, taking the rank stairs instead, and strode to the rack of mailboxes. He stripped three keys from his keychain: one for his apartment, one for the entry door, and one for his mailbox. He dropped them one by one through the slot in the superintendent's mailbox where they clattered to the bottom with finality.

Hefting his key ring, it felt much lighter than the loss the three keys could have caused. He turned and walked out the entry door feeling lighter, freer than he'd felt in ages.

As the entry door latched closed behind him, he turned to look one last time at the red brick building he'd called home. In the cold, grey light of that early February morning, it looked dirty, neglected. Streaks of dirt ran down the brick exterior, and the windows were opaque with layers of grime.

It struck him. This was no longer his home. He stared at it through the eyes of a stranger. Then, he turned and walked to his waiting pickup truck.

Maine's gotta be better than this.

He unlocked the door and climbed in, then fired the engine. "You ready, Fred?" he asked, looking over at the passenger seat.

Fred sat, unmoving, the seatbelt across his brown velveteen body, his black bear eyes staring, unblinking, straight ahead. He was a big bear, big enough to sit up with his head at the lower windshield level, like a little old lady peering out at a world too big for her.

"Since I'm not hearing any objections, let's get this show on the road."

Jim pulled away from the curb and headed out of the sleepy Sunday streets of Newark. Fred stared ahead in anticipation.

Jim and Fred had been close companions for more than four years. He'd taken Alicia, his girlfriend at the time, to a traveling carnival. She'd spotted the bear, told Jim she thought he was the cutest one she'd ever seen, and Jim laid down five bucks for the privilege of tossing three softballs at open baskets. He dropped them all into the same basket, and Fred was the prize. When he handed him to Alicia, she said, "Oh, no, Jim. You keep him. Think of me whenever you look at him."

Ten days later, Alicia was run over and killed by a hit-and-run driver as she waited for a bus. Her death left Jim drowning in a sea of emotions. He was angry at the unfair world, angry at himself. He blamed himself, telling himself over and over, if he'd only been with her he might have saved her. All the possibilities of a future together with Alicia would still be alive.

Jim glanced over at the bear he'd named Fred, and an image of Alicia washed over him. He gently shook his head from side to side until, once again, the image faded. Sadness marred his face as he stared at the road ahead.

***

The Roy Rogers restaurant on the Massachusetts Turnpike was surprisingly crowded, seeing as it was past two on a Sunday afternoon. Jim paid for what he dubbed a "Trigger burger". In addition to the tricked-out hamburger, the meal included fries and a soda.

He carried his tray to a small molded plastic table with an attached chair and sat down. He guessed it was attached so it couldn't be stolen. Then he caught himself, chided himself for hanging on to his Newark mentality. While he unwrapped his burger and stripped the paper from his straw, he glanced at the other travelers around him. He picked up snatches of conversation from those closest to him. There were families with young children and there were several couples—some young, some old. He didn't see any other single diners, which surprised him.

Curious, he scanned the checkout line for singles. Again, he saw families and couples. Then he noticed an attractive young woman pay for her tray of food and turn away from the register in search of a table.

Aha! I'm not the only single left in the world.

She walked purposely in his direction, and he reflexively pulled his tray toward him to make a space for her, thinking that she might take the seat across from him.

She surprised him. She stopped behind the open seat and looked him squarely in the eyes. "Is this seat taken?" she asked, smiling brightly.

"Not any more, it's not. Pull up a chair," he said, returning her smile.

"Good one, Jim," she shot back, then set her tray down and slipped into the immovable chair.

His first thought was that he'd met her somewhere before, maybe when things were chaotic, like in the ER, and he didn't remember her. Then he took another look and guessed that he couldn't have forgotten a previous encounter with this woman. Glowing red hair tied back in a loose bun, emerald-green eyes, an aquiline nose over full, wide lips, and a trim, athletic body. A hell of a package. Not in the least forgettable.

He stared at her, mouth likely hanging open a bit, and asked, "When did we meet?"

"Oh, we've never met before, Jim," she answered straight away, giving him a warm smile.

"Then how—"

"How do I know your name? That's easy. Tony Bonnano gave it to me."

"Tony Bonn..." Then he remembered. Tony Bonnano from the ER, the man who thought he'd saved his son's life. "So—"

"Let me explain," she interrupted as she swept an errant strand of red hair behind her ear. "I keep in touch with the people Tony decides he owes, and I remind them of Tony's promise. He doesn't want them to ignore his offer."

"You followed me so you could remind me that Tony Bonnano owes me a favor?"

"Exactly. Simple, really. I went to your apartment this morning, but you'd already left. I called Tony, who told me where you were heading and what you were driving. So I drove fast, maybe bent the speed limit a little, and here I am," she said as she unwrapped her hamburger then picked up a French fry.

"That was, what? Three weeks ago when Tony made me his offer? I can't think of anything he could do for me," Jim said.

"No problem. I didn't really expect you to. As I said, he pays me to keep track of you and remind you from time to time that his offer is still good."

He stretched his hand across the table and said, "Jim Booker."

"I know that, of course. I'm Merry Riddle," she offered, taking his hand in hers. "That's M-E-R-R-Y, like Christmas, because I was born on Christmas Day. My parents had a good sense of humor," she added, smiling at him.

"So, Merry, how did you get the job of reminding people that Tony Bonnano's offer is still good?"

"Good question. Believe it or not, he made a promise to me, like he did to you. After he'd settled what he called his debt to me, he asked me if I wanted a job. He explained what he wanted me to do. I knew Tony Bonnano's reputation, knew he was involved in some shady dealings, but I knew from personal experience that under it all, he had a heart of gold. He offered me a substantial salary, one I couldn't refuse, and here I am." She looked down at the lunch getting cold in front of her. "Let's eat."

Jim eyed his lunch and agreed, while silently thinking how weird this all was. He had Tony's card. Why the extra trouble to remind him? Seemed almost like Tony was *urging* him to ask a favor.

A not-uncomfortable silence ensued.

Jim swallowed, then asked, "What kinds of things do people ask Tony to do for them?"

Merry wiped her mouth with a paper napkin. "Good question. I've seen everything from a man wanting help convincing the woman he loved to marry him to a woman who wanted her husband killed," she said, looking up at Jim.

Curious, he asked, "What did he do to help convince the reluctant woman?"

"A number of things. The most creative thing was having someone he knew rig one of those things that you see at Christmas, projecting stars and snowflakes and trees on someone's house as a decoration. It got modified to project the man's face with 'Marry Me!' below it, in multiple images. The woman came home in the dark, and there it was. She wasn't convinced until she saw the airplane towing a banner that said, 'Marry me, Susie!'"

"That is creative," said Jim. "What did he do for the woman who wanted her husband killed?"

"Nobody knows for sure what happened to him. He disappeared without a trace," Merry said in a matter-of-fact manner.

"Tony takes care of lots of things, then."

"He does. He always writes three words on the back of his card: 'Say the word.'"

Jim finished chewing another bite. "Looks like he's true to his word."

"Uh huh," Merry nodded. "His word means a lot to him."

"So, where do you go from here?"

"At the moment, there are three other people out there who Tony wants to repay," she explained. "I'll be calling on them next to remind them of Tony's promise, and if any of them want to call in their marker, I'll pass it on to Tony and his, ah, associates. Then, before you know it, you'll see me again." She added her warm smile as a topping.

"How will you know where to find me?"

"That's easy. Tony Bonnano has an incredible search network. He knew you were taking a new position at a substance abuse treatment facility in Maine and was aware you were heading there today."

Jim didn't know how he felt about that. "So, how did you figure out what route I'd take when I left Newark?"

"Truth to tell, there are only a couple routes to consider, and the one you're following is the fastest and most direct, as you know. I took the chance that you'd take this route. As it turned out, I passed you in Connecticut, and then dropped back to let you take the lead in Massachusetts. By the way, I like your traveling companion. Does he have a name?"

Jim stared, dumbfounded, the realization of how well she'd studied him sinking in. "Fred," he managed to say.

"I like it," said Merry. She opened her purse and took out a business card. Reaching across the small table to Jim, she said, "Here's my card. If you want to call in your marker before we meet again, you can reach me any time at this number."

Jim took it from her, gave it a quick look. It was as simple as the one Tony Bonnano had slipped him. Her name and phone number were printed on the front. On the reverse side were three words: *Call Any Time.*

He slipped it into his shirt pocket and watched as Merry got to her feet.

"Nice meeting you, Jim. I hope you like your new job."

Jim wriggled out of the fixed table and chair arrangement and stood. He was surprised to discover that she was only a couple inches shorter than he was. He stood six foot one, so he guessed she was around five-ten.

"Thanks for stopping by for lunch." A warm smile creased his face.

"Safe trip to Maine, then."

"And a safe trip to you, wherever that's taking you."

"Thanks. Bye."

With that, she turned from the table and was swallowed up by the crowds of people moving about. He watched the back of her red head until she disappeared.

He sat back down, tempted to pinch himself to see if this was all a dream. It all seemed unreal, even after Merry's explanation. He decided to hold off making a final judgment until more time passed.

While he finished the last of the French fries and sucked up his drink, he found his mind flipping back to the nightmare scene with Dianne when he'd told her he'd accepted a position in Maine. The look on her face was permanently etched in his mind.

"Maine?" She'd stretched the word out, making it sound like two syllables. "Where in Maine?" Her voice was cold, flat.

"Cairo. At the Serenity substance abuse treatment facility." He'd struggled to keep his voice neutral.

"You're an emergency room PA. What do you know about substance abuse?" Her voice had climbed, reaching for the screech level.

"I'll be doing physical exams and handling sick call. Whatever I need to know about the treatment program they'll teach me, is how they explained it." He'd made it a point to keep his own voice calm.

"Why Maine? That's right in the middle of nowhere!"

19

He'd watched her struggling to keep from losing it.

"Why *not* Maine?" he'd asked her, his voice level. He could have spoken of clear lakes and the rocky coast, of fishing and hunting, of hiking and skiing, of a rural existence and a slower pace, and of many other changes he looked forward to making a part of his experience. He could have, but he didn't. In retrospect, he knew what effect his short reply would have on Dianne, and by being brief, he'd hoped it would speed up this final separation.

It had.

"You're doing this to get rid of me, aren't you?" she'd challenged.

"No, Dianne. We both know things haven't been going well between us for some time now. I don't think we have the right chemistry to make this relationship work." He struggled to maintain his calm demeanor.

"Oh, so you're just going to walk away from me, make your little escape to Maine, and make no effort to straighten out our little differences?" Her voice had reached a higher octave, shrill with the effort, her face reddening.

"We shared some good times together, Dianne, but I think we both know we won't be riding off into the sunset together." Jim had summed things up, albeit somewhat lamely.

"*Good* times? So all you wanted from me was sex, is that it?" Now her voice was truly shrill.

If sex was the only thing, we'd have broken up long ago is what he wanted to say. Instead he'd said, "Come on, Dianne. You know there was more to it than that. We had some good times together. But I'm a country boy at heart and you're a city girl. I'm lost in the city, and I think you'd be equally lost in the country." He recalled his voice getting a little louder, but he'd clung to calm and reasonable.

"Well, thanks a lot for making that big assumption about me," Dianne said. "How can you even think that, when you've never seen me in the country?"

"You know what, Dianne? You're right. Give me a chance to get settled up there, and then come on up and join me for a while, see what you think." He'd tried to picture her in a country setting with him. The image was always blurry, indistinct, unreal.

"Don't try and patronize me. I can take a hint. Right now, just about the last thing I'd want to do is go with you anywhere, least of all up to Maine, of all places." Tears were in control of her face, anger over the rest of her.

The scene had played itself out. She'd scooped up her coat and headed for the door. He'd offered to drive her home. She'd refused his offer, leaving him with the hope that he'd rot in Maine, for all she cared. Then she'd slammed the door behind her. Silence had settled over his apartment, and it was over.

Looking back on it, he could see that she'd handled it her way, shouting and accusatory, and he'd played it his way, calm and reasoning. Both of them had reached the same end point. In the end, he couldn't help but feel sorry for her. At twenty-five, she was forced from the security of a shared relationship to the insecure singles scene, to isolation and arranged dates and the sheer misery of being alone. Sitting there by himself in the restaurant with crowds of strangers passing by, Jim had a sense of how Dianne must be feeling now.

***

Two hours later Jim crossed over the Kittery Bridge, the high, curving iron that spanned over the Piscataqua River that separated New Hampshire from Maine. He'd felt exhilarated seeing the WELCOME TO MAINE sign halfway across the bridge. Until then, he'd been growing increasingly numb from the monotonous miles of interstate driving with only the radio and Fred for diversion.

Now, with the entire state of Maine before him, he felt awakened, invigorated, like the feeling he got when he stepped out onto a porch on a frosty morning. He supposed it had to do with the optimism he felt for his new job, but Jim had a sense of relief as well. Exploring the emotion, he guessed it had to do with leaving the city and returning to his country roots.

Jim hadn't been born in Maine. Pennsylvania claimed that honor. He'd been born in Pittsburgh, but his parents carried him back to their farm in the rural community of Ligonier before he'd opened his eyes. His memories were of the pungent, sweet smell of cows, and antiseptic, and raw milk, and freshly turned hay, of hot summer days in the fields, of races with afternoon thundershowers to get the newly baled hay into the barn. Then after, the smell of the rain and the sound it made drumming on the barn's metal roof, all coupled with the sweet smell of the freshly baled hay that had made it safely under cover.

There were other memories of the times when the rain won, drenching him and his load of hay before he could get it under cover. Or the times when he'd gone out after a rain, the sunshine returning, to turn the wet windrows of hay with the tedder so it could dry out all over again. It was always a race against the summer storms, and sometimes the storms won. When they did, baling was delayed for a day or two, and the resultant hay was leached of much of its nourishment by the rain.

The memory of the wonderful meals came back to him, too. He recalled the rich aromas, from the yeasty odor of leavened bread baking in the kitchen to the pungent smell of maple and hickory wood smoke, thick and clinging to everything when the smokehouse door was opened, and he went inside with his mother and two brothers to collect the hams and slabs of bacon that were ready for storage. When he was seven, he recalled the pride he felt at being able to shoulder a ham and struggle to the house with it. Later, as a strong teenager, he'd shouldered two slabs of bacon without a thought. A smile worked its way across his face.

Mostly, he remembered being busy all the time. A farm didn't allow you to be idle, unless you had no connection to it. There was always something to be done, something to finish. Spring and summer and fall were filled with planting and cultivating and harvesting. Winter gave him a chance to slow down and catch his breath, but also afforded him a time to help his dad check over all the farm equipment and fix the little things that had gone wrong, a time to make repairs to the barn, to clean out the manure and manage the silage that kept the cows contented and well-fed, producing as much milk as possible.

It wasn't all drudgery. Far from it. He recalled the numerous trips to the stream below the house for a chance to catch a few trout, maybe even set a hook in old Hook Jaw.

Jim smiled, thinking of the evening when he'd hooked into the fish, fought to land it for what seemed like an eternity but was likely only five minutes. He had it coming into the shallows at the stream edge, saw the massive, sparkling flank and his thick, irregular jaws. He'd felt victorious, elated, full of himself.

Then old Hook Jaw had rolled, flipped, and the line went slack, and Jim had a fleeting glimpse of its flashing tail as the fish streaked for its deepwater den. He reeled in his line. His hook was gone. Old Hook Jaw had collected another trophy.

Walking back to the house, disappointed, Jim had gained a personal understanding of the old saying *Don't count your chickens before they hatch.*

He was pulled back to the present when the car in front of him braked for the tollbooths on the Maine Turnpike. He dropped into one of the two open lines and reached the booth. He powered his window down and accepted a ticket from a pleasant, smiling middle-aged woman who made eye contact with him and said, "Have a safe trip."

"Thanks," he replied, smiling back.

It was a new experience for him. He couldn't recall a tollbooth attendant speaking to him, let alone making eye contact with him. Ever. As he headed north toward Portland, he realized he was relaxed and at ease, more so than he'd been in a long time.

He'd felt uncomfortable during his undergraduate days at Columbia. His dorm had security, with the entrance guards and his own door release card. But he remembered taking a walk in Morningside Park at night with an impulsive little blonde girl. Kay? Yes, that was her name. She'd pushed him into taking a stroll in the park just as the sun began to set.

At first he'd thought nothing of it, but when they were deep into the park, he'd realized that they were all alone. There wasn't another soul around. Suddenly every bush and clump of undergrowth was a hiding place for an ambush.

Realizing their potential danger, he'd turned Kay around, using the lame excuse that he was supposed to meet friends at the gate on 116th Street, and he'd convinced her to retrace their steps. They'd made it out safely, but the memory of it had made a lasting impression on him. In hindsight, there probably weren't any bad guys there. Even the dimmest of bulbs had to know that fools didn't travel in Morningside Park after dark.

Philadelphia, where he'd gone to physician assistant school, had been no different. He wasn't aware of daily dangers, what with classes and work in hospitals taking up most of his time. But when he was waiting in the subway late at night for a train to come in and haul him cross-town to the apartment he shared with three other students, he had a heightened awareness of his surroundings, particularly his backside, where a mugger could sneak up on him and gain the advantage.

He'd graduated and taken the position at the University Hospital Emergency Department fresh out of PA school, then made Newark his home for the next two years. He couldn't recall feeling unsafe in Newark. He guessed that after four years of New York's upper west side and two years of Philadelphia, he'd gone on autopilot, protecting his hindquarters without realizing he was doing so. After all, Newark had its seamy side, too.

So here he was, cruising up the Maine Turnpike, feeling more at ease than he'd felt since leaving the family farm and heading to New York more than eight years ago. Yes, he'd made it home numerous times during those eight years and remembered feeling a lifting of the pressure on him when he did. He'd thought it was simply a good feeling of being home.

Now he could see it differently. This new assignment in Maine was giving him the same sense of ease, a feeling that he didn't have to be on his guard all the time. He welcomed this new feeling. Jim hoped it would last.

The Kennebunk Plaza exit beckoned him, and he pulled in to fill up his gas tank and empty his bilge before the final leg of his journey to Cairo.

"A nice thing about being in Cairo," Brent Caldwell had told him when he'd been interviewed for the PA position, "is that we're east of Rumford's paper mill and its rotten egg smell. It's a rare event when the wind blows out of the east and carries the smell back to us."

Brent Caldwell, MD, the medical director at Serenity, would be Jim's new boss and mentor. Jim had taken an immediate liking to the man. In his late forties, an ex-military doctor, Brent still carried himself like a soldier. His round, rugged face on a slightly balding brown head, and friendly disposition had made Jim feel at home. He was energetic and had a solid, if somewhat dry, sense of humor.

My kind of guy.

In hindsight, it was a pivotal point in his decision to take the position. No matter how the job turned out, he had a good feeling about working with Brent.

He snugged his gas cap and stuck the nozzle back in the pump. Then he climbed behind the wheel and buckled up.

"You ready for the last leg, Fred?" he asked his glassy-eyed co-pilot.

Fred continued to stare at the road ahead.

"Let's do it," Jim said.

Chapter Three

"Okay, listen up everybody. We've got a lot to cover, and you've got somebody to meet!" Brent Caldwell's voice had started out gruff, then became excited as the scattered conversations died down and everyone's attention turned to him. "Meet our new physician assistant, Jim Booker," Brent announced, his manner smooth, mellifluous. He waved a broad arm as a greeting to Jim.

Jim looked at all the faces. He raised his hand and waved, a casual roll of his wrist acknowledging Brent's introduction.

"Jim comes to us from the smoke and pollution of Newark, New Jersey," continued Brent, "where he spent the last couple of years working in a hospital emergency room. He told me he was sick and tired of patching up bullet holes and stab wounds, and wanted to work in a place where his efforts could make a difference." Then Brent pivoted toward Jim and added, "Though why he chose to come up here to the wilds of Maine and work in our substance abuse treatment center is beyond me!"

Scattered laughter rippled through Brent's audience.

"Okay, let's do the intros. Jim knows me, so you start it off, Sally," he urged an attractive young woman to his left.

"Hi, I'm Sally Harpswell, the intake coordinator," she said, grinning at Jim. She had a thin, attractive face, short hair swept back on the sides. She looked to be in her late thirties.

"I'm Andy McMartin, clinical psychologist," said the thin, hawk-nosed middle-aged man to her left.

"Bill Thomas, primary counselor for the White team." Bill had a round face and florid complexion set on a stocky wrestler's body that had gone soft.

"Hi, Jim. I'm Martha Knowles. I work with Bill. I'm the associate counselor on the White team." She paired off well with Bill, with her full face and a body that wasn't aging gracefully. She gave Jim a smile that tempered her appearance.

"Breanna Fowler, primary counselor, Red team," an attractive redhead said as she stared candidly at Jim.

Three more counselors and two nurses introduced themselves. By then, Jim's head was swimming with a sea of new names and new faces. He gave up trying to recall all the names, and concentrated instead on making connections between the different teams of counselors. The names would come later. He hoped.

"And that brings us full-circle," concluded Brent, referring to the circle of chairs they occupied. He pressed his hands together in front of him like a priest giving a benediction.

"Nice to meet you all," Jim said to the circle of professionals surrounding him, his expression relaxed, beaming. "Hope you'll forgive me if I have to ask you your names for the next few days, though."

"Not a problem. What'd you say your name was?" asked the counselor he thought was Dave Levesque. Relaxed laughter rolled through the room.

"Hey, don't worry about that," said Brent. "That's why we all wear name tags. The clients think it's for their benefit, so they can tell who we are, but the truth is, it's so I can keep everyone straight, especially when I come back after being gone for a while. Like after a weekend," he added with a twinkle in his warm, brown eyes.

The grins on the faces of many of the counselors after Brent's comment led Jim to guess that Brent had used the line before. He decided to make a light comment of his own.

"I'll be relying on your name tags a lot during the next few days. I hope my looking at them doesn't make any of you uncomfortable."

Sharp, icy stares from every woman silently greeted his comment, while the men snickered. Jim realized he'd stepped over a boundary.

"Okay, enough of this idle chit-chat," Brent said, interrupting the chilly mood. "We have six teams to go over. Who's ready?"

The focus was directed to the business at hand and away from Jim. He felt relief, though he still sensed a cloud hanging over the room, like a dying balloon that had enough helium left in it to keep floating, but not enough to make it soar.

"White team'll go first," Bill Thomas volunteered. Jim remembered that he was the primary counselor for the White team. Short and wiry, he had salt and pepper gray hair.

"Good," chuffed Brent, his way of saying, *On with it, then.*

"This is the second team presentation on Harold B., a thirty-two-year-old alcoholic male from Rumford referred by his wife," Bill began. "She says she's ready to divorce him, but she's willing to wait until he completes treatment before she makes her final decision. Harold has a long history of alcohol use and abuse, and yesterday he admitted to having had blackouts. This was a big step for him because initially, he wouldn't admit he had a drinking problem when he came in two weeks ago."

Jim watched Bill pause for emphasis, then continue when nobody looked impressed.

"Treatment issues include denial, with partial breakthrough obtained, job loss secondary to alcoholism—he got sacked for taking too many sick days—and marriage breakup, though that's not definite and may not happen if he does well in treatment. Oh, and he has medical consequences, with his liver enzymes up from all the alcohol," Bill added.

Brent turned to Andy McMartin, the clinical psychologist. "What does his MMPI show?"

This confused Jim. "Before you answer, can you explain what an MMPI is?" Jim cut in, a quizzical look on his face.

"That's right, Jim, you haven't taken the test yet, have you?" Brent said. "How about it, Andy. Want to enlighten him?"

"Yeah, sure. MMPI stands for Minnesota Multiphasic Personality Inventory. It's a quiz, I guess you'd call it, with over five hundred yes/no questions. We give it to every client when they're clean and sober enough to focus on the questions. If they take it seriously, their responses can give us a profile of their personality, which gives us a big window into what they're really like. It helps us design a treatment plan to suit them," Andy said.

While Andy explained, Bill passed the patient's chart to him, open to the MMPI. His explanation for Jim complete, Andy eyeballed the MMPI graph.

"No big surprises. He's got the big central *fuck you* spike of the classic alcoholic," Andy said, holding the chart up so Jim and the others could see the spike in the middle of the graph.

Jim looked at it, then glanced around the circle to assess the effect Andy's little crudity may have had. He saw no obvious reaction on any of their faces.

Andy continued, "He's got a wimp kind of personality, though he's got the potential to be a wife-thumper if he gets sloshed. And he's a hard-ass when it comes to accepting things. Like treatment, for instance," he said, grinning at his own wit.

This drew a chuckle from the circle.

"We've already found that out," Bill said.

Brent cut in, "So where is he spiritually?"

"He and his wife don't go to church much, but he tells me he believes in a higher power," replied Bill.

"I can work with that," said Brent. "I'll give him my spirituality lecture."

"Okay, that'll help the cause," said Bill, giving Brent a thumbs up.

"Anything come out of men's group?" asked Andy, who had continued to scan the MMPI results.

"Ah, not really," answered Dave Levesque. "He pretty much just sits there and listens to the others. He's, you know, there, but he doesn't say much after he's said, 'I'm Harold B. and I'm an alcoholic.'"

"You think he's holding back on something?" asked Andy. "Reason I ask, he's got a homophobic semi, not a full-blown spike like his alcoholic one, but there's something there." Once again, he held the chart aloft and pointed at another, smaller peak on the graph.

"Maybe. I'm not sure," said Dave. "Yesterday, he seemed to key in on the discussion on sexual abuse, but he never opened his mouth."

"See if you can push him a little to open up next time. Sounds like he's hiding something," said Andy.

"Consider it done." Dave compressed his lips together.

"Anything else?" asked Brent.

There wasn't.

A treatment plan to cover Harold B.'s next week was quickly formulated, and they moved on to the next client.

"This is the third team evaluation on Mary T., a seventeen-year-old female alcoholic and drug abuser referred by her school counselor at Wakefield High because she was missing school a lot," summarized Breanna Foster from the red team, launching into her presentation.

She sat too far away for Jim to read her name tag.

"She started drinking and smoking pot when she was thirteen, and she's tried most of the street drugs over the last four years, including acid, PCP, speed, and a sprinkling of heroin and cocaine, which she literally sprinkles on her pot and then smokes it.

"Issues include sexual abuse at age twelve by a neighbor, her parents' divorce when she was thirteen, and a pregnancy which was terminated in a self-induced abortion at age fourteen. She lives with her mom, who doesn't know what to do with her."

"How's she coming along?" asked Andy.

"She's doing pretty well, all things considered. She asked for time in Women's group yesterday and talked for ten minutes about the sexual abuse by her neighbor. She did great, didn't she, Martha? Even had Alice P. shouting about finding the neighbor and cutting off his, ah, equipment," Breanna concluded, coloring slightly.

While Breanna continued her presentation, Jim looked at her more closely. He took in her youthful, shapely figure and her shoulder-length hair, more auburn than red, held back in a loose ponytail. He noted her thin nose above her full, wide mouth. He wasn't sure about her eye color from where he sat. Green? Hazel? He searched her left hand for a wedding ring, but could see none. He knew that meant nothing. Plenty of attached women didn't wear rings. He felt an attraction for her, but at the same time he sensed a defensiveness about her, a protective aura coming from her. It puzzled him.

General laughter at her last remark brought Jim back from his musings. He found himself smiling at her decorous choice of words.

"Did she get in touch with her anger?" Andy asked her.

"You better believe it," said Martha Knowles with enthusiasm. "By the time she was done, she'd screamed and cursed and threatened to track him down, and do to him what Alice P. suggested doing. With a pair of rusty scissors," she added, an impish grin spreading over her face.

"So what about having Mary bring charges against the neighbor?" asked Andy.

"We've notified the Department of Human Services about it, and they're going to investigate," said Breanna.

"Have you talked to Mary about pressing charges?" Andy pressed.

"Yes." Breanna nodded. "She's willing to do so. I wish all the abused women we get in here were as ready as she is."

"Good, good," said Brent, a pleased expression on his face.

"Sorry to break in, but can you tell me what the Department of Human Services—DHS—covers?" asked Jim. "I'm thinking it may be different than DHHS in New Jersey."

"No problem," said Andy, looking Jim's way. "It includes Child Protective and Adult Protective Services, the two areas of concern for us."

"Thanks. Got it," said Jim.

"Glad you asked," said Andy. "That's how we learn."

Four more team presentations were made. Jim was struck by the number of clients (not called patients, as he'd become accustomed) who had been sexually abused. Four women were presented, and every one of them had a history of being abused sexually. The two males presented hadn't admitted to any abuse, but Andy had suggested that one of them had been hiding something.

Jim was stunned by this. In his work at the emergency department at University Hospital in Newark he had seen the occasional woman who was brought in for an exam, mostly for rape, but he had no idea there were so many women out there who had been abused sexually, both as youngsters and as adults. He wondered if it was a Maine phenomenon.

When the team meeting broke up, he casually asked Brent about it, curious.

"Hey, Andy. Come over here a minute." Brent's booming voice rolled effortlessly across the room, and Andy responded by joining them.

"Andy, how about you take Jim for coffee and fill him in on our work with sexual abuse. I'd join you, but I got a conference call I can't dodge."

"Yeah, sure. Glad to, Brent," Andy said.

Andy and Jim walked out of the conference room and made their way to the elevators. The treatment unit was located on the fifth floor of the Cairo Community Hospital building.

As they waited for the doors to open, Andy quipped, "Hey, it's not every day I get a direct order to go have coffee. Glad you came on board, Jim."

"Is Brent always so, ah…" Jim considered his words carefully—abrupt, then short, then brusque, and finally settled on what he thought was the best choice. "…busy?"

"Yeah, but I'd say it's more like *harried*. Come on. Let's take the stairs. It's a lot faster."

Jim knew right off he was going to like Andy.

They reached the first floor and made their way to the coffee shop. At a quarter to ten, there were two other people at a table when they arrived. Blue-suited business types. Hospital administrators, Jim guessed. Or maybe drug company detail men. A marked contrast to Jim and Andy, who were dressed in shirt, tie, and slacks.

The woman behind the counter was short, trim, and looked to be in her mid-thirties. "Who's this with you, Andy?" she asked, her bright blue eyes taking in Jim as she spoke.

"Jenny, meet Jim Booker, our new physician assistant. He just signed on."

"I'm pleased to meet you, Jim Booker," she said, extending her hand to him.

Jim shook it and was surprised by the strength in her grip. *No dead fish grip here.* "Likewise, Jenny. I expect you'll be an important part of my life here," he said with a grin.

"Hey, he catches on fast, doesn't he?" Andy said to Jenny.

"Indeed he does. Now, what can I get you? Coffee and a slice of Mae's coffee cake?"

"Sounds great, but coffee's all I need," said Jim.

"Oh, I forgot to tell you, your first order's on the house. A 'welcome aboard' from me and the hospital," explained Jenny.

"Go for the coffee cake, Jim. You can't go wrong with Mae's cooking." Andy looked at Jenny. "Make mine the same."

"Have a seat, gentlemen, and I'll bring it right over."

The coffee cake turned out to be delicious, and Jim told Jenny as much.

"I'll be sure to tell Mae. She'll be pleased to hear she's got a new customer," said Jenny, as she got back behind the counter.

"This is really good," Jim repeated to Andy as he cleaned his plate and licked his fork.

"Mae's a first-rate cook," agreed Andy. "Wait'll you meet her. She's everyone's image of the perfect mother. Jenny's great, too, as you've already seen."

"A good combo," said Jim.

"So what'd we come here for, besides coffee?" asked Andy. "Oh, yeah. You had a question about the sex abuse thing."

"I couldn't help noticing how many of the patients, or clients I guess you call them, have been abused. Especially the women."

"Good observation for your first session. Yeah, we see a lot of it. We started tracking it about a year ago. At this point, we're finding that about ninety percent of the women and about fifty-five percent of the men have a history of being abused. We're sure our figure for the men is low because they have a tougher time admitting it. The macho thing, you know. And the deal that a man should be able to defend himself against such stuff. Of course, they never stop to think that they were weak, defenseless kids when it happened to them. They tend to remember the abuse through their adult eyes."

Jim nodded slowly, sipping his coffee. "Is this a Maine thing, then?" he asked, sure it must be.

"We thought it might be, but when we presented a paper on our findings at a national conference in San Francisco last fall, many people from several other states thanked us for bringing it up because they'd had similar experiences within their own programs.

"Here's how we think it works," said Andy, pausing to take a sip of coffee before continuing. "Sexual abuse leaves the victim feeling used, dirty, and unless they get some kind of closure, feeling guilty."

"Guilty? Of what?"

"They figure that it must've been their fault that it happened. Like maybe it was something they said, or it was the clothes they were wearing, or the way they acted, or they shouldn't have been where they were at the time. They blame themselves for what happened, and not the creep who abused them. So, how can they be angry? They can't be angry at the perp, but they can sure lay the anger on themselves. How do you think they feel about themselves?"

"Not too good."

"Not too good is right," Andy said. "Matter of fact, they feel like shit about themselves. So, what do they do to feel better?"

"They drink."

"Bingo! They drink. They also smoke pot. They do coke. They shoot up heroin. Et cetera, et cetera. Usually they do two or more drugs. And at some point, the alcohol and drugs lose their magic. Then, we might get them here to get a chance to sort it all out for them."

"What can we do for these people?" Jim picked up his cup to take a hit of coffee and was surprised to find it empty. He didn't recall finishing it. He set it back down.

"We help them get in touch with their anger. We take away their guilt by helping them see that it wasn't their fault. Once they accept that, they can redirect their anger at the perp, or perps, where it should've been directed all along."

Jenny came to their table, coffeepot in hand, and refilled Jim's cup.

"Help me finish this pot so I can make a fresh one," she said, filling Andy's cup.

Jim reached in his pocket for money, but Jenny put her hand on his shoulder, a gesture of gentle restraint.

"No charge, Jim. I'd have thrown it out anyway," she said with sincerity. She was back behind the counter before they could protest.

"Thanks, Jenny," said Jim.

"Yeah, thanks, Jenny," Andy echoed.

"My pleasure," she responded.

Jim took a sip. It smelled and tasted freshly brewed. He made a mental note of Jenny's generosity as he returned to the topic of discussion. "Who are the perps?" he asked.

"Fathers. Older brothers. Uncles. Next door neighbors. Someone they know and trust, mostly. As for the men abused as boys, ditto, plus those of the opposite sex."

"Mothers, older sisters, aunts, et cetera?"

"You got it. Plus, toss in older women who insinuate their way into their lives and get it on with them," said Andy.

"With all the information out there, on the internet and elsewhere, how can this abuse still be happening?"

"Yeah, I know what you're saying. Thing is, there's still a lot of sickies out there who prey on children. No matter how many times a mother tells her daughter to watch out for men trying to touch them, it still goes on. The sickies get better at what they do."

"Why don't they tell somebody about it right after it happens? Then maybe they wouldn't have to use drugs and booze."

Andy shrugged. "Some do, and if they're believed and action is taken against the offenders, they get over it. But when a lot of them tell their moms that their dad or stepfather or older brother or uncle diddled them, you know what? Their moms tell them they're lying, that it couldn't have happened, that so-and-so would never do such a thing. The ugly head of denial rears its head. And guess what? Boom! There goes the last possible family support for the poor kid. Those are the ones we get," said Andy. "Those, and the ones who never tell."

He paused a moment to let it all sink in, then continued. "But you know what? Most of them never say a word to anyone. Their guilt is so great, they believe so completely that it was their fault, they keep it to themselves and try to brick off the part of their minds that holds the memory. Or memories. It usually happens numerous times over many years."

"Why would they let it keep happening to them?" Jim asked, surprised.

"Sometimes the perp threatens them, sometimes threatens to hurt someone else, maybe a parent or other loved one. More often than not, the victim figures, 'What the hell, one more time isn't going to make a difference,' so they roll over and let it continue. The 'damaged goods' attitude."

"Damaged goods?"

"Yeah, you know. The box is already broken open, so what's it matter if more is lost out of it?"

"I get you. But why wouldn't they at least tell their friends, or maybe a best friend?"

"Something happens to them. They feel dirty, set apart from old friends, embarrassed to talk about the disgusting things that happened to them, afraid they'll be laughed at, ridiculed, or shunned. Or worst of all, not believed. So they keep their silence. Keep their secret."

"So they drink and use drugs."

"Yeah, to block out the memories for a time, and to help them feel better for a time. At least while the drugs and booze are affecting them. But you know what? While they're drugging and boozing, they're set up for more unwanted sex from opportunistic males and females, and that makes them feel even worse when they're sober again. So now they have even more stuff to block out, more reasons to get high. And on and on it goes."

"Until they come here for help."

"I wish it was that simple, Jim. If it was, fixing them would be easy. Unfortunately, damned few of them come here wanting help for their sexual victimization. By the time they come in here, most of them don't even realize that there's a connection between their being abused and their drugging and drinking. They've buried it away, bricked it off, as I said, and we have to chip away at their walls until we can get them to look at what they've hidden away.

"And if we can't get through, get them to deal with the abuse, we can't fix them. They'll go back out there and get right back into the drugs and booze. Maybe we'll get a second shot at them down the road. Maybe not."

Andy picked up his cup, tossed back the remains of his cold coffee, then set it back down. "Maybe we'll see their names in the obits, victims of their own hands," he added.

"Does being sexually abused affect everyone the same way?"

Andy shook his head. "No, not at all. One of my fellow psychologists

33

said that some of them flex and bend, some shatter, and some ring like a bell, or words to that effect. The ones who flex and bend are the ones who get support and closure right off, the ones who ring like a bell are the ones who stuff it away and end up coming in here, and the ones who shatter, well, we never see them. They're the ones who end up in the psycho wards. Or dead."

"I gotta tell you, Andy, all this talk about victims of sexual abuse makes me feel different, guilty in a way, out of place, because I've never been a victim myself. I guess I had what you'd call a normal childhood, all things considered."

"Yeah. Me, too. But don't let anyone tell you that that keeps you from being able to help those who've been sexually abused, because it's not true. All it takes is sensitivity, and I'm guessing you wouldn't be in medicine if you didn't have that. And don't worry, we get help from the staff who have been abused."

"I never thought of that," said Jim. "How many of them are victims?"

"The counselors, the six you met today, all are recovering addicts and alcoholics. Brent feels they make the best counselors, since they've been there themselves and can relate to the clients. All the women counselors are victims of sexual abuse, and one of the males. I'll let you figure out which one on your own," said Andy, his eyebrows dancing.

"So that's why I got the cold stares when I made that dumb comment about looking at their name tags."

"You got it. Their way of saying, 'Watch it, buster!'"

"I'll have to be more careful about what I say in the future. I've gotten used to making comments like that without thinking beforehand," said Jim.

"Hey, it's not all that bad. You'll see me get away with a lot of off-color comments, but they know me. When they get comfortable with you, they'll ignore all that stuff, too, or most of it. In the meanwhile, you'll need to be careful with what you say."

Jim nodded. "I've got another question. What happens to the perps when they're identified by one of our clients?"

"Depends. If it's been more than seven years, the State of Maine, in its wisdom, says the statute of limitations has run out, and there's nothing we can do. If it's been less than seven years, like with kids, we can work with them to press charges, get them into court, and hopefully get the perps sentenced to prison. But it's a long, painful process and it's the rare ones who face charges, and even rarer to see them do jail time."

"So these creeps probably go on to abuse others."

"Not probably. Almost certainly," Andy said in a serious tone. "We joke about hiring the Equalizer to come in and dole out some good old-fashioned frontier justice."

"Who's the Equalizer?"

"Don't you remember that TV program about the middle-aged, overweight ex-intelligence guy who went around kicking the butts of the bad guys, giving them some of their own medicine? We think he could work wonders with the perps we coax our clients to identify."

"Oh sure, I think I remember watching re-runs of the show."

Suddenly, Jim was hearing a voice he thought he'd left behind in Newark: *I want you to come to me any time you have a problem, no matter how big or how small. I'll take care of it. You got me? Say the word and I'll take care of it.*

He sat up abruptly, pushing back the memory. "Right, then. How do you see me helping the cause?"

"I guess Brent's talked to you about asking if they've been sexually abused when you do the history and physical with the new clients."

"Sure, though the thought of asking the question has me a bit nervous. It's never been a part of my routine before."

"Normal reaction, but I assure you, once you've asked a half-dozen clients, it'll be as easy as asking how old they are."

"Who said asking that was easy?" Jim joked.

Andy chuckled. "Probably a bad example. Anyway, we've found that the more times people ask the question, the more disclosures we get. They deny it to Sally, you met her, the intake coordinator, and they'll deny it to the nurse. Then, you come along in your white coat and ask, and they'll say something like 'how did you know?' and spill the beans.

"After you've got some experience, you'll know before you get to the question, so instead of saying, 'Were you ever sexually abused?' you'll ask, 'When were you sexually abused?' That really gets them. They'll think you're a mind reader."

"The Great Swami."

"You got it."

Jenny came to the table again.

"Would you boys like some lunch?"

"Oh, no thanks. I've got some paperwork to do," said Andy, pushing back his chair.

"Just thought I'd ask, since it's ten of twelve," she said.

Jim checked his watch, and saw she was right.

Andy drew his chair back in. "What's the special today?"

Chapter Four

"Did you pick up anything from Andy?" asked Brent, his fingers steepled in front of his mouth as he slouched casually in his desk chair.

"Plenty," said Jim, his expression serious. "He gave me food for thought for the next month." He sat in the padded armchair to the right of Brent's desk.

"Glad to hear it. Andy's come up with some great statistics which we presented at a substance abuse conference in San Francisco. Did he mention it?"

"He did. He said more than ninety percent of the female clients have been sexually abused, and at least fifty-five percent of the males. And those were the ones who were man enough to admit it," recalled Jim.

"Good memory. We think the real number for men is as high as seventy percent. Maybe higher. As we get better at asking the right questions, we'll get better data," Brent said.

"What do you mean, when we get better? What's to ask?" probed Jim, sensing this was the direction Brent wanted to go.

Brent leaned forward in his chair, his expression contemplative. "Imagine for a moment that you were sexually abused when you were ten or twelve, and that you've been hiding it ever since. Over the years, you've taken great pains to wall it away, to keep anyone else from knowing. And as time goes by, you even succeed in walling it away from yourself, so most of the time you've deluded yourself into thinking it never happened. You know you don't like yourself, but the reasons have gotten fuzzy over the years. You turn to alcohol, and maybe to pot and coke and heroin, to help make you feel better, and for a brief period of time, each time you use, you do feel better. Or at least, you get high. Then the effects wear off and you experience the natural depression that follows. So you use again. And again. Each time you hope to get that high, that feeling that everything's fine, and each time you crash back down to the pits.

"So somehow, you end up here at Serenity." Brent sat back in his chair.

"Maybe you got smart and realized you weren't going anywhere but down, maybe family or friends pushed you into coming, or maybe the law gave you the option of coming here for treatment instead of going to jail. Whatever. So here you are.

"You spend a day or two getting sober, and we do our magic so you don't see the pink elephants or get the shakes during detox. And you're starting to feel better."

Brent shot forward in his chair, his eyes fixed on Jim's. "What happens next? Some guy in a white coat with a stethoscope stuck in his pocket sits you down and asks you a whole bunch of questions. And one of the questions is, 'Have you ever been sexually abused?' What do you say? You say, 'Hell, no!' in a loud voice. Want to know why?"

"Why?" asked Jim, captured by Brent's presentation.

"Maybe you believe it yourself, for one. You've been building and reinforcing those walls so long that you've got yourself believing that nothing happened to you.

"Or two, you've been saying 'no', guarding your ugly secret from the world for so long now it's second nature, a knee-jerk reaction, a basic defense."

Jim leaned in closer. "Why would they be so defensive? Clearly, you're trying to help them."

"Okay. Do this. Picture yourself when you were ten or twelve, starting to feel your oats but not any kind of match for an adult, especially a scheming, planning, devious one. So there you are. And some older guy, probably a relative or a close friend of the family or someone you've grown to trust, he talks you into doing something with him, something that starts off innocent enough, but ends up with your pants off and maybe your mouth where it was never meant to be. Got it?"

Jim felt uncomfortable with this scenario, but said, "Got it."

"So afterwards, he tells you to never tell anyone or something terrible will happen to your parents, or some such a line, and then you go home. And from that moment on, you feel different. You go to school and see your friends, but nothing is the same again between you. Part of it is because you have that ugly secret separating you. Another part is that you *are* different. You've had a nasty, traumatic thing happen to you, and your friends haven't. You'd die of embarrassment before you'd ever tell them. Get the idea?"

"Got it," said Jim.

"And the worst of it is, once the guy does it once, it's easy for him to do it again. And again. Maybe he gives you little gifts, maybe he just gives attention that you don't get from your busy parents. The second and third and tenth time are never as bad as the first time because you've learned

37

how to go numb and get through it each time. If you were a girl, you'd think, 'Hell, I've already lost it. What's the difference if it happens again?' The 'spoiled goods' attitude."

Brent paused a moment to let Jim process what he'd said, then went on.

"So time passes, and you're a teenager, and the guilt starts sinking in. You're bigger now, and better able to defend yourself. And you find yourself asking, 'Why did I let him do those things to me? Why didn't I fight him off?' forgetting that you were much smaller, much more vulnerable and defenseless when it happened. But that doesn't help to make you feel better about yourself. Fact is, you get to feeling worse and worse about yourself, to the point of hating yourself. So what can you do to make yourself feel better?" asked Brent, his piercing blue eyes on Jim.

"Get high?" Jim offered.

"Exactly! You start with booze, and then try pot, and then maybe toss in a little speed, maybe LSD, and move up to coke and heroin, if you can figure out how to afford it. Some end up using their bodies to get coke and heroin. Kind of ironic, really. Do something completely degrading in order to buy some coke to make them feel good for a short time. But does it make them feel better? Hell, no. They feel worse, and they hate themselves worse, and they reinforce their belief that they're bad, all of which makes it easier to do the same thing to get more coke or heroin the next time."

"You're painting a picture here of a child alienated from his familiar world by a calculating and manipulative deviant. Is the end of the story always the same sordid one?" asked Jim.

"Good question, and the answer is no. If an adult intervenes, either by discovering what's going on and putting a stop to it and getting closure on it for the child, or the child has the guts to tell someone and the bad guy gets his comeuppance. Either way, the incident can be dealt with then and there, and the child doesn't have to carry the baggage into adolescence, maybe into adulthood. We don't often get those children, the ones who get saved, in here," said Brent, his arm sweeping around him to encompass the treatment facility, a wistful smile on his face.

"Okay, so how do you break through the defenses they've built? What do you ask them?" asked Jim, returning to the original subject.

"I thought you'd never ask," replied Brent, his face lighting up. "Tell you what. Instead of my trying to answer that, let's go down to the Detox unit. There's a guy who came in yesterday. By now, he should be sober enough to answer my questions. Maybe fuzzy enough to be caught off guard by them. I'll talk to him, you listen, okay?" He got to his feet.

It wasn't really a yes-or-no question, Jim realized. He said the obvious. "Sounds like a plan," he agreed, standing as well.

"I think you're going to take to this business just fine," said Brent, draping an arm across Jim's shoulder and giving him a reassuring squeeze. Then he headed for the door, Jim right behind him.

As they walked together, Brent talked about the role of the Detox Unit. "Detox is the first stop in the treatment facility," he explained. "It's where the clients who are ready to make a change in their lives or maybe get away from the demons that chase them, are housed while the chemicals leave their bodies. If they are pure drinkers—an anachronism today, since most substance abusers drink and do some drugs—they have their blood pressure, pulse, and temperature monitored for elevations. If their blood pressure and pulse rate go up, they get other chemicals fed to them to keep them from having DTs, or delirium tremens.

"DTs is a nasty condition, mostly relegated to the past, but still occurring to drunks who stop drinking on their own with nobody around to monitor them. This sometimes occurs to the drunk who swears off alcohol and they go into DTs. It more frequently occurs to the drunk who can't get the money to continue to drink, and as a result, goes into DTs. Modern medicine uses tranquilizers to chemically control the withdrawal period so the person withdrawing doesn't have to see pink elephants or risk convulsions from abrupt cessation of drinking." Brent glanced his way.

"The multi-substance user, the person who drinks, plus smokes pot or snorts coke or shoots heroin, is the more typical admission to today's Detox unit. Most of them admit to using alcohol because that's a legal substance, but few disclose their other habits when they first come in. It's up to the Detox detectives to find out what else the person has used."

He went on. "A simple screening test is used to break the code of silence. It's a urine test for drugs of abuse, which includes screens for marijuana, opioids, cocaine, amphetamines, and barbiturates. Cocaine is the first to go from the bloodstream, disappearing from drug screen detection after forty-eight hours of being used. Marijuana is a long-lasting drug, sometimes hanging around in the user's fatty tissue for several months. The other drugs of abuse fall in between. I'm sure you know all, or most of this, but once I get on a roll I can't stop," Brent joked.

They arrived at the Detox nursing station, and Brent casually pulled a chart from the rack. A male nurse, looking trim in a white shirt and pants, sat at the counter. He looked up from a note he was writing in a chart.

"Hi, Doc, how's it going?" the man asked, lifting his eyes to Brent. He had a short-cropped blonde head on a well-muscled body.

"Good, Larry. Meet Jim Booker, our new PA. Jim, this is Larry Morrissette, one of the best detox nurses in the world."

Larry stood and reached for Jim's proffered hand. "Good to meet you, Jim. Brent jests, though. I'm not the best in the world. I'm still working on it."

"That's what makes him the best, Jim," Brent said. "He spends his free time reading articles and journals to pick up the latest stuff." Brent ended his brief shower of praise by putting his big arm around Larry's shoulder and hauling him up against him for a second.

Jim noted how effectively Brent used physical contact. He also got the point about keeping up-to-date with articles and journals.

"How's the new guy doing, Larry?" Brent asked.

"Mr. Springer? He's coming along fine, considering his BAL yesterday was 2.1. He's had two PRNs of lorazepam and it looks like his BP and pulse are stabilizing. He's almost out of the woods, I'd guess," said Larry.

Jim knew a BAL was a blood alcohol level, a measure of the amount of alcohol in a person's bloodstream, usually put there by drinking. He also knew most states considered a person legally intoxicated if their level was above 0.1, so Mr. Springer came in well saturated at 2.1.

"Is he ready for company?" asked Brent.

"He's awake, and he ate half his lunch, so I'd say the time is right," said Larry, nodding his head in the affirmative.

"Okay, then. Let's go talk to this guy, Jim. See what he's made of."

Brent set Mr. Springer's chart back on the chart rack.

Jim noted that he hadn't opened it, only used it like a stage prop. He'd gotten what he'd needed from Larry.

When he and Brent entered his room, Mr. Springer was lying on his bed, dressed in maroon-colored hospital pajamas. The deep maroon of the pajamas was in stark contrast to his pasty-white face. Jim could see that Mr. Springer had reached a point several levels below his usual norm.

Brent wasted no time. "Hi, Mr. Springer, I'm Doctor Caldwell and this is Jim Booker, my physician assistant. How're you doing?" he asked, extending his right hand.

Mr. Springer blinked, then struggled to a sitting position to shake Brent's outstretched hand.

"Good, Doc. I'm feeling a lot better, thanks to you and the nurses here."

"Thank the nurses, Mr. Springer. They're the ones who do all the work around here," Brent said.

"Nelson."

"What?"

"Nelson. My name's Nelson. My father's name was Mr. Springer," he said, running his hand over his hair in a futile effort to straighten it. His other hand was still firmly in Brent's grasp.

"Oh, okay, Nelson. You can call me Brent."

"Okay, Doc," he replied through a half smile.

Brent turned to sit next to Mr. Nelson Springer on his bed, continuing to hold his hand captive.

"So what got you in here?" Brent asked him, his voice pitched low, conspiratorial.

"I got sick and tired of feeling sick and tired," Nelson said, his voice flat.

"Sounds like you've done this before, Nelson."

"Whatever makes you think so?" he shot back, still smiling.

"*Sick and tired of feeling sick and tired.* That old phrase goes way back," said Brent, his eyes on Nelson Springer's pasty-white face.

"Well, I don't feel very original today, for some reason."

"Understandable. What have you been using?" Brent asked, changing the subject.

"What else? Booze."

"You tell me what else. Booze and what?" Brent persisted.

"Why's it got to be booze and something else? Why not just booze?" asked Nelson, a hint of anger, maybe righteous indignation in his voice. He extracted his hand from Brent's grasp.

Brent clasped his hands in his own lap.

"Because you're too young to be a boozer. What are you, thirty-five?"

"Thanks, but I'm forty-one," said Nelson, somewhat mollified.

"So what else do you do?" Brent prodded.

"I smoke a little pot now and then."

"And?"

"And what?"

"And what else, Nelson?" Brent asked.

Nelson twisted slightly. "I've done a few lines of coke."

"A few lines? What's that mean?"

Nelson laughed mirthlessly. "A few lines here, a few lines there, until I'd sucked more than fifty grand worth of nose candy into my head, and the last snort was ten times, no, a thousand times, less pleasurable than the first!"

"Cocaine lie," Brent said.

"Huh?"

Jim was glad Nelson had said huh because he didn't know what Brent was talking about, either. At the same time, he guessed that Brent was glad Nelson had asked so he could inform both of them.

"You know, the big cocaine lie. The first few lines are such a rush that you can't wait to do it again and get the same high. But the next time takes a little more, and the time after that takes even more, and before you know it, you're snorting five hundred, maybe a thousand bucks at a whack, but that first big high stays just out of reach. Then you blow your wad and come crashing down, with no more money to chase the dream. It's the big cocaine lie that keeps you using until you're broke."

"Yeah, you got that right. I blew fifty grand, all I had. If I'd had a hundred grand, or a million, I would've done that, too," lamented Nelson.

"When did you start using?"

"What? Cocaine?"

"Whatever. Cocaine. Booze. Pot. Speed. LSD. Mushrooms. PCP. Glue. Gasoline. Whiteout. Whatever."

"Hey, shit! That was a long time ago. I don't remember."

"You remember. How old were you, Nelson?" Brent rested his hand on Nelson's shoulder in a neutral manner.

Nelson squirmed.

"I guess I was maybe thirteen when I snitched brews from the refrigerator. Not long after that I was doing speed. Then pot. Then I don't know what all."

Brent clapped Nelson on the back.

"Good work, Nelson. We covered a lot of ground today. Get some rest, and we'll talk more later."

He stood and turned to Jim. "C'mon, Jim. Let's leave Mr. Springer alone for a while so he can think about things."

With that, Brent left the room, Jim following on his heels.

When they got back to the nurses' station, Jim waited for an explanation for their abrupt departure. Brent appeared to be ignoring him. He had picked up Mr. Springer's chart and was thumbing through the progress notes, his back to Jim.

What the hell? Jim decided to ask, which looked like the only way he was going to find out. "So, Brent. Why'd we leave so abruptly?"

Brent faced Jim, a big smile on his face. "Way to go, Jim. That was a good observation, shows you were paying attention," he said. His big left hand reached out and squeezed Jim's shoulder in a friendly way. "We left when I knew he'd been sexually abused. He wasn't in any shape to get into it now."

"Okay," Jim said. "Now tell me how you know he's been abused?"

Brent pulled out a chair and sat down. Jim did likewise.

"There's no magic here, Jim," Brent said. "It's a matter of asking the right questions and listening well. Why don't you tell me what you heard Nelson say?"

Jim thought for a moment, feeling slightly uncomfortable. It was similar to the feeling he had when, as a PA student, he'd been asked to discuss a differential diagnosis, a disease process, or a procedure in front of medical students and residents. But he'd gotten through that, acquitting himself well, and there was far less pressure here. Still, the feeling was there.

"Okay. He started out telling us he was a boozer, and he got angry when you suggested there was more. Then he told us he smoked a little pot, like that was all, but when you pushed him, he admitted to a big coke habit that broke his bank. Then you asked him when he'd started using, and he got defensive, said he couldn't remember. When you told him you didn't buy that, he admitted to beer at thirteen, then speed and pot after."

"Couldn't have summed it up better myself. Now, what do you make of all that?"

It was Jim's turn to squirm. He knew Brent was trying to get him to see the clues suggesting that Nelson had been sexually abused, so he focused on that.

"Well, he was defensive about everything," Jim began.

"Good start," Brent said.

"And he downplayed his drug use, like it was no big deal," Jim added.

"Why do you think he did that?"

"Because he was ashamed of it?"

"Maybe," Brent shrugged. "So, which drug does he like best?"

"You never asked him that."

"I didn't have to. He told me anyway."

Jim considered this. Then it dawned on him. Cocaine had broken his bank, and he'd admitted that he would've spent more if he had it. Jim's eyes lit up. "Cocaine."

"Bingo! Go to the head of the class. Why?"

"Why?"

"Yeah. Why cocaine?

Jim ran over in his head the illicit drugs and the effects they had on the user. Cocaine, he remembered, offered the biggest high. "Because it made him feel good?"

"Damn, you're good! Why would he prefer it over, say, pot, that makes you feel mellow?"

"Because he doesn't feel good about himself?"

"You're on a roll. Why doesn't he feel good about himself?"

"He's been sexually abused?"

"Maybe. It's not positive proof, but it sure has me leaning toward that conclusion. There's one more clue in what Nelson told me that makes me ninety percent certain he's an abuse victim. Can you ferret it out?"

Jim frowned in thought.

"I'll give you a clue," Brent said. "It was one of the last observations he made."

Jim reviewed his summary, then knew. "How old he was when he started using."

"There you go, and without even a question in your voice. Remember what I said about guilt setting in, about their feeling that they should have been able to prevent the abuse from happening?"

"Yes. When they get older and physically stronger, they look back and blame themselves for not preventing it, but they forget how small and defenseless they were when it happened." Brent rewarded Jim with a gentle squeeze of his shoulder. "So, what do you think of Mr. Nelson Springer?"

"That maybe someone took advantage of him when he was around nine or ten, and when he got bigger and tougher at thirteen he got the guilts. Since he couldn't change anything, and he felt like a piece of crap, he tried things to make himself feel better for a while. He tried beer, but that was real temporary, and it made him feel worse the next day. Then he tried speed and pot, which probably worked to distract him a bit. But when he discovered coke, he knew he'd found a friend. He could jump on the soaring high, and as long as the money lasted, he could keep soaring."

Brent clapped his hands together.

"Maybe. You've got all the maybes that I got. They add up to a very high probability, but what do we need to be sure?"

"We need Nelson to tell us what happened."

"That's it! You've got the job. Did I tell you you've got the job? You've got the job." Brent stood and wrapped his big arm around Jim's shoulders and punctuated his comment with a mighty squeeze. Then he stepped away.

"So, when should he tell us?" Brent asked.

"He should tell us when he's damned good and ready."

"Jeez, you're good! Where'd you say you worked before, an ER? How'd you get so sharp working in an emergency room?"

"Must've been the weekend drunks and druggies," Jim replied, feeling the pressure lift.

"Well, you've earned your first day's pay. What do you say we get out of here?" Brent suggested.

Jim checked his watch, was surprised to find it was four-thirty. "Where'd the day go?" he asked.

"Time flies when you're having fun," Brent shot back.

The phrase was trite and time-worn, but Jim realized the truth in those words. It had been fun.

Chapter Five

"So you're the new hotshot PA, huh?"

Her sarcasm caught Jim short. He turned to see the counselor from the morning team meeting. He searched her face for a smile but found none. She'd removed her name tag, too.

"You must be confusing me with somebody else," he replied, trying to lighten the mood.

"I don't think so," she shot back. Still no smile.

"You're, ah…" he fumbled, looking for a rescue, his eyes skyward.

"You won't find my name up there. You won't find it on my chest, either."

Jim recalled his dumb morning remark, confirmed by Andy McMartin, PhD. So here was one of the abused women come to berate him for it. He remembered her presentation. He remembered her comment about removing a perp's "hardware." He remembered liking what he saw. But now he couldn't remember her name. Then, mercifully, a name came to him.

"Brenda, right?" he asked, knowing he was wrong the moment he said it.

"Something like that. It's about as much like Brenda as George is to Jim, though," she said, her blue eyes flashing.

"Okay, I give up," he said, raising his hands above his head in surrender.

"So soon? I didn't figure you for a wuss, Hotshot."

Mercifully, axons clicked in his grey matter. Pathways opened. "Breanna! Right?" he said with obvious relief.

"Let's see. How did that work?" she posited, running her fingers through her thick auburn hair. "I take a sidelong shot at your masculinity, and you reach down deep and come up with my name. Interesting, Hotshot. Very interesting." Still no smile.

"Hey, you weren't the only one I met today. There must be over twenty new names rattling around inside my head."

"Wow. You sure know how to make a girl feel special."

Jim stood, speechless. He couldn't recall ever having the wind knocked out of his sails so completely.

"Well, if that's all you've got to say, I'm off." With that, Breanna turned on her heels and strode toward her car.

Jim watched her retreating figure, knowing he'd just been worked over by an expert.

It took him less than ten minutes to drive to his new apartment in Cairo. There were no traffic lights to slow him down. There were three stop signs, none of which caused him any delays, just brief pauses to look both ways and make sure the coast was clear. The total distance was a little over four miles. In Newark, at the same time of day, four miles would've taken him an hour or two, sometimes longer. He was already more comfortable here than he'd been in Newark. Cairo felt more like home. His encounter with Breanna had receded toward the back of his memory by the time he got to his apartment.

Fred was there to greet him, perched forlornly on a high stool inside the entry door, black button bear eyes staring.

"Hey, Fred. How was your day?"

Fred considered the question.

"Well, hey, while you're thinking about it, let me tell you about mine."

Fred offered no objection, continuing to stare at a point somewhere near the entry door, unmoving since Jim had set him there before leaving for his first day at Serenity.

Drawn to the area of Fred's stare, Jim noticed pale rectangles on the hallway walls. Each had a small puncture wound in their upper center. Jim knew at once what they were, having seen them on other walls before. They were the shadows of a previous occupant's life, places where they'd hung pictures to remind them of other people and other places. As time passed, the paint surrounding the pictures faded while the areas under the pictures were spared. Jim knew it was up to him to cover them with his own memories, making this foreign place his own home for a while.

"I get it, Fred. You've made your point. I'll get pictures up after we eat. That work for you?"

Fred, true to form, made no comment.

"I'll take your silence as a sign of agreement. Hey, let me fill you in on my day at Serenity."

Jim recounted his day, covering the morning meeting and his faux pas with the name tag comment, then reviewing his lengthy and informative coffee break with Andy, followed by the session with Brent and the new admission. He told Fred that he couldn't remember having learned so much in one day. Then he touched on the angry meeting with the counselor, Breanna, and her reaction to his casual remark. He ended by telling Fred he clearly had a lot to learn.

Fred listened without interruption, his silence an indication of his non-judgmental nature.

"I like you, Fred. Have I told you that before? I like you because you never rush to judgment. You always take your time and mull everything over before making a decision. That's a really nice trait in a bear."

Fred, taking Jim's words to heart, held his tongue.

"Well, hey, let's get some dinner going, what do you say?"

Jim pulled open the fridge and immediately regretted not stopping on the way home for groceries. Three cans of Stroh's beer, brought along from Newark, looked lonely on the door rack. The rest of the fridge harbored the dregs of a quart of milk, a partial tub of So You Think You Know Butter, a large glass jar that held one lonely pickle spear, a plastic bag holding the remains of a block of Monterey Jack cheese, and a wrapper that held three slices of whole wheat bread, well past its prime.

"Not a pretty sight, Fred."

He lifted out one of the Stroh's and popped the tab, then took three long pulls of it.

"It's time for some magic, old buddy." He opened the cupboard to the left of the stove and spotted two cans of ravioli.

"Guess it's 'Chef's Special' again," he muttered to Fred, taking out one of the cans.

Jim found a small saucepan and the can opener, relieved the can of its top, and dumped the contents into the pan. Then he set it on the stove, turned the burner to medium. Instead of the *whump!* of gas igniting, there was an annoying tick-tick-ticking as the electric burner heated up.

One more difference, one more thing to adjust to.

He shook off the minor annoyance.

He knew that the act of preparing a meal, even one as basic as this one, would help to warm up the new apartment, make it less foreign. Something about sitting around a new apartment with a full stomach blurred the harsh edges, smoothed off the burrs.

The ravioli heated quickly. Jim dumped it on a plate, scraped the residue from the saucepan, and set his meal on the kitchen table.

He called out to the entryway. "Hey, Fred, dinner's on. Shake a leg!"

As he spoke, he strode to the entryway, picked up Fred and his stool as one unit, and brought him to the kitchen table. Fred stared at the plate of ravioli with a total lack of enthusiasm.

"Don't be so critical, Fred. Here, try a bite." Jim speared a block of ravioli and held it up to Fred's stitched mouth. Fred held his mouth shut.

"Okay, don't tell me later that I didn't offer you some." Jim steered the fork to his own mouth, chewed briefly, then swallowed the results.

"You don't know what you're missing, Fred." Jim considered his words.

"Or maybe you do, you sly old bear. It's downright awful, tell you the truth. But it's nourishment, right? We'll eat better tomorrow, I promise."

The ravioli gone, Jim stood and carried his plate to the sink, grabbing the saucepan off the stove on the way. He turned on the hot water, then glanced back over his shoulder at Fred.

"I wash, you dry, Fred. Shared responsibilities make for a harmonious relationship, I'm told. Can't recall who told me that, though."

Jim washed the pan, plate and fork, set them in the drain rack, then rinsed out the sink.

"Okay, Fred. Whenever you're ready." He walked behind Fred's stool and patted him gently on his soft, plush back. "I'll unpack the boxes while you dry."

His one-sided conversation with Fred was interrupted when his cell phone rang. He looked at the number, didn't recognize it, then muttered, "what the hell," and answered it.

"Jim Booker."

"Hi, Jim. It's Merry."

A long pause ensued while Jim screened his memory banks for the name, delayed because he thought it might have been new to him that day. Then he remembered.

"Merry, hi. What's up?" he asked, caution in his voice.

"Guess I didn't make as big an impression on you as I'd thought," she said, her voice challenging.

"Yeah, sorry about that. I had my first day on the new job and I was introduced to over six thousand people."

"Wow. You were busy. How many were named Merry?"

"Touché. Mind if we start over? Everything all right?" Jim asked.

"Everything's great. Thought I'd call, touch base with you, knowing this was your first day at Serenity. How about you? Any problems?"

"No, everything went well. I've got a lot to learn about substance abuse treatment, that's for sure. Hey, how'd you get this number?"

"My boss is very good at a lot of things," she said.

Jim got the point. Tony Bonnano's world wide web.

"Why do you have a lot to learn about substance abuse treatment? I thought you were a physician assistant. Don't you leave all the substance abuse treatment stuff to the specialists?" Merry asked.

"You're right. My main job is the history and physicals, plus ongoing care of the *clients*. They call them clients here. I'm more used to calling them patients. One more thing to get used to. Anyway, the director sees me being more involved with the clients than just the medical side. He figures that another perspective, another point of view, could make a difference in some of the outcomes," Jim explained.

"Sounds like your director's got it together," Merry observed.

"Yeah, he does. I took to him right away. He has a warm, hands-on approach that seems to work well. But keep in mind, that's from only one day on the job."

"Sure. Well, I won't keep you. Glad to hear you've made a good start. I'll check back in with you from time to time. I hope you've kept my card in case you want to call me."

"Yes, I've got it. I'll keep you and Tony in mind. Never know."

"You're right. Never know."

"Hey, Merry. Mind telling me what Tony did for you? You know, to repay you? Or maybe the first question is, what did you do that put Tony in debt to you?" he asked.

"Wow! You're full of questions. I'll tell you sometime, but not right now," Merry replied, her voice neutral.

"Okay. We'll talk later then."

"I have a feeling we will. Bye, Jim."

"Bye, Merry." He disconnected the call.

Jim thought a moment about Merry's last comment: *I have a feeling we will*. For a moment, he thought there may have been a deeper meaning in the way she said that. Then he dismissed the notion as the imaginings of a lonely guy in a new place.

He turned to Fred, glancing at the pot and dish that had air-dried while he talked to Merry. "Nice work, Fred. You're good at drying. Think I'll keep you."

Fred took the compliment in stride.

"Let's check out the TV, see what we get," Jim suggested. He recalled the landlord's comment when he'd asked if there was cable.

"Hasn't got out this way yet," was his dry reply. Then the man had added, "There's room on the roof for another antenna, if you'd like."

Jim turned on the TV and pulled out the rabbit ears on the indoor antenna. After some serious searching and manipulating of the rabbit ears, he was able to get marginal pictures on three channels: six, eight, and ten. He settled on fuzzy six and a familiar sitcom when the house phone rang. It startled him. The phone was on his bedside table, an old habit born of his emergency medicine days. *Phone rings, wake up and answer, run off to see a patient.*

He rushed to get to it before the caller hung up, picking it up at the end of the third ring.

"Hello?" he said, slightly breathless from the adrenaline rush of his first landline call.

"Hey, Hotshot. Big apartment, eh?"

Jim knew right off who it was.

"No. Small apartment, lots of boxes in the way," he said, keeping his voice neutral.

"You're probably wondering why I'm calling."

"That, and how you got this number." Jim struggled to keep his voice calm.

"New England Telephone Company information gave me your number. I asked for 'new listings' and there you were. Why I'm calling, though, I guess I was a little, ah, rough on you, you know, earlier."

"Oh, that. I've already put it out of my mind," Jim lied.

"Well, I've been sitting here thinking about what I said to you, and maybe more to the point, how I said it, and I wanted to, ah, apologize to you for being so nasty."

"Look, Breanna. It is Breanna, isn't it?" he asked.

"Yes. It's Breanna."

"Well, Andy filled me in about you, and I guess you had every right to jump down my throat."

There was a long pause before she spoke again. "What did he tell you?" Her question hung in the air.

"Uh, that all the women counselors had been, ah, abused sexually, which is why I got icy stares after my dumb comment about nametags," Jim struggled to say.

"So you knew what made me angry at you before I tore you up this afternoon? Why didn't you butt in and say something? I feel like an idiot now," Breanna breathed, her voice softened.

"You were on a roll. There was no stopping you." His voice carried the hint of a smile with it.

"Knee-jerk reaction, I guess. My way of getting healthy, taking care of myself, and you caught my best shot. Or my worst," she amended, a gentleness coming through with her words.

"If it was a knee-jerk reaction, I guess I'm lucky I wasn't any closer to you," Jim replied lightly.

"Touché. But anyway, I wanted to call you and say I'm sorry. It was a dumb way to start out, you being new and all."

Jim sat down on the bed, listening. "I'd accept your apology if I thought it was in order, but really, I'm the one who was out of line."

"Would you for God's sake just accept my apology? Then maybe I can sleep tonight."

"Okay, if it'll help you sleep, I accept your apology, even though it's not necessary."

"Thanks. By the way, which do you prefer? Hotshot or Jim?" she asked.

"Up to now, my friends have called me Jim, though I have to say, Hotshot has a certain ring to it."

"I'll think about it. Meanwhile, thanks for humoring me and hearing me out. Now I can sleep." She paused, then added, "I hope you can, too," completing the apology.

"I don't think it's going to be a problem," he said.

"Okay, then. See you in Serenity."

"See you in Serenity," he echoed.

Jim replaced the receiver and left the bedroom, shaking his head.

"That was an interesting call, Fred, my man. An apology from the woman who chewed me up and spit me out a couple of hours ago. What's your sense? Was she sincere, or was she covering her backside in case I decided to tell someone about it at work?"

Fred's response was, as usual, slow in coming.

"Tell you what, Fred. Mull it over, and we'll talk in the morning. You okay with that? Meanwhile, I'm hitting the sack, and so should you."

Fred stared straight ahead, seemingly lost in thought.

Jim switched off the forgotten TV and the living room light. The bedside table lamp shone through the doorway and washed over Fred on his stool. He sat alone in a sea of darkness.

"Remember, I'm here if you need me, Fred."

Jim hadn't considered that it went both ways.

Chapter Six

"You're up early, Fred. You didn't spend the whole night on that stool, did you?" Jim asked the bear.

As was his habit, Fred was studying the living room when Jim emerged from the bedroom, hair tousled, wearing only a smile. He gave Fred a pat and went into the bathroom.

A short while later, he emerged shaven, hair in place, his smile the only adornment on his lean, muscular body.

"Any thoughts about that phone call last night, old buddy?" Jim paused briefly, then returned to his bedroom.

A few moments later he was back out, wearing gray slacks, a green pinstripe dress shirt, and a solid dark green tie. Ready for the day ahead.

"It's breakfast time, Fred. What can I get you?"

While waiting for an answer, Jim busied himself with making coffee. It was the one thing he fussed over, his breakfast extravagance. He ground the beans, carefully measured the coffee into a cone filter, then poured four cups of just-boiled water over them to produce his morning wakeup. Most mornings he added toast or a bagel or a muffin, but without the coffee the rest had no appeal.

Finished, Jim poured himself his first cup. He took an exploratory sip, then gave his own imitation of the old Maxwell House "Ahhh!" He drank his coffee black, unsullied by sugar or cream. A rich coffee aroma filled the kitchen and overflowed into the living area.

"All's right with the world now, Fred," he said, sipping again while breathing in its thick fragrance.

Fred took equal pleasure in breathing in the rich aroma that surrounded him.

Cup in hand, Jim crossed the living area to the TV and hit the power button. Channel Six came on. Local news. He checked his watch.

"I want to get in early today, do some wandering around, get acquainted before everyone shows up. Means I've got twenty minutes."

Sipping his coffee, he stared at the TV with lackluster focus. Saw images of a big paper mill, heard something about a possible strike, but it wasn't registering. He looked at Fred. "Okay, what're your thoughts about the phone call from Breanna last night? You read anything into it?"

Fred returned his stare, his glossy black button eyes mirroring miniature TV images too small to decipher.

"That's what I came up with, too. Nothing. Guess her conscience got the better of her."

Jim stared, unseeing, at the TV screen while he replayed the phone call from Breanna. He turned back to Fred. "Nice way to sign off, though, don't you think? 'See you in Serenity.' It conjures up images of a warm, comfortable, peaceful place. But who knows? Maybe that's the way everyone says goodbye there, and it's only new to me. Time'll tell, eh, Fred?"

Sipping his coffee, he glanced at the TV. A weatherman, dressed in a sports coat and tie, and with a twisted wire protruding from the right side of his head, was sweeping a hand over a map of the northeast. He was saying something about a winter storm track, that it was likely to drop another four to six inches of snow on parts of Maine. There was a good chance that the low pressure area off the coast could draw the whole mess seaward, and if that happened, the total accumulation would amount to an inch or so. He concluded by urging viewers to stay tuned for updates as they came in.

Jim shook his blond hair from side-to-side, his lips turning up at the corners. This was a far cry from the spit and polish, the dead-sure presentations of the Newark stations. He liked the difference. He liked the casual clothes and the disregard for professionalism, as revealed by the loosely concealed wires. He especially liked the admission that the forecast was far from certain, something that was avoided in the big city, even if the outcome proved different.

"Refreshing, isn't it Fred? We're either getting another half a foot of snow, or we're getting a dusting by this evening. Do you care?"

Fred showed no signs of caring either way.

"Neither do I, old buddy. Neither do I. Let it snow. Or not. The folks around here have demonstrated their ability to clear it from the roads with speed and efficiency, so let it fall where it may. It can't hurt the skiing, no matter what."

He checked his watch.

"Time to go, Fred, if I want to get there a little early."

He poured the last of the coffee into his big orange travel cup, then put on his parka, wool cap, and gloves.

"See you, Fred. If you find the time, wash the breakfast dishes. If you can't get to them, I'll do them later."

Jim closed the door behind him, leaving Fred to contemplate the dishes and all the other important issues of the world.

Chapter Seven

"You're in early, aren't you?" asked Larry Morrissette, the Detox nurse Jim had met the day before.

"A little, but you beat me," Jim said, making solid eye contact.

"Nursing hours. I work seven to three-thirty. You just missed the shift change report by a frog's whisker," Larry said, showing off a huge grin.

"That close, huh?" he replied in response to Larry's witticism. "Anything I need to know?"

"We'll do a full report when Brent gets in at eight. Meanwhile, they said Mr. Bolduc in 214 is showing signs of being awake and alert. Do you want to go practice your interviewing skills on him? You've got a good twenty minutes," Larry added.

Jim studied Larry's expression, searching for signs of a setup. For his part, Larry returned his gaze, unblinking. Jim was unable to sense any warning signs. *What the hell. Nothing ventured, nothing gained.*

"Why not? Where is he?"

"He's in his room. Until Brent gives the okay, they stay in their rooms, usually for twenty-four to forty-eight hours," explained Larry.

"How long's he been there?"

"It was forty-eight hours at eight last night. He's been a tough detox," said Larry, still using the same bland tone, still maintaining solid eye contact.

A small alarm went off in Jim's head. He ignored it.

"If I'm not back here by eight, send in the troops," Jim said. Then he headed for 214 and Mr. Bolduc.

The door to 214 stood open. Looking in, Jim saw a short, stocky, florid-faced man sitting on the bed, his torso hunched forward. He wore hospital-issue pajamas and a cotton bathrobe, both a deep magenta. They closely resembled the man's complexion. His red eyes were set in doughy puff-pastry cheeks that looked like they'd been set out to rise far too long. The remains of his breakfast littered a hospital table in front of him. Much of it remained.

The man raised his eyes to see who had darkened his doorway. Both face and body showed signs of rapid aging. Once-sharp lines had coarsened, widened, grown indistinct. Jim concluded that Mr. Bolduc had been ridden hard and put away wet on more than one occasion. Despite his appearance, Jim guessed him to be in his mid-thirties.

"Mr. Bolduc? Jim Booker. I'm the PA here." Jim strode toward him, hand outstretched, smiling all the while.

"Goddamned coffee's fake! Fuckin' decaf. No taste, no nothing! Like drinking dirty water." He ignored Jim's hand.

"Well, other than the coffee, how're you doing?" Jim drew his hand back to his side.

"I'm fuckin' sober, that's how I'm doing!" Mr. Bolduc made his reply without looking up.

"How long's it been since you've been that way?" Jim asked, working to keep his smile intact.

"Beats the shit outta me. What's today?" asked a florid Mr. Bolduc.

"It's Tuesday."

"That's no help. What's the date?" he shot back at Jim.

"It's the seventh." Jim could feel his smile dissipating fast.

"Of January?" Mr. Bolduc's bushy eyebrows raised slightly, but his eyelids remained at half-mast.

"No. It's February." Jim gave up on what was left of his smile.

"Well, shit then. I've been drunk a fair piece. Last I remember was watchin' that fuckin' ball drop in Times Square! On the TV. I wasn't there," he explained.

"Sounds like it's been about five weeks," said Jim. "Are most of your binges that long?"

"If the money and the booze hold out," said Mr. Bolduc, a faint twinkle in his bloodshot eyes.

"Why do you drink?" Jim probed.

"To get fuckin' drunk! Why the fuck else would I drink?" parried Mr. Bolduc, a cynical sneer hauling at the left side of his mouth.

Jim knew this wasn't going well. He glanced at his watch. He still had ten minutes until report. He pushed on.

"Okay, so why do you get drunk then?"

"Because it makes me feel good," shot the irascible Mr. Bolduc.

Jim tilted his head, thinking. "So, you don't feel good when you're not drinking?"

"What the fuck. If I felt as good sober as I do drunk, I'd stay sober," reasoned Mr. Bolduc.

"Do you smoke pot?" Jim asked.

"Shit, no! Stuff makes me sleep."

"Do you use coke?"

"Too fuckin' expensive. I can stay drunk a lot longer than I can stay high on coke, dollar for dollar," said Mr. Bolduc.

"Have you tried any other drugs?" Jim prodded.

"Name some."

"Speed?"

"Yeah."

"LSD?"

"Sure."

"Peyote?" Jim asked.

Mr. Bolduc nodded. "Yep."

"Crystal?"

Mr. Bolduc gave Jim a sideways glance. "Crystal meth?"

"Yeah, crystal meth."

"Yeah."

"How about heroin?"

"You bet."

"Mushrooms?"

"Years ago."

Jim met his eyes. "You shoot up?"

Mr. Bolduc shrugged. "If I can get my hands on a needle and some good stuff, sure."

"What's your favorite?"

"Booze. It's cheap and dependable."

"If money wasn't an issue, which would you choose?" Jim asked, curious.

"No question. Coke."

"Why?"

Mr. Bolduc cocked his head to the side. "It takes me places nothing else can."

"You like getting high?"

"I like feelin' good. And coke takes me there better'n anything else."

Jim noticed that Mr. Bolduc had a dreamy, faraway look in his eyes. His voice had modulated. He guessed that the real Mr. Bolduc had stepped forward in the last few minutes. He considered the responses Mr. Bolduc had given and decided to ask the big question.

"Have you ever been abused, Mr. Bolduc?"

"What the fuck is that supposed to mean?" snapped Mr. Bolduc, his lower jaw thrust forward, brows lowered.

"In other words, did anyone beat you or do things to you when you were a kid?"

"Fuck, no. My parents loved me."

"That's good. But what about older brothers, older sisters, cousins, grandparents, teachers, people you trusted?"

"You are one sick sonofabitch! What'd you say your name was? Jim?" Mr. Bolduc looked Jim square in the face. "Listen, Jim. I don't know where you're comin' from, but you're startin' to piss me off real good with all your suggestions about people doin' sick stuff to me. Look at me! Do I look like someone who can't take care of himself?"

Throughout his outburst, Mr. Bolduc had grown increasingly animated and agitated. His magenta facial coloring had intensified, passing through crimson on its way to beet red. His hands darted and twisted through the air like barn swallows swooping at mosquitoes on a summer evening. A thin trickle of drool seeped from the left side of his mouth and hung, suspended, from his whisker-stubbled chin. His breathing had accelerated to short, rapid gasps.

"I take it that means no, Mr. Bolduc."

"You're goddamned right it does," Mr. Bolduc gasped, struggling to regain his lost composure.

"Sorry if I got you all worked up," Jim said sincerely.

"Well, you fuckin' pissed me off, saying I couldn't defend myself." Mr. Bolduc's color was lightening, his breathing easing.

"That was never my intention, I assure you," Jim said, his own voice calm.

The doorway darkened. Jim turned to see Larry there.

"Sorry to break in, but it's time for report," Larry announced.

"Thanks, Larry." Jim turned back to Mr. Bolduc. "See you in a little while, Mr. Bolduc."

"Yeah, yeah, sure. When can I have a smoke?"

The treatment facility had banned smoking on the units when there was a big push to make hospitals and associated facilities smoke-free. Now smokers had to be well enough to go outside if they wanted to smoke. There was irony in that. A smoker had to be healthy enough to go outside, often to face freezing cold or driving rain capable of toppling the toughest of them. Smoking had become a habit for the strong of heart, not for the weak.

"Dr. Caldwell and I will be back soon, Mr. Bolduc. He can tell you," Jim replied as he was leaving.

"Jesus H. fuckin' Christ! Caldwell. He'll come in here and put his big fuckin' arm on my shoulder and ask me if I'm tryin' to kill myself!"

Jim heard no more as he headed back to the nurses' station. He couldn't help wondering how much of Mr. Bolduc's prophesy would prove true.

"There you are. Getting right into it, I hear," said Brent Caldwell as Jim went to the nurses' station. Brent stood to greet him, enveloping Jim's strong hand in his own.

"I've been finding out a little bit about Mr. Bolduc," Jim explained.

"That's great. We'll go see him together after Larry briefs us on the night's events. Grab a chair."

Jim sat down and Larry Morrissette reviewed the five Detox patients, including the new admission who'd been brought in by way of the Bridgetown Emergency Room in the middle of the night. He ended by reviewing Mr. Bolduc's vital signs and clinical presentation.

"Thanks, Larry. Great job, as usual," Brent said, his eyes confirming his sincerity. "It sounds like Mr. Bolduc's ready for me. Let's go, Jim."

Jim was soon back in Mr. Bolduc's room. On the way, Brent hadn't asked him about what Mr. Bolduc had told him. Jim assumed they'd discuss it later.

"Good morning, Roy. How's it going?" Brent asked warmly, his hand extended.

Roy Bolduc held out his hand to be engulfed by Brent's. "Same old shit, Doc."

"In the same old crapper, too, right, Roy?" Brent sat down next to Roy, not yet releasing his hand.

Jim took a position nearby, observing.

"Yeah. Same ol', same ol'," Roy confirmed.

"How long were you wasted this time, Roy?"

"Well, thanks to your sharp assistant there, we figured it was about five weeks." Roy looked at Jim as he spoke.

Brent draped his left arm over Roy Bolduc's shoulder while continuing to hold his right hand captive.

"What're you trying to do, Roy? Kill yourself? Your liver can't take many more of your alcohol baths, you know," cautioned Brent.

Jim smiled inwardly at the accuracy of Roy Bolduc's prophesy. He'd obviously emerged from an alcoholic fog on Brent's Detox unit more than once.

"If I wanted to kill myself, I'd blow my fuckin' head off with a gun or try and move a bridge abutment with my car," snapped Roy.

"How old are you now, Roy?" asked Brent, changing the subject.

"I'll be thirty come April."

Jim remembered guessing that the man was in his late thirties. Alcohol and drugs had stolen ten years from him.

"You still going to the sex abuse group?" Brent asked.

"That fuckin' group? That doesn't do shit for me! I don't need that crap," spouted Roy.

Brent turned to Jim. "Roy had his uncle take advantage of him when he was, what were you, Roy?" he asked, turning back to Roy Bolduc.

"Ten, goddammit, and forget it, because I sure have," barked Roy.

Brent laughed, a short, guttural sound charged with disbelief. "Sure you have, Roy. That's why you're still trying to kill yourself with booze."

"Booze has nothing to do with it. I drink because it makes me feel good," he insisted.

"Sounds like you've got yourself believing that," said Brent, his voice calm, reasoning. "Do you still think it was your fault he did those things to you?"

"Damned right it was! I should've shoved him away, told him to leave me be."

Brent pulled back from Roy but left his hand on his shoulder. "How big were you when it happened, Roy? How much did you weigh?" he asked in a calm, matter-of-fact voice.

Roy stared at the floor, searching his memory. "Hell, I don't know. Probably five-foot-six and a hundred thirty pounds."

"Roy, you were in the fifth, maybe sixth grade. Think back. How big were you?" pushed Brent.

A big tear spilled from Roy's bleary eyes and slid down each puffy cheek. "I should've done something," Roy moaned.

"Yeah, you should've told your mom or your dad after it happened. But if you'd tried to stop your uncle, he'd have gone ahead and done what he did to you anyway. Wasn't he a big man?"

"Yeah," moaned Roy.

"How big?"

"Six-one, over two hundred pounds," Roy recalled miserably.

"So, what could you have done?" asked Brent, his voice gentle, his hand still resting on Roy's shoulder.

"But I didn't do anything! I let that sick fuck do that shit to me, and I never even tried to stop him," Roy said.

"So tell me, what *could* you have done?" asked Brent, his tone, his inflection unchanged.

"Jesus Christ! I should've done *something*," Roy wailed. "He kept coming back, doing more sick shit to me, over and over!"

"Okay, so what could you have done?" asked Brent, patience obvious in his voice.

"The sonofabitch did it to me for almost three fuckin' years, and I never tried to stop him. Not once." Both of Roy's cheeks were wet with tears.

"Do you know why it *wasn't* three years?" asked Brent.

"What do you mean?" asked Roy, staring at Brent, confusion in his voice.

"Did you ever stop to ask yourself why he stopped doing those things to you?" Brent's hand had stayed on Roy's shoulder the whole time, neutral, meant to comfort rather than threaten.

Roy shrugged. "He got tired of me," he said, his voice quavering.

"That's bullshit," snapped Brent, making Roy blink in surprise. "He stopped because you were getting bigger, and he got worried you'd fight back or maybe say something to someone about it. He got afraid of you! You think about that, Roy, and I'll come back and talk to you later."

With that, Brent stood up and walked out of Roy's room. Jim fell in behind him.

Ten paces down the hall Brent glanced toward Jim, his index finger across his lips as a warning not to talk. They walked in silence to the nurses' station, and Brent closed the door. They had the room to themselves.

"I go through this every time Roy comes in," said Brent, exasperation in his voice. "He can't stop blaming himself for everything that happened. I can't get it through his head that he was too small and weak to defend himself. Problem is, he looks in the mirror today at a six foot, two-hundred-pound man and figures he should've kicked his uncle's butt. He can't picture himself as a defenseless ten-year-old."

Jim considered this, then said, "Why don't you bring in a ten-year-old boy so Roy can see the difference between the youngster and himself?"

Brent's face blossomed. "That's a great idea! Wait a minute. That isn't a great idea. That's a brilliant idea! My son, Doug, is ten. I'll bring him in. Where did you get such a great idea? Great ideas like that don't come out of Newark, New Jersey," Brent joked.

"You're probably right. It's more likely the result of my exposure to the cold, clean air of Maine," Jim said, making light of Brent's comments.

"Well, wherever it came from, I figure you just earned your first week's pay, and what is this, day two? Keep this up and the Board will consider your present salary insignificant."

"You can always give me a raise, if it'll make you feel better," Jim suggested.

"Hey, you learn quick for someone who just crawled out of an asphalt jungle," said Brent.

"More likely the asphalt jungle made me a quick learner," Jim offered.

"Wherever you learned it, Newark's loss is our gain," Brent concluded, his right arm capturing Jim's shoulder. He squeezed it affectionately. "Come on. We've got to get to morning meeting."

Brent dropped his arm as they made their way to the elevator.

Jim was glad he'd come in early.

Chapter Eight

They walked side by side into the Gold Room, named for the color of the carpet, not for some benefactor named Gold. Brent took the same chair he'd been in the day before, and Jim did likewise, even though there were two others vacant. He wondered if the staff was such a collective creature of habit that he'd offend someone by sitting in the wrong chair. He decided he'd test his theory in a couple weeks when he wasn't so new, see what the reaction might be.

"We've got a good shot at getting Roy Bolduc to stay in treatment this time, and we can thank Jim Booker for that," Brent announced, his booming voice silencing the room.

Jim was impressed with Brent's ability to catch everyone's attention with a few words.

"Jim met with him this morning," Brent continued, making his voice softer for the attentive group, "and suggested to me that we bring in a ten-year-old boy so Roy can see how vulnerable a kid that size and age really is. Brilliant, don't you think?"

There was a general murmur in the affirmative from the staff. Embarrassed by the unexpected attention, Jim glanced around the room at the faces that looked his way. They wore smiling, friendly, open expressions. He returned their eye contact.

Then his eyes fell on Breanna. She wore a different expression. Mouth upturned, yes, but at the same time, he noted an almost imperceptible side to side wag of her head, a subtle sign of disbelief.

"Where's the ten-year-old boy coming from?" asked Andy McMartin.

Jim turned his attention away from Breanna.

"My son Doug'll volunteer, though he doesn't know it yet," Brent said. "He's an average ten-year-old, so if Roy can put himself in Doug's shoes, I'm hoping he'll finally accept how vulnerable he was to an adult as big as his uncle."

"Is Doug on salary or commission?" asked the tall, slender, soft-spoken intake coordinator.

Jim remembered his introduction to her the day before, but her name eluded him.

"Strictly commission, Sally," Brent said. "I'll probably have to buy him a double-scoop ice cream cone on the way home."

Jim silently thanked Brent for giving him half of the elusive name. *Sally.* He imprinted it in his memory banks.

"Ice cream in February?" asked Andy, disbelief echoing in his voice.

"Doug knows no seasons. Fact is, he likes it better in February because it doesn't melt so fast," Brent offered.

"Let me get this straight," said Andy. "You're bringing your ten-year-old son in here so a sexually abused guy can look him up and down, and who knows what else, and then you're gonna get him ice cream for being a good kid. Have I got that right?"

"Whoa, time-out," snapped Brent, the remnants of his smile hanging precariously from his lips. "Time to move on to other things. Who are we discussing this morning?"

Three hands raised.

"Dave?" said Brent, pointing at Dave Levesque, primary counselor for the Blue Team.

"Okay," Dave began. "This is the third team presentation on Judy W., a twenty-five-year-old separated mother of two children, ages seven and four, here for treatment of alcoholism and poly substance abuse, mainly pot."

Dave paused to draw a deep breath. "As you recall, she broke down in Women's group last week and described some nasty sexual abuse by her husband. One time he tied her up, and after he got off, he put a curling iron to her genitals and breasts. She has the scars to prove it."

Jim glanced at the faces around him while Dave spoke. All appeared calm. None showed signs of alarm or shock. He wondered what his own face looked like. Dave's graphic description had clearly shocked him.

"Yesterday, Judy received a phone call from the Belfast Police Department," Dave continued. "A customer found her husband lying on the floor of his garage. He was unconscious, and he'd been burned pretty bad. When he came to in the hospital, he couldn't recall what happened to him. Near as the police can figure, he was working on a truck exhaust using an acetylene torch to cut through the old pipe, and the pipe fell on his head, knocking him out. When he collapsed, the torch landed on his groin and did some serious damage."

"How serious?" asked Brent.

"He lost most of his penis. Too badly cooked to save. His testicles are in bad shape, too. The doctor in charge said he doubted if they'd ever work again."

"That's a perfect example of poetic justice," exclaimed Brent. "There is an Equalizer out there after all."

The faces around the room lit up. Dave Levesque and his associate, Betsy Loomis, high-fived.

"Here's to The Equalizer," shouted Andy, raising his coffee cup in a toast.

"Hear, hear," echoed the group with one voice, coffee cups raised.

"How did Judy react to the news?" asked Brent.

"At first, she was shocked, concerned for his safety. She loves him, you know, despite all the shit he's done to her," said Dave. "But Betsy pointed out that he'd gotten a dose of his own medicine, and she could see the justice in it."

"I told her she probably wouldn't have to worry about him messing with their kids now," Betsy added.

"Has he done anything to them?" asked Andy.

"She doesn't think so, not yet. But she voiced concern for them last week," explained Betsy.

"I'll meet with her to make sure she continues processing this in a positive manner," offered Andy. "The last thing we want is for her to blame herself for what's happened to him."

"How could she ever do that?" Jim asked, surprising himself with the question.

"Easier than you might think," Andy replied. "Since she's told us all the nasty things her husband's done to her, she's gotten in touch with a lot of the anger she has for him. Now this happens, and her mind will try to make her take the blame for it because of the guilt she's feeling for being so angry at the man she loves."

"Easy for you to say," said Dave, a sly grin flicking about on his face.

"Yeah, well, that's the long way around it. But keep in mind that she's likely been blaming herself for years for what he's done to her. Then add the guilt she's feeling for getting angry at him, plus some more guilt for feeling good about what's just happened to him, and you get a picture of a woman with a ton of guilt. Blaming herself for this is a piece of cake."

"I get the picture," said Jim. "Thanks."

"Anything else before we move on?" asked Brent.

***

While filing out after the last team made its presentation, Jim glanced at Breanna. She met his gaze, her eyes crinkled. He noted the barely perceptible *I don't believe you* shake of her head. Jim nodded his head, letting her know he'd gotten her message. A hand on his shoulder distracted him, and he turned, expecting it to be Brent. It was Andy.

"So you've already figured out how to get Brent's kid into the program, huh?"

"Brent made a big deal out of it," Jim replied, his exasperation magnified by Breanna's reaction.

"No, I think it's a great idea. Don't get me wrong. We like to yank Brent's chain when we get the chance, which isn't very often. You gave us the chance, is all," said Andy, his voice placating. "You got time for coffee?"

Jim checked his watch. Nine-thirty. "Let me call Larry down in Detox and find out if the new admit is ready for a physical. Will you be in your office?"

"Yeah. Stick your head in, let me know."

"Will do."

Jim walked into the Recovery nursing station and called the Detox extension.

"Detox. Larry Morrissette speaking."

Brief, professional, Jim noted.

"Larry, Jim Booker. Is our new admit ready for a physical?"

"She's starting to toss and turn, but she's still an hour or more from the awake and oriented stage," he replied.

"Okay. I'll be down after lunch."

"Sounds good. See you then."

Jim made his way to Andy's office, ready for a cup of coffee. He'd been surprised when Larry had said "she" because he'd assumed the admission was a male. The new admit's name was Sandy Collins. A natural mistake. Could have been either.

"Hey, Jim." Andy looked up from the papers on his desk when Jim poked his head in. "Be right with you. I'm looking for an MMPI," he said, holding up the clump of papers he'd been studying. "I'm reviewing Judy W.'s, the woman we talked about in team. Wanted to refresh my memory before I meet with her."

"Speaking of refreshing memories, who is this Equalizer everyone keeps mentioning?" Jim asked, taking another step inside the office.

"You remember the TV show a few years back? He was a retired agent, called himself McCall, went around helping people who were being victimized," Andy summed up.

"By con artists, thieves, angry husbands, people like that?"

"You got it. Advertised in the classifieds, New York City. Anyway, whenever we hear about a bad case of abuse, somebody usually pipes up and says, 'It's a case for the Equalizer.' It's not very often when we hear something that could have been the work of the Equalizer, like today."

"That's why everyone was so happy?" Jim said, sitting down in the chair across from Andy.

"Yes. Here's Judy W.'s MMPI," said Andy, handing Jim the sheets of paper.

A glance told Jim it was computer-generated. "A computer analyzes the results?"

"Yeah. We used to score them by hand, and then we compared the results to the different categories and made our assessments based on the numbers. Then somebody out there got the bright idea that a computer could do it much faster and more accurately. They're right. I've compared a slug of computer results to my own conclusions, and the computer's right on. We've let the computer do it ever since."

Jim flipped through six pages of single-spaced documentation interspersed with graphs showing peaks and valleys. It was from one of these, he supposed, that Andy had gleaned the big *fuck you!* spike of the classic alcoholic in Harold B.'s MMPI the day before. He returned the pages to Andy. "What's it tell you about her?"

"About what you'd expect. Passive dependent personality type. Probably pushed around by her dad, maybe even abused by him when she was a child. Low self-esteem. Lots of underlying mistrust of men. Stuff like that. Hey, what am I doing? Coffee time!" He dropped the MMPI results on his desk and led the way to the door.

Jenny greeted them when they entered the coffee shop. "Good morning, gentlemen. Coffee and—" she asked.

"Coffee only for me today," Jim replied. "I've got to watch my waistline, you know."

"Oh, don't be silly. You'll burn it off in a half an hour around here! Look at Andy. He's been eating Mae's coffee cake for what, Andy, ten years? He hasn't gained a bit," she bantered.

She was right. Andy was tall and trim. Jim acquiesced. "Okay, Jenny, make it 'and,'" he conceded.

"After that compliment, I don't have a choice," Andy protested weakly.

"Two coffees *and*, coming up!" Jenny said and hurried off to assemble the order.

Andy and Jim were seated at the same table they'd used the day before. Jim wondered if they'd always use it.

"How's it going?" asked Andy.

"Can't complain. I had a chance to see Brent in action again this morning. I came in early, ended up talking to Roy Bolduc, and got some information. Then Brent showed up and got a whole lot more."

"Don't forget, Brent knows this guy from several previous admissions, so he has the edge on you. Just as a suggestion, take a look at the old records, if there are any, before you go see a patient. Then you'll know as much as Brent does when you go in."

"Good idea, thanks. When I did ER work, I didn't need to look at a patient's records before treating them. Emergency medicine is pretty basic. If they're cut, they need sutures. If they're having a heart attack, they need oxygen and drugs."

"Yeah. Around here, though, anybody's been here before, we'll have a pile of good stuff on them. Some of it changes, but not much," explained Andy.

"Your coffee *and*, gentlemen," announced Jenny, setting down the coffees and two mouth-watering coffee cake portions.

Jim noted that she hadn't put creamers on the table. She'd remembered he took it black. He was impressed.

A comfortable silence ensued while he and Andy ate the coffee cake.

"Damn, that's good," said Jim as he set down his fork.

"It's hard to turn down Mae's coffee cake, or anything else she makes, for that matter," said Andy, dabbing his mouth with a napkin.

They sipped their coffee.

"Who's the admission on Detox?" asked Andy.

"Sandy Collins," said Jim. "A *she*, not a he."

"Doesn't ring a bell, but she may have been here before. Check, see if she has an old record," Andy suggested.

"Thanks. I will."

"Looks like you're one of them 'quick learners' I've heard tell of," Andy joked. "Hey, remind me to tell you about PES some time."

"What's PES?" asked Jim.

"I'll tell you when you remind me," said Andy, making a joke of it. He downed his coffee and pushed back from the table. "I've got to get going. I'll get this, you can pay next time."

"Thanks. I'll try to remember," said Jim, grinning on the inside over his dual reference to memory.

"You boys want me to save you some of Mae's Mexican pie for lunch?" Jenny asked them.

Jim checked his watch. Ten-thirty. "Sounds good to me," he said.

"Count me in, too," said Andy.

Andy paid the tab, and they left the coffee shop together.

Chapter Nine

Jim carried the wonderful aftertaste of Mae's delicious Mexican pie when he left the coffee shop after lunch. He vowed to make himself a small, simple supper after indulging in a lunch as good as that. He entered the nurses' station on the Detox unit and found Larry Morrissette writing a progress note in one of the charts.

"Hi, Larry. How's it going?"

Larry raised his eyes from the chart, saw Jim. "Hi, Jim. All's well. How're you doing?"

"Time is flying by," he joked. "Hard to believe it's almost one already."

"Time flies when you're having fun, right?"

"You got it. Hey, where do you keep the old records?" Jim asked.

"Over there, in that four-drawer filing cabinet," Larry said, pointing.

"Thanks."

Jim walked over to the filing cabinet and pulled open the top drawer, labeled A to E. He searched for Collins. There it was: Collins, Sandra P. He lifted out the file and carried it to the spare desk, opening it as he walked.

Sandra Collins had been here before, but the file was thin. Jim checked the admission date. She'd been admitted February 12, two years ago, and discharged two days later on February 14. AMA. *Against Medical Advice*. She'd decided that she didn't need to be here, but the doctor, the same Brent Caldwell, MD, felt otherwise. Therefore, when she made the decision to leave, it was against medical advice. She would've been told that if some medical problem occurred to her after she left AMA, neither the doctors nor the treatment facility could be held responsible. In spite of these admonitions, she had packed up her few belongings, signed out AMA, and stormed out.

Interesting.

What could've caused her to make that decision barely two days into her detox, Jim wondered. He turned pages until he found the discharge summary.

Like Sandra Collins' stay, it was brief and to the point. Her admitting diagnosis was acute alcohol intoxication. Urine drug screen was positive for cannabis, better known as pot, and for cocaine. Other lab work was normal except for an elevation in her liver enzymes, no doubt due to the effects of chronic alcohol intake. After twenty-four hours, pulse and blood pressure had returned to normal limits, and she was conscious and alert.

On day two, Jim read, she met with Brent Caldwell, MD, and a lively discussion ensued. Dr. Caldwell's note stated that Sandra Collins was a victim of sexual abuse, based on her presentation and her history of alcohol and substance abuse. Sandra Collins vehemently denied it, stating that he (Dr. Caldwell) "didn't know what the fuck he was talking about." She further stated, "When I have sex, it's on my own terms, and nobody ever forces me to do anything that I don't want to do." Dr. Caldwell had recommended that she enter the twenty-eight-day residential treatment program. Sandra Collins had replied, "I don't need your program, I don't have a problem I can't deal with myself, and you can stick your program where the sun doesn't shine." Soon after making these comments, Sandra Collins had stormed out, clearly against medical advice.

Now she was back.

Jim wondered what, if anything, had changed with Sandra Collins.

It was time to find out.

Jim met Carole Brown, the LPN—licensed practical nurse—on floor duty and told her what his plan was regarding the client. She went into the exam room to set things up while Jim headed off to collect Sandra Collins.

The exam room was at the midpoint of the Detox unit, opposite the door to the nurses' station. After he'd made his introduction to her, Sandra Collins followed Jim down the hall and into the exam room.

"Hi, Sandy," Carole said in greeting as Sandra entered the room. Carole Brown was mildly overweight and had plain features. Her warm smile and caring personality made her a winner. She exuded self-confidence. Jim took an immediate liking to her.

"Hi," Sandra replied, her voice neutral, no enthusiasm. She was tall and thin, her features sharp, angular. Her eyes and mouth showed remnants of makeup, giving her a neglected, unkempt appearance. Her dull brown hair hung in tangles to her shoulders. She swept a stringy clump behind her right ear as she sat down. Jim remembered from her chart that she was twenty-six. Time had not been kind to her, he could see. She wore a standard-issue deep magenta hospital Johnny with a magenta cotton bathrobe over it. She sat, slouched forward, no expression on her face.

The exam room was small and Spartan. It held a desk big enough to accommodate two, one person on each side, and there were three plastic chairs. The remainder of the room was dominated by the exam table and a small, single-drawer metal stand.

Carole had pulled one of the plastic chairs to the side and sat down while Sandra Collins was sitting in one of the chairs at the desk. Jim pulled out the other desk chair and sat opposite Sandra. He noted that Carole was positioned behind Sandra. Jim could see her, but Sandra couldn't unless she turned in her chair. He wondered briefly why she had chosen that vantage point.

"Miz Collins, I'm Jim Booker. I'm a physician assistant here on the Detox unit," Jim began.

"Forget the Miz thing," replied Sandra Collins. "Miz is for middle-aged spinsters, and that's not me. Not yet, anyway," she added with obvious sarcasm.

"Okay. Sandra then," Jim said, keeping his voice neutral.

"Sandy. Everyone calls me Sandy."

"Okay, Sandy it is. How are you feeling?" Jim kept the same neutral tone in his voice.

"Like shit. Food's lousy, beds're lousy, too much noise, can't sleep." Same monotone, same sarcasm.

"What brought you in here, Sandy?"

"I had a little too much to drink, or so they said at the hospital." Flat. Bored.

"Did you use anything else?" he asked.

"You got the lab results. You tell me." Short, unbending, sarcastic.

Jim glanced down at the lab results he'd brought with him. "Looks like pot and coke." Neutral, but emphatic.

"See? What'd I tell you? You already knew. Why ask?" More challenge. More sarcasm.

"How long have you been using?" Jim kept his voice calm, neutral.

"Ten years."

Jim tilted his head to the side. "No, I mean how long have you been using since the last time you were here?"

"I never stopped. Like I said, ten years."

"Did you try to quit after you left here?" He worked hard to keep his voice neutral.

"Why should I? I don't have a problem. If I wanted to quit, I'd do it." Irritation saturated her voice.

Jim made the decision to hold off on the questions. He didn't want to antagonize her to the point that she refused her physical.

"Okay, Sandy. Let's take a break and get your physical done. Can I have you sit on the exam table?" He kept up his pleasant expression. Calm. Professional.

"You're not touching my privates." It was a statement, not a question and with solid eye contact.

"When was your last pelvic exam?" Jim asked. Calm. Professional. Good eye contact.

"Not long ago. Everything was fine."

"Where was it done?"

"My own doc in Lewiston."

"Could you sign a release form, so we can get a copy for our records?"

"Whatever. I'll be out of here before you get it back." She shuffled over to the exam table and sat on the end, same stooped posture, her arms clutching her shoulders.

"You may be right, but we'll need it for our records anyway. Carole, could you get the form, have her sign it?" Jim asked with a brief glance toward Carole.

"I'd be glad to," Carole said, her voice bright, cheerful.

"Thanks. Okay, Sandy, no pelvic exam. Just the basics." He walked to the exam table and stood in front of her.

"Can I see your hands?" he asked her.

Sandy stretched her hands out toward him.

Before he took them in his own to begin his exam, he noted a fine tremor. "How long have your hands shaken like this?"

"Who knows. Why?" Sandy said, her voice flat. Uninterested. Unconcerned.

"Let me finish your exam and we can discuss it," he said.

Jim moved methodically through the exam. Hands for color, circulation, and uniformity of strength. Head. Eyes. Ears. Nose. Throat. Neck. Lungs. Heart. Abdomen. Pulses. Reflexes. Then a series of simple coordination tests to screen for neurological deficits.

The results were about as Jim expected. Sandy was in reasonably good health, but she had some tenderness and a palpable liver edge in her right upper quadrant. And there was the fine tremor of her hands noted at the onset.

Jim invited Sandy to return to her seat at the desk and sat opposite her.

"First off, your exam was mostly normal. I did find some tenderness in your liver when I palpated—poked it—and it's slightly enlarged, probably because of the alcohol you've been drinking. There's also that fine tremor you have in your hands," Jim summarized, his voice calm, professional.

"What's that mean?" she asked, but with no indication in her voice that she cared.

"The liver's a wonderful organ. It's overbuilt so it can survive a lot of insults and injuries over the years. But it has its limits. When the insults and injuries reach a critical level, and I have to add that everybody reacts differently to different problems, then the liver can no longer keep up with the work it's called upon to do. When that point is reached, you have liver failure. Then you die."

Jim watched Sandy's face as he said this, looking for some reaction. She was good. She showed none. "How long have I got, Doc?" she asked.

"Nobody can answer that. If you stop drinking, the inflamed areas of your liver will heal. The areas you've already killed are gone forever, though."

"You're telling me part of my liver is already dead?" she said, with a little more interest. She gave him solid eye contact, listening.

"Yes, I am." Short, to the point. No embellishing. Jim gave her solid eye contact back.

"Oh."

The first real reaction. She put her head down, thinking.

"What's the shaking in my hands got to do with it?"

Finally, some curiosity.

"Your fine tremor is your liver's way of telling you that it's struggling to keep up."

"Oh." She put her head back down.

Jim glanced over at Carole. She gave him a thumbs up sign for a job well done. He nodded, acknowledging her gesture. He now knew why she'd sat where she was.

He turned to the contemplative Sandy Collins. "I'm going to go write this up. Thanks for your help, Carole. A pleasure meeting you, Sandy." Jim left the exam room and headed for the Detox nurses' station.

Larry looked up when Jim came in. "How'd it go?" he asked.

"Not too bad. I got her thinking about the damage she's done to her liver."

"Hey, that's good. Make sure Brent knows it. Maybe he can use that," Larry suggested.

"Use what?" asked Brent as he strode into the nurses' station.

"The man's clairvoyant. Does this all the time," Larry exclaimed, referring to Brent's entrance.

"I just finished Sandy Collins' physical. I told her that she'd killed off part of her liver with her drinking. I think she heard me," Jim said.

"Tell me about it," urged Brent as he settled into one of the chairs.

Jim reviewed his interview with Sandra Collins, including her refusal of a pelvic exam and his physical findings.

"I'll bet it's been a while since she's had a pelvic exam," mused Brent. "Make sure you document that she refused it."

"Will do. I read her old record, saw she left AMA right after you discussed sexual abuse with her," said Jim.

"What was your impression after you spoke to her?" Brent asked.

"She's got all the symptoms. Drinking and drugging since she was fifteen or sixteen. Use of cocaine. I'm not sure about her refusal of a pelvic exam," Jim added.

"Interesting observation. Many sexually abused women don't protect that area of their body, figuring there's no reason anymore, what's the point. Maybe she hasn't been sexually abused. Or maybe she's throwing us off by defending that part of her anatomy. Let's go talk to her. Maybe we can find out."

"Now?"

"Sure," Brent nodded. "Maybe you got her guard down."

Sandy lifted her eyes to them when they entered her room. Her face clouded over when she saw Brent.

"Hi, Sandy. Remember me?" He reached his hand out to her, his expression open.

"How could I forget? Last time I was here you pissed me off with your stupid questions, and I left. You back to do it again?" She glared, challenging Brent. Ignoring his outstretched hand.

"I hope not," he replied. "How have you been?" His hand dropped to his side.

"Fine," she said, but a little of the edge had dropped from her voice.

"Where are you living now?"

"I've got an apartment in Lewiston with a friend. A *girl* friend," she added with emphasis.

"Good." Brent ignored the connotations. "Are you working?"

"I had a waitress job, but they fired me. Said I broke too many dishes."

"Did you?"

Sandy shrugged. "A couple times things slid off my tray. Could've happened to anybody." She was still defensive.

"Can I see your hands?" Brent asked.

She held them out. Jim could see the tremor.

"How long have they been shaking like that?" Brent said evenly, concern in his voice.

"It's not a big deal. They always shake a little when I haven't had a drink in a while."

She was rationalizing now.

"Maybe it *is* a big deal. A tremor can be a sign of liver damage."

"Oh, yeah! Next, you'll be telling me I need to get honest about having been sexually abused. Well, you can forget that bullshit, or I'm out of here. You hear? Out of here!" Anger had taken control of her fear.

"Come on, Jim. Sandy wants to be alone." Brent's voice was quiet, radiating compassion.

Together, they returned to the nurses' station. Brent closed the door behind them.

"Not much progress, I guess," Jim said.

"You never know. That may have been the storm before the calm, as they say." Brent grinned at his misuse of the phrase. "Anyway, finish dictating your physical, and that ought to do it for today. See you tomorrow."

Brent stood to go, then stopped. "By the way, Jim, you did some real good work here today." He punctuated this by clapping his arm on Jim's shoulder. Then he turned and strode from the room.

"Sounds like you're fitting right in around here," observed Larry. He was serious. Sincere.

"I hope so," Jim said. "I like it here."

"Then it's a win-win situation, I'd say. For my part, I'm glad to have you with us." He consulted his watch to confirm what he already knew. "I'm out of here, too. Nancy Dutton's my evening replacement, and she's making rounds on the clients. I've already given her my report. She's a…"

Larry was cut short by Nancy's arrival.

"She's a what?" Nancy asked Larry, her eyebrows raised.

"I wasn't going to tell Jim all the bad things about you, Nancy. I'll let you do that. Nancy Dutton, meet Jim Booker," he said by way of introduction.

"Hi, Jim. Nice to meet you," said Nancy in a voice full of enthusiasm. She stepped toward him and shook his hand firmly.

"Same here," Jim replied. He saw a solidly built woman in her mid-thirties. Her warm features and open manner suggested a caring, compassion nature. Jim knew right off that they'd get along fine.

"Okay, I'm gone," said Larry, "before I get into any more trouble. See you both tomorrow."

Jim and Nancy waved good-bye as he left.

"Larry told me a little bit about you in report," Nancy said. "Welcome to Serenity."

There was that phrase again. Nancy said it like she meant it.

"Thanks, Nancy. It's good to be here. Since you know a little about me, how about telling me a little about you?"

"Not much to tell, really. I'm an LPN, working on my RN. Married. Two kids, a boy, five, and a girl, two. Been working here for almost three years now, and I like it. Most of the staff's great. Clients can be an occasional pain in the ass, but we have our miracles here that make it all worthwhile."

"Miracles?" Jim raised an eyebrow in question.

"Sure. Only way to describe it when one of them sees the light and stops drinking and drugging," she said. "It's an emotional rush for me. I never get tired of it."

"I get what you're saying," said Jim. "I'm sure I'll enjoy working with you. Right now, though, I've got to dictate Sandy Collins' physical before I start forgetting stuff."

"Hey, go to it. We'll talk later. I've got my own paperwork to do."

Jim sat down with Sandy Collins' chart, reviewed the current information, gathered his thoughts, and picked up the phone to access the dictation system. In no time, he was immersed in the task of dictating a clear, coherent history and physical, being sure to mention her refusal of a pelvic exam.

Nancy, on her part, busied herself with writing notes in other charts.

He was putting the finishing touches on his dictation when he sensed a figure in the doorway. He turned to see Sandy Collins standing there.

"Hi, Sandy," said Nancy, also aware of her appearance. "Can I help you with something?"

Sandy stood there, framed in the doorway. "I want to speak to the doc there," she said, and pointed at Jim. Her demeanor was calm, purposeful.

"Jim, do you have a moment to talk to Miss Collins?" Nancy asked, her attitude protective.

"Sure, I do. Give me a minute to finish this, and I'll meet you in your room, okay, Sandy?"

"Okay." She shuffled off, stooped, clutching her wrinkled hospital-issue bathrobe to her with both hands.

"Wonder what that's all about?" mused Nancy.

"I don't know, but you're coming with me," Jim said.

"Glad to."

Jim finished his dictation, put a note in the progress notes that stated he'd dictated the history and physical, and closed the chart.

"Let's go." He glanced at the wall clock. Four-fifteen. Fifteen minutes til he was done for the day.

When they walked into Sandy's room together, Sandy asked, "Does she have to be here?"

"Yes, she does. For legal reasons," he explained, his voice calm, neutral.

"Okay. Well, it's True Confessions time, and I want you to hear it, not that smug sonofabitch Dr. Caldwell," Sandy stated matter-of-factly.

"I'm ready," replied Jim, sitting in the spare chair to face Sandy, who perched on the side of her bed.

Sandy paused a moment, gathering herself, then began. "Well, it's true. I was sexually abused. I've never told another soul. You're the first," she said, looking through Jim with hollow, haunted eyes, her blank face still masking the turmoil inside.

Jim remained silent, waiting.

"It was my daddy. My daddy did it to me." As she spoke, her voice changed from that of a woman to a child.

Jim sat still, silent. Waiting for her to continue.

"It started when I was ten," Sandy said. "He used to come into my room at night to read me a story and tuck me in. He'd tickle me and make me laugh. Then, without me realizing it, his hands were tickling me on my chest and in my private area. At first I thought it was an accident, that he touched me there because I'd moved suddenly or maybe because he wasn't being careful. But with each passing night, he spent more time touching me. Then one time, he put his hand inside my pajama bottoms and pushed his finger inside me. It hurt a lot, made me cry out. He put his other hand over my mouth to cover my cries. He whispered to me that he was going to make me a woman and sometimes it hurt a little to become a woman. I was a kid. What did I know? He was my daddy. I trusted him." A large tear rolled down Sandy's cheek.

"Sandy, why don't you hold off until tomorrow to tell the rest?" Nancy interrupted.

"If I don't tell it now, I may never share it," she replied in a calm, mature voice.

"Each night after that, for maybe a week, maybe two, I don't remember, he came into my room to tuck me in. And I would go numb."

As she spoke, Jim noticed her voice changed back to that of a child's.

"I stopped feeling the pain because my mind would just go numb. I didn't feel anything. He must've thought that my pain was going away. Maybe he thought I liked it. I don't know." Sandy brushed away tears with the back of her hand.

It was Jim's turn to try. "Are you sure you don't want to wait until tomorrow to finish this?" he asked.

Sandy ignored him.

"Then one night, everything changed forever. He came in and closed the door. He turned out the light before he came over to my bed. He pulled down the covers. My mind went numb, like always. And then he told me it was a special night because he was going to make me a complete woman. He pulled off my pajama bottoms and lifted me up, and I felt the worst pain of my life. I was being split open and I screamed. I couldn't stop screaming, but he had his big hand over my mouth and no sound was coming out because he was holding his hand so tight on my face. I knew my mommy and my younger brother couldn't hear me." Sandy sat dry-eyed, staring ahead, remembering the horror.

"Come on, Sandy, let's hold the rest until tomorrow," Nancy begged, her voice soft, coaxing.

Sandy was somewhere else, somewhere where Nancy's voice couldn't reach her.

"When he finished with me, he pulled the covers up around me. The blankets always made me feel safe. He told me I was a woman after that, and it was our secret. I mustn't ever tell anybody about it because if I told anybody, he would go away and never come back, and then I wouldn't have a daddy. I didn't want that to happen. I couldn't imagine what it would be like not to have him around."

"Sandy, why don't we stop here, and you can tell me the rest tomorrow," Jim suggested, trying to break through to her. He fought to keep his voice calm, matter-of-fact, professional, far from what he was feeling. He knew victims who blurted out their long-guarded secrets often flipped back into denial. They would abandon any hope of recovery. Delaying their telling of the whole story made it easier to get them to resume later on.

"No, it's all right. That was the hardest part. I want to get the rest of it out now." Her voice was flat. Clearly, she was feeling numb now.

"After that," she continued, "he came into my room and forced himself on me on a regular basis. It was never as bad as that first time, but I never felt anything, never found any enjoyment in it. I would go numb when he came in, and stay numb until after he'd gone away. Then I'd cry myself to sleep."

Tears streaked down her cheeks. She had the haggard look of a defenseless woman.

"This continued for four years, and it probably would have gone on longer. I got pregnant when I was fourteen, and my daddy was the father," Sandy recounted in a high-pitched, thin voice of the child she'd lost so many years ago. "But only he and I knew that. My mother and my younger brother thought the father was some boy I'd slept with. As if I had any interest in any boys. So my mother and father arranged a quick abortion. I was so sick of his attention that I ran away from home. I was barely fifteen. Not long after that was when I started drinking and doing drugs."

Jim blinked, felt bitter tears run down his cheeks.

Sandy continued to stare down the long tunnel to her childhood, oblivious.

Nancy saw, reached out with a box of tissues, and regarded Sandy. "How do you feel about your father now?" she asked.

Sandy continued her silent stare.

Jim, recovering, thought she hadn't heard. But she had.

"I hate him. I hate him for taking away my childhood. I hate him for the pain he caused me. I hate him for making me run away from home. But more than anything, I hate him for taking away my feelings. All the times I've been with a man, I've never felt *anything!*" The child was gone. The woman spoke now.

"Those are four good reasons," said Nancy. She turned to Jim. "Jim, why don't you write a quick note about the good things that happened in here this evening. I'll stay and talk to Sandy a little longer, make sure she's okay."

Jim realized that Nancy was in control of her emotions, realized he was not, and was thankful for her suggestion. He stood up. "Good idea, Nancy," he said, but his voice was shaky.

He took Sandy's hands in his, drew a deep breath to regain control. "Thank you for trusting me with your story, Sandy. I'm honored. I'll come in to see you first thing in the morning."

"Thank you for hearing me," she replied, looking him in the eye.

He knew she meant it.

Jim went back to the nurses' station and pulled out Sandy's chart.

Shit. His emotions were awash with Sandy's flood of memories. He stood motionless a moment, his own mind numbed by the deluge.

He sat and wrote in her progress notes: Client disclosed that she was sexually abused by her father when a child. Full note to follow tomorrow. He signed his name.

That was the best he could do right then. He left the chart on the table and walked from the room. It was four forty-five by the wall clock.

He headed for his office to hang up his white coat and pick up his overcoat. As he pulled his office door closed, he heard a familiar voice.

"Hey, Hotshot. Working late?"

Then she saw his face. "Jeez, you don't look so good. You feeling okay?"

"No, I'm not," Jim said. "A client just told me a horrible story." His voice was a low monotone.

"What do you mean?" asked Breanna, though he suspected she'd already guessed.

"She told me her father sexually abused her. In detail," he added, visibly shaken.

"Look, ah, Jim, do you have somebody you have to get home to?" she asked, her voice softened, concerned.

"Just Fred."

"Who's Fred? A dog? A cat?"

"No. A bear."

"A *bear?* You live with a bear?" she said, incredulous.

"A big, stuffed bear. I'll introduce you to him sometime," Jim said, his voice still flat, far away.

"Oh, a *stuffed* bear. That's cute. Well, look. If he doesn't mind waiting, why don't we go get a pizza and talk things through a bit. What do you say?" she asked, looking into his eyes.

He turned to look at her, looked into her eyes, saw her for the first time as a rational human being. "Sounds good to me," he said, recovering somewhat.

"If you can keep up with me, I'll lead the way to Pop's Pizza, the best pizza parlor in all of Cairo." Then, in a stage whisper, she added, "It's also the *only* pizza parlor in Cairo."

Jim half-smiled. "Lead the way."

They walked together to the staff parking lot and went separate ways—Breanna to her sedan, Jim to his pickup.

Chapter Ten

As Jim walked in, he took in the atmosphere of the place. Pop's Pizza was like most pizza parlors in small-town America. It had six booths along the outside wall and six small, round tables grouped in the center of the seating area. The kitchen was in the back with a unisex bathroom opposite it. The paper placemats featured Italy, with stereotypical Italian phrases printed around Italy's boot. There were large, framed posters of Italian cities hanging on the walls. The lights were dimmed. It wasn't a place for reading while you sat there, unless you wanted eyestrain.

Jim and Breanna took one of the two empty booths. Pop's was busy, considering it was just past five. Breanna waved to two other couples they passed before she sat down.

"Popular spot," Jim said above the general hubbub.

"I wouldn't take you to a dump," said Breanna, attempting to sound wounded, but smiling to show she wasn't.

"I never thought you would," Jim replied, still fighting to regain animation after listening to Sandy's traumatic story.

"I'm glad that's settled. You want to start with something to drink?"

"Sounds good. I'll have a beer. How about you?"

"A cola's fine."

"I'll have a cola, too, then," Jim said.

Breanna laughed. "Don't be silly. You want a beer, have a beer!"

Jim raised an eyebrow. "You sure you don't mind?"

"Course I don't mind. Why should I?"

"Well, if you don't drink, I thought it might bother you if somebody else did."

"The answer is no. As the saying goes, 'I don't drink, but I don't mind those who do,'" quoted Breanna, a smile working at the corners of her mouth.

"You're sure?"

"If you ask me again, I'll yell. Order a beer!" Her voice raised a notch. "Besides, I do drink sometimes. I happen to be on call tonight, or I'd gladly join you."

Jim registered the smile on her face, raised his hand to signal the waitress.

She brought them two menus. "Hi, Brie."

Breanna said, "Hi, Sue."

They ordered, and the waitress left to get their drinks.

"Everybody knows you," Jim commented.

"Small town. No secrets. By the time we get the check, they'll know who you are and be planning our relationship," Breanna said in a matter-of-fact voice.

"Sounds like where I come from," said Jim.

"Where's that?"

"A small town in western Pennsylvania. My family has a dairy farm there."

"What's the name of it?" she asked.

"Reynardia. It means 'land of the foxes'."

"Hmm, I've never heard of it. What's it near?"

"The farm?"

She gave him a weird look. "That's the name of your family's farm?"

"Uh huh. Reynardia."

"Okay, I got that. What's the name of the *town*?"

"Ligonier. It's about fifty miles east of Pittsburgh."

"I know Ligonier! There's a classy club there, and they have steeplechase racing in the fall," said Breanna.

Jim nodded once. "That's right. How'd you know that?"

"I was there, let's see, four years ago, with a college friend who went to Pitt. She took me to the horse races when I drove down to visit her. We had a great time. There's a lot of beautiful homes around there."

"You're right, there are. A lot of business people from Pittsburgh live in Ligonier. Where'd you go to college?" Jim asked.

"Syracuse. It's an easy hop to Erie, then zoom! Right down to Pittsburgh."

"I guess our paths wouldn't have crossed back then. Four years ago I was in Philadelphia at PA school. I haven't been back for the steeplechases for six years."

Sue brought their drinks. "Are you guys ready to order?" she asked with a smile, a pad in hand.

"What do you like on your pizza?" Breanna asked Jim.

"Mushrooms, black olives, stuff like that," he recited after a quick glance at the menu.

Breanna leaned closer. "How about onions and green peppers?"

"Sure, that'd be fine."

"Okay, Sue, bring us a large pizza with mushrooms, black olives, onions, and green peppers on it," said Breanna.

"Coming right up, Brie," replied Sue. Then she was gone.

"She calls you Brie. I like that."

"My friends call me that. And my family," she added. "Mom wanted to call me Brie, like the French cheese, but Dad wanted it to be fancier. So they agreed on Breanna, but everybody calls me Brie. Guess Mom won," she added, smiling.

"Well, my full name's JimDanBob, but everyone calls me Jim."

"Seriously?"

"No. It's real traditional. James, shortened to Jim."

"Wise guy!"

Jim grinned. "Had you going, though."

Breanna shook her head. "Not really. I could tell you were lying. Your nose twitched."

"It did not."

"Did, too!"

"I find that hard to believe. I've been working for the past six months on lying without having my nose twitch."

"Well, you need to keep practicing. It still twitches," Breanna said, wrinkling her own nose.

They both took sips from their glasses. There was a brief silence, but neither was uncomfortable with it. Breanna was first to break it.

"Do you want to talk about what happened this afternoon?" she asked, her eyes holding his.

He frowned, remembering Sandy's story. "Yes. I guess I do."

Realizing Breanna was waiting for him to begin, he drew a deep breath and began, leaning towards her and speaking softly to avoid being overheard.

"First off, I've got to tell you, all this sexual abuse stuff is new to me. I mean, there were women who'd been raped and were brought to the ER for what we called a rape exam, but others heard their stories. I was only involved in checking their physical condition and collecting samples." Jim paused, sipped at his beer, then set it down. "So I wasn't prepared for what she told me today."

"Whose story is this?" asked Breanna, her soft voice washing over him, encouraging.

Jim glanced around to see who might be close enough to hear. Satisfied no one was nearby, he continued, his voice slightly above a whisper. "Her name is Sandra Collins. Twenty-six. Single. Been through detox before but refused the twenty-eight-day program when Brent offered it to her," Jim reeled off from memory. Clinical information. Calm. Professional. He drew a deep breath. "She was admitted again for alcohol abuse two days ago. Her drug screen showed pot and cocaine."

"I've heard the name, but never met her," said Breanna, speaking low.

"On her previous admission, Brent thought she had all the symptoms of a sexually abused woman, and he told her so. She told him he was crazy. Then she told him what he could do with his program, and left AMA.

"I went in to do her history and physical this afternoon. She was adamant that I wasn't going to do a pelvic exam, so I deferred it. I reviewed her labs and told her that she'd done some damage to her liver. I think she heard me."

Jim took a sip, then continued. "Then Brent showed up, and we went back to see her together. She immediately got defensive about his previous guess that she'd been sexually abused. He dropped the subject and reinforced the issue of liver damage by pointing out the fine tremor in her hands. Then we left her alone to ponder.

"I was dictating her history and physical when she came to the nurses' station, asking if she could speak to me. I finished my dictation and went back to her room with Nancy Dutton."

"I work a lot with Nancy," said Breanna, giving Jim a chance to prepare for the next part. "She's a good nurse."

Jim nodded in agreement.

"Sandra told Nancy and I everything. Once she started, there was no stopping her. Her voice changed while she was telling her story. It was like she was ten years old again, reliving it. Jesus, Brie, how can a father do that to his own child?"

Breanna listened and watched him. He reached up, self-conscious, and brushed away a tear with the back of his hand. "Damn! Something in my eye," he muttered.

"Yes," she said softly. "Compassion. You can't wipe it away. It's a gift not all of us are blessed with."

Jim raised his eyes to meet hers. "You're pretty perceptive."

She returned his gaze.

"Large pizza with mushrooms, black olives, onions, and green peppers," announced Sue, holding a pizza aloft.

Jim cleared a place for it, and Sue set it down between them. Then she set a plate in front of each of them.

"Refills on the drinks?" she asked.

Jim noted that both glasses were empty. "Bring us two colas, Sue."

"Two colas it is. Be right back. Oh, and watch that first bite. It's always the hottest," she cautioned as she pivoted and headed toward the kitchen.

"Comic relief," said Breanna, looking at Jim.

Jim laughed. "Good timing!"

"Amazing how this old world works."

"What do you mean?"

"I believe everything happens for a reason. Even little things, like waitresses arriving with pizzas," she said.

Jim served each of them a slice of pizza. "And big things, like being in the right place at the right time so Sandy Collins could get rid of that ugly secret she's been carrying around all these years," said Jim.

"Yes, like that. But she isn't rid of it. Not yet," Breanna added. "Are you familiar with Elizabeth Kubler-Ross' five stages of grief?"

"Denial. Anger. Bargaining. Depression. Acceptance. Right?"

"Yes. Well, Sandy has to go through the same process, all the way to acceptance, before she'll be whole again. And right now, I'd guess she's somewhere between denial and anger."

"And I thought I'd cured her," Jim joked.

"You did a very important thing to start the process. You listened to her. And you didn't judge her."

"Two colas," announced a happy Sue. She set them on the table. "Need anything else? How's the pizza?"

"Everything's great," said Jim, trying to match her enthusiasm.

"Okay, enjoy! Wave if you need me," said Sue, before heading off to tend to other customers.

Jim and Breanna ate in thoughtful silence for a few moments, each immersed in their own thoughts. Jim considered what she had said, recalling his conversation with Sandy Collins.

"What did you study at Syracuse?" he asked.

Breanna's laugh bubbled out of her, soft but insistent, like foam from a shaken beer bottle. It surprised them both.

"I'm sorry," she offered after she'd regained control, "but that was perfect. I was trying to think of something neutral to talk about when you came out with that question. You beat me to it!"

Jim grinned. "I have a huge inventory of inane questions ready at the tip of my tongue for situations like this."

"Anyway, to answer your question, I was an English major. I was going to get my teaching certificate—" A chirp sounded, and she stopped mid-sentence.

"Oh, damn!" She reached for her purse. Opening it, she took out her phone and looked at the text message that had caused the interruption.

"I'll be right back. I've got to use a land line to call in," she explained. She slid out of the booth and walked to the back of the restaurant.

Jim watched as Sue held out the phone to her. No question, this wasn't the first time she had been interrupted here. He wondered who she'd been with and was surprised to feel a small pang of jealousy. Then he thought back over all she'd said about Sandy Collins and sexual abuse. He remembered Andy telling him that all the female counselors were victims. He wondered who had abused Breanna. The anger welling up inside him at the thought of someone violating her took him by surprise.

He shook his head to clear the thoughts and spotted her returning to the booth. She was smiling at him. If she'd seen a change in his facial expression, she didn't comment.

"Guess who that was?" she asked, sitting down.

"The President. He needs you at the White House," Jim said lightly.

"No, that's my other phone." She paused, then said, "It was Nancy Dutton."

"The LPN on Detox?"

"The same. It seems that Sandy Collins has slipped back into denial, and she's demanding to leave AMA."

"I thought the next step was supposed to be anger," said Jim, recalling the five stages of grief.

"It is, if it progresses normally. The problem is, she's been denying the abuse for so long that it's more natural for her to slip back into denial than it is for her to go forward. She exposed a lot of painful nerve endings when she told you about it, and she wants to get back to where it doesn't hurt. For her, that's back in denial, back behind the walls she's built up over the years," Breanna explained quietly.

"What're you going to do?" Jim asked.

"I'm going in to talk to her. I'd like you to come, too, if you're feeling up to it," she added, assessing him.

Jim stared at the half-eaten pizza as Sue approached them.

"Want me to box it up to go?" she asked, guessing.

"Yes, thanks, Sue. And bring me the check, please," Jim said.

"No problem. Be right back."

"So, what do we do?" Jim asked, by way of an answer.

"Mostly, we just listen. I'll probably do most of the talking, but you can help by being there to remind her that she told you about it, and it's not going to go away."

***

Their footsteps echoed through the tiled hall leading to the Detox unit. The overhead lights had been dimmed for the night. It made Jim feel like an intruder. Breanna pushed open the Detox unit door. The feeling dissipated in the brighter light. Nancy Dutton looked up at them, her eyebrows raised at seeing Jim.

"Hi, Nancy. I brought Jim along to help," Breanna said.

"Glad to have you both," said Nancy. "Sandy's been screaming at me and threatening to leave in her hospital Johnny if I don't get her clothes. To buy some time, I told her we had to get them from the laundry room. Good luck."

"Thanks. Let's go in," said Breanna.

Nancy led the way to Sandy's room. The door was closed. She knocked.

"That better be my clothes," screamed Sandy.

Nancy opened the door, walked in. "You have visitors, Sandy," she announced in a soft voice.

"Who…?" Her question died when she saw Jim.

"Hi, Sandy. I want you to meet Breanna Fowler," Jim said, gentleness in his voice.

"Hi, Sandy," said Breanna, holding her hand out.

Sandy ignored her hand and turned to Jim. "Listen, all that shit I told you, that was a lie. I made it up because I thought it was what you wanted to hear."

"What was the lie, Sandy?" asked Breanna, her voice calm, unruffled.

"It's none of your concern."

"Well, yes it is. I'm the keeper of the clothes, so if you want them back you need to tell me the lie you told Jim."

"Bullshit. I'll leave in this stupid Johnny! Keep the clothes," shouted Sandy, spittle flying as she marched toward the door.

"Be my guest," said Breanna, keeping control of the situation. "But there's a policeman outside who'll bring you back here for indecent exposure."

Sandy spun around. "Got it all worked out so I can't leave, don't you?" she shouted, her face crimson.

"I told you I'd get your clothes when you tell me the lie you told Jim, and I will," said Breanna. Her voice was soft, reasoning with Sandy.

"All right, I'll tell you. I made up a story about being abused by my father."

"Tell me."

"I told him that my father did stuff to me when I was little," said Sandy, her voice dropping to a normal level.

"How old were you?"

Sandy glared at her. "I told him I was ten."

"What did he do to you?" Breanna pressed.

"I told him he fondled me."

Jim noticed Sandy's voice had dropped to a whisper.

"What else did he do?" prodded Breanna.

"He… Oh, Christ! He had sex with me." With those words, Sandy's

86

voice changed to the little girl voice Jim had heard before.

"How long did it go on?"

"Until I got pregnant. Four years."

Breanna asked, showing her surprise in a tactful way. "Your father got you pregnant?"

"There wasn't anyone else. I hated sex."

"Thinking about what he did to you, aren't you angry?"

"How can I be angry?" Sandy asked in her little girl voice. "He's my daddy. Anyway, it was my fault that it happened."

"How so?" asked Breanna, caring in her voice.

"I did something to make him do those things to me."

"That's what I used to think, too."

Sandy jerked her head up, stared at Breanna. "What do you mean?"

"I used to think it was my fault I was abused, just like you," she said, her voice calm, steady.

"Someone abused you?" Sandy asked, her woman's voice returning.

"You think you're the only one?"

"No, but... Well, you...I mean, you don't act it," Sandy blurted.

"How *should* I act?" Breanna asked.

"I don't know. You seem so...so confident," said Sandy.

"I've gotten help, learned how to deal with it," she said. "Through a treatment program."

"So, a treatment program's going to change my life?" asked Sandy, her challenging voice full of doubt.

"No. *You're* going to change your life, with the help you get from treatment," said Breanna.

Sandy fell silent, considering.

After the pause grew, Breanna spoke again.

"Look, Sandy, right now is the absolute worst time for you. You've made a hole in that wall you built to protect yourself from the pain and the hurt and the humiliation you've been carrying around all these years. Now all those raw nerve endings are open and exposed, and the pain you're feeling is making you wish you'd never said anything to Jim or to me."

She paused, letting her words sink in. "Here's what I want you to do. I want you to put that wall back up for now. Don't use cement, but put the bricks back in place so you're shielded from the pain. You know how to do it."

"Yes," said Sandy in a quiet voice. "I know how to do it."

"Good. Get those bricks back up, so you can rest. We'll talk again in the morning about where you go from here. And remember, if you want to talk to me again tonight, just tell Nancy. She'll call me, and I'll come in."

"You'd do that?" asked Sandy, surprise in her voice.

"Are you forgetting I've been in your shoes? Of course I will."

"I…I think I'll be okay," said Sandy.

Jim thought she seemed calm, almost introspective in her mannerisms.

"So do I," said Breanna. "You're a survivor."

"A survivor. Yeah. Thanks, Breanna."

"Call me Brie. Nobody I care for calls me Breanna." She smiled in Jim's direction when she said it.

"Okay, Brie," said Sandy, smiling for the first time.

"That's a pretty smile, Sandy. You need to do that more often. Tell Nancy if you want to talk to me again tonight, okay?"

"Just knowing you'd come back if I needed you helps a lot. See you tomorrow," said Sandy. The smile remained.

"See you tomorrow," echoed Brie. She turned to Jim.

He'd been a quiet observer since they'd arrived, as he listened and watched Breanna—Brie.

"Ready, Jim?"

"Ready," he confirmed. "Good night, Sandy."

"Good night, Jim." The smile was still there. "And thanks again."

He understood, returned her smile. Then he and Brie made their exit from Sandy Collins' room.

After Brie made a note in Sandy's chart, they headed for the parking lot. Once there, she faced Jim. "I'll follow you," she said. Calm, direct.

"Where to?" asked Jim, feeling stupid for asking.

"To your place. We've got pizza to finish. And have you forgotten? You wanted me to meet Fred." Brie stomped her feet on the snow-covered ground but maintained solid eye contact.

Jim, his mind reeling from the tidal wave of emotions that had washed over him in the last two hours, almost reached out to envelop Brie in his arms. *Almost.* He caught himself. "Oh, Jeez, yes. Where are my manners?"

"You're forgiven this time. Let's go!"

Jim, in his pickup, led the way.

Shortly, he pulled into the apartment parking lot. Brie parked next to him and got out.

"Fairview Apartments. I should've guessed. Did Brent set this up?" she asked, her brows raised in question.

"Brent, or somebody at Serenity. I'm not sure who. They handed me the keys when I got here. Why?"

"Oh, it's fine. Don't get me wrong. Clean. Safe. Convenient. Just a little pricey."

"I thought it was reasonable," Jim said.

"That's because you're from New Jersey. Everything costs less up here in the boondocks of Maine." She was kidding with him, he noticed. "How long is your lease?"

"A year."

"Well, if you're still here in a year, I'll show you some other places just as nice, and for a lot less money."

"If I'm still here? Where am I going?"

"We see a lot of people come to work here from away—that means from out of state—and they find out Maine wasn't what they'd expected. They move on."

"I expect to *stay*," said Jim, putting an emphasis on stay.

"You've got the right transportation for it. Half the vehicles in Maine are pickups."

"Then I fit right in." He gave her a broad smile.

"Enough of this idle chit-chat. I'm starting to freeze in place. Lead me to your palatial abode and your faithful companion, Sir Knight." She linked her arm through his.

He held the pizza box in the other arm. "At your service, fair lady."

They went inside, stomped the snow from their shoes, and climbed the stairs to Jim's apartment. Jim unlocked the door, then looked at Brie.

"Please excuse the mess. I asked Fred to tidy up the place when I left this morning, but he's lazy and probably didn't get much done."

Brie shivered. "Enough of your excuses, Sir Knight. Open yonder door!"

Jim unlocked the door and reached in to turn on the lights.

Brie walked in.

Fred was on the stool where Jim had left him. His black button eyes reflected the light from the table lamp.

"Fred, meet Brie. She's the young lady who called last night. Remember?"

"Hi, Fred. I've heard a lot about you. It's good to meet you," said Brie, putting a hand on Fred's shoulder.

Fred didn't reply, but there was a hint of polite acceptance in his fixed bear expression.

Jim hung their coats in the hall closet. Then he took the pizza into the kitchen, almost stumbling over the two pairs of skis, downhill and cross country, leaning against the wall. Composing himself, he chided, "I see you didn't get to the breakfast dishes, Fred."

"I've got an idea, Fred," said Brie. "While Jim gets us a beer and washes the dishes, we'll have a chat. What do you say?"

"You want a beer?" Jim said, surprised.

"Oops! Don't you have any?" Mild embarrassment could be heard in her voice.

"Sure, but I thought you didn't drink when you were on call."

"That's true, I don't. But today, and what you've been through, makes it time for an exception. One beer, which I will consume over a long spell.

Anyway, I've got a feeling we won't hear from Nancy or Sandy again tonight."

Jim noted her use of "we." Curious, he asked, "Did you ever have a problem with drinking?"

"Yes. For a while I drank a lot, trying to block out the bad memories. But when I learned to deal with those memories, I no longer had a reason to get drunk. I didn't drink for more than two years after getting my head on straight. Then one day I said, 'What the heck!' and had a beer. I found I could have one and not crave another, so I knew I was all right. Drinking wasn't the problem. It was one of the things I did, trying to block out the real problem."

"Two beers coming up!" Jim said cheerfully, sidestepping the real question.

"No rush. Take your time. Fred and I'll have a chat."

"Your wish is my command, fair maiden." He put the oven on low to warm the leftover pizza, then ran water in the sink to wash the breakfast clutter.

"So, Fred. Tell me a little about your handsome friend," she said.

Fred sat quietly, staring, attentive.

"Is he as nice as he seems, or does he beat you for no reason?"

Fred's expression didn't change.

"I assume your silence means he's nice to you. What else can you tell me? Does he like the outdoors? Does he ski? Forget I asked that, Fred. I have visual confirmation."

Fred, quick to obey, remained silent.

"Okay, Fred, what about the romance angle. Is there a girlfriend back in New Jersey?"

"No," answered Jim, leaning around the refrigerator to make eye contact with her. He grinned like the Cheshire cat.

"You're supposed to be doing the dishes!" She tried to cover up her obvious embarrassment.

"I've done them in my usual, efficient manner," Jim said, handing her a glass of beer. "Fred, where are your manners? Why didn't you ask Brie to sit down?"

"Oh, he did, but we were having such a good chat that I didn't think to sit."

She walked to the couch and sat down, leaving room for Jim. Then she held her beer glass aloft. "To your first success," she proposed.

Jim's face was blank as he sat down next to her.

"Sandy Collins," Brie added.

"Yes, Sandy Collins," Jim echoed, clinking his glass with hers.

They sipped their beers and the motion relaxed Jim enough to open up.

"This sexual abuse business is new to me. I can't help feeling angry."

"At who?" she asked.

"At the creeps who do those things. I don't understand how men can hurt people that way."

"Women, too, don't forget," added Brie.

"Women?" he said, a question in his voice.

"Sure. Women aren't above doing things to young boys. Or to girls, either, for that matter. It can be just as bad. Sometimes worse."

"What makes them do it?"

"Many were abuse victims themselves, and they're simply carrying on an old family tradition. Others do it because they need to feel powerful, in control over someone. Kids are logical targets."

"What you say makes sense, but I still feel angry," said Jim.

I want you to come to me any time you have a problem, no matter how big or how small. I'll take care of it. Jim shook away the memory of Tony's words.

"It's okay to get angry, but draw energy from it so you can help those who've been abused because, in case you didn't notice, it steals a lot of energy from you."

"I noticed. While I was washing the dishes, I checked my watch. I couldn't believe it's only eight-thirty. Feels like it should be much later."

"Time flies by. What's that smell?"

"Our second dinner," Jim said. "I put it in to warm. Must be ready."

Jim scooted into the kitchen and was back in no time with a plate of pizza slices and two paper towels. He set the plate on the coffee table and handed Brie one of the paper towels. They each picked up a pizza slice and munched in silence.

"I think pizza tastes better the second time around," said Brie. "I always try to take some home."

"It's true," Jim agreed. "It's like stew, gets better with age."

"Fred, you want some pizza?" Brie asked the taciturn bear.

"Don't offer him any. He's supposed to be on a diet, for obvious reasons."

"Well, I think he's cute the way he is. I can't imagine what he'd be like if he was skinny," Brie observed.

"Careful, or you'll sabotage his diet. He's been sticking to it pretty well."

Brie grabbed a slice. "Then we'll just have to eat the last two slices ourselves."

"That reminds me. Fred told you a lot about me, I gather. What did he learn about you?"

"Not much. I hardly let him get a word in edgewise," she replied, giving Jim a coquettish smile.

"Okay, then. I'll ask. Who are you?"

"Who am I? That's an interesting question. Let's see," said Brie. "I'm Breanna Fowler, primary counselor for the Red Team, but friends call me Brie, and you'd better be calling me that by now."

Jim inclined his head toward her in obeisance.

"I'm a Mainer through and through. Or a Mainiac, if you prefer, since I was born within the borders of this glorious Vacationland. Even though it wasn't planned, I'm entitled to carry the lofty title of native, for what it's worth. The long and the short of it is, my parents were vacationing here, my mother a comfortable four weeks from her due date, and I persuaded her to step up the delivery. So I was born here, not in Rhode Island, which is where they returned to when I was fit to travel. My birth certificate says I'm a Mainiac. As soon as I was old enough to choose, I came back to live here and claim my rightful title. But I'm getting ahead of myself."

Jim chewed on his pizza and waited.

"I was raised in Jamestown, Rhode Island, a navy brat. My dad was a career navy man who worked across the bridge in Newport most of his career. He was in security, so he didn't get moved around a lot. I made it through elementary and high school with the same friends. Unusual for navy kids. But I digress…

"Somehow, I graduated from high school with grades good enough to get me into Syracuse. My freshman year I took Psych 101, probably because I was messed up, looking for answers. The professor was perceptive, sensed I had problems, and got me to see a counselor at the student health center. It was the start of my healing process.

"By the time I'd gotten my head screwed on straight, it was time to declare my major. It seemed only natural that I should give back what had been given to me, so I got my bachelor's in social work."

She took a sip of her beer, then continued. "The problem I took to college was being gang-raped by two of my older brother's friends," she said in a calm, steady voice. "I played with them, guess I was a tomboy, and never thought I needed to be careful around them. I was twelve. They were sixteen or seventeen, both navy brats like me. They got me alone one afternoon. It happened fast. I had no idea what was going on until it was going on. They must have planned it ahead of time. When they were done with me, they told me not to tell anybody about it or they'd do it again, and then they'd kill me. I believed them. So, I buried my terrible secret inside of me for six painful years.

"After I got help, I tried getting in touch with them, to confront them. Both had moved away, but the navy keeps good records. I tracked them down. One of them had died in a car wreck when he was eighteen. Probably drunk. The other had enlisted in the navy, lost both legs in an accident on an aircraft carrier. I guess they both got what they deserved, but I felt cheated, not able to tell them what I thought of them for what they'd done to me." Brie made eye contact with Jim, unblinking. "Guess that's about it."

Hearing her story, Jim felt the urge to put a protective arm around Brie, to comfort her, reassure her that she was safe with him. He thought the gesture might be misinterpreted and resisted the urge.

But she surprised him.

"Would you mind putting your arm around me? I won't bite, and it's comforting with someone I trust."

"You're a mind reader. I was thinking of doing just that, but I didn't know how you'd take it." He encircled her shoulders with his arm and Brie leaned into him.

"Every time I tell someone my story, it gets easier. While telling you, I focused on the facts and blocked out the emotional side of it.

"But it wasn't like that until fairly recently," she said. "You noticed that Sandy Collins' voice changed to that of a young girl's. She was reliving the whole sordid situation in her mind. She probably had flashbacks of pain and shame and frustration because she was unable to change what was happening to her. I know, because that's what happened to me when I first began dealing with it.

"What I told Sandy is true. The first time you talk about it is the worst. The next time is nearly as painful. As it's shared with others again and again, it gets easier. It's a slow process, nothing she'll notice day to day, but one day she'll tell it and she'll realize the pain is less. She'll know instinctively that it was easing a little each time, but she won't have noticed it happening.

"Then, she'll be able to tackle the last obstacle in the grieving process: acceptance of what happened. It's the last step toward being whole again. And that's not a single step, either. Looking back on my progress, there were many times when I thought I'd accepted what happened to me. Then I'd roll backward into anger and bargaining and depression again, when the old memories overwhelmed me. That's when I had to hitch up my britches and start all over again."

Jim sat quietly next to Brie as she spoke, his arm resting neutrally on her shoulders, a gentle offering of comfort and protection. Her words stirred a mixture of feelings in him. He felt anger at the abuse she'd suffered, frustration at his inability to intervene and protect her, and admiration for her strength and determination to move beyond her pain.

He also felt a closeness to her that both surprised and confused him. He liked her company, but beyond that, he felt the urge to draw her to him, encircle her with his arms, be her shield and protector. Her knight. He smiled inwardly at the thought. He was deterred from doing so by the abuse she suffered. He never wanted her to feel that he might take advantage of her. With all these thoughts busy in his head, he did his best to remain passive and supportive.

Brie seemed to sense some of the conflict he was feeling, and reached her hand out to gently stroke his face. "You're a great listener, Jim. Thank you."

Then she leaned toward him and kissed him lightly on the mouth, a feathery touch charged with implications.

He didn't know how to respond.

After she sat back, contentment dominated her face.

Jim's mind raced, struggling to assimilate all this.

"And thanks for the pizza and the company," she said. "I've had a great time."

Jim finally found his words. "You know, you're the first date I've had who ended up taking me to a substance abuse treatment center."

"Wait a sec. Who took who?" Brie challenged.

"Good point," said Jim. "I guess we took each other."

"That's a nice way to put it. It was mutual," said Brie.

Brie stood and walked over to Fred, who had sat through the entire conversation without batting an eye.

"And thank you, too, Fred, for being such a good listener." She enveloped him in her arms, giving him a huge, drawn-out squeeze. Then she released him, repositioned him on his stool.

"I think we're going to be good friends, Fred. You're kind and gentle and you don't force anything. I like that in a bear."

She glanced at Jim, who had taken in every word and realized her words were meant for him more so than Fred.

"And now, Sir Knight, if you will be kind enough to bring me my cloak, I shall retire to my own castle."

"Straight away, fair lady!"

Jim got her coat from the closet, helped her into it.

"I'll follow you home," he said.

"Heavens, no! We've already given the town enough to talk about. Besides, it's less than a mile away and my car's reliable. Thanks for the offer, though. Very chivalrous."

Jim bowed, knight-like, then walked her to her car.

After she'd driven away, he returned to his apartment, shivering, wishing he'd grabbed his own coat on the way out.

He opened the door to Fred's glassy stare. His apartment was just as he'd left it, but it felt empty, like someone had sneaked in while he was seeing Brie off and stolen something vital.

"Fred, what's missing?"

As usual, Fred made no reply, but as Jim moved toward him, the overhead light reflecting in Fred's button eyes moved from top to bottom, looking for all the world like tears tracing their way toward his velveteen cheeks.

"What's the matter, Fred? You sad?"

Fred, muted by an overwhelming sadness, made no reply.

"Do you like her?"

Jim thought he saw confirmation in Fred's eyes.

"Me, I'm confused. She started out by beating me up every chance she got, and now she's done a flip-flop. Which one is the real Brie, do you think?"

Fred offered no comment.

"I guess time will tell. If she doesn't bite my head off tomorrow, maybe I'll need to change my first impression. You only saw the peaches-and-cream side, Fred. Too bad you weren't at work to see how she reacted to me in the first go-round."

Fred continued to stare back, unblinking, his expression unchanged.

"Maybe Mom has some sage advice. Besides, I owe her a call."

Chapter Eleven

Soon after his conversation with Fred, Jim sat on the bed and dialed the number from memory, then waited for the familiar voice. After a short delay, a woman answered.

"Hi, Mom. How're you doing?"

"Who's this?" she asked.

"It's Jim, Mom," he said into the phone.

"Jim who?"

"Your famous son, the PA!"

"You mean my infamous son, the one who never calls me?"

"Don't be mean, Mom," Jim said. "I'm not infamous. And it hasn't been *that* long since I called you."

She sighed into the phone. "So, how's New Jersey treating you?"

"I'm not calling from New Jersey. I'm in Maine now, at my new job. I've been here for a week. I'm sorry I didn't call you sooner. Won't happen again."

"Now, where have I heard that before? How was the drive to Maine?"

Jim switched the phone to his other ear. "No problems, and they had a nice apartment waiting for me. There's a bedroom, and a pull-out couch in the living area you and Dad can sleep on when you come to visit."

"You know your father's back won't do well on a pull-out couch."

"Okay, I'll take the couch and you and Dad can have the bedroom. You drive a hard bargain, you know. How's Dad?"

"He's good, Jim. Still doing all the farm work, same as before."

"He's tough. And how's my younger brother, what's his name?" Jim grinned.

"You think that's funny, pretending not to remember your own brother's name?"

"I'm kidding, Mom," Jim said. "It's Todd, I know. What's he up to?"

"He's studying hard at Penn. He's decided to take up biology."

"A biology major? When did he decide that?"

Mom sighed again. "You know he looks up to you and all you've done.

It helped him make the decision."

"He looks up to me?" Jim asked, incredulous. "Did you tell him that was a bad mistake?"

"Nooo, I told him to go with his gut feelings."

"And he wouldn't change his mind? Guess I'd better call him myself, try to warn him off. What's his number down there at Penn?"

She gave him the number and Jim scribbled it on the pad by the phone. "Got it, Mom. Thanks."

"How is it going for you in Maine so far?"

Jim scrunched up his face, thinking. "I've been on the job a few days, but I like it so far. People are nice, and it's good to get out of crazy Newark. Oh, and I met a girl."

"Nothing unusual about that. There's girls everywhere, I'm sure you've noticed. What's with this one?"

"Not a whole lot to tell. She's young and good-looking and lots brighter than I am." Jim came close to telling his mother about Brie's issues, but thought better of it. *Not my story to tell.*

"What's this girl's name?"

"Brie. Breanna's her full name."

"That's an unusual name. I like it."

"Yes, it is different. Her mother wanted to call her Brie, after the French cheese, but her dad wanted something more formal. So they named her Breanna, but everyone calls her Brie."

"Good luck with your cheese lady, Jim. Isn't life grand? You never know where life leads until you find yourself following it."

He could hear the smile in her voice. He was glad he called.

"You're right, Mom. Time will tell."

***

After he'd finished his call home, Jim dialed the number his mother had given him.

"Todd?" As soon as his question was out there, he realized the voice at the other end wasn't Todd's. "Is Todd there?"

"Which Todd should I inform of your call?" the male voice asked.

"Todd Booker."

"I shall do my best to track him down."

Jim listened to background voices and waited, wondering how many Todds lived in that dorm. Then Todd—his brother, Todd—was on the line.

"Hey, bro. How goes it?" Jim asked.

"Are my ears deceiving me? Is this *really* my long-lost brother, James?"

Jim laughed. "Yes, it's *really* your brother calling. Don't give me any shit. I just got off the phone with Mom, and she gave me enough for both of you."

Todd chuckled. "Glad to hear it. So how's it going?"

"Good. Settling in up here in the boonies of Maine, and I like it. Word's out that you've decided to major in biology."

"Ahh, the jungle telegraph is alive and well. Did Mom tell you?" Todd asked.

"Yeah, Mom told me," Jim said. "That's why I called. Are you out of your mind?"

"No more out of my mind than you are out of yours. I remember you sharing the agony of PA school with me, bro."

"That's true. You don't have to go into medicine. You could teach. Professor Todd Booker has a nice ring to it."

"Or Todd Booker, MD, specializing in clinical research."

"Sure, research, too. Or maybe get a job in a zoo figuring out the estrus cycles of white rhinos and giant pandas so they can breed successfully in captivity. How's that sound?"

"You know, I never considered that option. Thanks, bro, for adding that to my growing list of possibilities."

Jim conceded. "You're right. You have plenty of time to decide, no rush. What else are you up to?"

"I've discovered intramural soccer."

"Intramural soccer, hmm? How many times a week?"

"Twice. Tuesday and Thursday. Gives time in between for my wounds to heal."

Jim grinned at his brother's humor. "Sounds like fun. But a word to the wise from your older brother. Find something you can play with one other person, or something you can do solo. Ten years from now, you'll exhaust yourself trying to round up twenty-one other guys for a game of soccer. It'll be a lot easier finding another guy for a game of squash or tennis or racquetball. Even easier to pull on a pair of running shoes or biking shorts."

"Don't forget, I'm an accomplished skier."

"Yeah, you're right. That's a good solo sport. We had a great time together at that ski lodge in Pennsylvania last year, remember? I've got to get back to it. Here I am, right in the middle of ski country and I haven't hit the slopes yet."

"Trying to get everything done in the first week, that's the brother I know," Todd said.

"True, I've only been here a few days, but hey, it's already February.

Tempus fugit! You been yet?"

"Yeah, couple times, to a small slope west of here."

"Nice! Oh, to be back in college when everything took priority over studying."

"I'm doing my share of that, too, since I've seen the light."

"Yeah, well, that's good you're studying," Jim said. "It can't hurt. Any love interests?"

"Interests, but I wouldn't call it love. More mutual release, if you get my drifty."

"Smart man. No need for a serious love interest if you haven't decided whether you want to inseminate orangutans or root around in DNA strands."

"What about you, bro?" Todd asked. "Planning your wedding day yet?"

Jim chuckled. "Far from it. I met a sweet woman here, but we haven't set the date yet."

"Set the date for what? The stuff that usually comes before the 'I do's'?"

"Don't be crude, little brother. She's someone I work with. Name's Brie, like the cheese. She's a counselor. An LCSW, Licensed Clinical Social Worker."

"So you like her."

Jim thought a moment. "Yeah, she seems nice, although she started off treating me like crap—until this afternoon."

"Really? What happened to change things?"

"A female client chose to tell me how she'd been sexually abused. It really got to me. I mean, I've seen badly mutilated bodies brought into the ER, but this woman's story hit me far worse. Brie ran into me afterwards, and I guess she could see I was in shock. To make a long story short, she took me for pizza, and I told her the story. While I explained the woman's experience, a tear ran down my cheek. She reacted differently to me after that."

"I like it. Nice touch. I'll have to try that on my next girlfriend."

Jim shook his head. "There you go, getting crude again. You kids are all alike."

"Yeah, and then we have to grow up."

"You'll get used to it. By the way, how many Todds are there in your dorm?"

"I'm it."

"You're the only one?" Jim asked, surprised. "The guy who answered the phone said, 'Todd who?'"

"Yeah, that was Mike. He likes his weed."

"Ah, that explains it. Is there a lot of pot there?"

"If you want it, you can get it."

"Sounds like my college scene. Hey, I'll let you get back to your studies."
"Yeah, thanks for the call…and the advice." Todd laughed.
Jim laughed with him. "Talk soon."

Chapter Twelve

The *uh oh* feeling hit Jim's gut as he walked by Brie the next morning. She didn't make eye contact or acknowledge his existence when he passed her. He sat down four chairs from her, out of her line of vision unless he leaned forward in his chair. Or she did.

When Brent kicked off the morning meeting, Jim's thoughts were elsewhere, but when he heard his name mentioned, he tuned in.

"...only been on the job for a week now, and he got Sandy Collins to talk about her sexual abuse issues, something I wasn't able to do. Let's give him a hand," said Brent and began the applause. The rest of the staff joined in.

Jim felt his face flush with embarrassment. During the applause, Brie and the others leaned forward to look his way. She had a neutral expression on her face, Jim noted. The applause died, and Brent continued.

"But we came close to losing her, in spite of Jim's efforts. Last night she had a change of heart, slipped back into denial, and was ready to walk. Would have, except for Brie coming in and convincing her to stay. Give Brie a big hand, too!"

The room filled with applause, and it was Jim's turn to lean forward. He saw her smile, saw her eyes move from face to face in silent acknowledgement until the clapping ended. She had avoided eye contact with him.

"Which confirms what I've maintained all along," Brent said, "things get done around here, and get done well, because of teamwork. I applaud you all!" He clapped vigorously for some ten seconds, grinning and sweeping his eyes over the staff, who sat in silence, embarrassed.

Andy broke the awkwardness of the moment. "Hey, you're doing a hell of a job yourself, Brent. You deserve your own hand." He started the applause, and everyone quickly joined him. The tension lifted from the room.

After the applause ended, but before Brent could continue, Andy added,

"There! I guess we all got the clap."

The laughter that followed was genuine.

"We can always count on Andy to put things in proper perspective," Brent commented. "Okay, who's got team presentations today?"

Three hands shot up.

"Martha, I saw yours first."

Jim glanced at the list of staff names he kept with him, his way of learning who was who. Martha Knowles was down as the assistant counselor for the White team. He looked her way as she began her presentation. Short, dark complexion, moderately overweight, hair cropped on the short side. She had a baby doll face which Jim found appealing. She maintained the hint of a smile on her face as she spoke, an expression that said, "Like me, because I like you."

"Patti R. is a seventeen-year-old single female admitted for drug and alcohol abuse and dependency. She—"

"Which is it, Martha? Abuse or dependency?" Andy cut in.

"Dependency."

"Okay. Why do you say so?" Andy persisted.

"In Women's group yesterday, she admitted to drinking whatever she had until it was all gone. Or until *she* was all gone," explained Martha, her eyebrows arching at her turn of the phrase.

"Okay. Sorry to interrupt."

"No problem," Martha said. "Anyway, Patti started using alcohol when she was eleven, pot at twelve. She has all the classic signs of sexual abuse. She sat through Women's group and listened while two women described being abused. She never batted an eye. I mean, she didn't even show the usual sympathy for the two women. Sat there stone-faced, showed no reaction. So I'm thinking, either I'm wrong about her being sexually abused, or she's the coldest fish I've ever seen."

Martha shifted in her chair, pulled her skirt down over her legs, then continued. "After group, she came up to me. She's smiling, calm. She asks if she can talk to me about something in a voice like she wanted to borrow a cup of sugar.

"We went in my office and I closed the door, then I asked her what's up. And she tells me she was sexually abused, but she didn't want to talk about it in front of all those other women."

"Who did what and when?" asked Brent, cutting to the chase.

"Ray Barribee did everything he could think of to her when she was eleven and kept it up for another two years. The abuse was interrupted when he was sent to jail for unrelated charges."

"Why does that name ring a bell?" Andy asked.

"He's the same creep who molested Carrie T., the woman we got to testify against him. Her testimony got him sent to Thomaston for three to five. He's back out, by the way. Served two and a half. Fully rehabilitated, they say." Martha's voice was thick with sarcasm.

I want you to come to me any time you have a problem, no matter how big or how small. I'll take care of it.

Jim shook off the thought.

"Sure. Rehabilitated. Wonder what little girl he's homing in on now?" said Brent, his anger showing in his voice.

"Some eleven-year-old who'll come to us for help after her childhood's destroyed and her adolescence is in tatters," said Andy in a serious tone.

"There's another job for the Equalizer," said Brent with vehemence.

"The ultimate solution," seconded Martha. "And the best one!"

Jim heard Tony's voice again: *I want you to come to me any time you have a problem, no matter how big or how small. I'll take care of it. You hear me? Say the word and I'll take care of it.* He wondered how far Tony Bonnano's pledge went, wondered how he might deal with a creep like Ray Barribee. Jim blinked, forcing the thought into the dark part of his mind.

"Okay, back to reality," Andy said. "What's the plan, Martha?"

"Patti's agreed to bring it up in Women's group today. It was a tough sell, but she said she would."

"Good work. Keep us posted. Who's next?" Andy asked the group.

Two more presentations were made. Jim caught himself fantasizing about calling Tony Bonnano and asking him to take care of Ray Barribee. He even went so far as to conjure up several responses for Tony, ranging from *Whoa, we don't do that kind of shit!* to *Where do we find this asshole?* The first scenario left him feeling disappointed. The second one scared him.

The meeting broke up, and Brent stood in front of Jim, bringing him out of his contemplations.

"Great job yesterday, Jim. Keep this up, and you'll have me out looking for a new job." Brent wore a wide, disarming grin.

Before Jim could think of a response, Brent continued. "I'd like to have you go to Men's group this morning. Get the flavor of it. See how you might fit in."

"Be glad to. Where and when?" asked Jim.

"It's at ten. You've got half an hour, so go grab a coffee. You deserve a break."

"Can you join me?" Jim cocked his head at Brent in question.

Brent glanced at his watch, considered. "Hey, why not? I've got an outpatient coming in at nine-forty-five, but he's usually late. My secretary will text me. Let's do it."

They rode the elevator to the lobby and entered the coffee shop. Jenny greeted them.

"Good morning, gentlemen. Two of my best customers, and here together. You do me a great honor," she said, punctuating her words with a half-curtsey.

"Hi, Jenny. You haven't lost your gift of gab," Jim said.

"Or bullshit," added Brent, pitched loud enough for Jenny to hear.

Jenny chuckled softly. "Coffee all round? Some of Mae's coffee cake?"

"Sounds good," Jim confirmed.

"Hold the cake for me," said Brent. "I'm on a diet."

"You know perfectly well, Doctor, that Mae wouldn't make fattening coffee cake," said Jenny, with a twinkle in her eye.

"Okay, Jenny. When my wife asks, I'll say it was diet cake," responded Brent, pleased with Jenny's solution.

"And you won't be lying, either, Doctor Caldwell. Mae's coffee cake is on most everyone's diet around here," she added with a sly grin.

Jim and Brent pulled out chairs and sat down while Jenny went behind the counter for the coffee and cake.

"The Men's group, as you might suspect, is a place for the men to talk about things they'd feel uncomfortable talking about in front of women. The main topic, as you've probably guessed, is sex. Sexual inadequacy, sexual identity, sexual dysfunction, sexual abuse," Brent recounted, grasping a different finger for each. "If they stray from the subject, the counselor's work is to steer them back on track. For today, and until you're feeling comfortable in there, sit quiet and soak up as much as you can, okay?"

"Here you go, gentlemen," announced Jenny as she approached the table, her way of staying out of earshot of any confidential information. She set down the coffees and plates with practiced efficiency. "*Bon appétit!* Enjoy the diet cake," she added pointedly.

"We will," said Brent, answering for Jim.

They were silent while they ate. Brent finished first, dabbing at his mouth with his napkin.

"You're right, Jenny. I didn't taste a single calorie," he said loudly, beaming.

"It's amazing how Mae does that, isn't it?" answered Jenny from behind the counter.

"She's got a natural talent, and she knows how to use it," added Jim.

"I'd say that describes you, too," said Brent, fixing Jim with his eyes.

"Thanks, but part of it is good old beginner's luck, I'm sure."

"Wrong. There's no such thing as luck. There's being in the right place at the right time, and there's the results that come from persistence and hard work and paying attention, but luck?" Brent shook his head. "If you want to use the term, I say people make their own luck. It isn't something that's given to them on a silver platter," he said, keeping the discussion light.

"What about the guy who buys a single lottery ticket and wins the megabucks?" countered Jim.

"He buys a chance with his ticket, and once in a while his number comes up. Luck would be more like walking down the street and having John Baresford Tipton stop his limo next to you and handing you a cashier's check for a million dollars. Course, you could argue that you were there at that spot and at that time because you made plans that took you by that spot, so is that luck? And what kind of luck is it? If a part of the million dollars goes to buy you a plane ticket, and the plane crashes and you're killed, did the money bring you good luck or bad luck?"

"So you don't believe in luck," said Jim.

"I believe we're able to control what happens to us, while luck suggests that we're not. I believe we have a hand in our destiny, that our actions matter. Otherwise, the alternative is to go around doing nothing, waiting for the limo to stop or the number to come up. Or the plane to crash," said Brent.

Brent's cell phone chirped, interrupting their discussion. Jim heard the secretary's soft voice announcing that Brent's nine-forty-five appointment had arrived.

"Gotta run!" Brent stood up, grabbed the check, paid Jenny. Then he turned back to Jim.

"Men's group starts in ten minutes. Good luck, Jim." He waved a farewell.

"Luck has nothing to do with it," Jim fired at Brent's retreating back.

In acknowledgement, Brent held his thumb aloft.

"Sounds like you got the Luck Speech this morning, Jim," said Jenny as she cleared the dishes.

"Yep. I kind of like the idea of it."

"Me, too. Makes you master of your destiny instead of a puppet on a string."

Jim smiled at her, thinking that she'd summarized it better than he could've. He took a dollar from his pocket, set it on the table.

"Hey, didn't you see my sign?" asked Jenny, pointing at it. "Tips aren't accepted."

"That's not a tip. It's a contribution to your children's scholarship fund."

"You mean my grandchildren's?" asked Jenny, smiling.

"You can't be old enough to have grandchildren," countered Jim.

"Flattery will get you everywhere. Want me to hold a special for you for lunch?"

"Darn right I do. See you in a couple hours."

Jim left, curious about what the special was but he didn't wonder if it would be good. He knew Mae's cooking wouldn't disappoint.

Chapter Thirteen

Dave Levesque met Jim at the door. "Hi, Jim. Brent told me you were coming. You remember Ted Aaronson?" Dave nodded at the associate counselor striding toward them.

"Sure. Hi, Ted, how's it going?" He silently thanked Dave for refreshing his memory. Names were his weak suit, especially when they were thrown at him in bunches, and especially when he had no contact with the faces for some time after.

"I'm good, Jim. Welcome to Men's group," Ted said.

Dave turned to speak to the men standing around in groups of twos and threes. Jim could feel the tension in the room.

"Okay, guys, grab a seat and let's get started," said Dave, who set the example by sitting down first.

Jim saw Ted move to a chair halfway around the circle from Dave and took his cue from that. He sat midway between the two, a client on either side of him. There were just enough chairs to go around, leaving no gaps in the circle. Jim recognized the thoroughness of Dave and Ted's preparations.

"As you've no doubt noticed, we have a guest today. Meet Jim Booker. He's our new PA. You may have already met him if you're a newcomer," added Dave.

"He's gotten to know my ass," muttered one of the clients, a short, stocky dark-haired man, alluding that Jim had done his physical. Jim remembered him. A wise guy.

"Mine, too," echoed another. Brief, tight laughter erupted from the group, then it died just as quickly. But the tension was still there. Jim recalled the second man, too. Quiet, shy, spare of words. He wondered what had prompted him to speak out.

"Let's go around the circle and introduce ourselves," prompted Dave. "I'll start. I'm Dave, counselor."

"I'm Nelson. I'm an alcoholic."

"I'm Harry. Alcoholic and drug addict."

And so it went around the circle.

"Thanks. Now, let's get started," said Dave. "Yesterday, Harry told us he was sexually molested by a man named Ray Barribee when he was ten. He told us this a few minutes before the group ended, so we didn't hear the whole story, did we, Harry?"

Jesus! Ray Barribee again. Jim couldn't believe it.

Harry, alcoholic and drug addict, shook his lowered head and studied his clasped hands in his lap with particular intensity. Jim guessed he was in his late teens or early twenties, but time hadn't been easy on him.

I want you to come to me any time you have a problem, no matter how big or how small. I'll take care of it.

Jim wondered what Tony Bonnano's boys would do to Ray Barribee. Kill him? That would be unacceptable.

"Are you ready to continue?" prompted Dave.

Harry nodded, still studying his hands.

The group waited, silent, expectant, all eyes on Harry.

"He got a bunch of us kids over to his place after school," said Harry.

"By *he*, you mean Ray Barribee?" asked Dave.

"Yeah," Harry began, "I guess we figured, since there was a bunch of us, it'd be okay. Well, anyway, he gave us alcohol. Beer and wine and the hard stuff. That was really cool for a bunch of ten-year-olds, you know. At first, we just tasted it and then went home. But as time went on, he pushed us into drinking more and more. Some of my friends got up and left, but I was stupid. I stayed. It didn't take him long to get me drunk enough to get into my pants. And *my* pants weren't the only ones he got into. He got us to play around with each other while he watched the show. Then he got me alone one afternoon and had my ass. Literally." His voice broke with his last word.

Nobody in the circle thought it was funny.

Harry's hands fluttered above his legs. Tears rolled down his cheeks and fell onto his pants. He stared at the dark spots they made, looking puzzled, like he was unsure what was causing them.

"How long did it go on for, Harry?" asked Dave, his voice calm, gentle.

"Oh, fuck, I don't know," Harry said. "Maybe a year, maybe a little more. One of the girls told him she'd told her parents on him, and the next thing we knew, he'd moved away."

"Did you like it?" asked Dave, his voice was soft, but intending to trigger a reaction, any reaction.

"Fuck you!" It was the first sign of animation from Harry.

"Well, help me to understand, Harry. You let it go on for a year, and it might still be going on if one of the girls hadn't scared him off," reasoned

Dave, still pushing Harry's buttons.

Harry drew in a deep breath, blew it out. "I was scared of him. He told me he'd cut off my balls if I ever told anyone. And I got so I needed the alcohol. It numbed me so I could go on taking his abuse, so I could go on abusing the others." Harry's hands were white from squeezing them together, and now his hands shook.

"What'd you do to the other kids?" asked Dave, his voice calm, urging him on.

"You name it. Ray had me—us—do it," Harry said, his voice distant.

Jim considered all the young lives that this creep, Ray Barribee, had screwed up. He counted the ones Harry spoke of, plus the ones he'd heard about in the morning meeting. He remembered Martha saying he'd been released from the Maine State Prison at Thomaston after serving barely two and a half years. Rehabilitated? Jim guessed it was more likely he'd be picking up where he'd left off.

I want you to come to me any time you have a problem, no matter how big or how small.

"I was at Tommy Town with Ray Barribee."

Everyone turned to see who had spoken. Jim's eyes came to rest on a man with black hair and an acne-scarred complexion. He was slouched down on his chair, across from Harry. Jim guessed he was in his late twenties. His nose was set left of center on his pockmarked face, testament to a left cross he hadn't ducked.

"Welcome to the group, Jack," said Dave. "I told you we'd never bring up that you were in prison, but if you want to talk about it, that's fine."

"Yeah, well, shit happens to all of us," said Jack. "I did eighteen months for taking cars that didn't belong to me. I made the mistake of taking the mayor's car. The cops didn't think it was funny."

This drew a few chuckles, but most sat silent, waiting.

"How'd you meet Ray Barribee?" asked Dave.

"He was my cellmate. What a creep. He bragged about all the kids he screwed when we smoked pot at night," Jack explained.

"Pot in Thomaston?" someone asked.

"Shit, it's easier to get pot in Tommy Town than on the street," answered Jack, sarcasm in his voice.

"What kind of stuff did Ray say?" said Dave, leading the group.

"Ah, you know, shit like how he loves young kids, how easy it is to get them to do what he wants, how he couldn't wait to get out and get some more."

"When was that?" asked Dave.

"Right up to when he was paroled. They let him out a month ago," Jack said.

I want you to come to me any time you have a problem, no matter how big or how small. I'll take care of it.

While listening, Jim felt an overwhelming urge to make a phone call.

Chapter Fourteen

Jim had eaten dinner, washed the dishes, and put everything away. He sat, staring at the business card. *Merry Riddle* and her phone number was on one side, and printed on the back *Call anytime.* He sucked in a long breath, exhaled, and picked up the phone.

What the hell. I'm only calling to get information.

He dialed the number on the card.

It was answered on the third ring. "Hi, Jim. How's it going?" asked Merry, her voice cheery and bright.

"How'd you know it was me?" he asked, surprised.

"You're on my contact list," she said. He could sense her smile.

"This is my land line," he said, still surprised. "How'd you get this number?"

"I called Information. They were very cooperative." He could really feel her smile now.

"I gotta say, you're good at what you do."

"I suppose I am, with Tony's help. Tell me why you called. Or did you just want to hear my voice again?" she asked, flirting.

She'd given him the opening he could use.

"Both, Merry. I like your voice, and I wanted to bounce something off of you."

"Ouch! Hope that doesn't turn out to be as painful as it sounds," she joked.

"I'll try to be gentle," he fired back. "Tell me, Merry. What kind of stuff does Mr. Bonnano do for people like me?"

"Ah. The sixty-four-million-dollar question. Let me answer your question with a question of my own. What's going on in your life that's brought Tony Bonnano's pledge onto the table?"

Jim paused a moment to collect his thoughts, then continued. "As you know, I'm working in a substance abuse treatment facility."

"Yes, and I think that's noble work."

"Okay, here's the thing. As it turns out, the vast majority of the women being treated are victims of sexual abuse, and surprisingly, a significant percentage of the men are victims, too." He paused, letting that sink in.

"I guess, thinking about it, that makes perfect sense," said Merry.

Jim thought he detected a slight change in her voice.

"Yes. They use alcohol and drugs to blunt the pain that it's caused them," Jim said.

"So they're doing more harm to bodies that are already harmed," summarized Merry.

"That's correct. The thing is, when they break down and talk about the abuse, they often give up a name, or names, of those who have abused them."

"I see where this is going," said Merry. "You have a name, or names, and you're wondering what Tony could do, am I right?"

"That's it in a nutshell. I'm thinking that he and his boys could be very persuasive in altering a perp's perspective about continuing to abuse," explained Jim. "That is, short of causing their death."

"There it is," said Merry. "You want these creeps to pay for what they've done, but you don't want them killed. Have I got it right?"

"You got it. I couldn't live with myself if I knew that my actions resulted in someone's death."

"I hear what you're saying, Jim. Now, what about personal injury as a means of altering their attitude?" Merry probed.

A silence ensued while Jim considered. Finally, he said, "I can see that this discussion can go on for a long time. I guess if personal injury is appropriate to the abuse inflicted on a perp, and it was effective, then it would be justifiable. Thing is, I wouldn't want to know about it, if you get what I mean."

"I get it. 'What you don't know can't hurt you,' or something like that."

"Yeah. I could sleep at night, not knowing the gory details."

"I think I've got a clear picture of your problem, Jim. Let me touch base with Tony and see how he might react to your, ah, situation. I'll get back to you as soon as I can, okay?"

"That'd be great, Merry. Remember, we're just talking in generalities."

"For sure. Nothing can or will be done until you give us a name," she reassured him.

"Thanks, Merry. I'll wait for your call."

"We'll talk soon. I promise."

Jim hung up the phone, wondering if he'd gone too far. He was comforted by Merry's words: *Nothing can or will be done until you give us a name.* The question was, was he ready to unleash the Equalizer?

He caught Fred looking his way. "Hey, Fred. What do you think about all that?" he asked, his voice a whisper.

Fred never responded quickly to important questions. He was no different now.

"Take your time, pal. I know you want to choose your words well before you answer me."

Fred listened politely, then went back to his considerations.

"While you're working on it, I'm going for a beer," Jim said, then turned and made tracks for the fridge.

He pulled out a cold bottle of a local Maine brew, popped the cap, and tilted back a quick slug. The taste hit him solidly. *A long way from New Jersey. His old beer didn't hold a candle to this stuff.* His thoughts were interrupted by the phone ringing.

Now who could that be? Brie came to mind as he picked up the receiver. "Hello?"

"Hey, Jim. Told you I'd get back to you quickly."

It was Merry.

"You're true to your word, I'll give you that," said Jim. "What have you got?"

"As soon as I hung up with you, I called Tony. Miracle of miracles, I got right through to him. Bottom line is, he wants you to call him right away—now—to discuss things."

"Now?"

"Yes. He wants to know more about your situation so he can offer some constructive suggestions," Merry explained.

"Okay, I can do that."

"Have you got his number handy? If not, I can give it to you."

"Thanks, Merry. I've got it."

"Okay, then. Let me know what you work out."

"Will do. Thanks."

Jim hung up the phone and sucked in a huge breath. His actions had brought him to a pivotal point, this point of no return. He exhaled, hoping he was making the right decision.

He took Tony's card from his billfold and dialed the number.

Chapter Fifteen

"I'm calling to speak with Mister Tony Bonnano." Jim's voice sounded hollow even to him, like someone else was making the call.

"Who's calling?" asked a deep, harsh voice on the other end.

"Jim Booker."

"Hold on," said the New Jersey-accented voice. The delay gave Jim's conscience the chance to ask once again what the hell he was doing.

"Hey, Jim. How're you doin'?" Tony Bonnano came onto the line. No question about who it was.

"I'm good, Mister Bonnano. I'm up in Maine, took a job at an alcohol and drug treatment program."

"What the hell you go and do that for? You saved lives at University, now you're working with drunken bums in Maine?"

"It was time to get away, do something different," Jim said. Once out, his explanation seemed inadequate.

Tony surprised him. "Hey, I know what you mean."

Jim thought better of asking him to elaborate.

"So I got a call from Merry. She said you might have a problem I could fix," Tony offered.

Jim explained his situation. Tony listened in silence, interspersed with expletives that showed he was hearing Jim, and hearing him well.

"You told me to call you if I had a problem, so I'm checking to see if you can arrange to scare this guy, make him stop. I know it's a long way from Newark to Maine," Jim added, giving Tony an out.

"The distance is nothing, Jim. I'll make a phone call and have my associates up there take care of your problem," said Tony, casual, offhand, like he was going to call and order a pizza.

"You aren't going to do anything more than rough him up a little, are you?" asked Jim, concern in his voice.

"Hell, no. We'll arrange somethin' that'll get his attention, you know? Somethin' he'll remember," said Tony Bonnano, his tone reassuring.

"Thanks, Mr. Bonnano. I won't bother you anymore."

"Hey, bother me! This is nothin' compared to havin' my son Nick alive and well."

"As far as I'm concerned, this more than makes up for anything I did for your son."

"Hey, Jim. You got a problem, you call me. I'll never forget what you done for Nick."

"Thanks, Mister Bonnano," Jim replied.

"Thanks, nothin'. And you call me Tony. We're connected, you and me."

"Okay, Tony." Using the man's first name made him feel a bond, a connection had happened. Regardless of how lightly Jim took it, Tony Bonnano believed he'd saved his son's life. Hell, maybe he had.

"That's more like it. Keep in touch, okay? And don't worry. I'm goin' to take care of your little problem."

The line went dead. Jim listened briefly to the garbled and distant crosstalk between Newark and Cairo, then put the phone down. He wondered if his call would produce any change in Ray Barribee's attitude. At that moment he could only guess at the results his call would bring about in the man.

Chapter Sixteen

Sitting at the bar, Ray Barribee was drunk, and he knew it. Whenever he got drunk, he thought about young girls, young boys. He sometimes thought about all the shit the other inmates did to him when he was in prison after they found out what he did to kids, but that was a long way off now. If he listened to his conscience, it would tell him he shouldn't think about screwing kids. But he couldn't stop the impulses he had, especially when he was drunk.

He slouched forward on the barstool and let his mind slide over the intimate details. The alcohol numbed any conscience he had left, turned his mind loose. He loved tricking them into doing what he wanted, what he needed.

He'd had his fill of grown women and all their disgusting hair. He couldn't stand them. No matter what he did, he couldn't satisfy women. They always wanted more, more than he had. Then they'd laugh at him, call him Speedy, joke about his size.

"Fuck 'em!"

The man sitting next to him turned when he spoke, then turned back to his drink. More important things to tend to.

Ray took a slug from his glass, felt the brown liquid warm his throat, his gut. His mind returned to the pleasures of the past, pleasures that only kids could give him. He felt a stirring in his gut that wasn't from the booze.

Mandy. His kid sister's little girl. Now there was a kid worth his trouble! He remembered the last time he'd dropped by, how she'd climbed up onto his lap and hugged him and called him "Unka Ray." Then his sister was looking at him sideways, her expression sending him a silent warning not to fuck with her kid. She couldn't see the rise in his pants, but little Mandy had to be feeling it. She'd bounced up and down like it was a special treat.

Guess I'll have to get to know Mandy a lot better.

Had he spoken the words, or only thought them? He glanced around to see if anyone was paying any attention to him. Nobody paid him any mind.

He guessed he hadn't spoken out loud, guessed it was just a good thought. Ray massaged his crotch, Mandy on his mind.

No time like the present. Strike while the iron is hot.

He chuckled at his choice of words as he patted his crotch. He stood up and tested his balance, found he was up to the challenge of walking. He turned and headed carefully for the door, expecting a betrayal from his legs at any moment.

The icy February night air punched him in the face as he walked out. He paused to zip his jacket tightly up to his neck, an action that undoubtedly saved his life.

"Hey, Skinner!"

Ray squinted at the short, stocky man who stood in the shadows across the street from him. He didn't recognize him, shrugged his shoulders and began weaving his way toward his sister's place. The Leaky Bilge, the tavern he'd just provided with serious financial support, sent out a diluted wash of light, ineffective, watery, like its drinks.

"Hey, Skinner," the short, stocky stranger hissed again.

"You got the wrong guy, mister. Name's not Skinner," Ray answered, his words slurred.

While Ray spoke, the stranger crossed the street toward him. As he moved into the watery light, Ray made out a dark complexion which blurred the lines, made it hard to read his features.

"Fuckin' guinea from away," Ray muttered to himself, a wheezing chuckle escaping through his broken, nicotine-stained teeth. "Got lost up here in the back country. Needs directions. I'll give him directions!" He balled his fists at his sides while another wheezing chuckle erupted.

The stranger shuffled casually toward Ray, his hands shoved deep in his overcoat pockets. Ray could see that he was smiling. The pale light reached down Harbor Road and outlined his teeth.

"You lost?" asked Ray, his horsey laugh punctuating his query.

The man got right up in Ray's face and stopped, but his grin kept right on going.

"I know who you are. You're Ray Barribee," he hissed through his clenched teeth. "You're a goddamned skinner!"

The man's meaning poleaxed Ray. He knew what a skinner was from his time in Tommy Town. It was jailhouse slang for men who got off on kids. Ray had sweated through his jail time, forever on guard against inmates who hated skinners. Sometimes skinners turned up dead in prison, and nobody ever knew what happened. Or cared. He'd been careful, and he'd made it through. A missing tooth. A nose that no longer looked the same. Memories of beatings, rape even. Could've been worse. He could've died.

Ray's alcohol-saturated brain wasn't cranking over at peak efficiency, but he knew he didn't want this guy in his face and acting ugly. He cocked his fist to give this piece of shit his famous haymaker, and the next thing he knew, his famous haymaker was cranked tight behind his back. The resulting pain put a watery film in his eyes, blurring his vision. He sucked in a breath to scream for help just as the stranger drove a fist into his side. A whistling grunt was all that came out. Ray doubled over in pain, but the stranger cranked on his arm and persuaded him to stand upright.

Through glazed eyes, Ray saw car headlights approaching, felt a surge of hope. It was going to be someone he knew. They'd get him out of this nightmare. The car stopped. Ray strained to see the driver. Then the passenger door opened; the dome light came on. He could see the driver. It was nobody he knew. It hit him, then, that his troubles were just beginning. He searched desperately for a way out.

"Get in," snarled the short, dark stranger at the other end of Ray's right arm. Ray was propelled into the front seat.

The stranger jammed himself in next to him and slammed the door. The dome light winked out. Ray was sandwiched between the two strangers in the dark. He tried to make out the features of the driver, but the dashboard glow wasn't much help. He could only tell that he was dark complexioned and squarely built. Ray could smell the man's aftershave. He couldn't identify it, but knew it wasn't what he used.

"Do I know you? What d'you want?" asked Ray, his voice coming out high-pitched and hoarse, betraying his fear. His effort to regain control was failing miserably.

"We're here to do you a favor, Ray. We're goin' to help you keep your pecker in your pants where it belongs and away from kids, if you get my meanin'," hissed the man on Ray's right, that same quiet, menacing voice that struck fear into Ray's besotted brain.

"What're you talking about?" croaked Ray, his voice flying high and reedy, bubbling with panic.

"Hey, Ray. It's not so much *what* you've done as *who* you've done, if you get my drift. I'm talkin' about kids, Ray. All those kids you got off on." The man's voice carried more threat than Ray wanted to think about.

"I did my time for that! I was in for two and a half years," Ray said, abruptly sober, shouting.

"That's not true, Ray. You haven't paid. Not yet."

The words hit Ray like a judge's sentence.

Ray's sphincter muscles sagged with the overwhelming fear. He felt warm urine dampening his crotch, struggled to shut down the flow. Ray didn't know what these strangers had in mind for him, but they scared him, scared him bad. They knew things about him, secrets he didn't like other people knowing. He guessed they must've been in Tommy Town, only he didn't remember them.

He stared down the road ahead, hoping for a car. If one came, he'd grab the wheel, swerve into it. He'd take his chances getting hurt in a crash. The prospect was less threatening than these goons. But no cars came at them. He figured he'd put up a struggle, work his arms up and flail out, get free, get away.

"Give it to him," the driver said in a calm, reasonable voice.

"Okay," answered the dark stranger.

Ray turned to see what he was going to give him, disarmed, curious. He felt a sharp, stinging jab of pain in his right arm, saw the stranger pull a needle out. Realization flooded his inebriated brain.

"Jesus! What did you do to me?" Ray whined. More urine flowed, but he was no longer aware of his weakness. Terror gripped his mind, numbing him, like he was falling into the icy waters of the Gulf of Maine.

"You'll see, Ray. You'll see," said the dark stranger.

His cold, threatening words chased Ray into the dark tunnel that appeared before him.

***

Ray's return to consciousness was slowed by the alcohol he'd had. He came back by degrees. Conscious. Unconscious. Each time he opened his eyes, the sky was lighter. He sensed a great hurt somewhere, but he couldn't pinpoint it. He was also aware of a deep, penetrating cold that enveloped him. The alcohol he'd downed, together with the drug they'd given him, still clouded his mind. He slipped under once again.

Time passed.

Ray became aware that he was lying on the icy ground, and he was cold, very cold. At the same time, he sensed a deep pain radiating outward from his groin.

"Maybe the cold's causing the pain," he mused. But Ray knew in his heart that this pain was worse. Far worse.

The enveloping pain clicked up another notch as the world moved more and more into focus. He could smell whiskey on his clothes now, and the smell of urine. He sensed a cold wetness in his crotch, remembered pissing his pants.

"I'm alive. They didn't kill me! I'm gonna be all right," he said out loud to himself, relieved.

He became aware of something in his mouth that made breathing difficult. He opened it and spat out a messy blob. His breathing improved at once. He felt a flood of relief.

Prob'ly bit off a hunk of one of those goons.

A wheezing laugh bubbled out, shaking him. The movement sent a message to his brain that the source of the pain was his crotch.

"Them sons of bitches kneed me in th' balls," he whined. His hand went to his crotch to explore for damage. He felt a wetness and a numbness that confused his efforts to define his injury. He brought his hand up to his face and was puzzled by what he saw. In the uncertain light of dawn, his fingers were black. He stared, unable to understand the importance of what he saw. Then the pain surged through his core, and his mind withdrew once more to the sanctuary of merciful unconsciousness.

When he opened his eyes again, the sun had appeared. Ray could see clearly. He remembered the riddle of his fingers and held them in front of his eyes again. They were no longer black. They were red. Blood red.

"Oh, shit! Oh, shit! Oh, shit," Ray moaned, the truth finally reaching his brain. "They cut me! Those motherfuckers cut me. I'm bleeding!"

His eyes locked onto the bloody blob on the ground in front of him. He remembered something in his mouth, something choking him. He recalled spitting it out, feeling instant relief. He stared at it, curious. He saw pale skin, saw long hairs on it, saw two oval lumps. Blood and spittle clung to it. He still didn't get it.

"What the fuck is that shit?" he asked, staring down at it with bloodshot eyes.

Then the pain in his groin crescendoed, and he knew. He stared in horror at the mess that was his testicles, his scrotum, and then he plunged into the dark tunnel once more.

Chapter Seventeen

"As you see, people, we have a guest today," Brent said, his voice cutting through the banter, bringing silence in its wake. All eyes fixed on the stranger, a tall, stocky man whose limp suit and wrinkled tie looked like his closest companions. He had short cropped, black hair over a round, thoughtful face. The man radiated fitness, confidence.

"This is Detective Denton Coe of the Maine State Police. He's asked for a few minutes of our time this morning," said Brent, by way of an introduction.

"Thanks for the intro, Doc. I go by Denny," began Detective Coe as he got to his feet. "As some of you may have heard, one of our more celebrated perps met with a strange accident the other night."

Hearing this, Jim's senses elevated to high alert. He struggled to maintain a mask of calm curiosity, praying that he wasn't blushing or blanching, implicating himself.

"Seems that a couple strangers jumped him, cut his balls off." Detective Coe paused for effect, then continued. "Perp's name is Ray Barribee." Again he paused, his sharp, coal black eyes jumping from face to face, searching for a reaction.

"Looks like the name rings a bell with you, young lady," said Coe, staring hard at Brie.

Brie colored under his scrutiny.

"Want to tell me the connection?" he asked.

"Sure," said Brie. "His name's come up many times over the past several years. He sexually abused three of our female clients that we know about, did it when they were kids. And last week, we had a young man tell us he'd been abused by him six, maybe eight years ago. Yes, Detective, we know the name Ray Barribee. Sounds like he got the right therapy for his problem." She smiled defiantly at the detective.

Everyone laughed, dumping some of the tension the detective had brought into the room.

"Yeah, well, I've been assigned to find out who's responsible for this assault on his person," said Coe. "Whether or not you think he deserved it, he's still entitled to protection in the eyes of the law."

"You speak of protection, Detective?" said Betsy Loomis, her voice shrill. "What kind of protection did those poor kids have when he took it upon himself to ruin their lives?"

"This Ray Barribee, he's one sick fuck, Detective Coe," Andy McMartin cut in, speaking his mind. "There isn't a soul in this room who isn't cheering over Ray Barribee's recent loss. He's fucked up more lives than we'll ever know."

"You people aren't making this easy for me," complained Detective Coe.

"We'll do whatever we can to assist your investigation, Detective," Brent said, restoring order. "But as you can see, you can't expect us to show any sympathy for the creep."

"Thanks, Doc. I won't take up any more of your time right now, but I may need to talk to some of you individually." His eyes swept over the group.

He walked to the door, then turned back to the room. "Oh, by the way. None of you should leave the state without telling me first. Until this thing gets solved, you're all suspects." With that he left, closing the door behind him as his threat settled over the room.

There was silence.

Finally, Brent spoke. "There is an Equalizer. He lives!"

"Long live the Equalizer," cheered Andy, his coffee cup raised above his head.

The room erupted in a groundswell of support for the unknown benefactor who had made their day.

***

Detective Coe, who had been listening outside the door, whistled low, hearing it. "Hell, I'm the Equalizer, as someone will be finding out. Meanwhile, though, they're not making my job any easier," he muttered as he strode away.

***

Jim rode a roller coaster of emotions. Tony Bonnano told him they'd just *rough him up*. But this was more than roughing up. A lot more. He had worried that they might get carried away, that they might kill him. He couldn't live with that. He was a P.A., pledged to save lives, not take them. When he learned of Barribee's fate, he was both shocked and relieved. Shocked at the mutilation his actions had caused another human being. Relieved that he hadn't caused the man's death. And shocked at the exhilaration he felt for the justice he'd meted out.

"Who do you suppose did that to him?" asked Dave Levesque.

"Who knows?" answered Andy. "Could've been any number of people. A prior victim. The father or relative of a victim. Maybe even somebody right here in this room," he added, smiling wickedly.

"Wish I could take credit for it," said Ted Aaronson, grinning from ear to ear.

"Don't we all," agreed Bill Thomas.

Jim searched the smiling faces. Everyone seemed delighted with the news. A few grinned in his direction. He wondered if his face had already betrayed him, wondered if anyone guessed that he was responsible. As the newest newcomer to the group, he guessed he could be the most likely suspect. He'd have to be careful.

"Hey, Jim. Did you arrange this little accident by any chance?" It was Brent, a sly grin creasing his face.

Everyone turned to look at Jim. He felt the color rising to his cheeks.

"Jim didn't do it. I set the whole thing up." It was Betsy Loomis. "I've been scheming over the best way to even the score with good ol' Ray for a long time now, and I finally got my chance."

"You can't take the credit," complained Breanna. "I cannot tell a lie. I set it up."

"The heck you did," Dave spoke up. "I'm responsible."

"Okay, okay. I confess. I paid the right guys to relieve ol' Ray of his family jewels," confessed Andy.

"I hope you pickled them in formaldehyde, so we can put them on display for everyone to see. Think of the therapeutic value," said Brent.

"We'll label them 'Barribee's Balls' and put them on a special shelf in the group room," suggested Martha, grinning impishly.

Thanks to all this bantering, Jim recovered enough to risk joining in. "And we'll ask Detective Coe to come for the dedication ceremony," he offered, smiling.

"Bad idea. Then he'll know someone here did it, and he'll hound us forever," lamented Bill Thomas.

"I hope Detective Coe never finds out who's responsible," said Martha Knowles. "This is justice, not a crime."

"Hear, Hear," shouted Andy. "May the Equalizer remain alive and well."

"On that note, let's end this most productive meeting," suggested Brent.

"We didn't get any team presentations done, so plan on doubling up tomorrow. Those of you who're presenting, keep them short and sweet so we can get them all in. Let's go to your groups now. Oh, and make sure all our clients hear the great news."

Everyone got up to go. The room buzzed with positive comments about Ray Barribee's fate. The mood in the room was upbeat, almost festive, like the atmosphere in the campaign headquarters of a successful politician. An outsider might have concluded that they had pooled their money, bought megabucks tickets, and won the big jackpot.

Jim filed out, responding to comments made to him. He was still in shock. He was also stunned by the overwhelming support for Ray Barribee's mutilation. Everyone was overjoyed by what had happened.

But he was responsible.

He had acted impulsively, out of anger and frustration over a sexual deviant's acts. He had asked a powerful man to have him roughed up enough to get his attention. Well, he guessed they got his attention all right. They caused serious bodily injury. That was more than Jim bargained for. Did Ray Barribee deserve that punishment? Those in the room with him clearly felt he did. But did that make it right?

Jim didn't think so. He needed time to digest it all.

"Way to go, Jim. I knew you were our man." It was Andy.

Jim struggled to regain control before he spoke. "Hey, Andy, don't try to foist the credit onto someone else. I know you've got his balls curing in your desk drawer, ready for the grand presentation," Jim teased him.

"You got in my drawers without me even knowing it, didn't you?"

"I couldn't help myself," said Jim, going along with the double meaning. "And I have to confess, I was amazed at all the weird stuff I found."

"Okay, I'll tell you what. I'll buy you coffee in exchange for your pledge of silence. I can't have this getting out," Andy said in a mock-hushed voice.

"Done."

"Sally's meeting us down there. I've got to stop by my desk to check on some things. Then I'll be right along. See you there?"

"Okay. And Andy. Give the jar a little shake. It'll make them cure faster that way."

"Sounds like you're an old hand at this," Andy shot back.

"Nothing gets by you, does it?"

Andy raised his eyebrows suggestively, then made his way to his office.

Jim went to the stairway, his long legs closing the distance quickly while his mind continued to review the shocking results his phone call had caused.

Chapter Eighteen

Jim strode into the coffee shop and eyeballed the customers. No Sally. He took a seat at an empty table. Although Jenny was waiting on two people at another table, she took the time to make eye contact with him and mouthed a "Good morning."

"Morning, Jenny. Take your time. I'm waiting for Sally and Andy."

"Here's one now," said Jenny, nodding toward the door.

Jim turned to see Sally Harpswell coming in. She wore a bright floral print skirt that reached to her knees and a pale pink blouse with enough buttons left undone to show off a small gold pendant on a short chain. Her light brown hair was in a bun today. She wore practical sneakers.

She paused, then spotted Jim who gave her a quick wave. She waved back at him and made her way to his table.

He stood to greet her.

"Hi, Sally. Good to see you. Andy said he'd be right down."

"Good to see you, too, Jim." She pulled out a chair and sat down. "How are you liking it here so far?" She was relaxed but interested.

"In twenty-five words or less? I like the people, I like the program, and I like the town. Guess it's unanimous."

"Oh, that's good. I'm glad it's working out for you. I can't imagine what a drag it would be to move all the way up here, only to find out you didn't like it."

"You're right. I'm a lucky guy." Jim realized the truth in his words. "What about you? Are you from around here?"

"No. I grew up in South Carolina. I met my husband in Washington, on the Mall near the Washington Monument, at a rally. He was just back from Iraq, and he had a lot to say about his experiences. We hit it off from the start. We got married, and he dragged me up here to Maine. He was raised here. His dad was a game warden out in the Sebago area. I love it here," she said, giving him a warm smile.

"You love your job?" Andy said, surprising both of them. He pulled out a chair and joined them.

"Oh, well, maybe not my job. But everything else." Sally's warm expression radiated from her face.

"That's more like it," said Andy. "Sally's got the hardest job around here. She has to put up with more shit than that guy who had to clean out the Aegean stables, what's his name?"

"Hercules?" answered Sally and Jim as one.

"That's the guy. She has to put up with clients who don't want to be here, and social workers who want her to take every client, and Brent, who only wants the cream of the crop so his statistics will shine at budget crunch time. Other than that, it's a cushy job, hey, Sally?" Andy asked, smiling.

"I couldn't have said it better myself."

"Barkeep, coffee all round!" Andy waved in Jenny's direction.

"Coming right up, cowboy," said Jenny without hesitation.

Jim guessed she was used to Andy's ways.

"I had a great conversation with your old friend Mary Evans this morning," Sally said to Andy.

"My *old* friend? Where'd you get that idea?" countered Andy.

"From her. She said you two go way back," said Sally, her eyes twinkling.

"That's a lie! I deny everything."

"Well, she spent the better part of a half hour complaining to me about her PMS, and then she wanted me to take one of the most underqualified clients I've ever been presented. I guess she thought I'd feel sorry about her PMS and take on her client," concluded Sally.

"PMS, huh? Do you believe that stuff?" Andy asked.

"Oh, I don't know. I've never had it, but a lot of women claim to," said Sally, ever the diplomat.

"If you ask me, it's a convenient little catch-all condition designed for women who need to complain about something to get through the day," said Andy. "Hell, it can't be anything as bad as PES."

"Oh, yeah. You told me to remind you to tell me about that," said Jim, remembering. "What's PES?"

"You're a PA and you haven't heard of PES? Unbelievable," said Andy.

"Not yet. Care to enlighten me?" said Jim, sensing the onset of a leg-pulling.

"It stands for Prostate Enlargement Syndrome," Andy explained.

"Doesn't sound like anything that I could complain about," said Sally with her usual dry humor.

Andy shook his head. "Nope. It's something for us men."

"Are you talking about BPH? Benign Prostatic Hypertrophy?" asked Jim.

"That's the deal that happens to men when they get older and have to get up ten times a night to pee, right?"

"You got it," said Jim. "It's the gradual enlargement of the prostate gland. It narrows the urethra and makes it harder and harder to empty the bladder. The end result is peeing smaller amounts more often. That's what causes the frequent runs to the can at night."

"Nope. BPH and PES are totally different," said Andy. "BPH is a problem for men later in life, right? Well, PES strikes men in their prime. Fact is, it usually starts in adolescence, but it can be a problem at any age. Perhaps you know it by its older, cruder name. BB."

"BB?" said Jim, puzzled.

"Correct. The full scientific name is Blue Balls," said Andy, straight-faced.

"Oh, sure! Good old Blue Balls," Jim concurred, laughing.

"I remember being blamed for that when I was in my teens," said Sally, grinning. "His name was Billy Wilson, and after we'd been making out in the back seat of his dad's Pontiac for an hour or so, he tried to have his way with me. When I told him that wasn't part of my plan, he started wailing about me giving him blue balls, and what was I going to do about it? I asked him what he suggested, and he gave me several options. None of them appealed to me. That was the last I saw of him."

"That's it exactly," said Andy. "You women have no idea of the seriousness of the condition. It's only recently that the scientific community has explored the condition and come up with far more information about the causes and effects of it. I'm surprised you haven't read about it in your medical journals, Jim."

"Hey, there's so much to read and so little time," Jim complained, all the while smiling.

"Isn't that the truth? Well, let me tell you what I know about it," offered Andy.

"Hold on. Is this your own personal anecdote or is this from the scientific community?" asked Sally.

"Ow, that hurt! Do you think I'd make something like this up, based on my own personal experience alone?" Andy fired back.

Sally looked at him, her eyes crinkled with merriment. She made no reply.

"Forget my question," said Andy. "While some of the results of the study are based on personal experience, there is also a significant amount of corroboration from other males who have experienced the symptoms."

"You've got me on the edge of my seat," said Jim. "Tell me about PES."

"Okay. First of all, the only thing new is the name. Men have suffered from it for years. It's like PMS in that regard. Women throughout history surely haven't suffered the symptoms of mood change, bloating, cramps, depression, and all that other crap, in grim silence. Now they have a syndrome they can blame for all their problems, and look how many more women suddenly suffer from it as a result.

"The same is true for men now, with the official recognition of Prostate Enlargement Syndrome, or PES. Now men no longer have to sneak around, hiding their pain and frustration from the world, commiserating with other men as their only way of gaining sympathy. Now men can proudly proclaim that they're suffering from PES, and the world will know what their problem is, and be sympathetic, just as the world is sympathetic toward women with PMS," Andy summarized, his voice rising in a crescendo.

"Hey, that's fantastic," said Jim. "You told us you'd tell us what you know about it."

"Sure, sure. Well, it was originally believed that sexual stimulation that was, shall we say, unfulfilled, caused pressure from too much blood flow to the testicles, and this pressure caused the painful and long-lasting condition known previously as Blue Balls. The term itself was crude, and obviously didn't attract much sympathy, especially from women. And this was compounded by the fact that women caused the problem in the first place.

"So, with all the sex research and the new openness toward sexual issues, the condition was studied scientifically. What they found was, the prostate gland was the real culprit. Sexual stimulation causes an increase of fluid in the prostate gland, and if sexual release doesn't occur, there's no place for all that fluid to go. The result is, the prostate is stretched beyond its normal parameters, enlarged if you will, and this enlargement causes a stretching of the nerve endings, which is the pain a guy feels," explained Andy.

"So why does a guy say his, ah, balls hurt if it's really his prostate?" Sally asked, coloring slightly.

"A very good question, Sally, and one I'm sure Jim can answer as well. In a word, referred pain," said Andy.

"Good old referred pain," said Jim.

"Okay, I'll bite. What's that?" Sally glanced from Jim to Andy.

"It's when pain that's occurring in one part of your body is perceived to be occurring somewhere else. For example, heart attacks can cause jaw pain, arm pain, shoulder pain. Pneumonia can cause abdominal pain," explained Jim.

"So what's the cure for PES?" Sally asked, guessing already.

"It's simple. A regular and complete emptying of the prostate before the fluid level reaches a critical point. And now that women can understand the key role they play in this critical male health issue, they can be proud of themselves for the importance of their part in maintaining male harmony," said Andy, grinning broadly.

"Jeez, if Billy Wilson had told me all that, it might have changed my whole life," said Sally, smirking at Andy.

"A little education, coupled with some good old down-home scientific explanations, and you have a totally new perspective on this age-old problem," said Andy.

"And I thought women had a monopoly on pain and suffering since PMS was recognized," said Jim.

"Not any longer," Andy shook his head. "With widespread acceptance of PES, men now have an equally convenient syndrome to lump their symptoms under. That's the beauty of it."

"Well, I'm impressed," said Sally.

"Now, if you'll spread the word amongst your female friends, help to disseminate the word, if you will, you'll be doing your part to speed universal acceptance of this terrible syndrome," Andy said.

"You know you can count on me." Sally winked at him. "By the way, that bit about referred pain brings up a question. Where did Ray Barribee feel it when his, ah, balls were removed?"

Jim, absorbed by Andy's explanation of PES, had pushed thoughts about Ray Barribee to the back of his mind. Sally's question jarred him. Fortunately, Andy jumped in.

"You heard about that?"

"Sure," Sally said. "It's the topic of conversation amongst the entire staff. Everyone's cheering the news."

"Comments from the medical side, Jim?"

Jim had recovered his composure. "My best guess, not having any personal experience with that kind of injury, is that disruption of the testicular and scrotal nerves would likely cause pain deep in the pelvic area. There may be some referred pain in the thighs as well." Jim felt a sympathetic twinge of pain in his groin as he spoke.

"Well, everyone I've spoken to hopes his pain lasts a long, long time," said Sally.

"I think we can safely say that it's worse than your basic PES pain," said Andy.

A pot in hand, Jenny asked, "More coffee?"

Andy glanced at his watch, groaned. "Lunch would be more like it."

"I can do that, too," Jenny said, waggling the coffee pot in her hand.

"Seeing as it's quarter to twelve, let's do it," said Andy.

Jim and Sally seconded the motion.

"Mae's special of the day?" Jenny asked.

Seconded and passed.

"Be back in a jiff," said Jenny, returning to the kitchen.

"Okay, listen. If anyone asks where you were all morning, tell them we had a meeting to discuss men's issues," Andy proposed.

"And we did," said Sally.

"Amen to that," Jim agreed.

***

When Jim got to his desk after lunch, he found a note. It said, "Dinner. My place. Seven. Regrets only. B."

He hadn't a clue where Brie lived. Then it occurred to him that it could be an invite from Brent.

He looked more closely at the note. The handwriting confirmed that it was from Brie. He'd need to get directions from her before the end of the day. It was curious, getting a dinner invite from her when she seemed to be studiously avoiding him. Though lunch was still fresh on his mind, he found himself thinking ahead to dinner and all its possibilities.

Chapter Nineteen

"Good, you found me," said Brie, opening her door.

Jim stepped inside an apartment similar to his own in its dimensions, but totally different. It was warm, cozy, something his apartment lacked. He surmised that it had something to do with a 'woman's touch.'

"Nice place," he offered, summarizing his feelings.

"Thanks. Take your coat?"

Jim handed it to her.

While she hung it on a hallway hook, he searched for the subtle touches that made the space inviting. He came up empty. Had to be a combination of things.

"Come on in and have a seat. Dinner's under way," said Brie, ushering him into the living room.

The aroma of garlic and a mix of other, subtler herbs and spices wafted in from the kitchen, which he could see was similar to his own. He felt his stomach twitch in anticipation, realizing with a jolt that he was ravenous.

"Smells wonderful. What've you got cooking?"

"You're my first guinea pig for chicken tetrazzini," Brie said, watching him for a reaction.

Jim didn't show any. "Need any help?"

"Nope. Everything's under control. Can I get you a cold beer? A glass of wine?"

"A beer sounds perfect."

"You got it. One cold beer, coming up." She headed for the kitchen.

Jim heard her lift the lid from a pot on the stove and stir the contents. There was a pause. He pictured her tasting the sauce. "How's it taste?" he asked, guessing.

"Mmm. It's coming along."

He heard her open the refrigerator door, then the sound of a beer can being opened. *One* beer can. *Uh oh.* She came in carrying one beer can and one glass.

"Aren't you joining me?" he asked, certain of the answer.

"I've got a glass of wine in the kitchen," she replied, her expression saying *You thought you got me*. He'd guessed wrong.

She returned to the kitchen for her wine glass, then came back and sat in the padded chair opposite him.

"What a wild day this has been," she said.

"You mean the Ray Barribee business?" He took a long swig of beer, bracing for what might come.

"That, and the detective showing up, and then the support from the staff. If I'd been the one who did that to Old Ray, I'd probably be encouraged to go out and do it to somebody else. Maybe to several other someone else's," she added, looking steadily at Jim.

"I hadn't thought about it that way, but I guess you're right," said Jim, returning her gaze.

Brie shifted in her chair and sat upright, facing Jim directly. "Jim, I need to know. Did you do that?"

She caught him by surprise with her abruptness, but he managed to answer without hesitation.

"Sure. I called my Mafia friends in New Jersey and they took care of it." His parents had drilled into him that the truth was easier to tell than a lie, so that's what he did.

"I'm serious, Jim. Did you personally do that?"

"Heck, no! Do you think I could take a knife, or whatever, and do something like that to another human being? I'm a PA. I took the Hippocratic oath." He held her gaze and clung to the truth.

"I'm sorry, Jim. I feel stupid now. You were the last one hired at Serenity, and I saw you react strongly to the sexual abuse of the women. And when you reacted to Old Ray's track record. I felt I had to ask you, before we go any further."

"I understand," he said, at the same time wondering what she'd meant by her last remark.

"So, who would do such a thing?"

"Probably some Mafia hit men," he said, adding his disarming smile.

"Oh, come on. There's no Mafia in Maine. They'd starve for lack of business," Brie countered, laughing at the thought.

"No kidding? I assumed they were everywhere. Well then, who do you think might have done it—other than me?"

"It could've been any number of people. Maybe a victim, grown up and wanting revenge. Maybe a parent or a victim's relative wanting revenge. Maybe some counselor or social worker, maybe even one right here at Serenity, who decided that Old Ray needed a comeuppance," she offered.

"What about you?" Jim teased, trying for a reaction.

"Don't I wish. But I know my physical limitations," she confessed.

She stood and sauntered over to him. "But you, on the other hand," she said as she grasped his right bicep with both hands, "You have the ability to carry it off." She sat next to him on the sofa, her hands still grasping his arm.

"Are you suggesting we join forces? Your brains and my brawn?" Jim asked, his eyebrows raised with the question.

"Am I that transparent? You see right through me." Brie laughed.

"No, to be honest, you've kept me guessing all along," said Jim, holding her gaze.

"Then here's to a new era of openness and honesty," she proposed, raising her wine glass.

"I'll drink to that," agreed Jim, clinking his glass against hers.

They sipped, regarding each other.

"It's back to the kitchen with me," Brie announced, breaking the silence.

"Can I help?"

"You can, if you can boil water," she said with a grin.

He chuckled. "That's the one thing I've mastered."

"Okay, then. You're the official pasta chef."

"I accept," he said, following her into the kitchen.

She tasted the sauce while he filled a big pot with water.

"So you think Old Ray got what he deserved?" Jim probed.

"You're damned right I do. I've been in this business long enough to see the incredible damage creeps like Ray do to innocent kids. Damage that can last a lifetime. We see the tip of the iceberg here, and we're successful with only a fraction of those we see. The rest either never get help or are too messed up to get anything from the help we offer them."

He set the pot on the stove. "Has anyone studied why one victim can get better while another can't?"

"I haven't seen any actual studies, but there are observations people have made, maybe not scientific, but valid, I think, in spite of that. It might go back to genetic strengths and weaknesses. Some people are inclined to illness, while others sail through life healthy. Until the end, anyway," she added as an afterthought.

"So you think some people can handle problems better than others?"

"Exactly. I've worked with women who were horribly abused as children, who got into heavy drug use, who ended up on the street, prostituting themselves for drugs and food, and who made the choice that they wanted to get better. And when they confronted all their demons, they were able to put the horrors in the past and begin leading productive lives.

"I've also worked with women who were sexually abused as children," she said, "and they were so overwhelmed by the abuse that they became

133

borderlines."

"Borderline, as in borderline personality disorder?"

"Exactly. A psychological disorder, mostly seen in women, but you probably knew that. They blame themselves for everything bad that's ever happened to them. They hate themselves. They punish themselves by cutting and disfiguring themselves, making suicide gestures and attempts, and sometimes killing themselves, though I think most successful suicides by borderlines are accidental."

"You're saying they make a suicide gesture, and it goes further than they expect, and they end up dead," Jim said.

"Yes. Borderlines love attention, and suicide gestures are a great way to get attention."

"So, what makes them crave attention?" asked Jim, dropping the linguini into the boiling water.

"My guess is, it makes them feel better about themselves, maybe even diverts their attention away from their general feeling of worthlessness. I've asked a lot of borderlines about their sexual activity. Most of them admitted to being very active, even to the point of being promiscuous. But when I ask them if they enjoyed sex, they say no, they don't feel anything. However, they like the attention they're getting while it's happening."

"Since they don't feel good about themselves or feel pleasure, they draw pleasure from the attention they get from their partners," Jim concluded.

"That's what I think. And that's what makes working with borderlines so difficult. They dominate the attention and the conversation in a group setting any chance they get. It makes the other group members mad because they can't get a word in edgewise to talk about their own issues. The more they get angry, the more the borderlines like it. It means more attention for them, even though it's negative. Negative or positive, it doesn't make any difference. It can get real nasty." Brie brushed a strand of hair away from her face.

"Why do you think they're so hard to treat?" asked Jim as he stared into the boiling linguini.

"There's probably as many answers as there are borderlines, though there are some common denominators. I think many of them have such low self-worth that they don't hear, really hear, the advice given to them. They're so intent on drawing attention to themselves that they hardly listen to what's said to them. Either that, or they're listening on a superficial level and aren't really taking it in. Another thing is, they think they're the reason for all their problems. The idea of blaming someone else is unacceptable. So, we keep banging our heads against their walls and hope for a breakthrough."

"Okay, so there are women who can shrug off the effects of their

134

abuse and lead fairly normal lives, and borderlines who are paralyzed, incapacitated by their abuse. What's in between?" asked Jim, absently stirring the linguini.

"Most of the women we treat fall in between. At one end are the easy ones, the quick learners, the ones who can accept they were victimized. At the other end are the almost-borderlines, or borderline borderlines. Some make pretty good progress while they're here, but most need long-term counseling so they can lead happy, productive lives.

"Our jobs used to be easier before managed care and DRGs came along. The program was four weeks long, and it wasn't all that difficult to get an extension of two or more weeks if we could show that a client was making progress and needed additional time in the in-patient setting.

"Now we get two weeks to accomplish what we used to try and do in four, and there's no extensions, no matter what. That puts a lot of pressure on us to make breakthroughs. Plus, it puts even more pressure on the aftercare people to carry the ball once we pass it to them," said Brie.

"No wonder borderlines are so hard to work with," Jim commented.

"Uh huh. Do you know what Andy says in Team Meeting when we get into a long discussion about a female patient? He says, 'She's got to be a borderline.' And he's right. Borderlines take up a lot of our time, and they're frustrating to work with."

"On that note, it's time to test the linguini," said Jim. He fished out a single strand with a fork, let it dangle, dripping, and then flipped it against the wall above the stove. It clung there, steam rising from it.

"Al dente!" he announced. "Let's eat."

"I had no idea I was in the company of such an accomplished pasta chef," Brie teased. "You do your pasta thing while I get the salad."

Jim drained the linguini into a colander and rinsed it while Brie took the salad from the refrigerator.

"Ranch or Italian?" she asked.

"Let's go Italian all the way," Jim said.

"On the side or slathered?"

"Slathered?"

"You know," she said, "slathered all over and then tossed for good measure."

"Slathered sounds good," he agreed.

Brie *slathered* the salad.

They served themselves chicken tetrazzini over linguini, with tossed, slathered salad on the side. Then they carried their plates to the small kitchen table that Brie had set with a red-and-white checkered tablecloth and a single candle in an old, drip-covered wine bottle.

Jim had a passing thought of who before him had borne witness to the wax build-up, then shrugged the thought from his mind.

"Oops! The wine," yelped Brie. She retrieved the bottle from the counter and poured wine in the glass she'd set for him, then placed the bottle between them.

He'd finished his beer, so he said, "Thanks, you did that like an old pro."

"Didn't I tell you? I was a waitress for three summers while in college."

"That explains all the professional touches I see about me," Jim said, glancing at the room.

"Don't get too carried away until you try the tetrazzini. I make no claims about my cooking," she confessed, watching him.

Jim took a forkful of tetrazzini and pasta, swirled it around, and swept it into his mouth. Then he chewed thoughtfully, smacked his lips, and gazed skyward. After, he leveled his gaze on Brie, his face was a mask of seriousness.

"You don't like it," she guessed, disappointment taking control of her expression.

"I hate to say it, but you're right." He paused a moment longer for dramatic effect. "I love it! It's absolutely the best chicken tetrazzini I've ever tasted."

"It's probably the *only* chicken tetrazzini you've ever tasted," she shot back, the disappointment leaving her face.

"Not true. I've had it before," he said, trying to look hurt.

"Once? Twice?" she pushed.

"Don't let's quibble over such minor details, Chef Brie. Take my word that it's *perfecto.*"

"Okay, no quibbles. Anyway, I agree. It's not half bad. And I've had it once before," she confessed, smiling impishly at Jim.

A comfortable silence ensued while they savored the meal.

Then, Brie spoke. "Hey, you want to go skiing this weekend?"

"Downhill or cross country?" Jim said as he stopped the fork midway to his mouth.

"Do I take that as a *yes,* pending a decision as to the skis we use?"

"Count me in. Either sounds fine. Do you have a preference?" He took the bite and chewed.

"It's supposed to be sunny and in the thirties Saturday. Let's go cross-country. I'll pack a lunch and you can carry it."

"I get it. You need a pack mule," Jim said.

"Am I that obvious?" she asked, batting her eyelashes at him.

Jim couldn't help but laugh out loud.

Chapter Twenty

Detective Denny Coe was ending a bad day. It wasn't his first bad day, and he knew it wouldn't be his last, but that didn't temper the funk he was in.

He had spent the whole day digging for a lead on the Ray Barribee mutilation case and had come up empty. He knew any number of vigilante-types could've done it to Barribee, including fathers of children he'd abused, or prisoners who hated him for what he'd done. Despite that, his instincts told him that the logical place to look was a drug treatment center, since the person or persons most likely to do something like that were either in treatment or providing treatment. It wouldn't be the first time a drug treatment counselor heard about a particularly nasty perp and decided to take matters into his, or her, own hands.

Denny hated what he'd been doing all day, because he had no sympathy, truth to tell, for Ray Barribee. Three years back, he'd been on the other side of the street on this one, chasing down leads and gathering evidence that would put Barribee in the slammer for the sexual abuse of little girls and boys. It'd pissed him off when Tom Lenihan, another detective assigned to the case, got the evidence needed to put Barribee away. He wondered if his boss, good ol' Captain Gagnon, had assigned him to the Barribee case because Lenihan had got the goods on Ray and put him away before he could. Speculation. He'd likely never know for sure, but it pissed him off just the same thinking about it.

He reviewed the places he'd been and the people he'd interviewed. He'd been to substance abuse treatment facilities in Bangor and Waterville where he gave his little speech and watched the faces carefully for reactions. He didn't think he'd seen anything, but he'd still check all the names and run them for priors. Never knew.

Yesterday had been a different story. He'd gone to that Serenity program, and those people were practically begging to be checked out. There were those two women who spoke right out about Barribee, and there was that new guy, that PA, who sat quietly while the room erupted around him. Being new there, it could make him more likely to react to guys like

Barribee. And do something. All three were worth following up on. Maybe place a couple discreet bugs. Never knew what might be said in what was thought to be a private setting.

Then Denny had gone down to Lewiston to check out their program and got a rise out of that middle-aged counselor when he disclosed what'd happened to Barribee. They were all good prospects. He couldn't recall their names, but names weren't his strong suit. He had them written down in his pocket notebook, and that's all he needed. Their faces were in his head, and that's what he worked on, that's how he found what he was looking for.

Denny considered what tomorrow would bring him. He had to go to Portland and do his little traveling act at the two treatment facilities down there. He didn't look forward to it any more than he'd looked forward to today's agenda.

He shut the door on tomorrow like a frustrated parent shutting a door on a screaming, demanding child. He parked in front of his apartment. He was home, his workday over. He'd learned a long time ago the importance of separating his work from his private life.

He laughed bitterly at the thought of what his private life had become. It had all gone up in smoke when Moira left him. What was it now? Jeez, more than a year ago.

He'd discovered he didn't miss his wife. They had drifted apart long before she walked out, so it was no big deal. But she'd taken Ellie with her, and he missed being with his little girl. At eight, she was growing up fast. Too fast.

Before the separation, he and Ellie used to talk about all the places they would see together. He'd come home and she'd get out the atlas. They'd look up a state or a country and plan a trip there. Ellie got good at it. She'd bring home books from the library about far-off places with strange-sounding names, and then she'd tie it all together, with maps of everything.

Moira tried to ruin it for them, saying that he was too busy to take them someplace close by, so how would he ever take them to another state or country?

Denny smiled inwardly. His trip plans with Ellie had never included Moira. Ellie had listened to her mother's rantings, but she kept right on planning trips with him. Denny supposed that she didn't want to give up the dream of traveling to faraway places any more than he did.

Guess I'll call her. See what she's up to. He opened his apartment door.

His apartment was cramped, dark, and dirty, but he hardly noticed. It was his place to come home to at the end of the day, his refuge from the unpleasant work he did, and it suited him fine. He had a small kitchen where he could microwave a simple dinner at night and make coffee in the morning, and there was a living area with an old couch and a TV. He had a bedroom to sleep in, plus a basic bathroom, so what else could he need? The kitchen was cluttered with unwashed dishes and pans, and the painted coffee table by the couch was littered with empty beer cans, glasses, and an ashtray full of cigar butts. He hadn't minded clutter when Moira was around, and he didn't mind clutter now.

He shoved his paper bag of groceries onto the kitchen counter, pushing old clutter out of the way to make room. He stored the freezer and fridge items, then left the dried goods for later. He hung his coat and hat on a hook by the door, shuffled between the couch and the table, and sank into the old couch with an audible sigh.

This was the worst time of day for Denny, the end of his work day, the start of his personal day. The transition was always tough. It was when he noticed the mess he lived in, and when he thought about the mess that was his life. Then he remembered Ellie and his plan to call her. The thought cheered him.

He retrieved the cordless phone from the coffee table and dialed Moira's number. She answered on the third ring.

"Hello." She sounded tired.

"Hi, Moira. How're you doing?" His voice carried no enthusiasm.

"If I thought for one minute you were asking 'cause you cared, I'd tell you," she responded in a voice as flat as his. "But I'm guessing you called to talk to Ellie."

"You know me too well."

"You got that right. Hold on."

Denny heard the muffled call to Ellie, heard his little girl ask who it was, heard Moira tell her it was her dad. Then Ellie was on the line.

"Daddy!" Her enthusiasm buoyed Denny up.

"Hi, Punkin. How're you doing?" he asked.

"Good, Daddy. Where're we going when you get time off?" She still clung to the idea of a trip with him.

"I don't know, Punkin. Someplace warm and sunny, don't you think?"

"Ooh! That sounds nice. We can take our bathing suits and our summer clothes, and we can swim and lie in the sun all day. Daddy, what if we went on a cruise?"

"Hey, what a great idea! Where did you come up with that?"

"Oh, there's a dumb boy in my class who went on a cruise with his parents. He told us about it in class. It sounded kind of fun."

"It does sound like fun, Punkin. We could stop and see a whole bunch of places that way, all on the same trip. Why don't you see what you can find out about cruises and where they go?"

"Okay, Daddy. I will."

"So, what's new?"

"The big news is I'm going to my friend Alice's house to stay the night tonight."

"Wow. That sounds like a lot of fun! Where does she live?"

"Oh, she lives a couple streets away."

"Is your mom taking you over?"

"No. She says I'm big enough to walk over there by myself."

"But honey, it's dark outside already," Denny protested.

"I know, Daddy. But the street lights are on, and I won't get lost."

Denny wasn't worried about her getting lost, or worse.

"I hope you have a good time but be careful." He struggled to keep his voice free of concern. "Any other news?"

"Oh, you know, Daddy. The usual stuff."

"Okay, Punkin. You be good and I'll talk to you soon. Put your mom on again for a second, okay?"

"Okay, Daddy. Bye."

"Bye, Ellie."

There was a soft clunk as she set the phone down, followed by a short pause, then Moira was back.

"What, Denny?" Moira was short on ceremony.

"What's this about her walking by herself to her friend's house this evening?"

"Oh, for Christ's sake! It's a five-minute walk on lighted streets. She could get there blindfolded."

"C'mon, Moira. Anything could happen."

"Jesus, Denny. That lousy job of yours has you thinking there's a pervert behind every bush. This is a safe neighborhood."

"Every neighborhood's safe until something happens," he countered, his voice rising.

"Don't you think I've talked to her about strangers and what they could do to her? And don't you think she knows it from your job and what you've told her, too?" she shot back.

"You can't be too careful, Moira. There's a lot of creeps out there."

Denny knew he was losing this one, but he had to make his point.

"Okay, Denny, I'll give her a quick refresher talk before she leaves, if it'll make you feel better. But I think she's perfectly safe walking over to her friend's house, or I wouldn't let her do it," reasoned Moira.

Denny accepted that he'd lost, glad for the small concession Moira offered him. He knew she was concerned for Ellie's safety, too. That wasn't the issue.

"I worry about her. Maybe I'm overreacting, but I worry about her," said Denny, his voice low.

"I know you do. I do, too," she replied, sympathy in her voice. "Between the two of us, we'll get her safely raised."

"I hope so, Moira."

"Take care of yourself, Denny."

"Yeah," he said. "Give Ellie a hug and a kiss for me."

"I will."

Denny disconnected the phone, set it on the coffee table. He fought to block images of Ellie being molested by one of the creeps out there. One of the creeps like Ray Barribee. Times like this, he hated his job.

Chapter Twenty-one

The dump master of a profitable, if loosely run enterprise, was Michael Hastings. The sanitary landfill operation outside of Norridgewock was one of the largest in Maine. Trucks from out of state were some of his biggest customers. They often arrived in the dead of night and deposited their cargoes of waste without leaving so much as a hint of what they contained. To say that it was a sanitary landfill was an oxymoron. The sealed barrels and other containers deposited within its boundaries were the leavings of a host of industries, some clean, most dirty.

There was serious speculation amongst the local citizenry that nuclear waste was indiscriminately buried along with the rest of the debris. To date, no untoward side effects had been noted amongst them, so they turned a blind eye toward Mike's operation. The tax advantage each gained by having such a profitable enterprise in their town was reason enough to look the other way.

Some thought Mike closely resembled a beached pirate than the man in charge of a sanitary landfill. He'd lost his right eye when he was a teenager during an explosives experimentation phase when he lingered a hair's breadth too long after lighting the fuse on his crowning achievement. He'd placed it in a neighbor's mailbox, and when the charge went off, the mailbox door blew off and flew in Mike's direction. It impacted the right side of his face with such force that three of the letters in US MAIL were permanently imprinted on his right cheek, and the door's handle had scrambled his right eye. Anyone who looked sharply at Mike's right cheek could see IAM there, just below the black eye patch that covered his empty right eye socket.

Curious people asked him what IAM meant, not recognizing it as MAI reversed. Some checked his left cheek for more information, but found none. It was an ongoing source of mystery few ventured to solve. His good left eye bore such a withering stare that any curiosity was promptly stifled.

Mike ran the landfill by what he liked to call a flexible attitude. Mostly, it involved looking the other way when trucks came in, but if someone rubbed him the wrong way, regardless of what they were dumping, he could be an almighty nasty prick. He once stopped one of the town selectmen and made him go through all the garbage he'd brought because he'd spoken at a meeting about how Mike turned a blind eye on the dumping that was going on there. The selectman had thought he was simply making a joke, what with Mike's missing right eye, but Mike hadn't taken it that way. Word of Mike's revenge spread quickly through the small town, and he was henceforth named Mad Mike. When he heard the new name, he approved. Nobody dared call him that to his face, but he knew folks remembered it when they brought their garbage to the dump.

On this cold February morning, Mike had arrived at the landfill an hour before what he called visiting hours, his usual starting time. It gave him time to fire up the temperamental bulldozer and lay a skim coat of fill over the new deposits. The bulldozer had a front end bucket that he'd load up with fill. Then he'd drive out onto the fresh waste and pack it down with the tracks. When he was satisfied with the compaction, he'd drizzle the fill onto it as he backed away.

Most of the time his thoughts were off somewhere else as he went about his nearly mindless task, and this morning was no exception. He was daydreaming about Mary Lou, his current girlfriend, who'd already taught him things he'd never even dreamed of doing.

He was backing up, looking over his left shoulder with his one good eye to maintain his pattern, when the trash shifted and he saw something. There was no mistaking what it was.

A human hand, fingers curled, reaching for the gray morning sky. He hit the brakes and shifted the bulldozer into PARK, then sat there a moment, studying the exposed hand.

"Shit," he growled, knowing what a stink this was going to make of his day. He pictured the swarm of cops and the coroner who'd descend on the scene. He imagined the dumbass questions they'd ask him, repeating them over and over until his mind was numb. He thought about the shutdown it would cause, and the mess when the dump was reopened and the backlog came rolling in.

What the hell! How many bodies get dumped here I never see? With that thought, he seriously considered looking the other way, getting on with his work.

In the end, though, curiosity got the better of him, and he climbed down from the cab and walked over to the hand.

"Probably some derelict that crawled in here and died from the cold," he speculated.

He reached down with his gloved hand and pulled a couple plastic bags away. His jaw dropped. He stared.

It was a man, all right. He wasn't dressed for the cold, Mike could see that. All he had on was a long-sleeved shirt and a pair of pants. No, that was wrong. He didn't have the pants on. They were crowded down around his ankles. They blocked Mike's view of his feet.

What really caught Mike's attention was the blood. The man's crotch and legs were covered with it, and then he saw why. His penis and scrotum were missing. In their place was a large, irregular, open wound. For a second, Mike considered that he must be wrong, that it was a woman he was staring at. But a glance at the man's beard erased that possibility.

Mike stared, fascinated for a moment longer at the mutilated body. Then he drew in a short breath and swore.

"Aw, fuck," he lamented, his breath making steam in the cold air. "There goes my day!"

He carefully lobbed the plastic garbage bags back over the body. Each made a soft *whump* as it landed, then settled. He left the pale claw hand exposed as before. Satisfied, he headed for the trailer that served as his office.

Time to make a phone call.

"Guess this is a job for the state cops," he said aloud. "Aw, hell. Time to call 9-1-1 and let them sort it out."

Chapter Twenty-two

Detective Denny Coe bent over the stiff male corpse. He scanned the bloody mutilation, knew he had another sex crime on his hands. It was his distasteful task to identify the body and search the surrounding area for clues.

He stood on the refuse heap, his feet snug in a pair of felt-lined boots he kept in his car for times like this, and pulled on plastic exam gloves. They would provide no warmth against the bitter cold, but they would protect his hands from contamination and keep his fingerprints off anything he touched.

He drew a deep breath, exhaled a steamy cloud into the air, then started his work. He lifted each plastic bag away from the corpse with care, then handed them off to another gloved officer who would label it and place it into the crime lab truck. It would be driven to Augusta where a thorough search of the bag and its contents would be made, in the hope that some clue to the killer's identity might be found.

When Denny had freed the corpse of any adjoining debris, save for what lay beneath it, more photographs were taken. They would show the body's position and capture any clues missed by the naked eye.

Satisfied that he'd missed nothing, he ordered a team of officers to pick up the body and move it to a clean canvas tarp set out for that purpose behind the crime lab truck. It was set down, as close to its original position as possible, not difficult in its frozen state.

Denny examined the area under the corpse for clues. He noted a minimal amount of blood pooled there, which confirmed his guess that the man had been killed elsewhere and then dumped here. After another series of photographs were taken, Denny carefully lifted out the rest of the bags and debris that had been in contact with the body, handing them off to the awaiting officers for labeling and loading.

Following this, Denny made his way to the canvas and searched the body. He probed the man's shirt pocket and found it empty. Then he tugged carefully at the man's trousers until he could access the pockets. He felt something bulky in the left rear pocket and carefully extracted a cheap, well-worn leather wallet. He turned it over in his gloved hands but noted nothing of interest on the outside. Then he flipped it open. There were slots on both sides where cards could be stored, and there was the usual compartment for paper money.

Denny pulled open the money compartment and counted two twenties, a ten, two fives, and three ones. Money didn't appear to be the motive, he guessed.

Then he reached into a right-hand slot and extracted a Maine driver's license.

"Bingo," he said under his breath, holding it up to read it.

The license belonged to William Prosson, age thirty-three, of Bangor, Maine. *Late of Bangor, Maine.*

Then it hit him. Billy Prosson. He'd dealt with this creep before, had seen him get off scot-free when charged with sexual abuse of several children. *Well, he won't be getting off again.* He smiled at the double meaning.

What's going on? First, Ray Barribee gets his balls cut off by a person or persons unknown. Now Billy Prosson gets his entire repertoire removed and gives up his life in the bargain.

Denny guessed that the two cases were related, and he didn't like the implications. Somebody out there was on a crusade to get rid of perps and was going about it with deadly efficiency. He wondered if this would be the end of it. Unless he did something, he guessed there'd be more deceased.

With the body temporarily identified, Denny put the license back in the wallet, same slot, and dropped it into a plastic evidence bag held out for him by one of the assisting officers. He'd leave the search of the rest of the pockets and a thorough exam of the body to the guys in Augusta. They'd go over everything with their fine-toothed combs, and Denny would get a complete report when they were done.

Meanwhile, he had a name to check out. First on the agenda was to find out if Billy Prosson was missed by anyone. *Who knows? Maybe this isn't Billy, just someone who looks like him, and someone planted his license on this body. Stranger things have happened.*

"I'll leave you guys to get this shit to Augusta," he said to the circle of officers. He didn't clarify what he was calling shit. Not surprisingly, nobody asked him. They all knew.

He stripped off the plastic gloves and tossed them at the uncovered garbage, then walked over to Mike Hastings, the dump master, who was leaning against an idling bulldozer.

"We're about done here, Mr. Hastings," Denny said in a polite voice.

"While you were waiting, did you think of anything you haven't already told me?"

"Nope. Like I said earlier, if the trash hadn't shifted and the hand hadn't stuck up, I probably would've missed seeing it."

"And the body would've been buried, and you wouldn't be so far behind in your work," said Denny, sympathy in his voice.

Mike nodded. "Guess I'm surprised you realize what this whole clusterfuck is to me."

"Yeah, I know. We appreciate you calling us. Could've been easier to bury it instead. Any guess as to when the body was dropped here?"

Mike shrugged. "Sometime during the night, is my guess."

"How do people get in during the night?"

"Where there's a will, there's a way," said Mike, leaving Denny to consider that.

"Okay. Here's my card in case you think of anything else, or come across anything you think might be connected," said Denny, handing him his business card.

Mike took the card, unzipped his coveralls and stuck it in his shirt pocket without a glance at it. "Can I get on with my work now?"

"Soon's the crime lab truck pulls out, the dump's yours again," Denny said. "Sorry for all the inconvenience this has caused you."

Mike looked into Denny's eyes, and smiled. "It's nice to meet a cop who knows what a pain in the ass he is to the people who have to stand around while he does his work."

"Yeah, yeah. Sorry about what it's done to your day."

"Glad to cooperate with law enforcement," Mike replied, a hint of sarcasm coming through.

As Denny strode purposely to his cruiser, he wondered how many bodies were buried under all that garbage. Then his thoughts shifted to the late Billy Prosson and what had happened to him. He guessed he'd pay another visit to the Serenity staff. This death smelled a lot like the Barribee cutting, and he'd gotten his biggest reaction from those people.

In particular, he wanted to observe two people real carefully when he broke the news. There was that angry young woman and another employee. What was his name? No matter. Denny had it all down in his notebook. He'd dig it out and refresh his memory before he got there. He'd be ready. Question was, would they?

Chapter Twenty-three

"As you can see, people, we have Detective Coe with us today," said Doctor Brent Caldwell to the gathering. The room had gone quiet when Denny entered the room, so the doc didn't have to raise his voice to get attention this morning.

"You undoubtedly remember Detective Coe from his previous visit," he said to the silent group. "He's requested a moment of our time."

While Caldwell made his introduction, Denny glanced from face to face. It was an ideal time to eyeball everyone without interruption, a chance to catch someone showing surprise, fear.

With his intro finished, Denny stood. He wanted to be as intimidating as possible. It also gave his six-foot height an unobstructed view of the room and its occupants, and allowed him to pick out the two people he wanted to question. He was pleased to see that only two seats separated them. That made it easier to observe how each reacted to what he was about to say.

He got right to the point.

"Have any of you heard the name Billy Prosson?" He watched the group carefully.

He noted a reaction in the woman, but nothing in the man. He scanned the room to see if anyone else had reacted, saw several other lights come on. *This isn't going to be easy.*

"His name's come up more than a few times," confirmed Caldwell. "Another one of Maine's better-known sex offenders."

"What's he done now?" asked one of the female counselors. "Or should I ask, *who's* he done?" Her voice was loaded with sarcasm.

"The fact is, somebody *did* him," said Denny, watching for any reaction. Of the two people he suspected the most, he thought he spotted a shadow pass over the woman's face and saw puzzlement on the man's.

"Did him how?" asked the man Denny remembered as the psychologist. Andy something.

"Did him in. Killed him," Denny said, his eyes busy.

"You won't find much sympathy from us," Caldwell said to Denny, acting as spokesperson. "What brought you here to tell us this wonderful news?"

"There are major similarities between what happened to Billy Prosson and what happened to Ray Barribee. They both had their genitals cut off, only Prosson died and Barribee lived. And since a majority of you were real interested in what happened to Ol' Ray, I guessed you'd want to know about Billy, too," he concluded, his eyes sharp.

"You think somebody here is responsible?" asked the psychologist.

"Until we catch the person or persons responsible, everyone's a suspect," Denny confirmed. "You're a suspect," he said, pointing a finger at the man. "You're all suspects," he concluded, his arm sweeping the room.

Denny thought he caught a reaction when he pointed at the woman, maybe a slight flinch when he pointed at the other man he suspected. It wasn't anything big, but his instincts told him it was worth pursuing.

"Jeez, Detective, are we your only suspects?" asked Andy. "Because if we are, maybe we should be calling our lawyers."

His sarcastic tone wasn't lost on Denny. He felt the atmosphere in the room warm slightly.

"Hey, I'm not accusing anyone of anything right now. I want to question some of you is all," Denny said, ever watchful for that tip of the hand that would steer him in the right direction. He saw none. He wasn't disappointed, though. He had a start.

"Come with me, Detective, and I'll find an office you can use," said Caldwell, ushering him to the door.

Denny, taking his cue, followed. "Thanks for your cooperation, Doc."

Caldwell turned to Denny. "We're always happy to cooperate with the authorities, Detective."

***

With the door closed, Andy spoke first. "Jeez, that's two down. How many more to go?"

"Should we get a list? I can think of three or four more deserving creeps right off," said Betsy, bubbling with enthusiasm.

"Me, too," seconded Martha.

"Hold on now," interjected Dave. "You women don't have a monopoly on perp lists. I can add a handful of names, too."

Jim remained silent, not adding his two cents.

"If you'll give me your lists, I'll see they get turned over to the Equalizer," Andy said. "Sounds like his work has just begun."

"To the Equalizer," toasted Bill Thomas, raising his coffee mug.

"The Equalizer!" Everyone joined in, raising mugs if they had one.

"Of course," said Andy, "if you or any of your IM Force are caught, I will deny your existence," he added, taking license with the *Mission Impossible* disclaimer.

Brent opened the door, silencing any further comment.

"Andy, he wants to see you first," said Brent, all business. "He's using my office."

"This should be fun," quipped Andy, standing. "How should I play it?"

"Play it straight, Andy. The last thing you need is this cop pissed at you for not taking him seriously. He could make life miserable for you, and for the rest of us, too," Brent added, his eyes sweeping the room.

"Okay. I'll let him run the show," Andy said, a serious expression settling over his face.

Jim wondered if he'd be next.

***

Brie's mind was racing. Jim had assured her that he hadn't laid a hand on Ray, and now Prosson was dead, mutilated like Ray had been. She wanted to believe Jim, but she thought it was a huge coincidence that these hits on perps began only a short time after he had arrived here.

What did she really know about him anyway? He'd told her about his family, and where he went to school, and what he'd done as a PA before moving to Maine. He'd let her know how he felt about men who abused women, too. So how far was he willing to go to stop them? How far would *she* go?

In a few minutes, she'd have to face Detective Coe. Not only would she have to acquit herself, but she'd have to divert attention from Jim, too. In her heart, she didn't think Jim could have done those things, but still, could she be absolutely certain?

***

Jim's head was filling with different thoughts. When Detective Coe had announced the death of Billy Prosson, a man who's name he'd never even heard, he wondered first at the coincidence and similarity to Ray Barribee's fate. Then Jim wondered who could have done it, wondered if his Mafia friends were ad libbing, giving him a freebie, no charge, no obligation.

He reviewed what he knew about the New Jersey Mafia, considered the distance between New Jersey and Maine. How could they find out about some low-life predator in the back country of Maine, get a location on him, and then "hit" him—wasn't that the term?—all with no help from the outside. Jim considered the power and the communications network of the Mafia, and accepted that they could do it if they chose to. So the question was, *did* they do it? Was it done on his behalf? He decided that he'd have to call New Jersey and get an answer.

Andy came back into the room, grinning, and interrupted Jim's thoughts.

"That was fun," Andy said. "Detective Coe asked some pointed questions and got the old mental juices flowing. I don't think he has a clue about who did those two perps. He's doing some fishing, hoping to get a bite somewhere. Oh, Brie. You're next. Give him hell."

***

Brie had been expecting it, but it still jarred her when Andy told her that she was next. She drew a deep breath, forced a casual smile, stood up. Jim watched her, a smile on his face. She wondered what Jim's smile meant. Encouragement? More deception?

Detective Coe was standing when she entered Brent's office. She'd been there many times before, but not under such unnerving circumstances. She struggled to appear calm, unconcerned, in control. The whole time wondering if she was pulling it off.

"Thanks for coming in," the detective said. "Have a seat. Let's see. Your name is Breanna Fowler, right?" He consulted his notebook.

"That's right," she replied, trying to swallow the lump in her throat.

"Is it Misses or Miss, or maybe Miz?" asked Detective Coe, a touch of sarcasm in his voice when he said Miz.

"Miss is fine," Brie said evenly, not taking the bait.

"Okay, then, Miss Fowler. What I'm doing is finding out who did all those things to Old Ray and Billy. It seems like you knew as much about those two as I do. Care to explain?" Detective Coe's dark brown eyes bored into hers.

"That's easy," Brie began, and hoped her explanation flowed out as easy as her first two words. She settled in her chair. "I'm a substance abuse counselor, and I work with women who abuse substances. Most of them have been sexually abused. We've documented that it's over ninety percent, and many of them were abused as girls or young women. Names come out when we break through to these women, and sometimes the names are repeated by many women over time. Ray Barribee's and Billy Prosson's names fall into that category, so I've heard them mentioned plenty."

"How do you feel about men like Ray Barribee and Billy Prosson?" asked Detective Coe, his face a neutral mask.

"Frankly, they're the scum of the earth. I don't condone what was done to them and would certainly never condone the murder of another human being, but I have to say that I'm not going to lose any sleep over what happened to them." She noticed her voice rising, her face flushing, and she took a breath to calm herself.

"Sounds like you've got a lot of reasons for wanting them out of the picture."

"Every time I hear another woman tell me she was abused by one of them, yeah, I have another good reason," Brie said, leveling her gaze on his.

"Is that enough to push you to take action?"

"Me?" Brie asked. "Even if I wanted to, I know I'm no match for any man, even creeps like them." She worked to keep her voice calm, matter of fact.

"So who helped you?" prodded Detective Coe, his eyebrows raising in question.

Brie sat forward, upright in her chair, her eyes locked on Detective Coe's. "You've got to be kidding! You think I had something to do with this?" she challenged.

"You told me yourself you've got a lot of good reasons."

"Oh, come on, Detective. Having a lot of good reasons and actually doing something is a huge difference. I told you, I'd never condone the murder of another person, even ones as low-life as those two," Brie shot back, fighting to bring reason, sanity back to the tone of her voice.

"Did that new PA, Jim Booker, have something to do with it?" he asked, a cockeyed smile playing at the corner of his mouth.

Brie wasn't ready for that, hoped her mouth hadn't fallen open with the question. She struggled for composure, forced a small smile to work the corner of her mouth, mirroring Detective Coe's.

"I have no idea, Detective, but from what I know of him, I'd doubt it very seriously," she managed to offer up.

"What do you know of him?"

"Not a whole lot, I guess," Brie said honestly, dodging his innuendo. "He seems nice. I can't imagine he's the kind of person to do anything like that."

Abruptly, he stood up. "You've been most helpful, Miss Fowler. Thanks for coming in and speaking with me. When you return to the conference room, would you mind asking Mr. Booker to come see me?" he asked, holding Brie's gaze.

"Gold Room," said Brie, in a knee-jerk reply.

"Gold Room?" asked Detective Coe, looking confused.

"That's what the conference room is called. The Gold Room," she clarified.

"Oh. Okay. Tell Mr. Booker to come see me," he repeated.

"Sure," Brie said, getting to her feet. Surprised by the abrupt way he had ended the questioning, she tried not to show it.

Detective Coe held out his meaty hand to her.

Brie reached out, shook it.

He held hers captive a moment. "I may have to ask you more questions down the line. Hope you don't mind," he said, looking into her eyes, probing.

For what? "Okay, Detective. I'm not going anywhere."

He released her hand.

She gave him a parting glance, then turned and left Brent's office.

On her way to the Gold Room, her mind whirled with thoughts stirred by Detective Coe's questions. Was Jim involved? Did Detective Coe think so? It seemed like he had strong suspicions, based on his questions. She acknowledged that Detective Coe acted very suspicious of her, too, which made her nervous, though she didn't know why. She hadn't done anything. As she opened the Gold Room door, she knew she wouldn't have the chance to speak directly to Jim, prepare him for what Detective Coe planned to ask him.

"Hey, welcome back, Brie. Did you have as much fun as I did?" Andy asked. "If not as much, close, I bet."

Brie forced a smile, tried for a casual appearance. "No problem," she said. "Jim's up next, and he'd better be careful. Third man's unlucky." She hoped Jim caught the warning in her words.

"That's for third man on a match, not third man on a detective," corrected Andy. "I'm sure Jim'll acquit himself well. Go get him, Jim!"

Brie watched Jim stand and head for the door. Then he turned back to the room. "I have nothing to fear but fear itself," he said in a poor imitation of Winston Churchill. He timed it so the door closed on his last word.

Brie hoped so.

***

Jim wished he felt the bravado he put in his voice as he went to the door and told the team it'd be a piece of cake. Brie's comment worried him. He guessed it was her way of trying to warn him that he needed to be prepared, on his guard.

Brent's office door was ajar when he got there. Jim could see Detective Coe waiting for him, slouched casually in Brent's chair. When he walked in, Detective Coe stood up.

"Thanks for coming. It's Mr. Booker, right?" Detective Coe asked, extending his hand.

"That's right," said Jim, reaching to shake the detective's hand.

"I won't keep you long. A couple quick questions. Have a seat." Detective Coe swept an arm at the chair across the desk from him.

"Thanks," said Jim, for both the offer of a seat and the promise not to keep him long. He sat down and leaned back, putting on the appearance of relaxed self-confidence. He wished he felt it.

"You've been here, what? About two months now?" Detective Coe began.

Jim nodded. "That's about right, yes."

"What brought you here?"

"Change of scenery, change of pace," said Jim easily.

"Enlighten me," Detective Coe prompted.

"I was working in an ER—an emergency room—in New Jersey, and I decided it was time to go somewhere peaceful and quiet." Jim shrugged. "This job meets all those requirements."

"I know what an ER is, wise guy. You don't need to lecture me," Detective Coe shot back.

His sudden abruptness caught Jim by surprise.

"I didn't mean to lecture," Jim said, chastened. "Believe it or not, there are still a lot of people who don't know what ER means."

"You call this place peaceful?" He'd ignored Jim's apology. "With one person maimed and another one dead in a little over two weeks?" The detective glared at Jim, waiting impatiently for his answer.

"None of that has anything to do with this place," Jim said, struggling to put confidence back in his voice. "All that violence happened miles from here."

Detective Coe leaned forward in Brent's chair. He held eye contact with Jim, a crafty smile creasing his face. "How do you know where the crimes happened?"

"I don't. I assumed they happened a long way from here. Those guys weren't from around here, I didn't think." Jim stopped, realizing that the more he talked, the worse he sounded.

"So, you know those things happened a long way from here, and you know those guys aren't from around here, but you don't know anything about any of it, am I right? Is that what I'm hearing?" pressed Detective Coe.

"No. Let me start over again. I have no idea where—"

"You don't have to start over again," interrupted Detective Coe. "You've told me a whole lot already. Now tell me what you had to do with the crimes that were done to Ol' Ray and Billy, okay?"

"I had nothing to do with any of it," Jim said, but struggled to sound indignant.

Detective Coe pushed on. "Did you do it all yourself, or did you have help from someone else? By the looks of you, you probably didn't need any help." His eyes bored into Jim's.

"You've got to be kidding! I had nothing to do with any of it," Jim protested.

"There you go, insulting my intelligence again. You're starting to sound like a broken record. Why don't you level with me and get it over with?"

"I have nothing to *level* with you," Jim fired back, his voice rising despite his efforts to remain calm.

Detective Coe leaned further across the desk, his bulky arms resting in front of him, invading Jim's space. "Let me tell you what happens to you if I find out you're lying, learn you're involved. You get the book thrown at you, you get the maximum sentence, you get no mercy. You'll end up behind bars for a long time, and you'll be there with a whole army of tough guys who don't take kindly to creeps who cut the balls off their friends. Do you catch my meaning?"

Jim stared straight at him, trying not to show any emotion.

"But if you tell me your involvement now, open up to me on your own, I'll do my best to see you get off as easy as possible," Detective Coe explained, a friendly tone returning to his voice.

"Jesus, Detective. Look at me! I could never kill anybody. I work under the same Hippocratic oath that doctors do. I work to *save* lives, not *take* them," Jim said, his voice rising close to a shout.

"Don't tell me about your hypocritical oath," Detective Coe fired back. "So what happened? You only *meant* to cut Billy Prosson's balls off, and he up and bled to death on you, is that what happened?" His eyes bored into Jim's soul.

"You've got it all wrong. I've never even laid eyes on those men, let alone laid a *hand* on them."

"So that's your story, is that right?"

"Yes, that's my story," confirmed Jim, nodding his head in agreement.

"For your sake, I hope I don't learn something that blows your story to hell," said Detective Coe, with an edge to his voice. "Because if I do," he sighted down his extended index finger at Jim like he was leveling a gun at him, "it's you who'll go to hell, and that's a promise."

"Is that all then?" Jim asked.

"That's all for now." Detective Coe paused. "But something tells me that we'll be having another little talk sometime soon." His threat was clear.

Jim stood, extended his hand. "Until then."

Detective Coe enveloped Jim's hand in his, held it a moment, his eyes locked on Jim's. "Until then," he echoed. Then he released him.

***

Denny watched the man go, thinking there was more going on inside Jim Booker's head than he'd been willing to let out. Denny made a mental note to run a check on him through the New Jersey State Police database, as well as through NCIC.

Maybe there was nothing there, but he knew it was worth a shot. It wouldn't be the first time a routine database search solved a case for him.

***

Everyone turned toward Jim when he came in. He was expecting it, had put on his best face for their scrutinization.

"Hail to the returning cross-examinee," said Andy. "Did you give him what-for?"

"I hate to tell you this, Andy. I broke under pressure and told him *you* did it," Jim said, trying to appear contrite.

"Aw, jeez. And after all the money I gave you to keep quiet. Who can you trust nowadays," Andy lamented, going along with Jim.

"Sorry. I'll give half of it back, but I spent the rest on sympathy cards for Ray and Billy's next of kin," said Jim, smiling broadly.

After the laughter died down, Brent broke in. "Okay, enough of the comedy routines. We've got team presentations to get done."

Order restored, the staff turned their attention to the usual business at hand. But Jim couldn't help feeling that he was being watched.

Chapter Twenty-four

After the morning meeting ended, Brie approached Jim. "You feel like pizza for dinner?"

"Sounds good. Your pizzeria or mine?" he asked with a wink.

"I thought they were the same," said Brie.

"You mean Pop's?"

"The one and only," she said. "Best pizza in town, remember?"

"Sure. You want to leave from here?"

"Works for me. See you at five?"

"Yup. See you at the checkout counter." Jim referred to the door that led to the parking lot.

"You got it," she confirmed.

Jim was pleased that she'd asked him to meet for dinner. He wanted to know how her interview with Detective Coe had gone. Sharing a pizza would give him the opportunity to find out.

They left the Gold Room, heading in opposite directions—Jim to do the admissions workup on a young male detox patient and Brie to see female clients assigned to her. Jim's thoughts were miles away from the task at hand.

It was nearly ten past five when he finished his last chart note and made his way toward the back door. He cursed himself for not keeping better track of the time. Brie would be pissed, and why shouldn't she be? They'd agreed on five, and it was already ten past.

He searched for an acceptable excuse for his lateness but couldn't come up with a plausible one. Late was late. He had no excuse.

He rounded the corner and found the entryway empty. No Brie waiting by the door. *Dammit. I wasn't there when I said I'd be, so she's taken off without me.*

Jim pushed open the heavy steel door and peered out into the parking lot, trying to spot Brie's car. The winter darkness defeated him.

Letting the door close behind him, he ducked out to search for it. He found it where she always parked. Surprised, he headed back inside. As he swung the door open, he saw Brie standing there just inside the doorway.

"Oh, Jim, I'm sorry," she said. "Have you been waiting long?"

He heard concern in her voice and had to smile. "I'm late, too. I went out to check the parking lot, thinking you'd already gone."

"Oh, thank the Lord. Looks like we're both running late. I got tied up with one of my clients." She linked her arm through his and steered him through the door into the icy night. "Let's get out of here and I'll tell you about it at Pop's."

They drove separately to Pop's. It was busy, the number of cars parked outside proof of it. As they went in, Jim noticed that the booth they'd shared the first time was empty, so he led Brie toward it. After they were settled in, Sue appeared, menus in hand.

"Hi, Brie. Hi, mister," Sue said in her cheerful voice.

"His name's Jim," Brie corrected her. "And he works with me at Serenity." She smiled at Sue.

"Well, hi, Jim. Nice to meet you." Sue was unruffled.

"Nice meeting you, too, Sue." Jim returned her smile.

"You guys want the usual? Beer and cola?"

"The usual? This is our second time here together," Brie said and laughed.

"Hey, I never forget a drink order," Sue said. "A pizza order, maybe."

"Well, I'm going to mess you up. We'll both have a beer," said Brie, ordering for herself and Jim.

"No problem. I'm on it." Sue disappeared toward the back.

"You were going to tell me why you were late. Even though you weren't," Jim said.

"Sure I was. Just so happened, you were late, too," she chided.

"Guilty."

"Anyway, I was late because I had to listen to a sickening story. You remember Nancy B.'s team presentation on Thursday?"

"Sure," Jim said, giving her his full attention. "Young woman, twenties, first time here, denies physical or sexual abuse. Am I thinking of the right person?"

"That's her. Turns out, she picked my last time slot of the day to open up. As I suspected, she'd been abused by several different men and one woman. The worst one was the first one, when she was ten years old. She told me about it like she was recalling her first trip to the zoo. Her casual attitude made it all the more appalling to me.

"A man named Jack Mignon, who was a friend of her father's, tricked her, bribed her with candy and trinkets into doing the most disgusting things you can imagine—to him and with him. She said it went on for over a year. Then he told her that he didn't want any more to do with her because she began growing hair, and it repulsed him. A true pedophile. I can't imagine what that did to her."

Brie paused while Sue set their beers on the table.

"Cheers," Sue said. "I'll be back in a few to get your orders, unless you're ready now."

"A few minutes is fine," Jim said.

"You got it." And she was gone.

Brie raised her glass. "Here's to one of the worst days on record. May it now be officially over."

Jim brought his glass to hers, clinking it gently. "Amen," he seconded.

They each took healthy swallows, contemplating each other over their glass rims.

"Anyway, this creep Jack Mignon has come up several times before, in Women's group and elsewhere. He's equally as bad as ol' Ray or Billy," she said, her voice grim.

"Hold on. Are you telling me all these perps come from the same sleepy town of Cairo, Maine?" Jim interrupted.

"Oh God, no." Brie shook her head. "We get clients in here from a fifty-mile radius of Cairo, and Barribee and Prosson operate that far away, probably farther. Jack Mignon, like all of them, moves around, so who knows where he really calls home."

"Why is it they aren't all in prison by now?"

She shrugged a shoulder. "They're good at what they do. They threaten their victims so well that most never tell of it."

"Maybe the Equalizer will get this Jack Mignon monster, too," Jim replied.

"We should be so lucky. Anyway, by the time Jack 'The Creep' Mignon was done with her, Nancy's self-esteem was so low she needed a stepladder to look in the mirror. She was easy prey for every guy who showed the least attention to her. She'd probably still be out there if she wasn't taken advantage of by a woman. After that happened, she got to thinking about where she was going and what she was doing, and decided her problem was alcohol and drugs. So she came in. After she'd heard a couple other women recount their stories of abuse, Nancy realized her problems went back to that, too. She picked this afternoon to tell me all the gory details."

"Of all days," he said.

"No kidding. I mean, I'm glad she did, but with Detective Coe coming in today as well. Did he run you through the wringer, too?"

"You mean it doesn't show? I thought the impact marks were still visible. I can still feel them. What did he ask you?"

"Ask? Not a thing. He as much as told me I was his prime suspect," Brie said.

"Are you serious? That's what he told me, too. So, we're both prime suspects," Jim concluded as he glanced around the restaurant. "We probably shouldn't be seen together. Detective Coe will figure we're planning our next victim. You don't see him lurking anywhere, do you?"

"That's not funny, Jim." But Brie couldn't resist scanning the restaurant for Detective Coe. She smiled at him when her search was complete.

"Guess he doesn't like pizza," she quipped. "We're in luck. For now, anyway."

A silence grew between them, each immersed in their own thoughts. They covered the silence by staring at the menus.

"Ready to order?" Sue was back, efficient as ever, jarring them from their thoughts.

"Want to do the same as last time?" Brie asked Jim.

"Sounds like a home run."

Brie turned to Sue. "We'll have a large pizza with onions, mushrooms, green peppers, and black olives heaped on it."

"Sweet choice. I'll get your order in right away." She turned on her heel and vanished.

While they waited for the pizza, Jim and Brie made small talk. They chatted about skiing, and Brie filled Jim in on the season's length. It was mid-March, and the sun was gaining strength, nipping away at the snow. Despite that, there was still plenty of cover on the slopes, and cross-country skiing would hold up in the higher elevations for at least another month. They made plans to go cross-country skiing that weekend.

Jim agreed it was a wonderful idea. He doubted that Detective Coe was a skier.

Brie laughed at that.

The pizza arrived, hot and steamy.

They dove in, being cautious with the first couple of bites to avoid burning the roofs of their mouths. Then they settled in, taking turns at making sounds of enjoyment as they worked their way into it. Appetites sated, conversation returned.

"How's Fred?" asked Brie, dabbing her lips with a paper napkin.

"He's good. He asks about you," Jim said, wiping his hands with his napkin.

"Oh, I like Fred. He's one of the sweetest bears I know. Do you mind if I stop by and say hi to him? It's been a while since we talked."

"Not at all," he said. "He'll be tickled pink to see you again."

They finished the pizza, washed it down with the last of the beer, and Jim got the check after a short protest from Brie. He paid the tab, leaving Sue a tip she'd remember, and they left, getting into their separate cars for the short drive to Jim's.

***

Detective Denny Coe watched the couple come out of the pizza place together from the relative warmth of his unmarked cruiser parked across the street. He noted with satisfaction that Brie followed Jim's truck. After allowing them a good head start, he followed, mindful of the attention he might attract on a road with so little traffic.

He smiled to himself when they both pulled into the Fairview Apartment parking lot.

As Denny drove by, he could see them going in together, into Booker's apartment, he noted smugly.

So they don't know each other very well, eh? We'll see about that. Looks like those two birds need to be watched carefully.

He parked his cruiser across the road and down a bit to avoid being seen. And waited.

***

Jim held the door open for Brie. She walked in and flipped on the lights. On his familiar perch atop the kitchen stool, Fred's eyes sparkled in the sudden brightness.

"Hi, Fred. Did you miss me as much as I missed you?" asked Brie as she walked toward him, shedding her coat.

Fred's eyes glittered. His bear smile held.

Brie turned to hand off her coat to Jim, then swept Fred up in her arms, hugging him to her. She held him as she walked toward the sofa. "So much has happened since we last talked. So much craziness, so much violence. I don't know where to begin to tell you."

Jim hung their coats in the hall closet and went to the refrigerator to get two beers. Brie was on the sofa with Fred when he came back. He set the beers on the coffee table, then sat next to her.

"Two of the nastiest men in the world had bad things happen to them in the last two weeks," Brie continued. "And one of them is dead, Fred. Can you believe it?"

Fred listened intently, his eyes riveted on Brie, not missing a word.

"They did terrible things to other people for a long time, and someone decided they'd done enough. They cut them up real bad. Once of them lived, one of them died."

Fred took it all in, his head cocked slightly to the right.

"And today," she said, "a policeman came to Serenity to ask us questions, to find out if we knew anything about it. He talked to me for a long time, and then he told me that he thought I had something to do with it. Can you believe it?" Brie's voice wavered. "But I told him I could never do anything like that, even if I wanted to and had the strength to do it. He smiled at me and asked me who helped me do it."

Listening, Jim realized she was speaking to him while directing her words at Fred.

"I told him he was crazy if he thought I had anything to do with those things, and you know what he asked? He asked, did Jim help me?" Brie's voice cracked.

"'No,' I told him. He asked me what I knew about Jim, and I said I didn't know much, but I doubted he'd do anything like that. Then the detective told me he'd want to see me again and told me to send Jim down to see him." Brie's face contorted as she finished her story, tears running down her cheeks. She hugged Fred to her, smothering him in her arms.

"I'm scared, Fred. Really scared," she sobbed. "I don't know what's going on. I don't know what to do." She rocked back and forth, clutching the bear.

Jim, just as shaken, put a hand on her shoulder to comfort her.

Feeling his touch, she turned into him. Tears flowed freely now.

Jim gently brushed them away with his fingers. "Don't worry, Brie. You haven't done anything wrong. Detective Coe can't do anything to you," he said, his voice soothing.

"But I'm afraid of what he *might* do," she cried. She reached out for him, letting Fred slip from her arms.

Fred bounced gently on the edge of the sofa and landed softly on the floor. His black button bear eyes stared up at them, watching Brie hug Jim as if he were life itself.

Jim stroked her hair and face, whispering assurances that all would be well, that no harm would come to her, he would see to it.

Brie eased her hold on him and looked up. For a moment, they held each other's eyes, silent.

"Do you mean that? I have nothing to worry about?" she asked in a whisper, still anxious.

"You have nothing to worry about. Detective Coe has nothing on you. He can't do anything to you," Jim reassured her, gazing into her deep blue eyes, transfixed.

Then they were kissing.

It was a mutual response. A long, deep, tasting, testing kiss. Out of breath, their hands joined in, exploring, caressing, stroking, then massaging and stimulating.

Jim drew back, searching the depths of Brie's eyes.

Reading his thoughts, she whispered, "It's all right."

To Jim, Brie's whispered words came not from her but from Fred, who lay still on the floor, staring silently up at them. Jim looked down at Fred. A blurry, indistinct image of Alicia stared up at him. She was smiling and nodding her approval at him, and then her image faded away to nothing. Jim stared at Fred a moment longer, but no image of Alicia appeared to him. She was gone.

Then he pulled Brie closer, tighter. He was ready to move forward with her.

This time, before their kiss deepened, Jim whispered that his bedroom was more comfortable, his voice thick with emotion.

In answer, Brie stood up and grabbed for Jim's hand.

Fred stared up at them from the floor, his black button eyes reflecting their united forms until they disappeared from his sight.

Chapter Twenty-five

L ying next to Brie, Jim marveled at the depth of emotion he'd experienced with her. Something had reached into a secret place in his soul, a place he was unaware even existed, and stirred an emotion so intense that he was left in awe. As his hands gently stroked and explored Brie's body, he could feel his desire building again.

Brie, as if sensing Jim's growing urgency, said softly, "I want you, too. But before we do, I need to know the truth. Did you have anything to do with Ray and Billy?" Her eyes held his.

Jim hesitated an instant, drew a deep lungful of air, and exhaled. "Yes and no," he said.

Brie waited, hitching herself up on an elbow.

Jim told her the whole story, of saving Nick Bonnano's life, to his phone call to Tony Bonnano, and the subsequent injuries to Ray Barribee.

"He was only supposed to be roughed up. I thought I'd made myself clear about that. I thought Tony understood. I never meant for him to get hurt like that. I only wanted them to scare him, put the fear of God in him. The whole thing went too far, got out of control. And I'm responsible. If I hadn't called Tony Bonnano and asked him for a favor he felt he owed me, none of this would have happened.

"But," Jim said, "I have no idea what happened to Billy Prosson, I swear. I don't think Tony's men had anything to do with it. I called to find out if he had, and he told me he wasn't in the habit of making hits like that, with no orders, no reason. I don't think he'd lie to me. What reason would he have?"

Brie continued to listen.

"As for how I feel, if I had to choose over again whether or not to make that phone call, I'm not sure what I'd do. I know it was wrong, it goes against all my principles. But my God, Brie! Ray Barribee is an animal, a ruthless predator. He has no more concern for his victims than a lion has for its prey. I take that back. He has *less* concern. At least a lion dispatches its prey quickly, mercifully. When Barribee's done with them, they suffer for years, maybe for the rest of their lives." Jim went silent a moment, considering.

Then, he went on. "To tell you the truth, I have such anger and disgust for Ray Barribee that I'd probably make that call again."

***

Brie listened in silence to Jim's explanation, watching his eyes, his facial expressions as he spoke.

"I understand, Jim," she whispered, reaching to stroke his face with her fingers. "God knows, if I had the chance to see justice done, like you did, I'd probably have made that same phone call. I know I don't have it in me to do something like that myself. But having it done by someone else makes it less personal.

"As for what they did, it was horrible, far beyond what you asked them to do. Their idea of roughing someone up is a lot more extreme than yours, and you had no idea they'd do what they did to him. I know you feel terrible about what they did, but Ray Barribee is truly a monster, and let's face it, he got what was coming to him.

"But what do we do about Detective Coe?" she whispered, her anxiety returning with the mention of his name. "He's suspicious of you. Of both of us," she amended. "And I know he'll be back with more questions, more accusations. What can we do to make him go away?"

***

Jim considered the dilemma of Detective Coe and the threat he posed. If Coe could somehow link him to Ray Barribee's accident, how easy would it be to link him to Billy Prosson's death? Cutting off someone's balls was one thing. Murder was another. Jim had no interest in going to jail for a death he had nothing to do with. None at all. And if Brie was implicated, too? The thought of her locked behind bars was more than he could stand.

"We'll have to be very careful," said Jim. "We'll have to be able to account for all our time. Then, if the man, or men, who killed Billy Prosson kill again, we'll be able to prove that we had nothing to do with it."

"What if we can't?" asked Brie.

"You mean, what if we can't prove we're innocent?"

"Yes. Or better yet, what if Billy Prosson's death was an isolated act, and whoever did it has no plans, no reason to kill again? Then what?"

"Then we'll have to continue to answer him the same way we've done so far. I don't think Detective Coe has anything solid on me, or on you, either, or he'd have made an arrest by now. I think he's got his suspicions, and he's hoping we'll make a mistake. Or, he's hoping we'll break under his questioning and admit our guilt."

"And what happens if one of us lets something slip?" Brie said. "Then, Detective Coe will come down on you, or me, or us, and we'll be facing murder charges. That prospect has no appeal for me."

"It has no appeal for me, either," said Jim.

Brie sat up and pulled her knees in close to her body. "What do you think about this? What if you call your friends in New Jersey and ask them for their services one more time? And what if you and I go somewhere together that's miles away from the next incident, and we can prove beyond a shadow of a doubt that we were miles away from there. Wouldn't that put Detective Coe off our trail?" she reasoned.

Jim considered another call to Tony Bonnano, considered asking for another mutilation that he would be responsible for. The thought turned his stomach. The first time he hadn't known what they'd do to *rough up* Ray Barribee. Now he did. Could he live with himself if he was responsible for another mutilation, knowing full well what he was asking for when he called? He wasn't sure.

But what if he didn't make another call, and Detective Coe gathered enough circumstantial evidence to put him in prison, put Brie in prison, or both of them? Wasn't that prospect far worse? Wasn't the mutilation of another animal a small price to pay for her—their safety? He knew from following the news that there were many people behind bars who were innocent of the charges, but had been railroaded by the system. He didn't want to be one of them. Still unsure of what to do, he quizzed Brie.

"Where could we go where we'd have a solid alibi?" he asked.

"I think we could have our whereabouts vouched for if we were on an island, an island that's only accessible by ferry."

Jim cocked his head in question. "Where's such an island?"

"There are several of them in Penobscot Bay, some closer, some farther away. Vinalhaven's one that's pretty far out, which reduces the likelihood that we could rent or steal a boat to get back to the mainland to do our dirty work and then get back undetected. I've been there in the summer, and there's a motel and some bed-and-breakfasts."

Jim wondered who she'd went with but bit his tongue. "How do we get there?"

"The ferry leaves from Rockland, which is a little over two hours' drive from here. We could go early on a Saturday morning, spend Saturday night, and come back on the ferry Sunday," Brie proposed.

"Motel or bed-and-breakfast?" asked Jim.

"My guess is the owner of a bed-and-breakfast would be more aware of our goings and comings than a motel owner."

"Did you stay at one when you were there last summer?" There. It was out.

Brie appeared to take no notice of Jim's implication. "No, I wasn't there overnight. I went there on a bike trip for the day. You have a bike. We could take them and ride around while we're there, if the weather cooperates," she suggested.

"Great idea," said Jim, relieved that Brie's previous trip to Vinalhaven was only a day trip. He didn't want to face a ghost from Brie's past, not on their first trip together.

"How do we know which one of them is a good bed-and-breakfast?" he asked.

"That's easy. I've got a friend who works at a travel agency in Rumford. I'll give *her* a call and ask her to check them out."

Jim thought Brie gave slightly more emphasis than was needed to the word *her*. He wondered how much of his petty jealousy had come through to her in his voice.

"It looks like you've thought of everything. I guess my main concern is whether there's another perp as deserving as Ray."

Brie rolled her eyes. "I wish I could say there aren't, but that'd be a lie. Fact is, the one I told you about earlier, Jack Mignon, he's about as bad as Ray, maybe even worse, if you can measure such things."

"He doesn't live on Vinalhaven, does he?" asked Jim, trying for an out.

"Nope. Last I heard, he was doing his thing in Portland, which is another good reason to pick him. Portland's more than two hours from Vinalhaven, driving and ferry combined."

"You really believe we need to do this?"

"I've got to admit, being even a little responsible for getting Jack Mignon's manhood removed gives me a vicarious thrill after all the nasty stories I've had to listen to told by the young women who had the misfortune of making his acquaintance," Brie confessed. "But seriously, if we can come up with a simpler, less violent way to get Detective Coe off our butts, I'm all for it. Let's give it a week to see if we can come up with an alternative plan. If we can't..." Brie didn't finish. She didn't need to.

"Okay," said Jim, accepting the idea.

"You're easy," said Brie, moving against him.

She kissed him, lightly on his lips at first, then more intensely as their passion grew.

It didn't take Jim long to remember what he'd been contemplating before Brie began questioning him. Once remembered, he needed no prompting.

Chapter Twenty-six

Jim was closer to losing his lunch than he'd been in a long time. He'd interviewed a young male admission on the detox unit, the history part of the history and physical, and he guessed he was getting pretty adept at asking the questions because he'd sure gotten the answers.

Responding to a gut feeling, he'd modified the question. Instead of asking *were you ever sexually abused*, he said, "*When* were you sexually abused?" It removed the opportunity for easy denial. It also caught the young man flat-footed, making him think he'd said or done something to tip Jim off.

The young man had sat silent a moment, then asked, "How did you know?"

Jim said that it was written all over him. Then he said, "Tell me about it."

What he heard turned his stomach. It was a first-hand account of what a despicable character Jack Mignon was, if such a monster could be called a human being. He had violated the young man when he was nine years old, and had kept at him until he was eleven, doing the most degrading and disgusting acts imaginable, and forcing the young man to perform like acts on him.

If Jim had any doubts about the socially redeeming qualities of Jack Mignon, they were dispelled completely by the sickening story the young man told. As he related his story to Jim, his voice had risen in pitch, had cracked on several occasions. Jim was hearing a nine-year-old's voice, not an adult's. The shame and guilt rang out in every word. Jim watched the bitter tears roll down the young man's face as he recounted the nightmares of pain and misery he'd kept locked inside him all those lost years.

He was aware of the important breakthrough the young man had made. He'd taken the first tentative step toward healing the deep childhood wounds he'd borne in silence all these years. Jim also knew that this young man was only one of Jack Mignon's many victims, that there were several who were unaccounted for, many who would never be accounted for. He also knew that Jack Mignon was out there now, inflicting pain and shame on young, innocent, and trusting children, perhaps laying plans for his next victim.

Jack Mignon had to be stopped, and Jim had the means to stop him. He no longer had any reservations about asking Tony Bonnano for one last favor.

He picked up the phone on the break room table and keyed Brie's extension. She answered on the first ring.

"Brie Fowler," she said, all business.

"Hello, Miss Fowler. This is Mr. Booker," said Jim, imitating her business-like voice.

"Oh, hello, Mr. Booker. I'm with a client right now. What can I do for you?" Her voice was cool, professional, all for her client's benefit.

Jim considered saying something to shock her from her clinical demeanor, then opted not to. Instead he said, "We've got to talk. Dinner at my place, okay?"

"That sounds fine, Mr. Booker. I'll be there."

Jim pictured her struggling to remain cool, intent on convincing her client that the relationship was one of business. It was a fine line she walked, he knew.

"See you after work, then. Come over as soon as you can," said Jim.

"Fine. I'll do that, Mr. Booker. Good-bye," said Brie, maintaining her cool.

"Good-bye, *my beauty*," whispered Jim, then set the phone down. *Had she blushed, giving herself away?* He doubted it.

Thankful that he was alone in the break room, he stood up from the table, still feeling queasy and unsteady. He crossed the room and drank long at the water fountain. The cool water helped to soothe his spasming stomach.

Then he drew a deep breath and headed to the young man's room to finish his work—the easy part, the physical exam. He could do that on autopilot.

***

Jim opened the door to Brie's light knock, and she stepped through and into his outstretched arms. She hugged him tight for a moment, then kissed him warmly. Jim responded in kind. She pulled back and looked into his eyes.

"My beauty, eh?" she smirked.

"You heard that, heh? Yes," he said softly. "You are a beauty."

"If you had a gravelly voice, you could pass for a pirate," teased Brie. "Argh, my beauty!"

"If I were a pirate, I'd carry you off to wondrous, far-off places and heap treasures at your feet." Jim did his best as a pirate-growl.

"Don't get carried away. I might hold you to it," she said.

Fred watched this interplay from his usual perch on the living room stool, his eyes reflecting the scene in miniature. He gave no indication of the joy he was feeling, a result of the attention he garnered from Brie. He kept his emotions carefully concealed, in true stuffed-bear fashion.

"You can hold me to it any time you want," Jim said, grinning.

"Now, don't be naughty," she said in a sultry voice, her eyebrows dancing.

"Let's put that thought in the bank," suggested Jim. "First, though, can I tempt you with some fresh grilled salmon with a nice dill sauce?"

"How'd you know that's the second thing I've been lusting for all day?"

"So now I'm a *thing*?" asked Jim, trying his best to look hurt.

"What makes you think I'm talking about you, smarty?" she replied, giving him a playful push.

"You got me!" He sagged to the floor like he'd been shot.

"I could be more specific about the thing I was referring to, but I think I'll quit while I'm still ahead," said Brie, the coy look was back.

"Now who's being naughty?" He stepped forward and enveloped her in his arms.

"You said grilled salmon with dill sauce, right?"

"I did, and I will," he nodded, getting back on track.

The fish was masterfully cooked, and they agreed that the key to it was the fresh dill. The white wine was cheap, but it fit well with the salmon.

After they'd finished, they sat comfortably together in the living room, the last of the wine in their glasses. Jim told Brie about his young male patient who had mentioned Jack Mignon. She listened in silence as Jim recounted the extent of Mignon's abuse, her expression mirroring her disgust.

"I'm ready to call New Jersey, Brie," Jim said, meeting her eyes.

"Then we need to pick a weekend and make a reservation," said Brie, moving to the next step. "Do you think two weeks from now is enough time?"

"It should be. I'll call, explain the situation, and ask Tony how much time he needs to set things up. Once we know, we can plan our trip together."

He picked up the phone, stared thoughtfully at it for a moment, then replaced it.

"Change your mind?" asked Brie, a quizzical expression on her face.

"What if Detective Coe is monitoring my phone calls?"

"I never thought of that," whispered Brie, clearly afraid she might be overheard.

"Let's go find an old pay phone," Jim suggested, standing. "There must be one or two that still exist."

"There is. I know the place. Follow me," said Brie, leading the way to the door.

She drove with him to a gas station that had closed for the night. Jim spotted a pay phone on the outside wall. They pooled their change together, then Jim dialed the number from memory.

After a brief delay, Tony Bonnano picked up.

"Hey, Jim. How you doin'?" Tony asked. "Nick's doin' fine. Older and wiser, you know what I mean? You comin' back to Jersey?"

"Hi, Tony. I'm glad to hear Nick's doing well. No, I'm staying here. For now, anyway," he added, tempering his words.

"Aw, that's too bad. We can use a good doc like you down here. So what can I do for you?"

Jim explained the problem with Detective Coe, then told him about Jack Mignon, and finished by telling him his plans for an alibi.

"Sounds like you got it figured out good, Jim. I'll have the boys set up their meeting with Jack Mignon two weeks from Saturday. They'll give him the same message the other asshole got, okay?" he said.

"Ah, okay, yes," Jim replied, giving in to the inevitable, but not without a serious internal struggle. "This is the last time I'll trouble you," he added.

"Trouble? You don't know trouble! This is no trouble. This is a pleasure," Tony said. "Trouble woulda been if Nick had died."

"It was no big deal," said Jim, remembering. "Just doing my job."

"I'll be the judge of that," said Tony, a sharp edge to his voice. "Nick bein' alive is a big deal to me."

"Thanks, Mr. Bonnano," said Jim, chastened.

"Will you for Chrissakes call me Tony?" he shot back, the usual ebullience back in his voice.

"Thanks, *Tony*," Jim said with emphasis.

"Don't you worry about a thing, Jim. Two weeks from Saturday. Count on it."

The line went dead.

Jim shivered, only partly from the chilly night air of early April in Maine. He hung up the phone and turned to face Brie, who had stood quietly at his side during the call.

"It's all set up. Two weeks from Saturday," he said in a quiet voice.

"I'll call and make reservations for a Vinalhaven bed-and-breakfast tomorrow," she conspired.

***

Detective Denny Coe, watching from across the road, waited until they were out of sight, then drove across to the station. He climbed out of his unmarked cruiser and read the phone number off the pay phone. After writing it down in his notebook, he returned to his cruiser and called in.

The dispatcher answered.

He gave her the number and told her to call the telephone company, ask what number was called from that pay station number five minutes ago.

"Roger that," she said.

"Guess we'll find out what was so important and so secretive that he had to come out to a pay phone instead of using his own phone," Denny whispered to himself, pleased with the way things were going.

Chapter Twenty-seven

Brie pulled in alongside Jim's pickup, and they climbed out. A small, nondescript sedan sat idling next to Jim's truck. Jim gave it a brief glance, dismissing it as another tenant, coming or going. Then the driver's window powered down and a female voice said, "Got a minute, Jim?"

Startled, he peered at the open window, trying to see in.

"It's Merry, Jim."

"Merry, what brings you here?" He could feel Brie's eyes probing from behind.

"Get in. We need to talk. You, too, Breanna."

Jim got in the passenger seat, Brie in the back.

"What's going on?" Jim asked.

Merry turned in her seat, extended her hand to Brie. "I'm Merry, Brie. I work for the man in New Jersey."

Brie reached, shook her hand, clearly unsure where all of this was going.

"Let me explain," Merry began, addressing them both. "I'm not the only one working for Mr. Bonnano. Our associates here in Maine are watching a Detective Denton Coe. He appears to be taking a strong interest in both of you, maybe more in you, Jim, since you're new on the scene.

"Today, they observed him entering your apartment. When he left, our associates went in and did a sweep. He put a listening device on your phone. He's done the same to your phone, too, Breanna."

"Holy shit," Jim said. "We had suspicions. We're coming back from calling Tony on a pay phone."

"Where's the pay phone?"

Brie told her.

"We need to think that Detective Coe watched you make the call and is using his police connections to find out who you called," Merry said matter-of-factly.

"Dammit! We're screwed," Jim lamented.

"Not so fast," said Merry, her voice calm. Mr. B.'s number is private, and the telephone company won't give it up without a fight. I'm betting that Detective Coe will get tired of waiting, and he'll call the number himself to see who answers."

"And then what?" Jim asked.

"Give me some reasons why you'd call a number in New Jersey."

Jim thought a moment. "Friends, associates, the usual."

"Businesses?" asked Merry.

"I suppose. Maybe medical-related," said Jim.

"That's good. Medical supplies," said Merry. "I like it."

Merry looked up as a car passed on the road. "There goes our Detective Coe now," she announced. "Checking to make sure you're in for the night."

"He scares me," said Brie in a low voice.

"I don't want either one of you worrying about Detective Coe. We have him covered. Do what you do every day, and let us take care of him," Merry reassured them.

"I had no idea all this came with Tony's promise to me," Jim said, clearly impressed.

"You have no idea. You've seen the tip of the iceberg," Merry said, smiling.

The comment reassured Jim. "We'll leave it all in your capable hands."

"Thanks, Jim. Oh, by the way. You asked me what I had Tony do for me? I can tell you that it was remarkably similar to your request," she confided.

A look passed between Jim and Brie with this disclosure.

"Hope to see you again," said Merry. "Both of you," she added, smiling at Brie.

"You take care, Merry," said Jim.

"It's been a pleasure meeting you, Merry," added Brie.

They climbed out of Merry's car, eyes on the road, and walked quickly into Jim's apartment.

Once inside, Brie turned into Jim's arms and snuggled against him. "I'll never again question the power of the Mafia in Maine," she whispered.

"I'm going to overuse my phone, give Detective Coe lots to listen to. Mom, Dad, Todd, and, of course, you." He smiled.

"Me, too," said Brie. "We'll fill his tapes with the most boring stuff he can imagine."

"Full speed ahead. Vinalhaven, here we come!"

Chapter Twenty-eight

They made the Vinalhaven ferry with ten minutes to spare. The line of vehicles ahead of them was fairly short. They had no problem getting on. The summer visitors would change that. The only way to guarantee a space on the ferry in June, July, or August would be by buying a reservation ahead of time. Either that, or show up an hour, maybe two before departure, and sit in line.

Since the number of vehicles boarding was easily managed, the ferry-ticket taker was open, friendly, even chatty. Jim made a point of talking to him, hoping he'd remember him if a policeman showed him a photograph in a couple of days. Brie joined in for the same reason.

Once they'd boarded, they left Jim's truck and climbed the stairs to the observation deck. There was a nip to the mid-April breeze, even with the sun out. The ocean temperature was still in the forties, and the air was cooled by it. Jim zipped his jacket, then helped Brie turn up her collar. They were alone, the only passengers willing to put up with the biting breeze on the open deck.

"Hey, hey! We're on our way," Brie said with enthusiasm.

Jim wrapped a protective arm around her trim waist and drew her to his side. The deck vibrated under their feet as the twin diesels were fed more fuel and the deck lines were released. The vehicle ramp was raised, safety chains were rigged across the open stern, and the engines shifted from reverse to forward. The acrid stench of diesel fumes mixed with the sharp salty air. Slowly at first, and then faster, the ferry plowed into the light chop of Penobscot Bay and set a course for Vinalhaven.

Once the Rockland shoreline was blurred by distance, Jim and Brie turned their attention seaward to search for their destination. They could see a land mass on the eastern horizon, still too far away to discern any landmarks. Jim searched for the buoy route the ferry would follow, but the distance defeated his efforts.

"What a beautiful day," said Brie, breaking the silence. "Last time I made the trip it was so foggy I couldn't see the bow of the ferry. I was scared the whole way. They blew the foghorn about every minute. I kept thinking, if I can't see, how can the pilot see?

"The trip seemed to take forever, and then unbelievably, we arrived," recounted Brie, remembering.

"Truth of the matter is, they don't need to see," Jim said. "With the navigational technology today, they know where they are within a couple of feet. The big problem is avoiding other boats, especially small ones. They can see most of the boats on their radar, but small sailboats, canoes, and kayaks don't show up too well."

"Where'd you learn all that, smarty?" asked Brie, smiling up at him through windblown hair.

"I guess I've always been fascinated by how people get from point A to point B, from the Vikings and Columbus down to the present. Nowadays, the GPS system is so precise that it's nearly impossible to get lost."

"GPS?" asked Brie.

"It's called Global Positioning Satellites, GPS for short. It's a worldwide network of satellites in stationary orbits. Each satellite sends out a constant signal, and receivers on boats, planes, and even hand-held devices pick up the ones within range. The receiver uses the signals to triangulate a position. It's so accurate that you know where you are within a foot or two. With that accuracy, it's easy to pull into a ferry dock, no matter how thick the fog is," Jim said.

"Wow, that takes all the fear out of fog," said Brie. "Wish I'd known that the last time I made the trip. What else can you do with GPS?" she asked, encouraging him to tell her more.

"One of the most fascinating uses is being able to come back to the exact same spot on the ocean without having to rely on a visual marker, like a buoy. Treasure hunters, once they locate a sunken ship, simply have to plug in the coordinates, and then go there. No more telltale surface markers for rival treasure hunters to find. The *Titanic*, once found, can be relocated any time. It also helps search-and-rescue operations, especially if the one needing rescue has a device that sends out a signal."

Jim put his hand on the fiberglass container on the deck next to him. "There's an inflatable life raft in each of these canisters, and each one has a signaling device that allows a rescue ship to pinpoint it within a foot or two, wherever it is," he explained.

"Bring on the fog," chirped Brie with enthusiasm.

Jim drew her close, kissed her lightly on her forehead. The ferry rolled easily on the light seas, adding a sensual motion to their body contact.

They stood together at the rail, bodies touching, for the remainder of the trip. They spotted cormorants, gulls, and a scattering of early sea ducks. At one point Brie thought she saw a porpoise, but they decided it must've been a whitecap because neither saw it again.

Hearing the ferry engines slow, they looked out to see land a short distance ahead. The ferry made a sweeping right turn and followed along the land mass. Soon they reached a channel, then turned into it. The sea was calmer in the sheltered water, the breeze less nippy. Jim and Brie scanned the numerous small islands they passed, noting a few with seasonal cottages perched on them.

At length, they made a sweeping left turn into Vinalhaven harbor. It was a wide, sprawling basin, well-sheltered from the wind and waves. In April, lobster boats made up the majority of the craft in the harbor, though affluent summer visitors would soon change that. For now, the lobster boats reigned supreme.

The ferry approached the landing, slowed, then eased into the wedge-shaped crib. Prior to its making contact, Jim and Brie retraced their steps to his truck, ready to disembark when the ramp was lowered into place and safety chains removed.

One of the ferry attendants casually directed the exodus of vehicles, smiling and waving to the regulars, clearing one lane at a time. Then it was Jim's turn, and after calling out a cheery "See you Sunday!" to the attendant—a final attempt to be remembered, he drove his truck up the ramp. It gave out a dull metallic clunk when it settled under his truck's weight, and then he drove up onto the solidity of the Vinalhaven pier.

It was Jim's first experience driving on an island accessible only by ferry, and he had an eerie feeling of isolation, knowing that all the roads were essentially dead end. The sea limited their range of movement, and the only way back to his familiar world lay behind him now. It wasn't a feeling of claustrophobia. It was more a sense of being in a finite space, of limiting boundaries, limiting options. He was contained within a huge fenced-in area, with the sea serving as the fence. He began humming "Don't Fence Me In."

"What's that about?" asked Brie, snuggled at his side.

He told her.

"I know what you mean," she agreed. "I get the same feeling, too. It passes, though."

They drove slowly down the narrow lane leading from the ferry landing to the island's commercial center. The initial surge of traffic generated by the ferry's arrival had passed, leaving traffic light, giving them the opportunity to check out their surroundings. They eased past numerous buildings on their right, the water side of the road. Some were identified by signs, others not. They passed the seafood co-op building where they could buy fresh fish and lobsters, and Brie suggested stopping on their way home to get a fresh meal for Sunday dinner.

A car passed them on its way to the ferry landing, and Jim was surprised when the driver waved at him.

"Did you see that? I guess he thought I was somebody he knew."

"No, everyone on an island waves to everyone they pass. It's a friendly gesture, a tradition, really. I'd forgotten about that," said Brie.

"I like that. If everyone waved at everybody else in this world, we'd have far fewer problems," Jim commented.

They drove slowly through the cluster of buildings, passing a grouping of condos on a hillside to their left, the town dock on their right. Then they passed a collection of small shops, and a restaurant, on both sides. The road sloped upward from there to a fork in the road, and Brie told Jim to keep left.

A small, unassuming signboard pointed the way to their bed-and-breakfast, and after two short turns, they arrived. Brie went in to register, leaving Jim to take the bikes off the rear rack so he could open the cap hatch and retrieve their bags.

He wheeled the bikes up onto the mid-April matted grass lawn and leaned them against a huge old maple tree, knowing the kickstands would be useless and sink into the soft soil. Then he returned to get the bags and carry them inside.

"This is Jim, my wonderful other half," Brie told the owner by way of introduction.

"It's nice to meet you, wonderful Jim," said a smiling middle-aged woman dressed casually in navy blue slacks and a faded blue blouse. "I'm Mary. You be sure and let me know if there's anything I can get you."

"Thanks, Mary. I can tell already that you have plenty of peace and quiet here, the two things I'm looking forward to most," Jim replied.

"That we have, especially this time of year. Oh, if you want to put your bikes under cover, there's a shed on the side of the house, always unlocked. We don't worry about people taking things here. Being on an island, there's only one way for a thief to escape, and that's on the ferry," she said with a grin.

"That's thoughtful of you. I'll put them in there at the end of the day," said Jim.

Mary led them to their room, a large, high-ceilinged bedroom that easily accommodated a compendious queen-size bed topped with a thick, flower-pattern quilt. The bathroom, in true bed-and-breakfast style, was in the hall. Mary told them they were her only guests for the weekend, so they had the bath to themselves. She left them to get settled.

Jim set the bags down. "Wonderful other half, huh?" he said to Brie.

"I had to think of some way to describe you to our hostess," she replied, a coy expression on her face.

"I like it, my beauty," he whispered, then surrounded her in an embrace and kissed her.

Brie responded, then eased back to break the moment. "What time is it?" she asked, her voice husky.

Jim glanced at his watch. "High noon, my beauty," he said.

"Want to ride our bikes down to that little restaurant in town for a fresh fish sandwich, and then bike around the island while it's sunny and warm?" she suggested, giving his hands a squeeze.

"That sounds perfect." He leaned into her and kissed her lips lightly. "Nothing like fresh air and exercise to sharpen the appetite," he murmured in her ear.

"Sharpen it for what?" she asked, drawing back, her voice low.

"Exactly," he replied, his eyes dancing.

***

They both ordered a haddock sandwich and fries, plus a fruit juice to share, then carried them across the road to the public pier. They staked claim to an unattended bench and sat down to enjoy their lunch. The water was calm in the harbor, and with the sun high overhead, there was no glare off the water to make them squint.

They watched a lobster boat thread its way through the moored boats to reach the floating lobster pound. Once there, the stern man unloaded several crates holding the morning's catch, watched while they were weighed, then got a voucher showing how much was due them. At this time of year, only the hardiest lobstermen were fishing. They had tended their traps through the winter, pulling in a diminished harvest, but the price per pound was generally higher. In a month, the lobster fleet would swell to more than triple the current number as weather and water conditions improved. The increasing volume of lobsters taken would meet the demand of the increasing numbers of tourists who came to Maine seeking the sweet crustaceans during the warmer months.

"That was incredible," said Jim, wiping his fingers with his paper napkin.

"Nothing like a fresh fried haddock sandwich," Brie agreed.

They tossed their trash in a nearby barrel and got on their bikes.

"Which way?" Jim asked.

"Take your pick. Almost every road we take will end up coming back here. Look," she said, holding up a map of the island she'd picked up at the landing.

Jim saw what she meant. There were a few roads that ended on peninsulas, but most joined others and weaved their way around the island's perimeter.

"Let's go back toward the bed-and-breakfast and take the road along the shore," he suggested.

"I'm with you," she said.

The road led them past island homes and cottages. Some showed signs of life, but most would be lifeless until their summer owners arrived to break the winter seals and let the homes breathe again. They passed tiny inlets that sheltered a few lobster boats. Their owners, most of whose families had probably been island residents for generations, preferred quiet isolation to the hubbub of the harbor area of the island.

Jim had his smart phone, and they stopped at scenic spots to take pictures of each other and their surroundings. They found many scenic spots and made as many stops. Brie got creative with her poses, hamming it up for Jim's benefit. He laughed and shot the pictures.

At road junctions Brie checked her map, and they chose the next road they'd take. Since they wanted to see as much of the coastline as possible, they chose the turns accordingly.

It was a clear, crisp April day, a gift for that time of the year. The sun cooperated by staying out, providing diluted warmth for them. That, combined with their biking efforts, kept them comfortable. They cycled along at a leisurely pace, completely absorbed by the beauty of the changing vistas, and with each other. And Jim tried to forget all about the snooping Detective Coe.

Chapter Twenty-nine

Leo Jenkins headed down the road to Rockland, his thumb held out to the passing vehicles. Waiting for a driver to stop for him, he passed the time by daydreaming about Sally. He'd been working on her for a couple of weeks, prepping her slow and easy, and had finally got her to cooperate two days back. She was new at it, but she caught on quickly with good directions from him. He'd gotten off on it as much from the pleasure he got from controlling her as he did from the act itself.

Three months had gone by since he'd gotten sprung from Tommy Town. While there, they'd filled his days with psychologists and group meetings and dull books to read, and he'd walked the walk and talked the talk so well that they showed him the door after three years of a six-year sentence. He'd been pronounced a rehabilitated man.

Now he was on his way back to Rockland and another go-round with Sally, as he liked to call it. A Saturday soiree. This time, he'd tease and tickle and stimulate her, and she'd let him do a little more with her. The present he bought her would help break down her resistance, too. He knew she'd like the little stuffed rabbit. She'd told him how much she liked bunnies, how her mother had told her that she'd get one for her when she was ten. This wasn't a real one, but she'd like it anyway. It was small enough so she could keep it a secret from her mother, in the same way she'd keep their other secret from her mother. If she knew what was good for her...

A car passed, went a fair piece beyond him, then braked to a stop. Leo stared at it. Was he stopping for him or pulling off for some other reason? Maybe it was one of those jerk-offs who stop down the road and then peel out as you run up to them.

The car horn sounded, *beep-beeeep*. The driver stuck his arm out to beckon him, get his ass in gear.

"Fuck it," mumbled Leo. "I ain't runnin'. He wants to give me a lift, he'll be there when I get to him." He continued to walk, slow and easy, down the shoulder to the waiting car.

When Leo reached the passenger side door, he looked in. "Hey, man," he said, surprised to see a familiar face, though he couldn't come up with a name right off.

"Hey yourself, Leo. You need a ride? Get in," the driver told him.

Leo got in and put his duffel bag on the back seat.

"Where you headin'?"

"Rockland, man," Leo said, still trying to come up with a name.

"Me, too."

"Beautiful!" Leo settled back against the stained, weathered passenger seat.

"You got some weed?"

"Nah. Wish I did, man," Leo answered truthfully.

"How much you want?"

"You got some?" asked Leo, his hope rising.

"I'm on my way to score a quarter bale," the man said, his voice even.

"Jesus! A quarter bale? That's a shitload," said Leo, impressed.

"Tell you what. You give me a hand getting it, I'll give you a pound for your trouble."

"No shit. What do I gotta do?" asked Leo, his mouth hanging open.

"I gotta meet a guy in a boat offshore. You and me take a boat out, meet him, get the pot, come back. Simple. You help me with the lines, hold us alongside during the deal. That's it."

"When's this happening?"

"Four-thirty, I meet him. We'll be back by five, five-thirty tops."

Leo consulted his watch. It was almost three. They'd be in Rockland in forty-five minutes. He'd told Sally to meet him at six in the abandoned garage. He considered what fun it'd be to introduce her to pot.

"Can do, man," said Leo with enthusiasm.

"Thanks, Leo. You won't forget this."

Leo thought his friend must've got his words wrong, meant to say, "*I won't forget this.*" *What the hell was his name, anyway? Damn! It'll come.*

The boat was a deep-V hull, nineteen-foot inboard/outboard. Leo was impressed. He helped cast off the lines, and they headed east out of the harbor. There were small rollers once they cleared the breakwater and rounded the head, but it was nothing the boat couldn't handle. It pitched slightly with the swells. When he shoved the throttle forward, the hull came up and planed. The pitching was replaced by a rhythmic slap-slap of the waves against the hull.

Leo stared ahead, trying to guess where they'd meet the other boat, the boat with all the grass. He made out distant land ahead of him, had never been out there in a boat, didn't know he was looking at an island. He gripped the windshield brace to steady himself against the pounding and watched the land get closer and closer.

Not far offshore, the man backed off on the throttle and the boat lost headway, the stern squatting, settling once more into the water and resuming its gentle rolling.

"Where's the other boat?" asked Leo, searching. He noticed that they were in a cluster of lobster trap buoys.

"We're a little early. The boat'll be coming from down there, near Vinalhaven," he said, pointing. "You watch for it. I've got my hands full watching out for the fuckin' lobster buoys."

"Okay, man," said Leo, agreeable as ever. He searched the seas around them, could see no other boats anywhere near. He was impressed with the man and his planning. *What was his name? Damn!* It still wouldn't come to him. He remembered him from Tommy Town, but his name escaped him. It would come, though. He never forgot a name. For long, that is. He went back to searching for the boat.

Then Leo felt something below his left shoulder. He thought the guy had given him a shove. The air went out of him with a whoosh, and Leo felt an uneasy sensation, like something terrible was happening to him. He couldn't put his finger on it, but he felt no pain, even when he realized the man twitched a blade back and forth inside him, shredding his heart.

"What's happenin', man?" asked Leo, his voice sounded faint and far away to him.

"You're dyin, you fucked-up bastard. If I can't do it, then you can't, either!"

Leo felt weak, disoriented, and accepted that the man was killing him, though he still didn't understand how.

His pants were being dragged down, and he felt cool air on his buttocks and groin. Then he was aware of a tugging, sawing sensation, and the man was holding something bloody up to his face. He struggled to bring it into focus and Leo, at last, understood that the man was holding his severed genitals. He opened his mouth to ask why, but he had no more air for words. Then there was no more light. Only darkness. And he still couldn't think of his name.

The man let Leo slide down onto the deck. He stuffed the severed genitals into one of Leo's pockets and tied a rope around his neck. He worked quickly and efficiently, carrying out his disposal plan, all the while keeping an eye out for any other boats coming his way.

After he'd wrestled Leo's body over the side of the boat, he got out a bucket and sponge and swabbed away all traces of the blood Leo had left behind.

His cleaning chores done, he checked everywhere to make sure he hadn't missed anything. Satisfied, he stowed the pail and sponge, then turned his attention to Leo's duffel. A stuffed bunny came out first. He tossed it over the side, then searched further. He found nothing worth keeping. It was the usual shit a guy like Leo would carry. He tossed the open duffel over the side without a second thought.

"Fuck it. Time to get my ass outta here," he muttered to himself. He gripped the wheel, pushed the shift lever forward, and headed the boat back toward Rockland leaving the little stuffed bunny bobbing forlornly on the gently rolling seas not far from Leo's body.

Chapter Thirty

It was four o'clock by the time Jim and Brie pedaled back to the bed-and-breakfast. The sun had lost its warmth for the day, though it still shone brightly, and the air held on to some of its warmth.

Jim checked his watch, turned to Brie who had dismounted. "Hey, my beauty, if you don't mind, I'd like to take a fast bike ride to burn a few more calories, sharpen my appetite for dinner. And stuff," he said.

"By yourself?"

"If you want to join me, great," he replied, his eyes on hers.

"Thanks for the invite, but I've had enough for one day. I'll save my strength for tomorrow. And tonight," she added, responding to his innuendo about "stuff."

"You sure?"

"Sure. See you in a bit. Be careful, *wonderful* other half," she said, tossing him a look, her eyes twinkling suggestively.

"I will. And I'll keep some in reserve, too," he said in a husky voice.

"You better," she said.

Jim enjoyed going fast, enjoyed expending the effort it took to push his bike to the limits. It hadn't been that way when he was a novice biker. He'd hated the exertion, hated the ache in his legs or the pain in his lungs when he climbed hills. He especially hated shifting gears at the wrong time and in the wrong direction, shifting up instead of down, down instead of up. And when the hills were climbed and he faced the downhill, the developing speed often made him wary, uneasy, and he worked the brakes to slow his descent.

He would have given up biking if it wasn't for Pete, his college roommate. Pete had been biking for years, had even raced some in high school, and he knew bikes and biking inside and out. Although Jim had wanted to chuck biking, he stuck with it because Pete got such pleasure from riding that it spilled over onto him and kept him going.

Then one day, Jim surprised himself with the realization that he was enjoying the ride. His legs were conditioned and didn't complain as much, and his wind was better so the pain wasn't there in his lungs. He shifted without thinking, an automatic reaction borne of time, of experience, and the dreaded downhills became a rush as he built confidence in his ability to control the bike at higher speeds.

He felt the rush of the wind on him, cooling his brow and drying the perspiration drawn from him during the uphill climb. He finally discovered the pleasure of biking that Pete had been preaching about for so long. From then on, he was hooked.

He took the same roads Brie and he had followed before, but at a much faster pace, not holding back, not spending time checking out the scenery. At first, his legs and lungs protested after the holiday they'd had during the winter months. Then he settled into a pace he could sustain, and the protestations ceased.

He encountered no long hills to climb. There were short hills that gave way to short, flat stretches. Jim settled into a rhythm, peddling hard along the flats so the uphills were less effort. Once he crested a hill, he'd peddle hard to regain his pace.

With the views of inlets and houses blurred by his fast pace, he found himself thinking of Brie and what she meant to him. He realized that she had become a central focus in his life, an essential piece of his own puzzle, a treasure to be cherished and held close to him. With those thoughts occupying his focus, he blew past a turn they'd taken before. He considered braking, turning around, and taking it, and then he remembered Brie saying that most roads linked back to the starting point. He pedaled on, deciding to take the next right turn. That, he reasoned, would lead him across to the road they'd taken, the one he'd missed.

The new road ran inland in a general northerly direction, he guessed, from his impression of fading sunlight on his left. The road had flattened out, allowing him to set a steady pace.

He'd covered several miles before it hit him that he hadn't come to another right turn. He decided to push on, figuring that he'd come to another right turn sooner than if he turned around and retraced his steps to the missed turn.

It was a mistake.

He continued on in dogged fashion, expecting at any moment to find a right turn that would lead him back where he belonged. The land to his left grew hilly, though the road he traveled remained relatively flat. Undulating, perhaps, described it better.

Then he saw a sign telling him he was approaching a boat landing which would take him, if he had a boat, to North Haven. He remembered from Brie's map that North Haven was another island just north of Vinalhaven. He wished he'd brought the map with him.

What the hell. I've come this far. Might as well see the water. So, he pedaled on until he came to a drop to the shore where a substantial dock had been built. There were no boats in sight. He looked across the passage that separated him from North Haven, saw several large houses which dotted the shoreline. Some were impressively large. He guessed wealthy summer visitors occupied them during the prime summer months, then shuttered and secured them the rest of the year.

He pulled out his cell phone and took a picture. Done, he glanced at the clock. Five o'clock.

"Damn. I've got to move it. Brie'll be getting worried," he said aloud to himself.

He climbed back on his bike and began retracing his route, pushing himself.

It seemed like an eternity before he reached the left turn he'd missed, considered taking it, then decided it would be faster to go straight ahead and back to the bed-and-breakfast the same way he'd come.

By the time he reached the bed-and-breakfast and Brie, it was nearly six. The sun was down, and twilight was near. If he'd been another fifteen minutes slower, he'd have had trouble seeing. He wheeled his bike into the shed, seeing Brie's bike already there, and hurried into the inn.

When he pushed open the front door, Brie jumped out of a chair in the entryway and rushed to meet him.

"What happened to you?" she asked, her voice filled with concern, worry.

Jim held her to him, felt her heart fluttering against his chest.

"I'm so sorry, Brie. I missed one of our turns, ended up all the way up by North Haven," he explained.

She listened, silent in his arms, content to be held by him.

When he'd finished his explanation, she stretched up to kiss him. Then she settled down. "You had me worried, you know. I thought something had happened to you," she scolded.

"I know. It was dumb. I should've turned around when I missed the turn. I kept thinking I'd come to another right and get back on track."

"Okay, well, you're here now. Run and take a shower so we can get some dinner, you sweaty man. Mary gave me directions to a good restaurant. I'm starving. Off with ye," she ordered him, smiling broadly.

"On my way," Jim said, releasing her.

Chapter Thirty-one

The microwave beeped, prompting Denny Coe to take out the reheated pizza slices. He knew he should eat healthier food, at least some of the time, but when he got hungry, he chose the easiest solution. Fast food had become a bad habit with him. He carried his plate to the couch and sank into it, sighing as he did so.

The pizza tasted like the cardboard box it came in, and the pepperoni, curled and desiccated, hadn't stood up well to three days of refrigerator life. He hardly noticed. Food didn't give him any pleasure. It was something he put into his body when hunger screamed. Or when he was bone-weary. Or both.

He pressed the remote, bringing the TV to life. He joined a sitcom already in progress, something about a family in California. Denny munched a slice of pizza. The show held no interest for him, but he made no attempt to change the channel. The TV voices filled his empty apartment, displacing some of the loneliness. That's why he had the TV. That, and for the morning news.

He set his empty plate on top of one left from a breakfast or dinner past and checked his watch. Nearly ten. Too late to call Ellie, and Moira wouldn't be sitting around waiting to hear from him at ten on a Saturday night. Or at any other time of day, truth be known.

His phone rang, jarring him from his Saturday night depression.

"Coe," he answered, automatic, his voice neutral.

"Denny, this is Lenihan."

Lenihan. That son of a bitch detective who beat me to the punch on Barribee and got him sent to Thomaston.

"Yeah, Lenihan. What's up?" he asked, fighting to keep his voice neutral.

"I'm down here at the ER at Maine Med. There's a guy here had his balls cut off. Captain told me to call you, thought this sounded like another case you're working on. What are you, the new castration expert?"

Denny ignored the sarcasm. "What kind of shape is he in?"

"About what you'd expect from someone who had his balls cut off against his will," said Lenihan.

"No other injuries?"

"Not unless you count his manhood separately."

"What'd he say happened?"

"Says he was walking back to his apartment building about five-thirty when two suits stepped out of the shadows, one on each side of him. Says one flashed a badge, asked if he was Jack Mignon. He says 'Yeah. What of it?' and the suit says he needs to ask him a few questions, does he mind sitting in the car a minute so the neighbors don't hear. Mignon says 'Okay', and they walk back to the street and they climb into a big black Lincoln, with Mignon the baloney in the sandwich.

"So he asks what do they want, and the talker, the one with the badge, says they're there to help him out. He says he doesn't need any help, and the talker says that's where he's wrong. He tells Mignon he needs help controlling his sick interest in young kids.

"This gets Mignon's attention real fast, and the light goes on that these two aren't cops. He's getting into telling them to go fuck themselves, let him the fuck out, when he feels a sharp stab in his left arm. He looks over to see the other suit pulling a needle out of his arm. He says the talker held his attention, and he wasn't paying any mind to the driver when he up and stuck him.

"He says he has enough time to ask him what the fuck was that, then everything goes black. Next he knows, he's lying in some bushes a block from his apartment. It's three hours later, and his balls are missing and he's hurting and bleeding like hell. He lays there, hollering and bleeding until somebody walking by asks what's wrong? And calls 9-1-1. So he's here, and that's about it. Oh, yeah. The ambulance guys found a pair of balls in his back pocket. Guess they were his. Don't know who else they'd belong to," Lenihan joked.

Denny knew Jack Mignon. He'd heard plenty about what he'd done to kids before one of his victims agreed to talk in front of a judge. Mignon got a five-year paid vacation to Tommy Town for his part in the story, and then got himself paroled when he announced to the shrinks that he'd seen the light. They pronounced him healed after only three.

Healed, my ass.

Seemed the skinners learned fast to walk the walk and talk the talk, with the psychologists and therapists there to help them see the errors of their ways. Denny guessed their success rate must be right up there close to a hundred percent. No doubt the skinners got motivated by the desire of the other inmates to probe their anal orifices and rearrange their anatomy, too. Skinners were criminal deviants not well tolerated by the likes of thieves and killers. Truth of the matter, they had their own set of principles.

"They admitting him?" he asked Lenihan.

"Yeah. Overnight, anyway, to make sure the bleeding's stopped."

"They sew his balls back on?"

"Nope."

"Good."

"Yeah. Sometimes things work out," said Lenihan.

"Sometimes. Look, tell him to wait for me. I'll be down to get his story first thing in the morning. He can rest, get some sleep."

"I'll tell him, only I don't think he's going to sleep much, knowing his balls're gone," joked Lenihan.

"Hell of a shame."

"Right. Couldn't have happened to a nicer guy."

"You got that right," Denny agreed, his dislike for Lenihan blurring some. "Thanks, Lenihan."

"Forget it," Lenihan replied.

Denny set the phone down, the wheels spinning again.

That makes three now. Who the hell is doing it, and why was one killed and deballed and the other two only deballed? Was Prosson more of a creep than Barribee or Mignon, earning him a knife in the back as well as one to the crotch?

A new thought hit him. *What if there turned out to be two independent operators out there, the one cutting, the other killing and cutting? If so, did they know each other? If they didn't, then it was one hell of a coincidence.*

He let those thoughts bounce around a while, considering the likelihood and the evidence.

It was possible, he had to admit. He had two perps who'd been castrated by two suits driving a big black car, maybe a Lincoln. Then he had a perp found in a dump with a knife wound to his back and his entire repertory slashed off, probably by the same knife, the forensics boys had said.

He guessed the suits could've done all three, but why kill one and only cut up the other two? He couldn't see how there was any difference in the three victims. What the hell, they were all sick fucking men. Denny could spare no sympathy for any of them, dead or alive.

It struck him how much he hated this job, working his ass off to catch a guy or guys out to do society a favor. He forced his hatred to the back of his mind. *Fuck it. A job is a job. It's what they pay me the big bucks to do.*

Denny felt bone-tired, and his Sunday was already planned out for him. *So much for weekends off.* First, he had to go see hurtin' Jack Mignon in Portland, hear his sad story all over again, see if he remembered anything more. Then he'd have himself another talk with those two lovebirds at Serenity, find out where they were when Mignon got cut. He was getting close to answers. He could feel it.

Chapter Thirty-two

Jonas Welch cast off the mooring line and let the *Wendy Jane* drift astern a moment before shifting into Forward and bumping the throttle. The Cummins' diesel responded with a throaty rumble. He turned the wheel to port to clear the dinghy tied to his mooring, then trued his course for the cove opening.

He glanced over his left shoulder at the trim cape-style home sitting solidly on the receding Vinalhaven shoreline, sensibly built well above the high water line by his grandfather. His judgment had turned out well. It had survived two generations of storms and was well into its third generation without suffering a mortal blow.

June, his wife, had risen with Jonas before dawn to prepare his breakfast and share a quiet moment with him. She likely watched his departure from the kitchen window. Wendy and Jane, his two daughters whose names were carried on the stern of his lobster boat, were asleep in their beds, perhaps dreaming of the young couple who had waved to them as they rode their bikes past their isolated home the afternoon before.

Jonas turned and waved a farewell, knowing June would be watching and would return the wave. He was too far away to see her, had never seen her return his wave, but it was a ritual he never neglected. She once told him how thoughtful he was for this simple gesture, and he never forgot it.

As the *Wendy Jane* gathered headway, the chill morning air probed at his thick canvas overcoat, prompting him to secure the top button. The sun began to climb from the ocean to the east, bleaching the colors from the clouds as it rose.

Gulls, alerted by his diesel engine's rumble, flew up from the water and circled noisily above the stern, beseeching him to throw them a portion of the fish parts he carried in five-gallon pails. Their treats would come later, when he'd rebaited his traps and tossed the old remnants overboard. Jonas was thrifty, like his forefathers who'd struggled to earn a living here before him.

He turned and ran the same channel used by the island ferry and all the other boats running between the island and the mainland, heading westerly away from the brilliant morning sun. He was alone on the water at this early hour, which suited him fine. He had enough to contend with on some days with fog, wind, and high seas. Having to deal with other boats, both working and pleasure, was an added burden he preferred to do without. That was one reason why he began his workday at dawn. The other was his love of the early morning. It was quiet, peaceful, and generally calm.

His line of traps was strung along the southwesterly shoreline of Vinalhaven, as were his grandfather's and his father's before him. It was an unwritten but respected territory that the other lobstermen acknowledged. They would no sooner set their traps within his boundaries than he would within theirs. Violation of this age-old law could lead to violence. Nobody messed with another lobsterman's livelihood. Men had died over such disputes.

Although his trap buoys were less colorful than some, he never had a problem spotting them. His were painted with alternating bands of bright red and yellow, the same as his grandfather and father had done. Some of the newer lobstermen were using bright fluorescent colors now, and the sea surface was festooned with blaze oranges and pinks and greens where they had staked their claims.

The *Wendy Jane* rounded the southwestern point of Vinalhaven and turned northwesterly. Her bow knifed effortlessly through the waves that had increased slightly as she cleared the shelter of Vinalhaven Sound and nosed into the larger expanse of the Gulf of Maine. Jonas guided her toward his trap line unerringly, having run it so many times before that it was second nature to him. He knew the winds and tides, and set his course to bring him to the downwind, or down current, end of his line. He would move against the current or the wind, whichever happened to be stronger, using it to drift him sternward while he pulled, emptied, rebaited, and reset each trap. He had set his trap line to take advantage of the prevailing winds and current. It made his work easier.

Today the current would be more of an influence than the light breeze, which barely ruffled the sea's surface, and he plotted his course accordingly. At the right moment, he turned the wheel to bring the *Wendy Jane's* bow into the current just before his first trap buoy and cut the throttle. The *Wendy Jane* settled, lost headway, then Jonas tweaked the throttle so she moved ahead at a creep.

When the buoy came along amidships, he leaned over and snagged the buoy line with his boathook, then pulled the shift lever into neutral. He looped the warp, or trap line, over the trap boom and winched the trap up and onto the side shelf. With practiced efficiency, Jonas opened the trap top, grabbed and banded the legal lobsters one by one, using his measuring tool to check the length of marginal ones. Shorts were unceremoniously tossed back in the water. If a lobster was carrying eggs on its underside, he notched the tail and tossed it back. It now bore the mark of a breeder, and if it was caught again, the notch would earn it another toss over the side.

His keepers were dropped into a tank with circulating salt water. When he returned to his mooring, they'd be transferred into floating boxes, called cars, or taken directly to the co-op.

Decent-sized crabs, ones his grandfather had tossed overboard as trash, were put in a separate crate. Though they didn't bring much, they helped to supplement his income, making their collection worth his while.

The trap empty, Jonas recharged the bait bag with the fish parts he'd brought, swung the trap over the side with the help of the boom, and dropped it back in the sea right where he wanted it. He then pushed the shift lever forward and idled up to the next trap buoy.

The fifth trap was coming up slow and heavy. Jonas guessed it had gotten fouled with a neighboring trap so he was pulling up two at once. It wouldn't be the first time it had happened. He watched the water, trying to get a glimpse of the problem as he worked the winch. Then he spotted the trap, saw something else, not another trap, trailing behind it. He thought it looked like a sack of something. There were lobsters hanging onto it in many places, blurring the lines.

Jonas winched the trap to the bottom of the boom and stared over the side. His eyes widened in surprise as he saw what hung there. The body of a man had been tied to his trap, the other end of the rope tied around his neck. There were close to a dozen lobsters clinging to the body, feeding on the exposed surfaces. He averted his gaze, gagged, fought to keep down his breakfast.

A glance at his trap showed close to twice as many lobsters in it as he usually brought up, not to mention the ones clinging to the body.

Being both thrifty and practical, he took up his long-handled landing net, drew a deep breath, and went to work scooping the lobsters off the wallowing body. Some, sensing danger, released their grip and disappeared into the depths, but most clung on until forced loose and into Jonas' net. He snagged ten that way, all good keepers.

With the body free of lobsters, Jonas could see it more clearly. The man's trousers floated about his ankles, and his groin area was a shredded, indistinct mess. He supposed the lobsters had done that. He turned away once more to regain control of his breakfast.

For a moment, he considered letting the whole mess drop back to the bottom. He remembered an old "Bert and I" record of Maine humor which recounted two lobstermen faced with the same problem. The body, a friend's wife, as it turned out, had attracted so many lobsters that they decided to "set her again."

Jonas chuckled at the memory, eerily similar to this, shook his head, then picked up his radio mike.

While he waited for the Coast Guard to reply, he bid a silent farewell to the serenity of his morning. Overhead, the ever-present gulls, sensing a potential feast, swooped and mewed in anticipation. Their shrill cries drew others, and soon the sky above the *Wendy Jane* was alive with hungry gulls.

Chapter Thirty-three

"Tell me what you remember about the two guys who did this to you," prompted Detective Coe, pointing at Jack Mignon's heavily bandaged crotch.

Jack Mignon lay flat on the hospital bed, a sheet drawn up to his shoulders, the bulky dressings obvious below it.

"Shit, Detective, it was dark and they were dark. I thought the sons of bitches were cops. I never thought to give them an eyeball until the driver stuck me. By then, it was too late."

Denny watched Mignon's hand move under the sheets and come to rest on the bandages. *Confirming his loss or maybe probing for pain?*

"So you can't recall anything that could identify them?"

"What I remember? They were in dark suits and they were big, I mean built solid. There wasn't anything that stood out, far as their looks went. Shit, Detective, they could've been cops. Maybe they were, I'm thinking. You have anything to do with this?" He stared up at Denny.

Fuck you, Denny wanted to say. *Wish I did have something to do with it, you sick fuck.* Instead he said, "No, Mignon. I'm here to find out what I can and try to catch the ones who did this." He kept his voice police-detective calm.

"Well, good fucking luck," said Mignon.

"The one who did all the talking, you remember anything? Moustache? Glasses? Scars? Warts? Tattoos? Anything?" asked Denny, unruffled.

"Bastard wore a hat, pulled low. I couldn't see much. He was on the street side of the car and the light was behind him. No moustache. No scars I could see. Light didn't come on when they opened the door. Must've had it rigged. They were smart. Had it all figured," mused Mignon.

Denny abandoned his efforts to get a description of the two men.

"What about the car? You said it was a black sedan," Denny prompted.

"Yeah, a Lincoln. Or some other big car like that."

"Was it a Lincoln or not?"

"I don't know what the fuck it was! I haven't sat in a lot of Lincolns. It was black, and it was a big fucking car, big enough for all three of us to sit together in the front. You figure out what kind it was," he screeched, his voice pitched high. Then, in a softer voice, he said, "Jesus Christ. My voice is already getting higher."

Denny stuffed his smile away and went on. "Did you see the license plate?"

"Why'd I want to bother checkin' the plates on a cop car? Shit, no," Mignon whined from his hospital bed.

"Can you think of anything else that might help?" he asked, running out of questions.

"Yeah. Go find a couple of sick fuckin' cops who get their jollies from cuttin' the balls off poor bastards like me."

"We'll check all possible angles, Mignon." Denny removed one of his cards from his shirt pocket, set it on the bedside table. "You think of anything more, call me at that number."

"Yeah, sure," said Mignon. He picked up the card, gave it a quick look, then let it flutter down to the table.

Denny showed him his back, thinking what a waste of time this trip to Portland had been.

Chapter Thirty-four

Detective Denny Coe reached the US Coast Guard station in Rockland at nine-thirty Sunday morning. He'd gotten their call after leaving Jack Mignon's room.

The State Police mobile crime lab arrived ahead of him. The three weekend duty officers were done with their work, were lounging about, waiting for Denny to show up so they could load everything up and drive back to Augusta. Two Coast Guard officers stood by, ready to answer Denny's questions. They'd been on the cutter that had responded to the lobsterman's call.

Denny stared at the body resting in the wire litter the Coast Guard had used to fish it from the Gulf of Maine. It was slightly bloated and bleached from its time in the salty waters.

"It's been shredded. What happened?" he asked.

One of the Coast Guard officers stepped forward. "There were a bunch of lobsters hanging on the body when the lobsterman pulled it up with his trap," he explained. "Looks like they had a meal off of him."

"Remind me to give up lobster," said Denny, deadpan.

Everyone laughed. Comic relief.

"We found these in one of his pockets, Detective." One of the crime lab techs held out a plastic evidence bag to Denny, who took it and held it up to view. Through the clear plastic he could see the partial remains of the man's manhood. The flesh was shrunken and bleached white from its time in the cold salt water. Denny thought the balls were surprisingly small, considering the reputation of the creep they belonged to.

"Find anything else?" he asked, passing back the bag.

"Wallet with a Maine driver's license in the name of Leo Jenkins of Collins Mills. Seventeen dollars. A Polaroid snapshot, in pretty bad shape. Looks like a young girl. Naked. Plain key ring with two keys on it. Thirty-six cents in change. About it," the tech finished, holding out a second evidence bag.

"Keep it. I'll check it later," Denny told him, holding up his hand, palm forward. "Coroner seen him?" he asked, the wheels turning.

"Yeah. Left ten minutes before you got here."

"What'd he find?" Denny asked.

"Cause of death appears to be a single knife wound to the left mid-back area, likely causing mortal wounds to the heart and major vessels. Cock and balls—excuse me, Detective, genitals—appear to have been cut off at or near death, based on the lack of bleeding into surrounding tissue. Coroner said he'd wait for the autopsy to confirm all this, though," said the tech, coloring slightly after correcting his poor choice of words.

"So somebody stuck him in the back, then cut off his cock and balls and tied him to a lobster trap," Denny summarized, excusing with his own description the crime lab tech's language.

Those within earshot grinned at Denny's summary.

"Yeah, that's about it," agreed the tech, a relieved expression filling his rugged face.

The wheels were clicking, meshing, in Denny's head. He knew Leo Jenkins, had sent him to Thomaston for child sexual abuse and molestation. He'd also gotten word he'd been released after only three years of his six-year sentence. The parole board declared that he was rehabilitated. No longer a threat to society. Denny wondered who the naked little girl in the picture was, where she lived, what Jenkins had done to her. He'd leave that search to the crime lab boys in Augusta. They'd tell him if they were able to identify her.

He wondered what the parole board would think of their rehabilitated Mr. Jenkins now, found with a picture of a naked little girl less than three months after his release. He'd make it a point to get the news to the parole board. Maybe they wouldn't be so quick to declare the next skinner fit to return to society. Somehow, he doubted it.

He thought about the body found in the landfill, that Billy Prosson creep, and he considered the similarities between Prosson and Jenkins. Both stuck in the back, both sexually mutilated. Then he thought about Ray Barribee, alive and well except he'd had his balls handed to him. And then Jack Mignon, just last night, same scenario as Barribee. All four in the last six weeks. All with big similarities. Clickety-click went the wheels in his head.

He reviewed what he knew about Jim Booker at Serenity. He'd taken a job there after leaving New Jersey a month before all this stuff started happening. He'd made a call from a pay phone to someone in Newark, New Jersey, two weeks ago, he knew that much. The telephone company person had told him they couldn't identify the name of the called party because it was a private, unlisted number.

He'd see about that.

And then there was that Breanna Fowler woman. Victim of sexual abuse herself, he'd learned. Counselor for women who've been abused. Openly admitted she didn't mind hearing about Barribee's and Prosson's accidents. Not very big, not strong enough to handle those two perps herself. But with help? With Jim Booker? He made a mental note to check on their whereabouts first thing.

"Where was the body found?" asked Denny.

The Coast Guard officer stepped forward. "Off the southwestern tip of Vinalhaven, sir, in about thirty feet of water. I have the coordinates if you want them."

"Never know," said Denny.

The officer pulled a notebook from his shirt pocket, found the page, copied the degrees and minutes onto a blank piece of paper, and handed it off to Denny.

"Thanks, Officer…" Denny dragged it out, prompting the officer to give him his name.

"Lieutenant Peter Maxwell, sir," he said.

"Thanks, Lieutenant," said Denny, smiling, writing the name on the paper Maxwell had given him.

"Anything more we can do for you?" asked Maxwell.

"No, I think this wraps it up. Thank you and your men for a job well done," Denny said, giving the Coast Guard a pat on the back. *Never know when you might need their cooperation again.*

He turned to the crime lab crew. "Guys need a hand loading?"

"Thanks. We got it, Detective," answered their spokesman.

The crime lab men transferred the body into a body bag and zipped it up. Denny watched, making sure nothing was left behind on the litter. They lugged the body bag to the van and strapped it to the stretcher inside. The door was closed, final thanks were given to the Coast Guardsmen, and the lab crew climbed into the van's front seat while Denny got in his cruiser. He checked his watch. Ten. Time to find out where Miss Fowler and Mr. Booker had spent their Saturday evening.

After checking his notebook, he called a number, listened a while, hung up and called a second number. That one wasn't answered, either.

"Well, well," he said to himself. "Where are you two? Go off on a little killing spree together? Time to find out."

Denny made a third call.

"Rumford Police Department," announced a matter of fact male voice.

"Yeah, this is Detective Coe, Maine State Police. I'm trying to locate a couple of citizens who live in Cairo."

"That's the sheriff's territory," said the voice. "You want a number?"

"Yeah. Go ahead."

The dispatcher read him a phone number. Denny thanked him, hung up, wrote it in his notebook, then called the number.

"Sheriff's Department. Sheriff McDermott."

"This is Detective Coe, Maine State Police. I'm trying to locate a couple of citizens who live in Cairo. I called their places, but they don't answer."

"What're their names, Detective?"

"James Booker and Breanna Fowler. They both work at the Serenity facility up there." Denny gave him their addresses and phone numbers.

"They wanted for something?"

"For now, just questioning."

"We find them, you want us to pick them up?"

"No. Let me know where they are, and I'll take it from there. What'd you say your name is?"

"Didn't I say? This is Sheriff McDermott."

"Thanks, Sheriff. I appreciate your help."

Denny wrote the name in his notebook. Then he gave Sheriff McDermott his cell phone number, told him to call when he had anything, and hung up.

Where could those two be?

Chapter Thirty-five

When Jim and Brie came downstairs, they found the dining room table set for them. They'd been alerted to the prospects of a hearty breakfast by the rich coffee aroma that wafted into their bedroom, prompting them to rise and shine. With their lovemaking appetites temporarily sated, the allure of a good cup of coffee was irresistible.

Blooming daffodils overflowed a vase set in the table's center. Next to it sat a generous platter of fresh fruit, sliced and attractively presented. Two place settings had been prepared, one at the end, the other next to it on the side. Each setting had a pale blue hand-stitched placemat with a matching napkin, anchored by a silver-plated knife, fork, and spoon. A small blue floral design plate rested in the center of each mat, ready for the fruit, and a matching cup and saucer sat on the left border, ready for coffee.

"Oh, that's so pretty," exclaimed Brie, taking it all in. "What a perfect way to start the day."

Jim, holding her chair out for her, leaned to her and whispered, "I already had the perfect way to start the day."

Brie blushed, her eyebrows dancing as she kissed him lightly.

Mary, hearing Brie's comment from her seat in the kitchen, appeared carrying a large ceramic coffeepot. Its floral design matched the table setting.

"Good morning," she said brightly. "Did you sleep well?"

"Oh, yes," Brie answered for the two of them. "The bed was so comfortable. I wish we could take it home with us."

"I have to charge extra for take-out beds," Mary joked.

"Then I guess we'll have to come back," said Brie, smiling at Mary.

"You're welcome any time. I love having easy guests like you two. Coffee?" she asked, holding up the pot.

"You bet," Jim said.

Mary poured the coffee, asked how they liked their eggs, then set the pot on the table and returned to the kitchen.

Jim held the fruit plate for Brie, then helped himself. They ate in silence for a moment. Then Brie broke it.

"Oh, this fruit is perfect. I can't remember when fresh fruit tasted this good."

"It is incredible," Jim agreed. "Why is it, do you suppose?" he asked, already knowing the answer. Brie did, too.

They had barely done justice to the fruit when Mary reappeared, carrying two large plates heaped with eggs, bacon, and toasted English muffins. She set a plate in front of Brie, then Jim. While they were marveling over the feast, she carried the fruit plates to the kitchen. Moments later, she returned with a dish of homemade raspberry preserves and a second plate of toasted muffins.

"Let me know if you need more," she said, setting them on the table within easy reach.

"This is fantastic! It's more than I can ever eat," Brie gushed.

Jim watched her as she forked food from her plate.

A short time later she said, "Call me a liar." Brie stared at her empty plate.

Jim, for his part, left half a muffin on the plate as proof they'd had enough. They had.

They sipped and sighed, working on their coffee refills.

Mary reappeared to clear away the dishes. "We had some excitement on the island this morning," she announced, eager to do her part to disseminate the news.

"Oh? What happened?" asked Jim.

"One of our local lobstermen pulled one of his traps this morning and found a body tied to it," she said in a conspiratorial tone.

"A human body?" asked Brie.

"Yes. The body of a man," said Mary.

"Oh, that's gross. What happened to him? How'd he get there?" she asked in a rush of words.

"They think somebody killed him and then tied him to the lobster trap. He'd had his, ah, privates cut off," Mary blurted, flushing slightly.

Jim and Brie were shocked to silence by this last revelation, but Mary hardly noticed. She seemed to assume they were horrified at the thought of it, as she obviously was.

"Who could do something like that?" Jim managed to ask.

"Lord knows. Probably someone from the mainland. We don't have such goings-on here on the island," she reassured them.

"What did they do with him?" asked Brie.

"The Coast Guard took him to Rockland. Said the State Police would take it from there," she added.

Both Jim and Brie sat in silence, absorbed in their own thoughts.

Mary, seemed to take their silence as an indication of their shock over the story, and apologized for mentioning it. "Nothing much ever happens around here so when it does, it's hard for me not to talk about it," she explained. "I'm sure it wasn't an island person who did it. Probably one of those drug dealers from the mainland. Jonas said he never saw the dead man before, and he knows everyone on the island."

"Who's Jonas?" asked Jim.

"He's the lobsterman who found the body," said Mary. "He and his family live out on the South Road. Moors his boat there, too," she added, making small talk, filling in the vacuum of silence.

"I'll bet it shocked him when he pulled a body up with his trap," said Brie, regaining her composure.

"You're right about that. He said he had all he could do to keep his breakfast down." She regretted her words as soon as they were spoken. "Oh, I'm so sorry. How thoughtless of me to bring this up right after you've eaten. Enough of this terrible talk."

"It's okay, Mary," Brie reassured her. "We won't have any trouble keeping *your* breakfast down."

"Oh, thank you. Can I get you more coffee? It's no trouble."

"None for me," said Jim. "I'm percolating already."

"Me, too," said Brie, flashing her a smile.

"All right, then. You two take your time. It's Sunday, and there aren't any guests coming in, so don't feel like you have to rush off," Mary said.

"That's so kind of you," said Brie. "We plan to get the three-thirty ferry, so if we can leave our stuff here until about three, that'd be great."

"It's not a problem. You two have been model guests. It's the least I can do."

"Thanks, Mary. And thanks for the fantastic breakfast. I'm all charged up for our bike ride," Brie said.

"Oh, you're welcome. You two have a nice ride, and I'll see you when you get back." She busied herself with clearing the table.

They returned to their room to get ready for their ride. Jim closed the door, and they turned to each other.

Jim spoke first.

"What the heck's going on? We come here so we'll have the perfect alibi, and somebody ends up dead and mutilated right under our noses. Detective Coe will have a ball with this when he finds out we were here on the island when it happened," he said.

"Hey, take it easy, big guy. I agree, he's going to want to question us about it, but there's no way he can connect us to it," Brie said, her voice a calm in the storm.

"For starters, how did we get this guy, whoever he is, to come to Vinalhaven? And then, if we did kill him, how did we get his body out to a lobster trap? We don't have a boat, and it won't take Detective Coe long to figure out we didn't borrow or rent one," she reasoned.

"Okay," he said, feeling less anxious. "We can expect Detective Coe to question us, but you're right. There's more he *can't* explain than what he *can*. We'll be open and honest with him."

"Honesty's the best policy," said Brie. She moved against him and kissed him lightly.

Jim drew her to him and kissed her urgently, with passion, not wanting to let her go.

"Mmmm," she murmured, melting.

He left a trail of kisses from her mouth to her left ear, then whispered, "Want to enjoy this great bed one more time?"

"I was thinking more of you than the bed."

"You always say the right thing," he whispered. He swept her up and carried her to the bed.

"Be gentle with my breakfast," she whispered in his ear.

He was.

Chapter Thirty-six

"Detective Coe?"

"Speaking," said Denny.

"Sheriff McDermott, up in Cairo. Got some information for you about Booker and Fowler, the two people you asked me to check on an hour ago."

"Good. Go ahead, Sheriff."

"Went to their apartments, got no answer. So I called up to Serenity, spoke to a woman who works with the Fowler woman. She says they went off for the weekend together. Left Saturday morning, early. Says they won't be back until tonight."

"She say where they went?" Denny asked.

"Vinalhaven. Said they were going to stay at some bed-and-breakfast. Said she didn't know the name of the place, though."

"Thanks, Sheriff. You've been a big help. I'll mention you in my report."

"Glad to help, Detective. Who knows? Might need a favor from you some day."

"You let me know if you do." Denny ended the call, the wheels beginning to mesh together. *Well, well, you two. You've got a lot of explaining to do.*

He called dispatch to get him a list of bed-and-breakfasts on Vinalhaven, then waited, considering his next move.

Dispatch called back with a short list, and he started making the calls. He got lucky on the second call. Yes, she had Mr. Booker and Miss Fowler staying there. Yes, they were still on the island, had gone for a bike ride, but she expected them back afterwards. They said they were taking the three-thirty ferry and would be stopping to get their belongings.

He thanked her, assured her it was nothing serious. Miss Fowler's brother had been in an accident, and the family wanted him to tell her before she heard about it somewhere else. No, the brother was going to be fine, nothing serious.

"Please don't tell her anything," Denny said to the woman. "I'll be over to meet her before the three-thirty ferry and tell her myself. And thanks again."

Denny checked his watch. It was eleven. He had two hours to get to Rockland and get the ferry over. Not a problem.

He reviewed what he knew. First, Leo Jenkins gets stabbed in the back, then has his genitals cut off and stuffed into his back pocket before being tied to a lobster trap off the southwestern tip of Vinalhaven, probably late Saturday afternoon or early evening. He's pulled up by the lobsterman who owns the trap early this morning.

Second, Jack Mignon gets his balls handed to him by two suits in Portland, some time around five-thirty Saturday evening.

Third, Jim Booker and Breanna Fowler just happen to be on Vinalhaven this weekend, close to all the action.

Denny thought a minute. "Shit." He realized that the two incidents happened at about the same time on Saturday. *How could they both be the work of one couple? Maybe they had help.* Not wanting to relinquish the belief that Booker and Fowler were the culprits. *Maybe Booker called down to New Jersey for help with all the dirty work. Could there be a better way of putting me off the trail than getting strangers to share in the slaughter?*

Denny's cell phone rang.

"Coe."

"Denny, it's Benoit, at the lab in Augusta. Found something that might interest you," said the French-accented voice.

"Whatcha got?"

"Piece of paper in one of Jenkins' pockets, a receipt from K-mart in Augusta for a stuffed animal. Bought last Thursday. Cost $3.99. Mean anything?"

Denny figured it was probably Jenkins' way of getting a child to do more with him, a bribe for favors. He wondered if Jenkins had had the chance to deliver it and collect his thank-you. The thought sickened him. He hoped he hadn't, for the kid's sake.

"Could be he bought it to give to the little girl in the picture," offered Denny. "You guys might start your search for her down in the Rockland area. I don't know what else could've got Jenkins down there. Maybe he got killed because somebody found out he was messin' with her."

"Hey, good thought. We'll check it out," said Benoit.

"Let me know if you find anything else, and call me when the medical examiner's done his thing, okay?"

"Sure, sure, no problem. ME's due in any time. You'll be first to know."

"Thanks, Benoit." He ended the call. It had left a bad taste in Denny's mouth. It was something he had to deal with a lot on this job. He still wasn't used to it. Never would be.

He forced the image of the little girl from his thoughts, focusing instead on what he'd ask Booker and Fowler when he met up with them. He had the drive to Rockland, plus the ferry ride to Vinalhaven to come up with the questions.

Chapter Thirty-seven

Jim and Brie noticed the black sedan parked in front of the bed-and-breakfast when they rode up on their bikes, but didn't make the connection until Detective Coe swung the door open and stepped out.

"Well, well. Good afternoon, you two. Remember me? Detective Coe, Maine State Police," he recited, fixing them with his steely gaze.

"Sure, I remember you, Detective. What brings you here?" Brie was the first to recover.

"Some strange things have happened in the last twenty-four hours, and I've got questions for you two."

"Anything to do with the body found tied to a lobster trap offshore?" asked Jim, fully recovered and taking the offensive.

"How'd you know about that?" asked the detective, suspicious.

"It's the talk of the island. Mary, the owner of the B-and-B here, told us about it this morning at breakfast. What's it got to do with us?" he asked, working to keep his voice calm and steady.

"It may have *everything* to do with you," said the detective ominously. "Tell me what you know about it."

Jim knew Detective Coe hoped he'd give him more details than were available from the island gossip sources, details not generally known, details that could be used to hang him. It made him smile inwardly because he knew only what Mary had told them at breakfast. Fighting back the smile that threatened to break free, he summarized what Mary had told them. When he finished, he felt good when he saw disappointment on the detective's face.

"Where were you two yesterday afternoon?" Detective Coe pressed.

"We took the eleven o'clock ferry over, and we've been here ever since," Brie said.

"Right here?"

"Except for bike rides and dinner, yes," she confirmed.

"Mind going inside with me and getting that confirmed by…" He looked at his notes. "…Mary?" the detective asked casually.

Mary met them in the entryway. "Is everything all right?" she asked.

"Yes," Brie answered, reading Mary's concern.

"Mary, I'm Detective Coe, Maine State Police. I spoke with you earlier."

"Yes, Detective, pleased to meet you." Mary extended her hand.

The detective shook it briefly, released it. "I wonder if you'd mind answering a few questions for me."

"Sure, Detective," Mary said.

"Can you tell me what time Miss Fowler and Mr. Booker got here yesterday?"

"Oh, let's see now. It must have been right around noon."

"Did they go out at all yesterday afternoon?"

"Why, yes, they went off on their bikes. They told me they had lunch down by the pier and then rode around the island. It was a perfect day for it," Mary added.

"What time did they get back?"

"I'd say it was around four o'clock, near as I can remember."

"And they were here after that?"

"Well, ah, no. Miss Fowler came in and said that Jim, I mean Mr. Booker, was going to take a short ride by himself."

"How long was he gone?" pushed the detective.

"Well, it turned out to be longer than he'd planned because he got lost," said Mary, smiling.

"Just how long was he gone?" prodded the detective.

"I'm guessing it was about six o'clock when he got back. It wasn't dark, but the sun was down," Mary recalled.

The detective wrote something down on a small notepad. "He was gone by himself for about two hours, from four to six yesterday?"

"Yes. That's right, Detective."

"And that's it?" he asked.

"No. They went out to dinner at about, oh, quarter to seven, and were back here by eight-thirty. But what's this got to do with her brother, Detective?" Mary was clearly confused.

"What about my brother?" asked Brie, concern in her voice.

"There's nothing wrong with your brother," Detective Coe said to Brie. Then he turned back to Mary. "It was my way of keeping you from telling them I was coming, Mary." The detective was clearly embarrassed, caught in a lie.

"So if this isn't about her brother, then what's—" Mary stopped short as the truth hit her. "Oh, my! You think these two nice people had something to do with that man they found tied to the lobster trap."

"Nobody here is a definite suspect, ma'am. I'm checking out all possible leads," responded the detective in his official police voice. He turned to

Jim, his tone blunt. "It seems like you've got some explaining to do for those two hours you were off alone, supposedly riding your bike."

"Sure, Detective." Jim had time to think about that while Detective Coe was weaseling his way out of Mary's question. "What can I tell you?"

"Where did you go, and who did you meet?"

"I meant to follow the same roads Brie and I took earlier, but I missed one of the turns. I ended up at the northern end of the island, at a dock on the shore. I could see North Haven across the water. I took a picture of it with my phone, if you want to see it. Then I came back down the road, passing the road I'd missed, and came on back here."

"Anybody you meet who can vouch for that?"

"No. I went alone, and I didn't see anybody along the way. But I can describe what I saw and where I went," he offered.

"What would that prove?" asked the detective, his voice charged with sarcasm.

"I've never been to Vinalhaven before, Detective, so the only way I could describe what I saw and where I went would be because I rode there yesterday," Jim reasoned.

"You mean that wrong turn you claim you took? You could've driven up there last night when you went out to dinner." His sarcasm was increasing.

"Except we didn't. Check the restaurant. They can tell you how long we were there. We wouldn't have been able to take the drive you're suggesting between the time we left and the time we got back here. Besides, there were things I could only see in the daylight, wouldn't have been able to see driving a car at night," Jim said.

"Yeah, so where did you go this morning that you're just getting back from?" asked the detective.

"We rode down to the southeast, across a bridge, and out to a nature preserve. Spent a lot of time on the shore. Could hear pheasants calling in the underbrush," Jim recalled.

"Anybody see you?"

"We met a young couple from Augusta there. George and Lucie Webster, they said." Jim felt smug satisfaction from taking the time to get their names.

The detective frowned, scribbled the names in his notebook. "Okay. Tell me something unusual about that road you took yesterday."

Jim did.

"That certainly sounds like the road up there, Detective," Mary commented, smiling pleasantly.

"Thank you, ma'am." His voice overflowed with irritation. He asked for directions to the restaurant, wrote them down, then put his notebook in his breast pocket. "That'll be all for now, you two. I'm sure I'll have more questions for you, so don't go anywhere."

"You mean we can't go home?" asked Brie, alarmed.

"I mean, don't leave the state without first telling me," he advised, all business.

"Oh, we have no plans to do that, Detective. Do we, Jim?" Brie said.

"No, we don't," Jim concurred, his eyes on Coe. "By the way, who was the man they found tied to the lobster trap?" He expected to hear Jack Mignon's name.

"I'm sorry, I'm not at liberty to divulge that information." The detective said, strictly official.

"Thank you all," he told them, then got into his car.

Mary was quick to comment. "What a grouch!"

"This isn't the first time he's questioned us, and it probably won't be the last," Brie said. She told Mary what Detective Coe had put them through, and why she thought he considered them suspects.

"Why, that's terrible," Mary exclaimed when Brie had finished. "Two nice people like you. Isn't that police harassment or something?"

"It feels like it," said Jim, "though I don't know if we have any legal recourse."

"If I were in your shoes, I'd call me a lawyer and find out," said Mary.

"That's a great idea," Brie agreed. "We'll look into it."

Jim checked his watch. It was two-fifteen. "We've got about forty-five minutes before we should head for the ferry."

"Do you still want to stop for fish on the way?" Brie asked.

"Right. I forgot that."

"The co-op's closed Sundays," Mary said apologetically. "What did you want to get?"

"Maybe some haddock for our supper tonight," said Brie.

"This is your lucky day! I bought haddock for dinner tonight, expecting guests, but they called and canceled. It's all yours," she told them.

"Oh, Mary, we couldn't do that," Brie replied, protesting. "Let us pay you for it."

Mary waved her off. "Don't be silly. I won't take a penny from you. Besides, it won't be fresh by the time I get to cook it, and I don't want to throw it out."

"That's very generous of you," said Brie, capitulating.

"You two have been lovely guests, absolutely no problem, and I hope you'll come back."

"Count on it, Mary, as long as we can have the same room," said Brie, offering up her warm smile. "That bed's to die for."

"Of course. I'm so pleased you like my accommodations."

"Everything's been great," joined in Jim, "except for the appearance of

Detective Coe. And you had nothing to do with that."

"Oh, what a terrible person he is," said Mary. "Imagine him lying to me, telling me your brother was in an accident. I hope he misses the last ferry and has to spend the night over here, just for punishment."

Mary's comment reminded them that they had to pack the truck and set the bikes on the rack before driving to the ferry. They thanked Mary once more, then hurried up to their room to change out of their bike clothes and finish packing.

The comfortable bed with its thick comforter beckoned to them. Jim smiled at Brie.

She read his mind. She encircled him with her arms and nuzzled his neck. "I'd love to, but if we miss the ferry we may have to share the room with Detective Coe," she murmured in his ear.

"Until next time, then," Jim whispered.

"Until next time," she agreed.

They changed clothes and packed. After a final check to be sure they weren't leaving anything behind, they said good-bye to the room and headed downstairs. Mary had the fish, packed in ice to keep it fresh, waiting for them.

"You're so thoughtful," Brie told her, accepting the package and giving her a warm hug.

"You two come back soon, now," she urged.

"We will," Brie and Jim said together.

After packing the truck and loading the bikes, they gave Mary a final wave and drove off toward the ferry landing.

"Oh my God, Jim, what a wonderful place to stay! I had a perfect time. Thank you," she murmured, snuggling against him inside the truck.

"Me, too," said Jim, "until Detective Coe showed up. What puzzles me, though, is he never said a word about Jack Mignon. Do you think the New Jersey crew grabbed the wrong man, ended up killing him?"

"I hope not," said Brie.

Chapter Thirty-eight

"I can't believe we were standing here a little over twenty-four hours ago," said Brie.

She and Jim were alone on the ferry's observation deck. They stood together, watching as the ferry reversed out of the crib. The captain turned the ferry in an arc until he had it pointed toward the southern end of the harbor and the route to Rockland. Then he shifted into Forward and advanced the throttles. The twin diesels responded with a thrumming sound they could feel through the steel decks.

"Of course," said Jim, his eyes on the cars and trucks on the deck below, riding backwards into Vinalhaven sound.

"What?" asked Brie, puzzled.

"I figured out how the ferry loads and unloads," he replied, grinning at her. "In Rockland, the ferry does a one-eighty and backs into the crib. The cars drive off. Then the cars load for the trip to Vinalhaven, and the ferry pulls out going forward all the way. That's why the cars are facing the stern now, but faced the bow coming over."

"I don't believe it. We're standing here after being grilled by Detective Coe, we're probably his prime suspects, and you're figuring out how the ferry maneuvers. What should I draw from that?" she asked, looking lopsided at Jim.

"That I'm not worried?"

"That you're crazier than a March hare," Brie shot back.

He cocked an eyebrow at her. "You know why they call March hares crazy? March is their breeding season and—"

"Stop it, Jim. You may not be worried, but I'm worried enough for both of us."

"I know," Jim said in a quiet voice. "But I think that if Detective Coe had anything on us, we'd be riding in the back of his cruiser, not standing up here by ourselves on the observation deck."

"You're probably right. In fact I know you're right, but I can't stop worrying. What went wrong anyway? And what about Jack Mignon? Did your friends from New Jersey mess up and grab the wrong man, and then mess up further by killing him?"

"When we get to Rockland, we'll find a pay phone and call New Jersey, get some answers," Jim said.

"Now there's a suggestion I can support wholeheartedly."

That seemed to appease her. With that, she turned and pointed over the starboard side. "Look, Jim."

The ferry had rounded the southwestern tip of Vinalhaven and began its swing northward to follow the channel. Brie pointed at a Coast Guard vessel anchored toward shore. An inflatable dinghy floated alongside it, and the heads of two divers were barely visible in the water next to it.

"Must be where they found the body," said Jim in a hushed voice.

A shudder passed through Brie. Jim, his arm around her waist, felt it. He drew her closer.

"Don't worry, Brie. No matter what they find, they can't tie it to us," he reassured her.

"I hope you're right. I got a picture in my mind of that man tied to a lobster trap in that awful, cold water," she said, shivering again. "Somebody killed him, took his life, and did it in a violent way. Maybe he deserved that death. I don't know. I only hope your New Jersey friends had nothing to do with it because if they did, then you and I are just as guilty as they are. We asked them to hurt someone, and it got out of hand." She shivered. "I'm cold, Jim. Let's go down."

They descended the steel stairway to the car deck and climbed into Jim's truck. Enclosed, out of the breeze, it felt warm, safer.

The reversal of the ferry's engines shook them back to the present. They watched as the ferry's bow swung around, then nosed into the crib in Rockland. The crew secured the lines, removed the safety chain, and lowered the ramp. Soon the first vehicles began their exodus. Jim waited for the attendant's signal, then drove up the ramp and back onto the mainland. He noted that it felt different from his drive onto Vinalhaven.

As they made their way out, Brie spotted a pay phone on a side street in Rockland, and Jim swung into a parking spot. They sat quietly, watching for any vehicles that might have been following them. Seeing none, Jim exited the truck and called the New Jersey number from memory.

"Hello?" The New Jersey accent was thick.

"This is Jim Booker, calling to talk to Tony."

"Jim, how ya' doin'? This *is* Tony."

"Hey, I didn't expect you to answer."

"It's Sunday. Maid's day off, if you get me," Tony joked.

"Oh, yeah. Keep forgetting that," he joked back.

"What can I do for you, Jim?" Tony was all business.

"A funny thing happened up here, Tony."

Jim told him about the dead and mutilated man tied to the lobster trap.

"The thing is, we went to Vinalhaven so we'd have a good alibi when your men met up with Jack Mignon, and now we're under suspicion because the guy got killed and disposed of right off Vinalhaven."

"What do you mean, you're under suspicion?" Tony asked.

Jim told him about Detective Coe and their run-ins with him, ending with their encounter that morning.

"So this Detective Coe, he thinks you had somethin' to do with this guy's death?"

"Yeah, and he'd like to pin Ray Barribee and another guy's death on me, too."

"Another death?"

Jim told Tony about Billy Prosson and the Norridgewock landfill.

"Jeez, Jim, you've been busy up there. Hey, I'm kiddin'. Anyways, sounds like this Detective Coe could be a problem. Lemme give this thing some thought."

"I take it your men had nothing to do with the dead man tied to the lobster trap."

"Hey, c'mon, Jim. We're pros! I ask someone to do somethin', they do what I ask, no more, no less. You didn't ask for that, they didn't do that. Simple."

"Who are *they,* Tony?"

"Hey, Jim, this is a big organization. I got somethin' needs to get done in Maine, I call the Maine chapter, if you get what I mean. I tell them what needs doing, they do it. Maybe next week, next month, they got somethin' needs doin' in Jersey, they call me, I take care of it. Understand?" Tony kept his voice even through his long explanation, like a teacher explaining something to a child.

"So there couldn't be a slip-up?" Jim pressed.

"No slip-up. They check back, tell me what they did, including if there was a slip-up. My boys didn't do that lobster-trap guy. Must've been some freelance deal."

"So they dealt with Jack Mignon?"

"Yeah, just like we planned. They posed as cops and got him in their car. The rest was easy. Saturday night, six o'clock, he got his balls handed to him, just like the Barribee guy."

"Thanks, Tony. I owe you."

"You owe me nothin'. My son's life is worth a hell of a lot more than two pair of balls off some sick perverts! Listen, Jim. I got an idea how we can get this detective off your ass."

"You aren't thinking of hurting him, are you?" Jim asked, shocked.

"Hell, no. That'd be stupid. Cops'd replace him, and you'd be worse off than before. Leave it to me, Jim. My guess is, you won't be hearin' any more from Detective Coe. Give it a week. Two at the most."

"Thanks, Tony. I owe you again," Jim couldn't help but say.

"Forget owing me. You want to do somethin', come back to Jersey. We need good docs like you down here."

"You never know, Tony. And you know I'm a PA, not a doc, right?"

"Yeah, yeah, sure. You're a doc, far as I'm concerned. Hey, keep in touch, Jim. I'm still a long ways from payin' you back. Don't forget that."

"I get the feeling you'll never think you've paid me back."

"Now you're catchin' on."

"So long, Tony." Jim hung up the pay phone and turned to Brie who had stood by him during the entire call, hearing his side.

"Come on," she urged him, "let's get in the truck. I feel exposed out here."

They got in, and Jim pointed the truck toward Cairo. As they drove, he filled her in on what Tony had said. They talked about Ray Barribee and Jack Mignon. They talked about Billy Prosson and the body tied to the lobster trap. They talked about what Tony might have in mind for Detective Coe. When they reached Cairo, they still didn't think they'd made any good guesses.

Chapter Thirty-nine

"Son of a bitch. Ain't this my lucky week," the man muttered to himself. He was on his way to Bangor, cruising up Route One because he had plenty of time and Route One wasn't busy like it got in the summer. And there was Willie, hitchhiking. No mistaking him, with his thick, flat nose, that white scar that ran from his left eyebrow down to his jaw, and those eyes. Dead eyes. They gave him the creeps, even from this far away. He jammed on the brakes, pulled to the shoulder, stopping fifty yards past Willie, and waited while he walked up to the car.

"Where you heading?" the man asked.

"Bangor." Willie made it sound like Bang-uh.

"Today's you're lucky day. Climb in."

Willie opened the passenger side door and got in. The driver stared at him the whole while, smiling his lopsided grin at him.

"You ain't one of those queers, are you?" asked Willie, hand on the door handle, ready to bolt.

"Willie Wainright. Am I right?"

Willie eyed the driver suspiciously. "How'd you know my name?"

"You don't remember me, do you? We did time together."

Willie stared at him a moment. "No, can't say I do," he replied, still suspicious.

"You were in Tommy Town with me. Got out not long after I got there."

"What were you in for?"

The man shrugged. "Same as you. Sexual abuse of a minor."

"They let me out when the guy who did it confessed," blurted Willie.

"Oh, yeah. Sure. I was innocent, too," said the driver, all sarcasm. "Only the guy who did it never confessed."

"No fooling? I couldn't believe how many innocent guys I met in there," he replied, missing the driver's sarcasm. "We got one hell of a fucked up justice system, you ask me," Willie added, relaxing some.

They were between towns and pine forest occupied both sides of the highway.

"Not to change the subject, but I gotta take a whiz," the driver told Willie. "Mind if I stop?"

"Go ahead," said Willie, feeling more at ease.

The driver spotted a turnout, an old logging road ahead on the right. He slowed and made the turn, going carefully over the ruts, and stopped about fifty yards in, out of sight of the highway.

"This should do it." He climbed out, stepping away from the car, unzipped his pants.

"Might as well join you," said Willie, getting out and facing away from the driver before unzipping.

The driver watched him over his shoulder. When it looked like Willie was fully occupied, he moved silently toward him. He drew his knife as he came around the back of the vehicle.

As he made his lunge, aiming at Willie's left mid-back area, a dry stick snapped under his foot.

Willie turned to his right with the sound. The movement saved his life. The knife sliced through skin and muscle, but didn't penetrate his ribcage.

Willie felt the knife hit a rib, slice into him. He felt no pain, just as there had been no pain when the knife opened up his face in prison. But he knew he was hurt, knew he was in trouble.

Instinctively, Willie swung his right arm around in a wide arc. It slammed into the back of his assailant's neck, driving him forward into the open car door. His head was driven through the window, shattering the glass and leaving him suspended in the opening.

His attacker was momentarily stunned. Then he drew himself back, shook his head, and glared at Willie. Small shards of glass sparkled in his hair, on his shirt. A line of drool hung from the left side of his mouth.

"You bastard! I'm gonna kill you," he snarled.

Willie knew he meant it.

To gain time, he lifted his foot and drove the open door into his assailant. The force caught the man across his chest, slamming him backward. The sound of the air expelled from the man's lungs was punctuated by the dull crunch of his head striking the car's roof. His head was driven forward and down at an impossible angle. Willie watched, fascinated, as the man's eyes dilated and he slumped to the ground like a puppet freed of its strings. The knife dropped from his lifeless hand and landed silently at his inert side.

For some time, Willie stared, half-expecting him to get up and come at him again. He couldn't see any movement in the man's chest.

Nervous, uncertain, he waited longer. Then he became conscious of pain in his rib, where he'd been cut. He stepped cautiously toward the man and kicked him hard in his side. There was no response, no reaction. Still cautious, he bent down and felt for a pulse in his neck. He couldn't feel one. It took him a moment longer to accept that his assailant was dead.

Willie considered his options. His first thought was to get out of there, run, but he knew he was hurt bad and would need a doctor's care. There would be questions. He made his decision.

He walked away slowly, painfully, back to the highway and flagged down a pickup truck. He told the driver what had happened, asked him to call the police. And an ambulance. The driver took out his cell phone and hit 9-1-1.

A State Police cruiser pulled up before the ambulance arrived, and Willie told his crazy story to the trooper who listened, took notes, and asked a few questions. By then the pain in his rib had grown so intense that any slight movement aggravated it. He'd lost blood, felt fuzzy, lightheaded.

Willie watched as the trooper searched through the dead man's pockets, saw him pull out a wallet, open it.

"What's his name?" asked Willie, his voice sounding far away to him.

"You don't know?" the trooper asked suspiciously.

"He knew me, but I didn't know him. Said he met me in prison. I don't remember him."

"His license says his name is Raymond Barribee. Mean anything to you?" asked the trooper.

Willie said it didn't.

The ambulance arrived, and the attendants removed Willie's coat and shirt, distracting him. The younger attendant confirmed the seriousness of the wound by blurting, "Jeez, look at that."

They secured a large compression dressing over the wound and started an IV. With the trooper's permission, they loaded him in the ambulance and transported him to the emergency room at Eastern Maine Medical Center.

Willie made it to Bangor after all.

Chapter Forty

"Raymond Barribee? You sure?" Detective Denny Coe asked. "That's what the driver's license says, Detective. And his face matches the picture on the license," the dispatcher told him.

"Tell 'em I'm on my way, don't move him," said Denny.

"Ten-four, Detective," said the dispatcher, neutral, professional.

Some time later, Denny pulled onto the old logging road. Ahead of him was a cruiser, the crime lab van, and an unmarked car. Four heads swiveled to follow his approach. Denny climbed out, exchanged greetings with the responding trooper, the crime lab crew, and the coroner.

He spotted the body, walked over, stared down at it. "Yeah, that's Ray Barribee, all right," Denny confirmed, seeing the all-too familiar face.

"So what's the story?" he asked the trooper. The version he'd gotten was skeletal.

The responding trooper took out his notebook. Speaking slowly, referring to his notebook from time to time, he recounted what Willie Wainright had told him. Denny let him speak without interruption.

"So, this Willie Wainright, they gonna keep him at the hospital?" asked Denny. He needed to question him, didn't want him walking.

"Yeah, Detective. The hospital says he'll be there twenty-four hours," the trooper confirmed.

"Good. You know, I remember that name. He did time at Thomaston for abusing a kid, a stepdaughter maybe. And then he got some hotshot lawyer who got the girl to change her story, finger someone else. Willie got out early, charges were dismissed. Ends up he was in there a short time with ol' Ray here." Denny pointed at Ray's bloodied corpse. "Wonder what ol' Ray had against him, why he'd want to kill him?"

"Wainright didn't have a clue. Barribee never said anything to him that made him think he had it in for him," said the trooper. "He came at him with a knife. If Barribee hadn't broken a branch when he rushed him, Wainright figures he'd be dead."

Denny turned his attention to the coroner. "Got an opinion about cause of death?"

"My guess, neck fracture, by the look of things. He put a pretty good crease in the car top there," he said, pointing at the dented passenger-side roof. "I'll let the boys in Augusta confirm it with the post," he added, referring to the post-mortem autopsy yet to come.

Denny thanked him. Then he turned his attention to the crime lab men. "Where's the knife?" he asked.

"Here, Detective." One of them held out a plastic evidence bag that contained Ray's knife.

Denny took the bag with care, turned it over, examined the knife through the plastic that preserved fingerprints and anything else that could provide evidence. The wheels in his head turned over with the knife.

"You guys might want to check this knife against the wounds on Billy Prosson and Leo Jenkins," he suggested. "Who knows? Might solve those two murders."

"Great minds think alike, Denny, but thanks for the suggestion." The crime lab spokesman smiled. The ritual of covering one's ass was as old as police work.

"You guys do good work," said Denny, being the diplomat. "Did you find anything in Barribee's car?"

"The usual crap. Nothing that we found could tie to this. We'll impound it and go over it in Augusta. We'll let you know if we find anything else," the tech said.

"Thanks. So that's it?" Denny clasped his meaty hands together at chest level.

"That's it for now, Detective."

"Guess I'll go see Willie Wainright then. Thanks, everyone." He turned and retraced his steps to his cruiser, leaving them to finish cleaning up.

***

Denny found Willie Wainright lying in his hospital bed, propped up on his right side, pillows supporting him. A large, padded dressing was taped across his exposed left mid-back area. Denny could see faint blood seepage at its center. He guessed that the late Ray Barribee fancied that area of his victims.

Willie's eyes met Denny's when he walked toward his bed. Denny saw fear in his eyes.

"Mr. Wainright, I'm Detective Coe, Maine State Police," he began, standing back from the bed and using his official police voice to allay

Wainright's fears. He could see it was working. Willie visibly relaxed.

"I don't know what I can tell you, Detective," he said, his voice fuzzy most likely from the effects of pain medication.

"That's okay. I came to hear the story from you, is all."

Willie drew a careful breath, then went over what had happened, going slowly and carefully, trying not to miss anything. Denny watched the fear reappear in his eyes when he recounted the details of Barribee's attack.

"So, Mr. Wainright, why do you think he wanted to kill you?"

"Wish I knew, Detective. He never gave me a reason. He just came at me, no warning. The only thing he said was, 'You bastard! I'm gonna kill you!' I believed him. Hell, I thought I was a dead man." Willie trembled, remembering.

"What about when you were in Thomaston? Did you guys have a run-in?"

"No, nothing I can recall. Hell, Detective, I don't even remember him from there, but he remembered me. Remembered me well enough to spot me when I was hitchhiking and stop for me. You know what, Detective? I think he flipped out. I think he was plain crazy. I don't know what else would make him want to kill me, except..."

"Except what?"

"Except, he made a point of telling me he was in for sexual abuse of a minor, same as me." Willie mulled it over a moment. "But I still can't figure why he wanted to kill me."

Denny thought about Ray Barribee. He thought about his criminal history, his jail time, the enemies he might have made over the years. He could think of plenty of people who'd want to see him dead, but what could he have against Willie, make him want to kill him? He agreed with Willie. It didn't make sense. Not yet, anyway.

He took one of his cards from his breast pocket, handed it off to Willie.

"Here's my phone number," he said, holding it out.

"Could I trouble you to put it on the table there? It bothers me to move." Willie sounded apologetic.

"Oh yeah, sure." Denny set it down. "Give me a call if you think of anything else."

"Okay, Detective. Am I under arrest?"

"Under arrest?"

"Yeah. I killed that guy."

"I think, when we go over all the facts, that you're likely to be found not guilty, that it was self-defense," Denny said. "Of course, that's after we go over everything in detail," he added. "We'll let you know."

Denny couldn't resist throwing in that little seed of doubt, knowing about Willie's past history. He watched the fear wash over Willie's face.

He left feeling as baffled as he'd been when he entered Willie's room. He reviewed the possibilities.

Maybe Willie didn't remember some key bit of information that would explain Barribee's murder attempt. Maybe it was something Willie didn't want to tell me. Or maybe Willie's right. Maybe Barribee flipped out, went crazy. Denny rolled that thought around as he returned to his cruiser.

His radio alert light shone brightly. Someone had tried to reach him. He grabbed the mike, called dispatch.

"Sergeant Gagnon wants you to call him," Dispatch told him. "You got his number?"

That was dispatch's way of advising Denny to call on a regular phone, for security reasons. Police radio transmissions were heard by far too many people every day.

"Yeah, I got it. Thanks."

"Ten-four," said Dispatch, signing off.

Denny pulled out his cell phone and called Sergeant Gagnon at the Augusta Crime Lab.

"Lab. Corporal Pierce," said a gruff voice.

"It's Coe. Gagnon there?" Equally brief.

"Yeah, Detective. Hold on," said Pierce.

Denny waited.

"Hey, Detective, guess what," said Gagnon, full of exuberance.

"I don't know. You had a baby. What?" Denny hated dumb questions, delays.

"Barribee's knife matches the wounds on Prosson and Jenkins. Looks like we got us a murder weapon, as well as a dead murderer. What do you think about that?"

Denny didn't know what to think about it. "You sure?" he asked Gagnon, stalling.

"Let's put it this way. It's the right length and width, and it's double edged, which explains the extensive damage done to the insides of both victims. You know, stick it in and wiggle it back and forth, cutting in both directions?" said Gagnon.

"I get the picture. So it's the murder weapon?"

"The only way I can swear it's the murder weapon is if it's taken from the killer's hand at the scene of the crime. But it's one hell of a wild coincidence if Barribee didn't hold this knife to kill Prosson and Jenkins, is what I'm saying." Gagnon was starting to get testy.

"Thanks, Sergeant. That's good enough for me," said Denny, adopting a placating tone in response. No need to screw up the relationship he had with the crime lab over something stupid.

"Hey, that's what I'm here for."

Denny hit END, considering the implications. *If Barribee killed Prosson and Jenkins, then who cut Barribee's balls off? And what about Mignon? Did Barribee cut his balls off? If so, why didn't he kill him, too?* It didn't add up.

Okay, if Barribee loses his balls to an unknown assailant and then he goes out and kills Prosson, and then kills Jenkins, and then tries to kill Wainright, where does that leave me? I'm wondering if the same guy who cut Barribee didn't cut Mignon, too. That makes more sense than saying Barribee cut Mignon but killed the other two. It also leaves Barribee as a loose end. I doubt Barribee cut his own balls off.

Denny laughed out loud, a sudden, explosive guffaw that drew stares from passers-by outside the hospital. He shut his cruiser door, still working it through.

So, what I'm looking for is the person or persons who separated Barribee and Mignon from their family jewels, assuming that Barribee killed Prosson and Jenkins. Who could've done that?

He considered Booker and the Fowler woman. He had to admit, it made more sense to go after them for the murders of Prosson and Jenkins. He couldn't see how they could have left Vinalhaven, gone to Portland and done surgery on Mignon, and then returned to Vinalhaven without being missed by Mary what's-her-name, the bed-and-breakfast lady. Unless she lied. But what reason would she have to lie? He could think of none.

Denny let his thoughts wander some more. Then he remembered something. *What if they arranged to have somebody else do the cutting?* He recalled the phone call Booker made that night from the pay phone, the call traced to an unlisted number in New Jersey. *Maybe it was nothing, since Booker lived there before he came here. Then again, maybe it was everything.*

He scribbled a reminder in his notebook to get a name for the unlisted number in New Jersey.

Next, he considered the implications of the deaths and castrations. There'd been three deaths and three de-ballings, since Barribee counted as one of each, in what? Six weeks? *Jeez, that's four perps out of commission. This keeps up, I'll be out of a job.*

The thought brought a smile to his weathered face.

Chapter Forty-one

Two days after Ray Barribee's death, the telephone company still hadn't come up with a name for the unlisted number in New Jersey. Denny had the pathology report on Barribee. The coroner had been right. Barribee's second cervical vertebrae had been broken in the collision with the car roof. A classic hangman's fracture. *Fitting.*

His desk phone rang. He picked it up. "Coe."

"Detective, there's a couple suits down here, say they need to talk to you," the desk sergeant told him.

"Tell them I'm on my way."

What the hell. Now what? He stood and made his way to the entry, puzzling over who it might be.

He spotted them immediately, young and athletic-looking in their dark suits, and walked up to them.

"Detective Denton Coe?" asked the shorter of the pair.

"Yeah, that's me." He was curious. He'd never seen either one before.

"There someplace quiet we can talk a minute?" the shorter one asked.

"Joe, the conference room open?" Denny asked the desk sergeant.

"Far's I know," he responded, not bothering to look up from his pile of paperwork.

"Follow me," said Denny.

He closed the door behind them, motioned them to have a seat. "What's this all about?"

The shorter man continued to take the lead. "Detective Coe, we're here from the governor's office on a matter of considerable sensitivity." He removed an ID from his inside coat pocket, waved it briefly at Detective Coe, put it away, then went on. "As we understand it, you're the officer assigned to investigate the, ah, castration of Jack Mignon and, until his death, Ray Barribee. Is that correct?"

"That's right," Denny replied, still puzzled.

"Well, sir, the governor requests that you discontinue your investigation, and he asked us to give you enough information so you'd understand the reason."

Denny waited.

"For some time now, the governor has been concerned about the high incidence of abuse, and particularly sexual abuse, that has plagued our state. As a result, he formed a clandestine committee to look into it and make suggestions."

The man had Denny's full attention.

"The long and the short of it is, the committee came up with several suggestions, as you might have guessed. One of them was pretty radical." Shorty paused, letting this soak in.

"The suggestion was to, shall we say, make examples of some of the sex offenders in the state, with the idea that the word would get around and other offenders would think twice about committing more sex offenses."

Denny thought he could see where this was going.

"So the governor gave this some serious thought, liked the idea, and made arrangements for a small task force to carry this out. He didn't want to know what was done to the offenders, only that nobody was killed. The task force has carried out his wishes. I assure you that the deaths of Prosson, Jenkins, and Barribee were not connected in any way with the task force's activities."

"That's not entirely true," Denny interrupted. "My guess is, getting his balls cut off turned Barribee into a killer."

"That's one conclusion you could draw, Detective. But you know you could never prove it," said Shorty, a sly smile creasing his face.

Denny had to admit the guy was right.

"So you want me to put this thing to bed? What do I tell my superiors?" asked Denny.

"Tell them you got it all wrapped up. Barribee killed the perp who cut him, and now Barribee's dead," said Shorty in a reasonable voice.

"What about Mignon? Who do I say cut him?"

"Barribee. Put in your report that someone surprised him in the act so he didn't have time to follow through and kill Mignon, only got so far as to castrate him."

"Why should I go along with this? I don't give a shit who authorized these castrations. It's still unlawful, and it's my duty to find who did it and see they're prosecuted for it," said Denny, his voice rising, defending the center of his belief system.

"What're we talking about here? A couple castrations of a couple low-life perps? You're ready to throw away your career to see the people who did this brought to justice? Because that's what we're talking about here, Detective. Your career will end in a heartbeat if you pursue this, and you know it. You won't be able to get a job as a night watchman after people get done reading all that nasty stuff about you in the papers."

Shorty punctuated his last remark with a straight index finger directed at, but just short of connecting with Denny's chest.

Denny had a fleeting image of his daughter, Ellie, staring in shocked disbelief at him when he tried to explain to her it was all lies.

"You guys're very persuasive," he said, his voice low. "By the way, how much more of this is gonna go on?"

"The task force's work is done," replied Shorty, grinning at Denny. "With all the extra help we got from Barribee, the fear of God is out among the scumbag community. Any cuttings or killings from here on out are all yours to investigate."

"Okay. I want you, I want the governor, and I want his task force to know that I don't approve of these actions. But okay," said Denny, conceding but making a last-stand defense of his ideals, his authority.

"Thanks, Detective. And the governor thanks you, too, for what it's worth."

With that, Shorty and his silent partner got up and headed for the door.

With his hand on the door knob, Shorty turned back to Denny. "Not a word of this to anyone, Detective Coe. This meeting, none of this ever happened. You good with that?"

"I hear you," said Denny, chastened.

The two men left Denny sitting alone, weighing what he'd heard. He thought back on other threats he'd gotten over the years, reviewed how he'd handled them. This one was different. This one could cost him his career. His reputation. His daughter's love.

He considered the impact that a smear campaign could have on Ellie. He really didn't give a shit what people thought of him, as long as he did his job and he knew he was right, but Ellie, she was another matter. He'd think it through in his head before making a decision.

Maybe the best thing would be to take their advice, but if he could figure out a way to go after them without getting smeared and shit-canned, he'd do it.

***

The two men in dark suits strolled out of the State Police substation and made their way to their car, a black Lincoln.

"You think he bought it?" Shorty asked his tall, silent partner.

"Yeah, I think so. You were damned persuasive, Lou."

"Hey, that was more fun than cuttin' balls off, you ask me," Lou said, smiling.

"All I got to do was jab 'em with the needle."

"C'mon, Jimmy, I'm not tryin' to take any credit away from you. You done your job great, no complaints," soothed Lou.

Jimmy smiled down on his partner. "Thanks, Lou." The brief storm had passed.

"Let's get outta here. We gotta call Tony in Jersey to tell him everything went like he planned it," said Lou.

Chapter Forty-two

Denny thumped his palm against his forehead, wondering why he hadn't thought of it before. He blamed it on his having a lot on his mind. He also knew that the telephone company had always given him the information he'd requested, usually promptly.

He took out his cell phone and punched in the New Jersey phone number Booker had called from the pay phone. "Screw the phone company. They won't tell me, I'll find out myself."

He heard it ringing at the other end. "Now I'll get some answers," he grunted, waiting.

"Dalton Medical Supplies," announced a male voice in New Jersey.

"Dalton Medical Supplies?" repeated Denny, surprise dominating his tone.

"Yes, sir. How may I help you?" asked the thick New Jersey voice.

"You can tell me why you have an unlisted number," said Denny, recovering from his initial shock. "That doesn't sound like it'd be good for business."

"Oh, but it is, sir. We give this number out to our regular customers so they don't have to worry about getting busy signals. Our regulars appreciate it."

"What are your hours?" asked Denny.

"We're here to take orders from eight to eight, and after hours we have an answering machine you can leave your order on," explained the man.

"What do you sell?"

"Everything medical, sir. May I ask where you got our number?" asked the polite New Jersey voice.

"An associate. I'm not placing an order now, but thanks for the information," said Denny, attempting to sound sincere.

"That's perfectly all right, sir. Call us when you're ready to place an order. We pride ourselves on same-day shipping."

"Okay, thanks," said Denny. "I will." He hung up.

The call had answered all but one of Denny's questions.

Why had Booker gone to a pay phone to make the call? Was he hiding something? Could there be more to that unlisted number he'd just called than what he'd learned? Or maybe Booker just happened to remember he needed to order something and called from the pay phone while it was on his mind.

Questions, questions, questions. And where was it leading him? He considered that for a moment. He thought about precious Ellie. He thought about his career. He thought about a future without a career. He thought about a future without Ellie.

"God damn it, those guys're right," he hissed through clenched teeth. "Barribee's responsible for everything." He knew in his heart that it was true. He picked up a pad of paper and began drafting his report that would close the case.

His phone rang, interrupting him.

"Coe."

"Denny, Captain Ross."

"Good morning, Captain." Without realizing it, he straightened in his chair. *Now what?*

"I'm going over last month's crime stats, Denny, and I noticed something I thought you ought to know." Captain Ross' voice was neutral.

"What's that, sir?" Denny hoped it wasn't bad news.

"The number of reports of sexual abuse is down. Way down. What do you think caused that to happen?"

"Well, sir, that Barribee guy killed off two perps and castrated another, and then got himself killed, too. That took four of them out of circulation. I'm working on my report to you now, sir."

"Good work, but you know what? I think it's more than that. I think the word's out to the perps in this state that bad things are happening to their kind, so they better watch out," said the captain.

"You're probably right, Captain," agreed Denny, thinking of the governor's task force.

"Well, I thought you'd like to know. Keep up the good work."

"Yes, sir," Denny said.

The captain clicked off and Denny set down the receiver, his head spinning with his thoughts.

So those boys in the governor's task force were right.

Then he considered the possibility that someone from the task force had spoken to Captain Ross as well. He guessed they had. Captain Ross' thinking was too much like that of the task force to be a coincidence.

He turned his attention back to the chore of writing up his report, feeling even better about his decision.

Chapter Forty-three

Jim's cell phone rang as he and Brie were getting ready to head to work. Fred sat in his usual position of prominence, his black button eyes picking up all their movements.

Jim answered it.

"Hey, Mr. Booker. This is Nick's father down in Jersey. Wanted to call you to tell you how things went," said the thick New Jersey voice.

"Thanks for calling, but please, call me Jim."

"Hey, a little joke to remind you to call me Tony," he shot back, a smile pouring through the thick accent.

"Okay, Tony," said Jim, his own smile coming through.

"Anyway, here's what happened. A couple of my boys had a little talk with your Detective Coe up there. They managed to help clarify things for him, help him see the whole picture, if you get what I mean."

"Did they hurt him?"

"Jim, Jim. Of course not. They only presented him with a bunch of facts he couldn't dispute, if you get my drift."

"Does that mean he's off my case? And Brie's, ah, Miss Fowler's?"

"I don't think you'll be hearing anything more from him. Especially after his phone call to me yesterday."

"He called you?"

"Yeah. You and Merry were right. He's not stupid. Probably got my number off that pay phone when you called me."

Jim thought back on the call he'd made from the pay phone Brie had taken him to. If Detective Coe had been watching him, it would have been easy for him to get the number he called from the telephone company.

"Anyways," Tony continued, "it was a good idea you and Merry cooked up, having us answer saying 'Dalton Medical Supplies' for a while, in case he called. Confused some of my regulars, I'll tell ya', but they got the picture when I explained.

"So anyways, I knew it was him soon's he started talkin'. Had that police officer voice, if you know what I mean."

Jim did.

"He asked me a bunch of questions, no surprises, and I answered them all, nice and polite. When he was done, he sounded like he wasn't suspicious or anything. My guess is we've heard the last from him. I'll be Dalton Medical Supplies for a couple more weeks, in case he decides to call again, but I doubt he will. Looks like you're in the clear, Jim."

"That's great news, Tony. Thanks again for all you've done for me," he said sincerely.

"It's nothing compared with what you did for me, and don't you ever forget it," Tony fired back. "You let me know when I can do something more for you. And let me know when you're movin' back to Jersey. We need you down here."

"Okay, Tony. See you."

"See ya', Jim." Tony hung up.

***

It was a dreary, overcast morning, not unexpected for early May in Norridgewock, Maine. Mike Hastings climbed up onto the bulldozer and turned the key. These mornings, with the weather considerably tempered, the old diesel coughed and struggled to life without the need for starting ether. He waited while the exhaust cleared from sooty black to gray, adjusting the weathered black patch over his vacant right eye socket, killing time.

Satisfied that the old engine was performing well, he surveyed his domain. There was the usual mound of new shit, as he liked to call it, that needed burying.

Pulling the shift lever into gear, he let the dozer crawl over to the pile of fill while he let his thoughts crawl over Mary Lou. She really caught his attention the night before when she did those interesting things with his eye socket and her body parts. He grinned, remembering.

With the front bucket filled, he reversed and headed for the fresh waste, ready to begin the packing down and burying process. He'd done it so often now he could keep both Mary Lou and his work in focus at the same time, no problem.

He was on his third pass over the shifting mounds of bags and boxes, and his mind was on its third pass over Mary Lou, when he saw the boot sticking up. He thought nothing of it. Just another article of trash thrown there by a world grown accustomed to the creation of so much clutter.

Things changed for the worse on his fourth pass. The dozer's weight caused a further shift of debris in the vicinity of the old boot. Mike's good left eye saw more than he wanted to see, and he squeezed it shut to block the image. When he opened it again, it was still there, and it was unmistakable now.

It wasn't only a boot. There was a lower leg poking out of it. Mike saw a bare white calf where the pants had fallen away from the ankle. The plastic bags surrounding the rest of it obscured what lay beneath. He pushed the shift lever to neutral, stopping the dozer.

"Shit," he growled, thinking what a stink this was going to make of his day. He remembered February, remembered the time he lost, remembered the stupid, unending questions.

He climbed down off the dozer and walked gingerly across the shifting trash to the exposed leg. Standing over it, he ran his eye over the blanched, dead skin of the lower leg. A few pathetic strands of black hair protruded from it. The pants cuff, which belonged to a pair of old jeans, was frayed and stained.

"Damned if we don't get some interestin' shit brought in here," he mumbled to the vacant landfill.

He reached down and picked up a plump bag of garbage. Without hesitation, he dropped it onto the exposed leg. It made a soft *whump!* as it landed, settled. Then he lobbed four more bags around it for good measure.

"Outta sight, outta mind," he whispered to the booted leg.

Satisfied with what he'd done, he returned to the dozer and got on with the job of burying the trash. He put a little extra fill over certain parts of his handiwork for good measure. For some time after, he had trouble getting back to his thoughts of Mary Lou.

***

Jim related to Brie what Tony had said.

"I feel like a huge weight has lifted off me," she exclaimed when he'd finished.

"I hope you're not talking about me," he joked.

In response, she pummeled him lovingly on the arm.

"If I ever even think about doing something crazy like that again, kick me, okay?" said Jim, holding Brie loosely in his arms.

"Don't worry, I will," she promised.

Fred, watching from his vantage point on his stool, smiled his bear smile, giving his tacit approval. His button eyes reflected miniature images of them as they pulled on their spring coats and left the apartment. When they switched off the light and pulled the door closed, his eyes went blank, would remain blank until they returned.

Jim and Brie stepped out into the brilliant early morning sunshine of a late April morning in Maine. Both felt more alive and free than they had in months. They climbed into Jim's pickup truck together for the drive to Serenity.

"I've been thinking, Jim. Maybe I'll give up my apartment," said Brie, watching him for a reaction.

"Talk about coincidences. I've been thinking about giving up my apartment, too," said Jim, turning to Brie as he spoke.

Brie laughed, a light, easy bubbling sound that flowed from her. It was free of all self-consciousness, free of all reservation. She encircled Jim's right arm and hugged it to her.

Jim felt her happiness and leaned into her to share it. He nuzzled her forehead and kissed her. "You're pretty special, you know," he said, his voice husky with emotion.

"So are you, Mr. Booker," she murmured back.

Together, they drove to Serenity.

It was Monday morning at Serenity, and people were chatting about their weekends when Jim and Brie entered the Gold Room. They were the last to arrive, except for Brent who was always a minute or two late, by his own design. Several people looked up when they came in. Their relationship was no longer fresh news, but many were interested in its progress.

"Hey, good morning, you two," said Andy, seeing them. "How's it going?"

"Better and better," Jim answered, smiling.

Brent breezed into the room. His arrival brought the room to order.

"Good morning, everyone. It's Monday, in case some of you lost track over the weekend, and as usual we've got a lot to cover, so let's get started," he said in his usual rush of words.

"I imagine most of you saw the editorial in Sunday's paper," he continued, waving a section of the *Portland Herald* as he spoke.

Several people, including Jim and Brie, appeared puzzled.

"Some of you had better things to do besides reading the Sunday paper, huh?" he said, his eyes dancing around the room. This drew the usual chuckles.

"Well, it's about the drop in the number of sexual assaults and abuse in the past month or so. It's a good article. Anyone wants to read it, you can borrow my copy."

"Three cheers for the Equalizer," said Andy.

"The Equalizer!" shouted everyone in unison, coffee cups and mugs raised high.

"Thanks for leading the cheers, Andy," said Brent, a big grin spreading across his face.

"Glad to do it," said Andy.

"Okay, who's going first today?" asked Brent, getting back on track.

"Guess I am," said Martha. All eyes turned to her.

"This is the first team presentation on Andrea M., a twenty-two-year-old single mother of one daughter, age five, admitted for treatment of both alcohol and drug abuse," Martha began, giving her bare bones introduction.

"She was referred to us by Sandy Simpson at Crisis Counseling in Lewiston. Sandy has been seeing her for a couple of months now, gradually gaining her trust and confidence. Six days ago Sandy made a breakthrough with her, which brought Andrea in to us." Martha paused and drew a breath before continuing.

"After the usual questioning, Andrea broke down and told Sandy she'd been sexually abused when she was twelve by a friend of her father's, a man named Greg Frackle. The abuse continued off and on for four years. He got her pregnant when she was sixteen and left her when he found out."

Brie glanced over at Jim. He was frowning, deep in thought. She reached out with her right leg and kicked him.

Surprised by her kick, he looked at her. Their eyes met and understanding flowed between them.

Jim shook his head from side to side.

Seeing it, Brie chuckled softly.

They turned their attention back to Martha's presentation.

If you enjoyed *Say the Word,* you may like Charles DuPuy's EZ Kelly series.

Easy Kill

"EZ. Kelly is the next, great kickass heroine."
—EmKay Connor, award-winning author

Will dangerous lady EZ Kelly succeed in finding the real culprit?

EZ Kelly is intent on becoming a travel agent, but trouble finds her wherever she goes. It's good that self-defense was a high priority among the lessons taught to her by her Special Forces father.

Expecting a boring night shift at the hotel where she works, EZ is surprised when night after night the place is targeted by thieves. Taking the thieves down one by one is a simple task for her.

Unafraid of the threats, she continues to work at the hotel and cooperates with the Miami Police's investigation to discover the reason why the hotel is being hit.

As they dig further into the case, she discovers that terrorists have a plan to detonate nuclear devices in three large US cities simultaneously. Will EZ be able to take the terror cell down before she gets herself killed?

Here's a sneak peek at *Easy Save*, the 2ⁿᵈ installment in the EZ Kelly series.

Easy Save

EZ Kelly watched as the young couple huddled over the rack of tour brochures. She kept their images in her peripheral vision while doing her best to appear busy. The guy looked eighteen, the girl was maybe fourteen. Statutory rape came to mind.

The young man stood tall and lean, his light brown hair cut short. He had a thin blond beard that barely showed. His narrow face sported a long, narrow nose perched above a thin mouth. He looked energetic, robust, ready for what life brought him. Turned out, he'd need every bit of that.

EZ guessed the girl's height at around five-six, with a slim but shapely figure and cornsilk-blond hair held in a ponytail. She had an oval face with blue eyes, and lips most women would die for. EZ had no doubts that she'd draw stares wherever she went, despite her youth.

Most of the people who migrated to EZ's rack of Florida tour brochures turned out to be casual lookers, passing time glancing at the multi-colored pictures, their brains in neutral, nothing registering. That's maybe ninety percent of them. Sort of like people who stroll down the street and eyeball shop windows, nothing on their mind, nothing on their shopping list. Most of the other ten percent were what EZ's dad would call tire kickers. They're the people who go to car dealerships and ask endless questions about the different models, tying up the salesman's time, then end up giving the car's tire a kick on their way out, no plans to return, no plans to buy.

The guy plucked out a brochure and the two of them, heads together, examined it like Darwin eyeballing a new species. After a short exchange, they turned and approached EZ at her desk, smiling as they came. As they neared, EZ noticed a thirtyish-looking woman standing behind them at the brochure rack. *Maybe it's going to be a good day for me.*

The young man glanced at the nameplate on her desk, shifted his gaze upwards to look at her, a quizzical expression overspreading his brow. "E? Or is it E. Z.?" he asked, unsure what to call her.

"My name is E. Z. Kelly. Stands for Esther Zane Kelly. Confuses a lot of people, you're not alone. Call me Easy. Everyone does," she said, smiling at him as she got to her feet.

"Oh, of course," he said, getting it. "Anyway, Melissa and I think the Everglades tour sounds cool. What can you tell us about it?"

"It so happens that I'm going on that tour tomorrow," EZ replied. "It's my day off, and every week I go on a different one of the tours so I can tell my customers first-hand what to expect. I agree with you; it sounds like a blast. Ever been on an airboat?"

"No, I, we, never have," he said, speaking for the two of them.

"You'll love it. It's like riding in an open boat powered by an airplane engine. A little noisy, but you fly over the water. Then they slow down so you can see alligators and manatees, maybe snakes and turtles, plus a whole raft of tropical birds along the way.

"The bus picks you up here at the hotel and takes you to Everglades City where you board an airboat for the wild trip through the Everglades. Your guide will point out the wildlife as you go along.

"After the ride, you'll go to one of Everglade City's great restaurants for lunch. If you're the adventurous type, you can try alligator served many different ways. After lunch, you can walk around the exhibits and stores.

"The buses load up again at three for the return trip. You should be back here at the Adriatic Hotel by around four. How does all that sound?"

While speaking, watching their faces, EZ could tell that she'd made a sale. Their youthful enthusiasm cascaded out of them.

"It sounds perfect," the young man gushed.

"Yeah, way cool," agreed the girl, smiling up at him.

"Okay, when do you want to go?" EZ asked, trying to get them to pick a day.

"Will tomorrow work?" His eyebrows raised in anticipation.

"Let me check." EZ picked up the phone and punched in the number she'd committed to her unfailing memory. Meanwhile, the thirtyish-looking woman, brochure in hand, had taken up a position behind the two of them, clearly within earshot.

Waiting for the call to be answered, EZ asked, "Where are you folks from?"

"Columbia, South Carolina," said the handsome young man. "I'm Ted and this is Melissa. We're brother and sister," he added. EZ guessed that wasn't the first time he'd clarified the situation.

"Nice to meet you both." EZ reached out and shook their hands. Both offered firm handshakes. "You already know my name. I'm EZ Kelly," she added.

At that moment the call was answered, helping to mask her surprise. She'd assumed they were young lovers, not close-knit siblings. No statutory rape there.

EZ confirmed that they could join tomorrow's tour, and the two of them whooped and high-fived at the news. Then she had them sit while she got the information needed to complete the forms and collect their money.

While doing so, she learned a little more about them. Ted had graduated from high school and enlisted in the army. His parents wanted the two of them to take a trip together so they'd have shared memories. *Nice parents.*

"I spent time in the army, Ted. Hope your time is enjoyable."

"Oh, yeah? What branch?" he asked, curious.

"Special Forces," EZ said, smiling, making light of it.

"No kidding! That's awesome. That's what *I* want to do." His enthusiasm was infectious.

"Good luck with that. I think you have what it takes."

Ted's face reddened slightly with the compliment. "Thanks," he responded, his eyes holding hers.

EZ finished the paper work and collected their money.

"Be down here by eight tomorrow morning to meet the bus. Hope that isn't a problem," she added, thinking how teenagers liked to sleep in.

"No problem. We'll be here in plenty of time!"

"Oh, and bring sunscreen. It's likely to get hot out there on the airboat in June, and with the wind in your hair, you won't notice how intense the sun is."

"Thanks for the tip, Miss Kelly. See you at eight tomorrow morning," said Ted.

"No problem, Ted. And please, call me EZ. Calling me Miss Kelly makes me feel like an old woman."

"You're far from that," he replied, giving her a warm smile.

"Thanks, Ted. I hope my being along on the tour doesn't take the fun out of it for you and Melissa."

"Are you kidding? You being along won't change a thing. Everything'll be fine," he said, smiling broadly.

After a final thanks, they bounded off for parts unknown, and the woman behind them stepped forward. She had severe features over what had likely been a pleasant, youthful face. She looked strong.

EZ stood to greet her, extended her hand.

"Hi. I'm EZ Kelly. How may I help you?"

She gave EZ's hand a limp shake. *Ugh.* "I couldn't help overhearing about the Everglades trip. It sounds like fun. Is this the tour?" she asked, holding up the brochure in her hand for EZ to see.

She glanced at it, confirmed that it was.

"Thank you. I'm going to show it to my husband. He's not much of a tourist, but I think he'll like the sound of it. I'll get back to you if he does," she said, the attempt at a smile working on her face.

"Sure," EZ replied, smiling back at her, while guessing that she'd had her first tire kicker of the day and wouldn't have any more to do with her.

***

The woman moved away from EZ's desk and sat in one of the lobby's upholstered chairs, then took out her cell phone and punched in a number. When her call was answered, she spoke slowly, quietly, carefully.

"I've found a good one. Thirteen, maybe fourteen, blond ponytail, going on an Everglades trip with her brother." She recited the tour information from the brochure she held, then listened.

"Yes, tomorrow. Short notice, I know, but well worth it. The wheel chair and black wig should work fine," she added, then closed her phone.

EZ listened to the call, and shook her head. *What was she up to?*

Readers, check out this legal mystery novel by WGN-TV's political analyst, Paul Lisnek.

Assume Guilt

"*Assume Guilt* is the ultimate courtroom thriller about Murder, Marriage, & Money by lawyer extraordinaire Paul Lisnek. Can our hero unearth the sinister secret of a cold-blooded killer or will it remain entombed forever? Lisnek's debut novel is a fast-paced must read."

—Linda Kenney Baden, Author of *Remains Silent* and Criminal Trial Attorney

With loyalty, family secrets, and death involved, Matt Barlow must discover the real facts.

Attorney Matt Barlow vowed he'd never be part of a criminal case again, not after failing to save an innocent man from the death penalty. A jury consultant on civil cases, Matt doesn't waver until...

When Chicago's top real estate developer and aspiring politician Charles Marchand is charged with the death of his wife, Sandra, loyalty to an old friend pushes Matt into signing on as the jury consultant for the defense. But the case is about much more than guilt or innocence.

As Matt—and his staff—delve deeper into the evidence, they uncover information Marchand himself would just as soon stay buried, including the death of a college classmate that links him to the corrupt Leo Toland, Governor of Illinois. Before the truth and lies are untangled, Matt even finds himself secretly working with his half-brother, who just happens be on the governor's payroll.

Author's Note

In my former life, I worked as a physician assistant in a substance abuse treatment facility in Maine. Like Jim, my main tasks were doing the histories and physical exams of the admissions, so I witnessed first-hand the effects of both drugs and alcohol on the minds and bodies of my patients, called clients by the rest of the staff.

My director, who was the spitting image of Brent Caldwell, encouraged me to ask them the big question, "Have you ever been sexually abused?" and like Jim, as I got better at asking, I changed the question to "When were you sexually abused?" The positive responses grew as I got better and better at asking.

The hospital built a residential adolescent substance abuse treatment facility, and chose me to direct it. I insisted on doing the histories and physicals so I could continue to connect with the clients, but having to orchestrate the staff, the annual budget and the day-to-day management of the facility occupied much of my time. Having the opportunity to intervene in an adolescent's life and steer them to a healthy adulthood, despite their pasts, made it all worthwhile.

Final note: I never worked in New Jersey, nor did I have a Mafia don tell me to "Say the word." I've often wondered what I might have done, had that happened.

Acknowledgements

A hearty round of thanks goes out to all the professionals who shared the agonies and joy of working with those afflicted by drugs and alcohol in that treatment facility in Maine. Many of you will recognize yourselves in the characters of my tale, despite the fact that your names were changed to protect your innocence.

Thanks also goes out to Brittiany Koren, my publisher and editor and supporter at Written Dreams Publishing in Green Bay, Wisconsin. Her suggestions and encouragement have brightened my pathway.

Finally, I give heartfelt thanks to my fellow writers, family members and friends who have prodded me to keep the juices flowing and the words coming out. Especial thanks goes to my soul mate, Janet, who knows better than anyone how to keep me on course.

About the Author

Charles M. DuPuy was born in Pittsburgh, Pennsylvania, but grew up on a dairy farm fifty miles east of there. It was a wonderful bucolic life full of experiences great and small. In school, he loved writing stories to entertain his friends, and hung on to the memories through young adulthood. When he was twenty-one, his wealthy aunt planned a trip around the world with her son and daughter, and invited Charles to join them. He accepted with glee. That introduction to the world fueled a desire to travel that he still enjoys.

He's seen Africa as a Peace Corps Volunteer, drove with a buddy to Alaska on the Alcan Highway one summer, and has been to or through nearly all of the fifty states, including Hawaii. He's no stranger to Mexico and Canada as well.

Charles got serious about writing when he penned articles for an outdoors magazine, and the commitment grew when the editor took the position of managing editor at *Fly Fishing* magazine and offered him the editorship of the outdoors magazine.

With his depth of experience, it was natural that he began writing longer prose. Short stories came first, and finally a novel idea was born. ***Say the Word*** is his first serious full-length novel, and it's only a start. His EZ Kelly series has seen ***Easy Kill*** published, and the second in the series, ***Easy Save*** due out in late 2019. His third EZ Kelly novel, ***Easy Does It***, is growing daily on his computer! He invites you, the reader, to follow his progress on his website, CharlesMDuPuyAuthor.com or to find him on social media.

www.ingramcontent.com/pod-product-compliance
Lightning Source LLC
Chambersburg PA
CBHW050252110726
47898CB00007B/2382